Love Me Do

Lindsey Kelk is a *Sunday Times* bestselling author, podcaster and internet oversharer. Born and brought up in Doncaster, South Yorkshire, she worked in London as a children's editor before writing her first book, *I Heart New York*, and moving to Brooklyn. Lindsey's novels include the I Heart series, *The Christmas Wish* and *On a Night Like This*. She now lives in Los Angeles with her husband.

You can follow Lindsey on Facebook, Twitter or Instagram @LindseyKelk, and sign up for her newsletter at www.LindseyKelk.com.

Also by Lindsey Kelk

I Heart series
I Heart New York
I Heart Hollywood
I Heart Paris
I Heart Vegas
I Heart London
I Heart Christmas
I Heart Forever
I Heart Hawaii

Girl series
About a Girl
What a Girl Wants
A Girl's Best Friend

Standalones
The Single Girl's To-Do List
Always the Bridesmaid
We Were on a Break
One in a Million
In Case You Missed It
On a Night Like This
The Christmas Wish

Cinders & Sparks children's book series
Magic at Midnight
Fairies in the Forest
Goblins and Gold

Novellas available on ebook
Jenny Lopez Has a Bad Week
Jenny Lopez Saves Christmas
Jenny Lopez is Getting Married

LOVE ME DO

LINDSEY KELK

HarperCollins*Publishers*

HarperCollins*Publishers* Ltd
1 London Bridge Street,
London SE1 9GF

www.harpercollins.co.uk

HarperCollins*Publishers*
Macken House,
39/40 Mayor Street Upper,
Dublin 1
D01 C9W8
Ireland

First published by HarperCollins*Publishers* 2023
1

A catalogue record for this book is available from the British Library

ISBN: 978-0-00-840791-9 (PB B-format)
ISBN: 978-0-00-840788-9 (TPB, ANZ-only)
ISBN: 978-0-00-861964-0 (PB A-format)
ISBN: 978-0-00-861932-9 (PB, US, CA-only)

This novel is entirely a work of fiction.
The names, characters and incidents portrayed in it are
the work of the author's imagination. Any resemblance to
actual persons, living or dead, events or localities is
entirely coincidental.

Typeset in Melior by Palimpsest Book Production Ltd, Falkirk, Stirlingshire

Printed and bound in the U.S.A. by Lake Book Manufacturing, LLC

Dear Emma Guns . . .
It's me, hi, I'm the problem, it's me
(and the answer is more bralettes)

CHAPTER ONE

CHAPTER ONE

'If you ever want to know how someone really feels about you, ask them to pick you up from the airport at rush hour,' Suzanne said. 'No one in this town would willingly drive to LAX for anything less than true love.'

'Flattery will get you everywhere,' I replied as my sister pulled sharply away from the arrivals terminal of Los Angeles International Airport. She cut in front of ten other cars, all of them hitting their horns at the same time, sending us off with a chorus of discordant honking, as my suitcase slid back and forth across the boot of her SUV. I closed my eyes and clutched at my seatbelt, nerves already jangling with jet lag. It felt as though I'd left my brain somewhere over the Atlantic Ocean, several time zones behind me. Humans weren't meant to be up in the air for eleven straight hours, it simply wasn't right. My watch said it was 4 p.m. but my body said otherwise. Why was I awake? Why was it daylight? And why did I decide to watch the entire *Twilight* saga instead of sleeping? I had been a fool.

'You didn't have to come and get me,' I said, twisting against my seatbelt to get a proper look at Suzanne. 'I could have got a taxi.'

Life in California suited my sister. She looked happy and healthy, her blonde hair was freshly cut and coloured, her skin was glowing and there was something else I couldn't quite put my finger on, a kind of glossy sheen that she definitely didn't have when she worked in Slough.

'Phoebe Chapman, sister of mine, love of my life, you know I would go to the ends of the earth for you.'

I yawned and smiled at the same time, utterly exhausted but deliriously happy. It was almost two years since we'd been in the same place at the same time and they had not been the best two years of my life. The thought of this holiday was the only thing keeping me going for the last few weeks, sun, sea and sisterly bonding. It was just what I needed.

'Also, I was feeling guilty,' she added. 'I have to go to Seattle for a meeting. I'm leaving tonight.'

She slammed her foot on the brake, barking obscenities at a little red car as it pulled in front of us. The driver flipped up their middle finger and promptly sped away, drifting across another two lanes, the Fiat and the furious.

'What do you mean you're leaving?' I asked. 'They're making you fly all the way to Seattle for a meeting? Couldn't you Zoom in?'

'I'm so sorry, Pheebs, I need to be there. If I don't go and fix things today there'll be literally no internet by this time tomorrow.' She pursed her lips and two little lines, permanently etched between her eyebrows, dug their way deeper into her forehead. It was an expression I knew well. Standard Suzanne exasperation. She'd been working on it ever since I was born.

'But I was thinking, you could come with me if you want? You might like Seattle, it's an interesting place, there's plenty to do.' She paused to flick her fringe out of her eyes. 'Well, there's a few things to do. Not as much as there is in LA but there are shops and museums and things like that. There's the Space Needle. Oh, and there's this cool market where they chuck whole fish at you.'

'On purpose?' I asked, horrified.

A notification popped up on the screen of her iPhone and she actually growled. Whoever David Sales might be, I would not want to be him.

'The only thing is the weather isn't forecast to be that great this week,' she said, flicking the message off the screen without reading it. 'It rains a lot. And I mean, a lot.'

Seattle was sounding more and more appealing by the second.

'But if you want to come we could try to get you on my flight. Or the one after. Worst-case scenario, first thing tomorrow morning. I'll be in meetings most of the day but I could dinner in the evening, if you don't mind eating late.'

It was one thing to threaten me with a flying fish to the face but quite another to mess with my meal schedule. I looked out the window and watched my dream of a perfect holiday swim away upstream like so much Seattle salmon.

Suzanne glanced over at me, her hands gripping the steering wheel at ten and two. 'Or you could stick to the plan and stay at my house. If that's easier.'

'How long will you be gone?' I asked lightly.

'Two days. Three tops.'

She seemed to have forgotten I spoke her language fluently. 'Leaving soon' meant you'd be waiting an hour. 'On my way' almost always translated to 'I'm still at my desk' and two or three days meant she'd be gone for at least a week. Half my entire holiday.

'And you have to leave tonight?' I pulled at my suddenly too-tight seatbelt. 'You really have to go right away?'

Her tasteful diamond earrings caught the light as she nodded, dazzling me. 'Two trips to the airport in one day. Am I a masochist or what?'

'We've known that ever since you chose to do advanced maths at A level,' I said with a half-hearted smile. 'If you've got to go, you've got to go. Can't have the internet imploding just so you can babysit your little sister.'

'I'll make it up to you when I get back,' she replied, relieved. 'We'll go to a fancy spa or something, really push the boat out.'

Flapping a hand in the air between us, I waved away her non-apology. It wasn't her fault and it was only a few days. I could survive in LA on my own for a few days. And it was like Therese always said, there's no point getting frustrated about things you can't control.

'You can't help work,' I told her. 'I get it. I had to work last weekend, totally cocked up my plans.'

'Oh no, was there some kind of greetings card emergency?' Suzanne said, smothering a half-laugh with an apologetic grimace. 'Sorry, that was rude. I know your job is entirely as stressful as mine.'

'Rude but fair,' I laughed. 'The furthest I've ever travelled for a work emergency is to the big Tesco when we ran out of teabags.'

I smiled when she smiled, expertly pretending the jibe didn't bother me. I was used to it.

'Everything's going well though?' she asked as she fiddled with the air conditioning, setting it somewhere close to sub-zero. 'I *loved* that set of National Pet Day cards you sent me. Your best yet, I reckon.'

'Thanks,' I replied, shivering in my jeans and T-shirt and gazing longingly at the sunshine outside. 'They did really well.'

Head copywriter at the UK's third largest independent greetings card company was far from the worst job in the world but it didn't exactly inspire wonder and awe in people when they heard about it either. I couldn't quite remember her exact title, but Suzanne was head of something strategic for an app I refused to download for fear of never accomplishing anything meaningful ever again. Was she partially responsible for the downfall of civilization? Yes. Was she incredibly rich and seemingly happy? Also yes, so, did she care about the first bit? No, she did not.

'What else have you been up to?' Suzanne asked, steering the car and the subject in a different direction as she merged onto another motorway. 'Anything interesting?'

Nothing I wanted to tell her about, I thought.

'You know, the usual,' I said through a yawn. 'Working, reading, cooking. I'm halfway through a *Vampire Diaries* rewatch which is taking up a fair bit of my time.'

'*The Originals* as well?'

'You've got to do *The Originals*,' I replied, nodding emphatically. 'But I'm leaving *Legacies* alone for now. What about you? Anything you'd like to share with the class?'

'You'll love the new house, it'll be like staying in a hotel, only better,' she replied, shifting topics once again with alarming ease. 'The fridge is fully stocked, your bed is made and I've got every television channel on God's green earth. I can't think of a single thing you might want that I don't have.'

'A Cadbury Spira, Ryan Reynold's phone number and the Tamagotchi you dropped off the side of the ferry on that school trip to France.'

'Well the important thing is you're not holding a grudge,' she replied. 'Knobhead.'

With a tired smile, I squinted at the sun-bleached shades of blue and beige outside the car. The area around an airport was rarely glamorous but this was not how I'd imagined Los Angeles. There was plenty of sun but no sea, no sand, no seductive anything. Just small, squat houses, run-down warehouses and giant billboard after giant billboard, all of them promising the very best traffic accident attorney money could buy. Only the towering palm trees that shot up into the sky at oddly irregular intervals clued me into the fact I was truly in California, as though someone from the tourist board had taken this exact same journey, panicked that it looked a bit shit and done the best that they could with a very limited budget. Where were the mansions? The celebrities? The allure? Definitely not on the bumper sticker of the car in front that read 'If you're going to ride my ass, at least pull my hair'.

'Oh, look, look!' Suzanne yelled out. 'Can you see it?'

'See what?' I asked, blinking out the window. 'What am I looking for?'

'Obviously not the dead possum on the hard shoulder.' She reached over and physically turned my chin to the left before pointing out of her window. 'Great big bloody sign on the top of a hill. Can you see?'

And there it was.

Jumping out from the side of a far- off hill, nine bold white letters announcing I had arrived.

'Welcome to Hollywood, everybody comes here! Land of dreams,' Suzanne crowed in her best-worst American accent. 'What's *your* dream, Phoebe Chapman?'

'For you not to quote *Pretty Woman* at me right before you leave me in a strange house for three to four days,' I replied, eyes fixed on the Hollywood sign. Somehow it managed to be bigger and smaller than I'd thought it would be, closer and further away at the same time. But it was still thrilling, I could hardly believe it was real.

'That film is not a fairy tale, it's a nightmare. Please tell me Richard Gere isn't going to try to climb up the trellis to my bedroom in the middle of the night?'

'He's a bit old for it now, can't imagine his hips would take it,' she reasoned. 'And if he does, you can push him into the pool.'

My head whipped around so fast, I slapped myself in the face with my ponytail. 'You've got a pool? Why didn't you say you've got a pool?'

'Because I wanted to see the look on your face when I told you,' Suzanne said as she steered us confidently across three lanes of traffic, several smaller cars scattering out of our way. 'There's a hot tub as well.'

'Stay in Seattle as long as you like, I'm never leaving.'

My sister grinned, pressing down on the accelerator, the car vaulting forward as though we were on a roller-coaster. 'I've got a feeling you're going to love LA.'

'I've got a feeling I'm going to love your pool,' I countered, gaze lingering on the iconic white letters. 'As for the rest of it, we'll see.'

Forty minutes, fifteen honks of the horn and one wind-the-window-down-to-call-someone-a-wanker later, Suzanne pulled onto a curving driveway and turned off the engine.

'Here we are,' she declared. 'Home sweet home.'

I was thrilled to be off the road – Suzanne was a menace – and I unclipped my seatbelt with white knuckles as she opened the passenger side door for me.

The heat hit me like a brick wall.

'Fuck me, it's hot,' I gasped, Suzanne cackling with laughter as I clutched at the massive car. I'd never felt anything like it, the air so dry and intense, it felt as though someone had seared the insides of my nostrils. After eleven hours in a stale cabin on the plane and the icy conditions of her SUV, my body was not ready. But it was ready for the little white bungalow in front of me, with its quaint wooden roof and charming double stable doors. The only word to describe it was adorable. More compact than I'd thought after Suzanne's description but wasn't that always the way?

'Suze, it's so cute,' I gushed, breathing deep and slow as I adjusted to my new normal temperature. 'But where's the pool?'

'Behind the house, where most pools are?'

'Behind the house where?' I asked. As far as I could see, there was nothing behind the cottage but hillside.

Suzanne stared at me from across the car bonnet.

'Phoebe, this is the garage. The house is up there.'

Keys in the palm of her hand, she pointed towards a narrow, tucked away staircase that ran up to an impossibly beautiful white-walled, Spanish-style villa. Huge, sparkling windows glittered like diamonds in the sun and an infinite number of warm terracotta tiles rippled along the roof. In front of the villa, two towering palm trees swayed in a breeze that was too high up for me to enjoy and the sloping garden was filled with dozens of lush green succulents, stately cacti and beautiful blossoming bougainvillea, running all the way down to the quiet, winding road. The deep fuchsia pink of the flowers sighed against the stark white walls of the house. All of a sudden I felt so far away from home, I couldn't quite catch my breath.

'Can you manage the stairs with your suitcase or do you want to take the lift?' Suzanne asked as though it was a perfectly normal question when we'd both grown up in the same semi-detached house in a tiny village forty miles outside Sheffield.

'You've got a lift?' I replied, wrangling my suitcase out from the boot of her SUV. 'In your house?'

'Yes, I have a lift, but technically it starts in the garage.' She pushed her sunglasses onto the top of her head and winked. 'Well? What do you think?'

'I think you've got enough room to start your own cult and I think I'd like to join.'

She reached for my carry-on and started up the stairs, chuckling as she went. 'There's a white tracksuit waiting

9

for you in your room. I'll get started on the Kool-Aid while you unpack.'

'If you don't mind. I've always wanted to try it,' I replied, heaving my case behind me and climbing the stairs to the house, step by step by step.

'It's all about the flow,' Suzanne said. We finished our tour of the house on a stunning terrace that rolled over the edge of the hillside, affording us a breathtaking view over the city, and I stared off into the distance, dazed. It was all too much. Outside was even more glamorous than inside, the lush green lawn, the indoor-outdoor living space complete with gas grill and wall-mounted TV, not to mention the azure-blue pool and in-ground hot tub. 'The real estate broker explained it all. With the south-facing aspect, you get all this wonderful natural light that sort of pulls you through the rooms and out here to the deck. All the good vibes in the house? That's the flow.'

'Vibes are impeccable,' I agreed, digging my hands into the pockets of my jeans, too afraid to touch anything even outside. 'Makes perfect sense to me.'

'I looked at another place up the street but I didn't connect with it. It was gorgeous and I loved the tree-house yoga studio in the backyard, but the energy was off, you know?'

'No,' I replied with a bluntness I reserved for immediate family members only. 'But I do remember when you forgot to pay the gas bill when you were at uni and they turned your heating off.'

She glared at me, turning her back on the spectacular view and leaning against the waist-high wooden fence that stopped us falling off the end of the terrace and into the neighbour's garden below.

'Point taken. You think I've turned into an LA wanker.'

'I think your house is incredible,' I corrected. 'And you've every right to want to show it off.' Holding a hand over my eyes to shield them from the sun, I took in the view, shaking my head with disbelief. 'You've come a long way, Suze. It's not the village, is it?'

'Too right it isn't,' she replied. 'There's no bloody freezer shop for a start. Practically impossible to find a box of fish fingers at a decent price around here, and do you know they don't sell Birds Eye potato waffles in America?'

'No wonder there's so much political unrest,' I tutted.

We stood side by side, lost in quiet reverie, and I wondered if we were thinking the same thing.

'Gran would be so proud of you,' I said softly. 'I'm so proud of you.'

'She'd be proud of you too,' she replied. 'I don't doubt it.'

Which was exactly the sort of thing you would say if you did in fact doubt it.

I knew I did.

'I called Mum before I got on the plane,' I told her, brushing my frizzy, post-flight hair behind my ears. 'She said to say hello. Have you spoken to her lately?'

'Couple of weeks ago, maybe a month?' She rubbed her fingertip lightly underneath her eye and shrugged. 'Have you heard from Dad?'

'Not in a while. You know Dad: Christmas, birthday, the usual.'

'Same old, same old,' she agreed. 'I think I worry more when I do hear from him than when I don't.'

Neither of us had ever been especially close to either of our parents. They split up when I was one and Suzanne was four, and according to the people who could remember that far back, things were never quite the same afterwards. The story goes that Mum was struggling with us on her own so we all went to stay with Gran, just for a few weeks. A few weeks became a few months and, after a year or so, it was decided things would be easier for everyone if Mum sold our house and we moved in permanently. It all worked out perfectly, Gran was patient and loving and kind, and her house had an excellent back garden complete with swings, a slide and a see-saw. I was very easily bought as a toddler.

As for our dad, Dave Johnson had been a fleeting presence in our lives ever since the break-up. He also moved in with his parents after he and Mum split up, only his parents lived in Florida which meant his visits became sporadic at best. It helped me to think of him like a neighbourhood cat; his absence wasn't malicious, he simply had other places to be. He always seemed happy to see us when he saw us but we weren't his priority. Thankfully, there was one person who was always there for me and Suzanne. No matter what else might be happening in the world, when Dad was far away and Mum was working around the clock to make ends meet, we could always depend on clever, constant Gran. At least, we could until she passed away three years ago. Suzanne looked to be doing OK but things hadn't been quite right for me since.

'What's that over there?' I pointed at a cluster of tall shiny buildings in the near distance before the heavy silence overwhelmed us.

'Downtown.' Suze pushed her neat blonde bob behind her ears, exactly the same way I had a minute earlier. 'We're on the eastside now, in Los Feliz. Hollywood is to the west of us, then West Hollywood, Beverly Hills, Brentwood; you can sort of see Century City from here, at least on a clear day like today. All the way west is Santa Monica, Venice to the south, Malibu to the north, and if you keep going after that, you'll end up in the ocean.'

'What should I do first?' I asked even though there was no way I was going to remember anything she told me. Jet lag had poked so many holes in my short-term memory, I could barely remember my own name.

'It's got to be the Observatory.' She took hold of my shoulders and turned me around to see a big brown dome atop a huge white building that stood in stark contrast to the bright blue sky above us. 'If you think the views from the house are good, you should see what it's like from up there. Well worth the hike up the hill.'

'Hike?' I repeated. 'Uphill?'

'A scandalous thought, I know.'

Without warning, she pulled me close and wrapped her arms around me in an unprecedented hug. LA had changed her; my sister was not a hugger.

'I wish I had more time to catch up but the car will be here to pick me up in a minute,' she said, squeezing me tightly, her softly floral perfume making my nose itch. 'There's a house manual on the counter in the kitchen.

Everything is colour-coded and organized by room, and you can call me twenty-four-seven if you have an urgent question that isn't covered, although that's not possible because I compiled it myself.'

LA hadn't changed her completely.

'I'm sure I'll be fine,' I said as she released the hug but kept hold of my upper arms, giving me the big sister once-over. 'All I want right now is to stand under a shower until I can't smell the plane any more, then go to bed. I don't know how you cope with all the travel, or do you have permanent jet lag?'

'I don't believe in jet lag.' She let go of my arms, looking slightly disappointed in me. 'It's a matter of self-discipline, that's all. I don't have time for it.'

LA hadn't changed her one bit.

'You've got to fight it,' Suze said, dragging me away from her million-dollar view and back inside the house. 'Visualize yourself as someone who is wide awake.'

'I'm visualizing myself face down on the settee with my hand in a big bag of crisps,' I replied as she slid the huge glass doors shut behind us, all the outdoor noises replaced by a gentle hum. Probably the vibes she mentioned earlier. That or the air conditioning.

'Are you sure you're going to be all right on your own?' Her eyebrows knitted themselves together over her clear blue eyes. Just like mine, just like Gran's.

I smiled at the likeness. Gran really would have loved this house.

'More than,' I promised. 'I'm going to be fantastic.'

'So,' she said, picking up an apple then putting it back down. 'I saw on Facebook that Thomas is getting married in two weeks.'

Every muscle in my body contracted at once. Just when I thought it was safe to relax.

'So I hear.'

'And you're not bothered?'

'Nope.'

'You sure?'

'So sure,' I confirmed. 'I'm deeply, deeply over him.'

'Is that right,' she said with crossed arms. 'Because you haven't mentioned seeing anyone since the two of you broke up.'

'Just because I haven't mentioned anyone doesn't mean there isn't someone,' I replied, running my hand along the back of her buttery soft leather sofa. 'For all you know, I've had more men than you've had parking tickets and looking at the stack of them over there on the kitchen counter, that's a decent bloody number.'

'I've got an IQ of 152 and I still end up with at least one a month,' she muttered. 'Working out the parking regulations in LA is a full-time job but don't you go changing the subject. How many times have I tried to get you over to visit? And suddenly you're available? The timing feels like a bit of a coincidence.'

'The timing was entirely down to when I could get out of work,' I said, my voice as tight and brittle as my nerves. 'So what if Thomas is getting married? It's been two years, I truly do not care. I am unbothered, mois- turized, thriving.'

'At least one third of that is a lie because you defi- nitely are not moisturized.'

'Fine, I'm unbothered, deeply dehydrated but still thriving,' I said with a warning glance. 'Will that do, or shall we have a chat about your love life next?'

There were three things my sister refused to discuss: her love life (non-existent), her shoe size (massive) and the series finale of *Game of Thrones* (she was adamant Daenerys was justified in her actions and that she would have done exactly the same thing, including shag her hot nephew). Before I could press any further, her phone flashed to life in her hand. It was such fantastic timing, I could only assume she'd pressed a secret button that made it ring on cue.

'My car's here,' she said with more than an edge of relief in her voice. 'Fuck it, come with me. Seattle isn't that bad.'

'Apart from how it rains all the time and random people throw fish at you?' I stood in the middle of her living room with my arms open wide. 'Why would I risk an unexpected trout attack when I could stay in a real-life version of Barbie's dream home? Go, save the internet, bring me a nice present from the airport. I'll see you in two to three days.'

She paused for a moment, looked at me, down at her phone then back at me. 'It could be four.'

'Colour me shocked,' I replied. 'Now go. Before you miss your flight.'

The indecision on her face settled into reluctant resignation as she pulled me into another hug, full of powdery roses and coconut conditioner, and I only realized how tightly I was holding on to her when she pulled away.

'You're sure you'll be all right?' she asked, brushing a limp strand of hair out of my eyes. 'And that you'll stay out of trouble?'

'I wouldn't even know how to get into trouble if I saw any,' I promised, stumbling over a flash of a memory.

She pressed a kiss against my cheek, slung her handbag over her shoulder and grabbed the handle of the neat aluminium carry-on case that sat by the door, packed, locked and ready to go. 'Call me any time,' she said. 'I mean it – twenty-four-seven. Anything you need, I will fix it.'

'Suze, I am a perfectly capable thirty-three-year-old woman in an English-speaking country and I've already downloaded the American version of the Domino's app. You're only going to be gone a few days, calm down.'

I followed her to the door and wrapped myself up in my own arms as she jogged down the stairs to a sleek black car that waited with its engine running. Gran always used to say Suzanne had been rushing to catch up ever since she was born two weeks late. She never stayed in one place long enough for anyone or anything to catch her – people, thoughts or feelings – but I'd never been able to work out exactly what it was she was chasing. She climbed inside the car and waved as it pulled away, disappearing around the corner and down the hill.

And then she was gone.

'See you when you get back,' I said, taking one last look at the beautiful pink flowers in the front garden before closing the front door and locking it behind me. 'Let the holiday commence.'

CHAPTER TWO

Suzanne wasn't lying when she said the fridge was fully stocked. I'd never seen so much food in one place and a weekly trip to the big Tesco was one of the highlights of my existence, so that was really saying something. It was more of a walk-in wardrobe masquerading as a refrigerator, absolutely rammed with every kind of food-stuff you could possibly imagine, but somehow, still neat, clean and well-organized. Classic Suzanne. There were dedicated drawers full of fruit and veg, stacks of sliced meat for sandwiches, regular hummus, spicy hummus, chocolate hummus? And best of all, six different varieties of cheese. It was my dream come true. No one knew me as well as my sister.

Feeling like a teenager whose parents had gone away and left them alone for the first time, I wandered back out onto the terrace and settled on one of the sunloungers. With a bag of crisps big enough to feed a family of four in one hand and a perfectly chilled bottle of rosé in the other, I waited impatiently for my brain to catch up with my body. I'd never been a good traveller. I didn't sleep well in a strange bed and always managed to eat something dodgy and spend half my holiday in the loo. Thomas used to say it was the Chapman curse, that I was so committed to not enjoying myself, my own body revolted against the idea of having a good time like the other women in my family. I suspected it had more to do with him starfishing across every mattress and refusing to eat anything more exotic than a Nando's but who could say for certain?

'Enough of him,' I muttered under my breath. There was no one around to hear but saying it out loud helped the intention stick. There were much better things to think about than Thomas, like being eaten alive by zombie rottweilers or stabbing yourself in the eye with a stick.

Rather than dwell on the past, I concentrated on my immediate future and opened the wine to pour myself a generous measure. Might as well start as I meant to go on.

'Here's to getting away from it all,' I declared, lifting my glass to toast the city before taking a long, cool sip. Perfect, like everything else in this house.

I would be fine on my own. Better than fine. Suzanne would have scheduled every hour of my day, from dawn to dusk. I needed some sun, some fun and about a thousand hours of sleep, not wall-to-wall activities planned out by a perennial overachiever. This trip was supposed to be a chance for me to get away, relax and unwind. Forget about all the things that so badly needed to be forgotten.

'Which would take a lobotomy, not a holiday,' I muttered, pouring more wine.

With restless energy buzzing through me, I stood and stretched, glass in hand, and walked down the garden to the end of the terrace. It was so unbearably pretty. My brain was still Swiss cheese but I stared out at the city below, trying to remember everything Suzanne had pointed out to me but failing to spot a single thing.

But there was one thing that was impossible to miss.

The nearly naked man in the garden below, watching me through a pair of binoculars.

'Oh my God, pervert!' I yelled, chucking the contents of my glass over the edge of the terrace. 'I'm calling the police!'

'I'm not a pervert!' the man shouted back, setting down his binoculars. 'I swear, I wasn't spying on you!'

With shaking hands and a regrettably empty glass, I peered over the edge at the Peeping Tom and gulped. An honest to God, audible, cartoon character gulp. Pervert or not, he was the most handsome man I had ever seen with my own eyes, and that was coming from a woman who once spent an evening in the company of the UK's second most popular Channing Tatum impersonator. He was a lovely chap called Darryl. Couldn't dance to save his life but he tried his best.

But this man? He was something else. Tall, tanned and wearing nothing but swimming trunks and a smile, his bare chest glowed in the golden hour light, his muscular arms held up in mock surrender. And the body wasn't even the half of it. His face was a masterpiece. Full lips, square jaw and piercing green eyes, all anchored by the kind of perfectly masculine nose sculptors had been trying and failing to recreate for centuries. Michelangelo could never. When he shook his dark,

messy hair out of his face and our eyes met, I almost
fell over. It wasn't fair, people shouldn't be allowed to
walk around looking like that without a paper bag over
their head and a siren blaring to warn us normals. He
was a living, breathing, possibly peeping safety hazard.

'I wasn't spying on you,' the half-naked man called
out. 'I swear.'

'Then what were you doing?' I challenged.

His lips curved upwards on his irresponsibly beautiful face.

'Birdwatching.'

What an incredibly shit lie.

'I was looking at the bushtits when I saw a red-tailed
hawk land in that tree,' he added. 'It's up in those trees
over there. Can you see it?'

'Who are you calling a bushtit?' I replied, my cheeks
turning pink as I put down my glass and leaned over
the edge of the terrace, searching for this alleged bird.
'You're full of it, I can't see anything.'

He held out his hand and cocked his head back
towards his own garden. 'She's definitely in there, I
think there's a nest. Come down here and I'll show you.'

'Are you going to kill me and eat me?' I asked, peering
down at him and trying not to be blinded by his beauty.

'Not on purpose,' he replied. 'I'm vegan.'

It was still a pretty tempting offer. On the one hand,
I didn't know this man from Adam. Suzanne was
away, I didn't know anyone else in the city, no one
knew where I was and no one was expecting to hear
from me, so if this Bill-Oddie-wannabe-slash-demigod
turned out to be a serial killer, I'd be completely on
my own.

On the other hand, what a way to go.

'Everyone has at least one flaw,' I muttered, decision made. 'OK, let's see these birds. How do I get down?'

'This way, I'll show you.'

He jogged over to the back corner of his garden and I followed, keeping to the edge of Suzanne's terrace, tapping my hand along the fence to remind myself this was really happening and not some jet-lag-induced fever dream. Unless it wasn't, in which case I would be very happy to never wake up again. Right at the edge of the terrace, where the platform met the hillside, I saw a shallow set of stairs cut into the ground below.

'If you climb over the fence, you should be able to get down,' the most handsome man in the world assured me. 'There's an exposed tree root you can use as a handrail if that helps.'

'Nothing will help,' I muttered, throwing one leg over and trying not to look down as I straddled the fence. 'I'm not a naturally graceful person. Or flexible person. Or good at climbing. Sorry, why am I doing this? Does your house not have a front door?'

'My grandpa used to go up and down those stairs every day until he was almost eighty so I think you'll be OK,' he replied as I heaved my other leg over the fence and hurled my body at the side of the hill, clinging to the snarled knot of exposed root. 'I'm here. If you fall, I'll catch you.'

I dug my fingers into the dirt, my body pressed against the hillside like a cat that had collided with a patio door. All I had to do was concentrate on what was directly in front of me: muck, tree, fence, steps. I would not look at the city skyline behind me, I would not look at the underside of the terrace above and I would not look at the exposed nipples of the man below. I stared straight ahead, moving slowly, determined not to wonder whether or not that odd, musty odour I kept getting a whiff of was me.

'There you go!' I heard the Adonis say as my left foot found solid ground. 'You did it!'

Bolstered by a sudden burst of confidence, I turned around too quickly, beaming with pride and buzzing with adrenaline, only to slip off the last step and fall straight into his arms.

'I did it,' I cheered weakly, my face nestled against his broad chest. He smelled as good as he looked; a mixture of warm skin, sunscreen and a woodsy, leathery scent that made me ovulate fourteen days early. Either he'd been building an armchair naked in the forest or I needed to buy shares in whichever company made that aftershave.

'You do know you're not wearing any clothes?' I said, fingertips still glued to his pecs. He was so solid. I'd never laid hands on anyone so physically dense before and I had to admit, I didn't hate it.

'If I'd known you were coming, I'd have put on a tux,' he replied. I prised my hands off him and tugged at my jeans and T-shirt in a vain attempt to sort myself out. Not that he was even looking at me, his deep, beautiful green eyes were firmly focused on the treeline. 'They're so cool; almost any time you hear a hawk in a movie or on TV, it's a red-tail. Classic raptor cry, gotta be one of my top ten favourite birds of all time.'

'I don't know if I could even name ten different kinds of birds,' I replied, refocusing my efforts and searching the skies for signs of life. 'You're sure it's up there?'

He nodded without taking his eyes off the tree.

'Positive.'

'How big is it?'

'Bigger than a crow, smaller than a goose. Pretty big.'

I stood at the bottom of a stranger's garden, still in my travelling clothes, side by side with the fantastic-smelling, beautiful man and stared into the branches, willing the hawk to come into sight. But there was nothing. The longer we stood there, the more certain I was I'd caught him spying on Suzanne's house and instead of confessing, he'd lured me down here with a ridiculous story about a giant hawk so he could laugh at me later with his friends. It was like Thomas always said; I was so gullible, I would believe anything if someone said it with a straight face. My jaw tightened, my hands formed tiny fists and just as I was about to make my excuses and leave, I heard a rustling high in the trees. Up above me, was a beautiful bird, bigger than a crow, smaller than a goose, with a snowy white chest, speckled with tawny-coloured spots, and rusty red tail feathers. She opened up her brown wings and shook them proudly for her audience.

'Oh wow,' I gasped, placing my hands over my heart. 'There really is a hawk.'

'Yeah,' the man replied. 'There is.'

'And she's gorgeous.'

'Yeah,' he said again. 'She is.'

I looked back at Suzanne's neighbour and saw he was no longer staring at the trees.

'I'm Ren, by the way.'

He held out a hand and after a moment's pause, I took it in mine. Dry palm, good strong wrist, firm grasp but not too aggressive. Too many careers teachers had convinced too many men their masculinity would be questioned if they didn't break at least three fingers with every handshake. Ren had it just right.

'Wren like the bird? That's convenient.'

'Without the "W",' he replied. 'It's short for Efren, Efren Garcia.'

'I'm Phoebe. Phoebe Chapman,' I replied, reluctantly letting go of his hand and quietly wondering whether or not anyone had ever actually blushed themselves to death. 'My sister owns the house up there, I'm visiting for a couple of weeks.'

Before he could respond, the hawk stretched out her wings and rose from her perch, circling above us for a moment before swooping low then flying off up the hill, her namesake tail feathers on full display. The little hussy.

'Good to meet you, Phoebe Chapman,' Ren said. He rested his hands on his hips and his index fingers slid neatly into sharply chiselled lines below his waist I thought only existed on men called Chris who made action movies. 'So you're here on vacation?'

'Yep,' I confirmed, realizing how naked he was all over again. He seemed perfectly fine with it but in fairness, if I looked like him, I'd probably stop wearing clothes altogether. String bikini for the post office? Why not. A thong and pasties to pop to the bank? Almost too much coverage.

'First time in LA?'

'Is it that obvious?'

'A wild guess,' he grinned. 'Allow me to welcome you to Los Angeles. Spotting a red-tailed hawk has to be a good omen; they don't come that close to people too often.'

I turned my attention away from the treeline and took a look around his garden instead. It was so different to Suzanne's place, no hot tub, no outdoor kitchen, no gas grill or wall-mounted TV, just a quiet, peaceful little tree-lined enclave. He did have a pool but where Suzanne's was long and rectangular, Ren's was much smaller and shaped like a kidney bean. There was more grass too and so many different kinds of flowers. The back of the house was covered in dark green wooden planks which gave it the look of a rustic log cabin rather than a swanky Mediterranean resort. Past the pool I saw a shed, one side opened up to reveal a work bench covered in chunks of wood and well-used tools. Maybe he had been building an armchair naked in the forest after all. The mental image alone would be enough to keep me warm through the cold winter nights.

It was so odd. Two such different homes sitting so close together on the same street, Suzanne's facing south and Ren's facing west, down the hill and round the corner. They didn't look as though they belonged in the same time period, let alone the same postcode.

'So, you're a big birdwatcher then?' I asked, coyly brushing a strand of hair behind my ear and immediately getting it caught in my watch strap. Why did I even bother?

'Oh, yeah, huge. I'm obsessed,' he replied with all the confidence of a man who knew exactly how good-looking he was. I couldn't think of anyone else on earth who would admit to it quite so readily without fear of at least gentle mockery, but people probably weren't as inclined to take the piss when you were as beautiful as Ren. If I decided to take up trainspotting, I'd be laughed out of existence. If Scarlett Johansson did it, no one would scoff and call her an anorak. They'd be too busy nodding and stroking their chins and explaining why trains were actually incredibly cool on some pro-Scarlett SubReddit.

'My abuelito, my grandpa, was a big bird guy,' Ren explained, the Spanish tripping expertly off his tongue. 'He would lie out here for hours watching them, always trying out different bird feed recipes, building his own bird houses. He kept logs, journals, I still have them all inside. They're like his diaries, you know? So it runs in the family. Birds are fascinating if you pay attention.'

'Can't say I've ever really thought that much about them,' I confessed, still trying to work my watch out of my hair without scalping myself. 'They're just there, aren't they?'

Ren shrugged. 'They are until they're not.'

Right as I freed my watch from my hair and opened my mouth to reply, a huge flock of great big, noisy green birds swooshed overhead, cawing loudly. Instinctively, I ducked, covering my head with my hands, eyes tightly closed. What was going on? Why hadn't Suzanne mentioned she lived on the set of *The Birds*?

'Wow, OK, you can stand up,' Ren said with an astonished whistle. 'They're not coming for you.'

'Is it me or was that a bunch of parrots?' I asked, opening one eye at a time, still far from convinced that I could trust him.

'Traditionally we say flock but yeah. The story goes that they started out as pets until someone released them in the sixties and they've been living wild ever since. Now they're feral.'

I stood slowly, prepared for another attack, and opened my mouth to ask another question, but instead an enormous, unstoppable yawn escaped, shaking my whole body from head to toe.

'You can say if I'm boring you,' he said as I clamped my hands over the lower half of my face, eyes wide with apology. 'I know, I'm a bird nerd.'

'I'm so sorry, it's not that,' I exclaimed through a second, smaller yawn. 'I only landed a couple of hours ago and the time difference is killing me. It's a miracle I'm still awake, let alone standing up. I'd be much happier flat on my back in bed.'

The words were out before I realized what I'd said. Ren spluttered with laughter and I closed my eyes, willing time to do me a solid and rewind by about fifteen minutes or so.

'What I meant to say was, I really need to get some sleep,' I corrected, my cheeks burning with the heat of seven suns. 'A lot of it. Urgently.'

'Jet lag is a killer,' he agreed, reaching one arm across his chest and clasping the opposite shoulder, his triceps flexing casually. I wasn't even sure I had triceps. It was disgusting how handsome he was. 'But I'm glad you stayed awake long enough to see the hawk.'

'And I'm glad you're not a pervert.'

He laughed again as I groaned at myself. What was wrong with me?

'Sorry,' I said again. 'My mouth is completely bypassing my brain. I'm going to go before I say something *really* stupid.'

'Let me help you back up the stairs,' he offered. 'Unless you'd rather go through the house?'

I glowered at the steep, shallow steps that led back up to the terrace. The front door was locked and my keys were upstairs on the kitchen counter. There was only one way I was getting back up.

'I'm sure I can do it,' I said, steeling myself. 'But if I do fall, please leave me to die. Suzanne says you have to pay to go to hospital here and I forgot to get travel insurance.'

'OK, but I'm going to need that in writing,' Ren replied. 'I've heard your sister yelling at people on the phone. She wasn't even talking to me and I was still afraid of her.'

I smiled proudly.

'That's my Suzanne. Absolutely petrifying, isn't she?'

With the promise of a hot shower and a good night's sleep in a king-sized bed hovering in front of me, I grabbed hold of the exposed root sticking out of the hillside and scrabbled around in the dirt, trying to find my footing. Climbing up the stairs required a lot more strength and focus than climbing down, but I was determined not to embarrass myself in front of my sister's god-like neighbour. At least not any more than I already had.

'You said your grandad used to do this every day?' I huffed, looking back after climbing what felt like Mount Everest only to discover I was about three feet off the ground. 'Was he part mountain goat?'

'The stairs were cut in a little deeper back then,' Ren admitted, slapping his palm against the dirt. 'And there used to be a real railing at the side which made life easier, and abuelito didn't have to climb over such a high fence at the top – your sister added that.'

'Practically exactly the same as it is now then,' I said with a grunt, my foot slipping out from underneath me as I felt around for the next step. 'I'm OK,' I yelled, dangling precariously. 'But like I said, I've no health insurance. Unless I stop breathing all together, I'm sure I'll be able to walk off any injuries.'

'Let me help,' he offered. 'I've got you.'

'Got me how?' I asked, glancing down between my legs just in time to see him bend over and squat down, positioning himself directly underneath me before hoisting me up onto his shoulders. I shrieked with surprise, clamping my thighs around his neck and grabbing at his head, clutching handfuls of hair as tightly as I could.

'It would be great if you could take your hands off my eyes,' he said, arms outstretched like Frankenstein's hot monster. 'This feels like one of those moments where being able to see would be a real bonus.'

'Sorry,' I squealed, moving my hands from off his eyes and into his hair as we rose upwards. 'It's been a long time since I had someone's head between my legs. I mean, my legs around someone's head. I mean, well, both actually.'

'Please don't make me laugh or we're both dead,' Ren replied through gritted teeth, holding me steady as he climbed.

'My name is Phoebe and I say stupid things when I'm in awkward situations,' I whispered, ignoring visions of Therese smiling and shaking her head. The moment it was within reach, I grabbed hold of the fence and hauled myself up and over with all the grace of a drunken guinea pig, and only once I was sure there was solid ground beneath my feet did I turn back to see Ren casually hanging one handed from the tree root, muddy marks up and down his bare chest.

'Oh no,' I said slowly. 'I made a mess of your . . . body.'

'Pretty sure it'll come off in the shower,' he replied, dropping down into his garden and rubbing at his skin. But rubbing only made more of a mess, smearing it across his pecs and his abs and it was all too much for my tired, confused brain. I hadn't felt anything approaching a knicker flicker in so long and I was suddenly both intensely aroused and deeply confused, almost certain I was one bicep flex away from spontaneously combusting. He wasn't even my type, far too perfect, but some things were beyond reason and one of them was Ren Garcia's six pack. It wasn't my fault, it was the jet lag. Twenty-four hours without sleep combined with twelve plus hours of watching Taylor Lautner with his top off on the plane. It couldn't be helped.

'I'm going to go inside,' I announced. 'Thank you for . . . that.'

'Great to meet you, Phoebe,' he said, raising a hand in farewell. 'I hope you have a great vacation. Let me know if you need anything at all.'

Slack-jawed, I watched him walk back to his house, muscles rippling under the skin of his back as he brushed himself down, wondering just how far that offer extended.

I'd only been in LA for a few hours and I'd already seen a hawk, been attacked by a flock of parrots, abandoned by my sister and muddied the torso of a very handsome man.

The holiday was officially off to a great start.

CHAPTER THREE

'Good morning, sunshine, up and at 'em!'

Suzanne might not believe in jet lag but I did. When I opened my eyes, I had no idea where I was or who was talking to me. Everything was too bright, too loud, and my mouth tasted like the furry grey insides of that cup of tea I'd put down in the spare room when the postman rang the doorbell then found three weeks later.

'Did you fall asleep on the couch again?' a peppy voice called. 'Suzie, we've talked about this!'

I had indeed slept on the couch. Suzanne's couch? I was in Suzanne's house! And so was this complete stranger who had let themselves in without knocking. Frantically, I searched for a weapon and grabbed the empty wine bottle I'd finished off the night before. I prepared to strike, paused, and swapped the bottle for a massive paperweight from the side table. I didn't want them to think I was a lush. No one liked a judgemental burglar.

'Even if it's a late night, you have got to go to bed. It sets your intention and— Intruder! Intruder alert!'

A tiny brunette decked out in royal blue athleisure-wear appeared across the room, took one look at me and leapt into a defensive pose, producing a shiny silver canister from the hot-pink bag she had slung across her body. In my panic, I leapt off the settee, crashed into the coffee table and ended up face down on the rug, my weapon spinning away across the living room floor.

'Hands where I can see them, scumbag!' she yelled. 'I'm armed and I'm not afraid to use it! What have you done with Suzanne?'

'I haven't done anything with Suzanne!' I wailed, my face buried in the shag pile. It was actually quite difficult to put your hands in the air when you were lying on your stomach. I hoped she wouldn't be too upset that I'd only managed to lift them up three inches and, I don't know, shoot me. 'I'm her sister, Phoebe, I'm visiting from England. I'm Phoebe visiting from England!'

Turning my head was no easier than raising my arms but I managed to contort myself just enough to see her shrug, relax her karate stance and slip the silver canister back inside her bag. Her fancy trainers moved towards me and stopped right in front of my nose as my heart rate stuttered back down to something that wouldn't require medical assistance.

'I can't believe I almost maced you,' she said, smiling as she held out a hand to help me up. 'Nice to meet you, Phoebe from England. I'm Bel.'

My knees creaked with slept-on-the-sofa distress and as I pulled myself up to my full five feet five inches, I saw the full glory of my assailant for the first time. She was completely gorgeous. Her hair was long and dark, falling over her shoulders in glossy, undone waves, and thick sooty lashes framed the huge brown eyes that dominated her heart-shaped face, leaving enough room for her adorable snub nose and glorious smile. Her sports bra and leggings clung to her slender frame like a second skin. Was everyone in LA this beautiful? Everything about Bel was sparkling, shiny and box fresh, from her baby-pink trainers to her crossbody bag. The only box I looked fresh out of was a coffin. I looked down at my jeans and T-shirt, also clinging to the curves of my body but more like they were holding on for dear life. Not so much a second skin as actual skin, they were part of me now.

'Nice to meet you too,' I said eventually.

It was a lie. It was not nice to meet her. Her unexpected entrance had taken at least ten years off my life but I was far too English to tell the truth.

'This might be a silly question,' I said, discreetly wiping my face to make sure I hadn't drooled on myself in my sleep. I had. 'But what are you doing in my sister's house?'

She cocked her head to one side, planting tiny fists on her narrow waist like a Gen Z Peter Pan.

'I'm Bel Johnson? I'm her trainer?'

A question and an answer all at once.

'Suzanne has a trainer?' I repeated, blinking as I worked through my confusion. 'As in a personal trainer? Who makes her do exercise?'

It simply wasn't possible. Of all the random things my sister might have done since moving to America, hiring a trainer was the least believable. Suzanne hated exercise so much, when she was fourteen, she stole a notepad from the doctor's surgery and used it to get out of PE for the following two years. And now I was supposed to believe that same person was paying another human being to make her exercise? By choice?

'We have HIIT drills this morning,' Bel replied, checking the time on the huge smart watch that overwhelmed her slender wrist. 'Is she ready? She knows it's ten extra push-ups for every minute she keeps me waiting.'

Extra push-ups? As in there was already a designated number of push-ups to be completed?

'She's in Seattle,' I told her, my own over-cooked spaghetti arms flopping helplessly at my sides. 'She left last night.'

When she laughed, I half expected a flurry of blue-birds to flock through the patio doors to perch on her shoulders. It was the sweetest, most perfect sound I had ever heard, including but not limited to Harry Styles' entire back catalogue, both solo and with One Direction.

'I can't believe she took off without cancelling me,' she replied, shaking her pretty little head. 'Although it was bound to happen eventually, right? Can't keep that woman in one place for long, always on the move, zoom, zoom, zoom.' She danced around the low marble coffee table and launched herself onto the overstuffed settee. 'I guess I'm getting the morning off.'

Even though every cell in my body told me I shouldn't like this cheerful, confident, exercise-inclined woman, I couldn't stop myself from returning her smile when she beamed at me across the coffee table. As a general rule, I shied away from women like her, the glossy, put-together ones, the girls who knew how to curl their hair with a straightening iron and had a personalized, pre-set filter for their social media posts. They always made me feel anxious, less than. But despite the fact Bel had the definite look of someone who would ask you your sun, moon and rising sign within the first five minutes of meeting you, she also seemed kind, the type who would top off your wine without being asked then put a curse on your ex-boyfriend.

'So, you're Suzanne's sister,' she said. She sat up, stacking her lithe legs underneath her in a perfect lotus pose. 'How are you liking LA? Are you having fun? What did y'all do? Did she take you out for tacos yet? I bet she took you to Guisados, Suzie loves Guisados. Did you get the sampler? Which one was your favourite?'

I rubbed the sleep out of my eyes, trying to work out which one to answer first. 'No?'

'No what?'

'No tacos?'

Her expression instantly flipped and her face contorted in horror, as though Suzanne not taking me for Mexican food the moment I arrived was some sort of human rights violation. Which, now I thought about it, it was.

'I only got here yesterday afternoon and she had to leave almost right away,' I explained. My stomach grumbled loudly at the talk of tacos, reminding me I hadn't eaten a proper meal on this continent. Crisps and wine were admittedly a small part of the food pyramid, however important. 'We didn't really get the chance to do anything. Or eat anything.'

'Then I arrived at the perfect time!' Bel exclaimed, pulling her phone out of her bag and tapping away at the screen. 'We have to get some food in you, girlie, I'm taking you out for brunch. Let me see what's open, we'll do a little welcome to LA moment.'

'Oh no, you don't have to do that,' I said as my stomach howled in protest. 'I still need to shower and unpack and—'

But Bel wasn't having any of it.

'Little Dom's!' she exclaimed, cutting me off as she leapt to her dainty feet. 'It's the most perfect place, they have the most amazing pancakes you've ever tasted in your life.'

'Pancakes?' I whispered, my excuses fading away in an instant.

Her brown eyes glowed. 'Blueberry ricotta pancakes. With butter and warm maple syrup and freshly brewed coffee and—'

'I'm in,' I replied quickly. I knew when I was beaten. 'You had me at pancakes.'

'You're going to love it,' she replied with a wink. 'Wear something with an elasticated waist.'

I liked her more and more by the minute.

Not nearly soon enough, I was showered, dressed and sitting on a little folding chair outside the nearby restaurant. The sun shone and the sky was clear but aside from that, it didn't feel very Hollywood. For starters, we'd been sitting down for five whole minutes and I hadn't seen a single famous person. There were no palm trees, no fancy cars, no red carpets; just a lot of people wearing workout clothes and a surprising amount of buckled concrete. Across the road, I watched a woman, who had accessorized her neon-pink leggings with a matching Hermès Birkin, stroll into a shop called The Reckless Unicorn. If someone offered me a million dollars on the spot, I couldn't have guessed what they sold inside. Were unicorns known to be reckless? Maybe that's why there weren't any. Maybe they made bad investments and crossed the street without looking.

I rocked from side to side in my chair, riding the uneven pavement and testing the integrity of the wonky wooden table. It was propped up by three cardboard coasters rammed under one of its legs. Where was the glitz? Where was the glamour? Where were the flat surfaces?

'It's so busy,' I said to Bel, watching a waitress deliver several giant plates full of food to the table next to us. It was all I could do not to snatch it off the tray and stuff it in my mouth. Even after a skin-scorching shower and a change of clothes, I felt as feral as one of last night's parrots. 'I thought people didn't eat in LA.'

'That's a very 2006 vibe.' Bel waved a hand to dismiss the notion. 'Eating is so in right now, everyone's doing it.'

I looked up from my menu, expecting to see a smirk on her face, but no, she remained as earnest as ever.

'Then this might be the first time in my life I've been ahead of a trend,' I replied happily.

A waitress in a smart white shirt appeared at my elbow, pen and order pad at the ready.

'Can I start you off with anything to drink? Mimosa, orange juice, coffee?' She paused and gave me a knowing look. 'Hot tea?'

There was an entire page in Suzanne's house manual about ordering tea in and the gist of it was 'don't do it'. I had no idea how anyone could mess up boiling water and a teabag but the way the waitress had emphasized the word 'hot' was enough to make my Tetley senses tingle.

'I'll have a coffee,' I said appreciatively. 'Thank you.'

'Make it two,' Bel added, studying her menu like it was a map to the lost city of gold. 'So, we have to get the blueberry ricotta pancakes for the table. The steak and eggs are great, breakfast sandwich is to die for, everyone gets breakfast pizza, it's super popular, and I hear the yoghurt parfait is divine but I don't eat dairy. Except for the ricotta in the pancakes. And the cheese on the pizza. Do you like baked eggs? The baked eggs are so good. What are you thinking?'

It was a very good question.

'I have no idea. It all sounds amazing,' I hadn't heard a single thing after the word 'pancakes'. 'If the table is having the pancakes, I'll get the super popular breakfast pizza, when in Rome and all that.'

She reached across the table to touch my hand. 'This isn't Rome,' she whispered in a kind voice. 'It's Little Dom's.'

'My mistake,' I replied, wondering how she managed to survive in this cruel, harsh world.

'And that's how I ended up naked in the hot-air balloon.' Bel wrapped both hands around a sturdy stoneware coffee cup and smiled. 'But enough about my weekend, you've hardly said a word since we got here. I want to know everything about you – spill.'

I didn't have much in the world but I did have a very particular set of skills and one of the strongest of those skills was the ability to get other people to talk about themselves while sharing absolutely nothing about myself, and in the ten minutes that had passed since ordering our breakfast, I'd learned that Bel was originally from Wisconsin, she was twenty-six, moved to LA four years ago to become an actress and while she'd appeared as an extra in a few different things and had one whole line in a Netflix film about a boy that turned into an Alsatian every time he ate a hot dog, she was still waiting for her big break.

'There's not that much to say,' I replied, so breezy. Being breezy was a big part of throwing people off the scent. 'Suzanne is the overachiever in our family, I'm very boring and normal. Now tell me more about the audition you did with Bradley Cooper.'

'It was with Bradley Cooper's assistant's assistant and I passed out in the waiting room because I was too nervous to eat the three days before the audition. Now back to you.'

Pouring half a jug of cream into my coffee, I watched it surge back up to the surface, swirling white on black. 'What's to tell? I'm sure Suzanne has filled you in on the important stuff.'

'Suzanne tells me nothing,' she said with a pretty snort. 'For the first three months we were working together, I was convinced she was a spy. Talk about a closed book.'

'Yeah, she's never been especially forthcoming,' I admitted, picturing my sister's flinty glare. 'She had this boyfriend, Victor, years ago now. They met at university, moved in together when they graduated, the whole bit, and right when we thought they were going to get engaged, she dumped him. Completely out of the blue. They'd been together for years, he was devastated.'

Bel stared at me with wide eyes, rapt. 'And she wasn't?'

'You don't like to use the word sociopath about someone in your own family,' I said, sucking the air in through my teeth. 'But she's definitely someone who likes to stay in control of her emotions.'

'I don't know if she's a sociopath. This one time, I was dropping off her pre-workout and when she opened the door, her eyes were all red and puffy and I know she doesn't smoke, so . . . I think she'd been crying.'

I almost fell off my chair. 'Really? You saw Suzanne cry?'

'She was watching a cartoon? About dinosaurs? And there was a bunch of Kleenex on the sofa?'

'Well, that explains it,' I said, everything suddenly making sense. 'She was watching *The Land Before Time*. Littlefoot is her one weakness, it's enough to break anyone.'

'I was a little freaked out,' Bel confessed. 'It's the only time I've ever seen her emote. Mostly she seems super caught up in her job, I don't think she holds space for a whole lot else.'

I picked a packet of brown sugar from the bowl in the middle of the table and gave it a flick before tearing it open and dumping the contents into my coffee. 'She's always been ambitious and she's always been successful,' I reasoned. 'Our gran used to say Suzanne could achieve anything she put her mind to, and so far she hasn't been proved wrong.'

'What about you? Are you ambitious?'

'Depends on your definition of ambitious,' I said, stirring my coffee. 'I like my job but I'm not obsessed with success the way Suzanne always has been. That said, if you need to know when to celebrate World Veterinary Day, I'm the UK's leading expert.'

She clasped her hands together and squealed with delight.

'You're a vet?'

'Not quite,' I replied. 'I'm a greetings card copywriter.'

'Really? That sounds amazing, wow.' Somehow, she managed to make one three-letter word last for what felt like an hour. 'I mean, I have no idea what it is, but it sounds totally incredible.'

It was almost impossible to believe this woman was real. I've never met anyone so enthusiastic about absolutely everything in my entire life. She was hyperbole personified.

'I write the poems and things for cards,' I explained. 'Birthday cards, Christmas cards, administrative assistant appreciation day cards. There's not much else to tell you but do mark the last Saturday in April in your diary, poor vets never get their due.'

'I went on a date with a vet once,' she said, twirling a strand of glossy hair around her finger. 'So hot, but I couldn't stop thinking about how he spent all day poking around in a dog's butt.'

'Probably won't put that on the cards for next year.' I grimaced at the thought, now marginally less excited for my pancakes. 'You must have a lot of good dating stories – what's the craziest date you've ever been on?'

'Nice try but I don't think so.' She pointed at me with an accusatory teaspoon. 'We're talking about you. Tell me more about your super awesome job.'

'Bel,' I said, warming my fingertips against my coffee mug. 'Any chance you were a cheerleader in high school?'

'And in college!'

Shaking my head slightly, I smiled down at the table,

oddly moved by her unreserved enthusiasm. Usually, someone with such a complete and utter lack of cynicism was kryptonite to me, but there was something about Bel that made me want to lie down with my head in her lap so she could stroke my hair and tell me it was all going to be OK. She was a real-life Disney princess only with baby-pink Nikes instead of glass slippers. Much more practical when you thought about it, far less likely to slice through your Achilles tendon.

'OK, but remember you asked,' I said as she gazed at me from across the table. 'Basically, the sales team tells me how many different cards they want for each season or celebration, let's say fifteen cards for Mother's Day, and how many they want in each style, for example, they might want five cute cards, five funny cards and five modern cards.'

'Got it,' she said, her lips pursed with concentration.

'Once that's worked out, I sit down and write the words. Love poems for Valentine's Day, jokes about golf for Father's Day, that sort of thing.'

'Why golf?'

'Beats me, but we sell a lot of golf-related cards to dads. As soon as a man has spawned, his interest in hitting small balls with a big stick goes up by roughly 74 per cent.'

'I get it,' she replied. 'My brother's kids make me want to hit something. For real, they're monsters, you wanna . . .' She cut herself off and reset her smile. 'Thankfully I don't see them that often. So, Phoebe, do you like your job?'

No one had ever asked me that before. I wasn't sure how to answer. Did I like my job?

'I suppose I do,' I told her, almost surprised to hear myself say it. 'Writing and reading have always been my favourite things. I never thought someone would actually pay me to write, even if it is just making up jokes for birthday cards. I work from home, the money is decent, my boss isn't terrible. Yes, I do like my job.'

Bel rested her elbows on the table and cradled her face in her hands. 'You're so lucky, not many people can say that.'

'Do you like your job?' I asked, relaxing against the back of my rickety chair, warm in this new knowledge about myself.

She pulled her shoulders all the way up to her ears and held them there. 'I like some of my jobs. I have a bunch, I'm not just a trainer, you know? I walk dogs, I work as a cater-waiter, I lead meditation classes, I run a women's self-defence club, oh, and I'm an activist.'

'That's amazing,' I replied with genuine admiration. 'I always feel like I should be doing more for important causes, but I never know where to start, it's all so overwhelming.'

'Oh yes, I know, but I can't sit by and do nothing, not when there's so much injustice in the world,' she said solemnly. 'Show me an important cause and I will march for it. Sometimes I make signs, sometimes I hand out snacks.' She leaned forward, dropping her voice to a conspiratorial tone. 'Between you and me, I was *very* instrumental in the Free Britney campaign. My facialist's roommate's ex-girlfriend's cousin started the original hashtag.'

I bit my lip and nodded in solidarity. It was, in

fairness, a very important cause. Not one I was expecting but still.

Bel sat back and sipped her coffee. 'And obvs, I act.'

'Obvs,' I repeated because it really was just that. Why else would a gorgeous, charming, charismatic, pocket-sized human be in Hollywood?

'The problem is, no one in LA is hiring anything less than an eleven,' she said, trailing her fingers through her shiny, silky hair and letting it fall around her high cheekbones. 'And I might be a Wisconsin ten but that's only an LA six.'

'Christ,' I muttered, raking my tangled, still-damp hair away from my still-tired face. 'What does that make me?'

'You're a beautiful soul and no one could ever put a number on you.'

'Thank you,' I said with a smile.

'But if I had to, I'd say a four.'

'Thank you,' I said without a smile.

'Hey, it's brutal out here,' she commiserated brightly. 'I'm sure you're solid double digits back at home but think about it. In Los Angeles, you can run into Margot Robbie at the grocery store, Kristen Stewart might be filling up her car at the next gas pump. One time, I saw Emma Stone at my Pilates class and I simply could not concentrate on my roll-ups because I felt like such a troll. In real life, that woman *glows*.'

'I was in the queue behind Nadiya from *Bake Off* in the supermarket a few months ago and all I had in my basket was a bottle of wine and an entire cheesecake marked down to half off because it was almost out of date,' I said, enduring a full body cringe at the memory. 'So I think I get it.'

'I don't know who that is, but it sounds terrible and I'm so sorry,' she said, briefly touching my wrist. 'You know what they say, life is suffering.'

'The Buddha?' I replied.

'No, I think it was Aviva Drescher,' she said. 'She's like the wisest housewife.'

She pulled a tube of gloss out of her bag and stared off into middle distance as she slicked it across her full, pillowy lips. Two men at the next table watched, their tongues hanging out almost all the way into their lunch. I assumed being worshipped wherever you went was something you got used to when you were as gorgeous as she was, they probably hadn't even registered on her radar. I was constantly aware of every single thing happening around me every single moment and it was exhausting.

'Do you have a boyfriend?' Bel asked as one of the men unsubtly rearranged the crotch of his unfortunately baggy, pale grey shorts. 'Or a girlfriend? A partner?'

I shook my head, shifting my chair until both men were out of my eyeline. 'None of the above, as single as single can be.'

A fact that didn't usually bother me, but then again, my ex wasn't usually getting married in two weeks.

'Me too!' She smacked her lips together before she put the gloss away. 'I love being single. It's the only way to really get to know yourself, you know? I love dating around, meeting new people. Who wants to settle down? I wouldn't have it any other way, and oh my gosh, the love of my life is walking right towards us, whatever you do, don't look.'

I looked immediately.

It was Ren.

'I said don't look,' Bel hissed, mussing up her hair until her entire face was completely covered. 'He'll see us!'

'And you don't want him to see us?'

'No!'

'But you said he's the love of your life?'

'Yes!'

'Well, that's not confusing at all,' I said as she slid down in her chair, any part of her not covered by her hair now hidden by the table. 'How come you don't want him to see you if he's the love of your life?'

'Because he doesn't even know I exist,' she said quickly as Ren came ever closer. 'I see him all the time when I'm at your sister's house; he lives next door but I've never been able to work up the courage to speak to him.'

I could hardly believe what I was hearing. '*You* don't have the courage to speak to *him*?' I echoed. 'You, stunningly beautiful Bel Johnson, who threatened to mace a stranger then took said stranger out to brunch?'

'You don't get it,' she wailed. 'I can't talk to him, I like him so much and, oh jeez, is he coming over here?'

'Certainly is,' I replied as she frantically searched for an escape route. But it was too late.

'Hey! It's my new neighbour!'

I stood as Ren came over, Bel staring slack-jawed when he picked me up off the ground in a quite honestly over-familiar hug. But then again, it was only fourteen hours since he'd had his head between my legs. In return, I pulled a rubber-faced expression, doing my best to let her know I was as surprised as she was, while also giving him a good sniff. Still so delicious.

'For someone who arrived yesterday, you did a damn good job of hunting down the best brunch spot in town,' Ren said as he set me back down on the ground, as wobbly legged as my chair.

'That's because my very good friend, Bel, suggested it,' I replied, smoothing out my shirt and doing my level best not to rub my face into his armpit for one more blast of that woody, leathery, masculine scent. 'Have you two met?'

'I don't think so.' He shifted his smile to Bel, one hand stuck in the back pocket of his jeans, the other cupped around the back of his neck, the sleeves of his crisp, white T-shirt straining around his biceps. 'Hey, nice to meet you, I'm Ren.'

I glanced over at my brunch mate only to discover the beautiful, sweet person I'd been talking to moments before had been replaced with a woman-sized badger in people clothes. Her hair hung limp in front of her face, her lips were twisted in a grimace that revealed only her bottom teeth and the glazed look in her eyes screamed *Why yes, I would like to discuss the current market value of my Beanie Baby collection.*

'Snigh!' She threw one arm into the air, presumably aiming for a wave but ending up fascist salute-adjacent. I winced for her as she lowered it slowly back under the table.

'Snigh to you too,' Ren replied. His features softened with the same consideration you might show a small child or a very drunk man who has lost the rest of the stag party.

'We only met yesterday,' I added quietly.

'I'm glad I ran into you,' Ren said, turning his attention

back to me as Bel's bottom lip began to quiver. 'I saw our hawk again this morning. I think she might have a nest in the Bishop's Pine.'

'I do hope that's a kind of tree,' I said, looking over at Bel to give her an encouraging glance. 'How cool is that, Bel?'

'So cool,' whispered the breathing bundle of hair sitting across from me.

'Right,' Ren confirmed, his eyes flicking to her with mild concern. 'Anyway, I think I could get a better view from your deck. Would it be OK if I come over some time with my binoculars?'

Wow. This was the place where dreams come true. A beautiful man was standing in front of me, asking if he could come to my house to look at my birds. I'd been waiting for this moment all my life. The fact the birds were real and not a weird euphemism was a bit disappointing but beggars could not be choosers.

'Don't see why not,' I replied. 'If you have the hawk's consent, you have mine.'

'How about tomorrow? Around sunset is usually the best time to see them. Say six-ish?'

He looked delighted, I looked delighted, Bel looked like she was about to cry.

'Perfect, I'll make dinner,' I offered. 'Or to be more accurate, I'll order a pizza.'

Ren grinned. 'It's a date. I gotta go, I'm running late for an appointment, but I'll see you tomorrow. Nice to meet you, uh, Phoebe's friend.'

He leaned in for another quick hug before striding off, breaking into a jog the exact same moment as Bel's forehead hit the table with a resounding thud.

'So, quick question,' I said as I sat back down. 'What just happened?'

'Kill me,' she replied. 'Push me in front of the biggest, fastest car you can see. Make it quick, I'm begging you.'

'And "Snigh"? Please tell me that's cool LA slang I'm not aware of.'

'I started to say "so nice to meet you" and "hi" at the same time but it all came out together and then I think I blacked out,' she mumbled without lifting her head. 'I told you not to call him over, I told you I wouldn't be able to talk to him.'

'And you were not lying.'

Combing her hair out of her eyes, she peered up at me. 'It's bad, isn't it?'

'It's not great,' I admitted.

'I've always been a people person,' she sobbed. 'I can talk to anyone. You, Suzanne, that rando guy over there who can't stop staring at me,' she paused to point at the man who had been staring at her and fussing with his crotch ever since we'd sat down. 'I could talk to him all day long because I'm not attracted to him at all.'

The poor, awful man's face.

She groaned and pressed her fingertips into her temples. 'As soon as I meet someone I like, it's game over. My brain goes into shuffle mode, I forget how to sequence words in the right order. But I like him so much, Phoebe, I like him so much. Sometimes I lose count of Suzanne's burpees because I'm too busy staring at his garden, waiting for him to come outside. This one time, I made her hold a plank for two whole minutes because he was swimming laps and I forgot how to tell time.'

'Well, he seems really . . .' I paused as I searched for the appropriate words to describe Ren. Funny? Weirdly obsessed with birds? So hot you could fry an egg on him? 'He seems really nice.'

'And there are maybe four nice people in this entire city,' Bel said, nodding aggressively. 'I did a little light investigating and all the women on his Instagram are stunning. Like, they could be beauty influencers, they're so hot.'

'Bel, you are also beauty influencer hot,' I pointed out. 'If you told me to buy a mascara, I would.'

'That's so sweet of you to say,' she replied with a sniff. 'But it's not just that. He's a real intellectual, he posts pictures of books. Books he's read! On June 22nd, it was a Tuesday, I saw him coming out of the bookstore down the street with a whole stack of 'em in his arms. And now he thinks I'm a total weirdo dummy.'

'He does not think you're a total weirdo dummy.'

It was a lie. He did. And if he found out she knew what he was doing on June 22nd, he'd think she was a stalker as well.

'Don't you think he's handsome?' she said, practically swooning at the table. 'Don't you think he's the most gorgeous, amazing, incredible man with the best hair you've ever seen?'

'Yes, he is very good-looking and his hair is very nice,' I agreed. 'But don't you think he's almost too good-looking?'

She looked confused. 'No?'

'He's not a real person, is he?' I explained. 'I can't imagine doing normal everyday things with someone like that. He looks like a Ken doll.'

And it wasn't as though someone like Ren would ever look twice at someone like you, a familiar, dark voice whispered in my ear, someone so deeply, desperately ordinary. With a shaky hand, I picked up my coffee and took a deep, scorching swallow, doing my best to ignore it until it went away. It always did, eventually.

'My life is ruined,' Bel whined, faceplanting back onto the table. 'I might as well order the yoghurt parfait, lactose intolerance be damned. Screw it, I wanna go to Jeni's Ice Cream.'

'Let's not do anything drastic,' I said, gently patting the back of her head. Her hair really was incredibly soft. When she wasn't weeping loudly enough for everyone in a three-block radius to hear, I would have to ask what kind of shampoo and conditioner she used. 'Even if you didn't make the ideal first impression, you still have the perfect opportunity to dazzle him the second time around.'

She looked up with red-rimmed eyes.

'I do?'

'He's coming over to see the hawk tomorrow. You can try again then.'

'No way. I'm not, I can't, I'm too embarrassed.' Right as she dropped her head back to the table, the door to the restaurant opened and our waitress appeared, carrying a huge circular tray laden with plates. I tried moving our coffee cups around to make room for our food but the only thing that was really in the way was Bel's face.

'You're good at talking, I'm good with words. Between us, we can turn this around,' I told her, a plan starting to come together, as the waitress tried and failed to find a spot for all our food. 'We need to prepare. Find out what he's into, see if you have any shared interests, any hobbies, preferences, that sort of thing.'

'Like, sexual preferences?' she asked, her head popping up from the table. 'Like, is he kinky?'

'I was thinking more like the music he listens to, but if he's into dressing up as a baby and having pureed carrots thrown at him you probably would want to know before things go any further.'

'Eh,' she said, finally pulling herself upright. 'I've done worse.'

The waitress cleared her throat as she put down the pancakes.

'Can I get you anything else?' she asked in a strained voice.

I shook my head and made a mental note to leave her a huge tip.

'Ren is like my fairy-tale prince. I really think we're soulmates,' Bel said, resting her chin in her hands as the waitress made a hasty retreat. 'I'm serious, he's all I can think about. His Instagram is the first thing I look at when I wake up and the last thing I check before I go to sleep.'

'Well, we don't want to scare him off so let's keep that little nugget of information between us,' I suggested as I tucked into the heavenly pancakes. 'But I will make you a promise. By the time my holiday is over, you and Ren will be well on your way to your happily ever after.'

CHAPTER FOUR

The light was different in LA.

Even though I knew it was the exact same sun in the exact same sky, everything was more magical here. Someone had turned the brightness up and the contrast down then added a 10 per cent fade across the whole city, tinkering with reality just enough to make me question whether or not the waitress had slipped a light psychedelic into my coffee. According to Bel, weed was legal in LA and mushrooms were 'totally having a moment' so it wasn't completely beyond the realms of possibility.

After Bel drove off to one of her many jobs, I left Little Dom's and strolled up a leafy street, wandering in the general direction of Suzanne's house. I was too curious and too stuffed full of pancakes and pizza to go straight home, I needed to keep moving. So I walked aimlessly, taking in the neighbourhood and bathing myself in the beautiful light.

Los Angeles didn't feel like any kind of city I'd ever visited before. There was a mountain right in the middle, for a start. Well, Suzanne's manual said it was a mountain but as I strode onwards and upwards, I reclassified it as a very big hill. Admittedly, a great big, massive people-come-from-miles-around-to-see-it sort of a hill, but not the kind of thing that required dedicated footwear. If you could climb it in Converse, it wasn't a mountain.

The roads weren't the kind of city roads I was used to either. Wide, leafy streets led away from the restaurant before twisting themselves into a narrow ribbon of a road with slivers of pavement disappearing and reappearing at will. I picked my way carefully around the blind bends, sticking close to the parked cars that lined the streets bumper to bumper whenever the pavement ran out, wondering why anyone would choose to drive one of the ubiquitous Range Rovers I saw everywhere when I wouldn't have trusted myself with anything bigger than a pushbike.

I'd been wondering a lot of things since brunch. Like, how come so many people had time to hang out at a restaurant on a Tuesday morning when they should be at work? Did anyone in LA wear anything other than jeans or leggings? And how could someone like Bel genuinely believe there was a single person alive who wouldn't fall in love with her as soon as they met her? It simply didn't make sense; *Love Island* would have turned her down for being too hot, and if being gorgeous wasn't enough, she also had the audacity to be a lovely human. I mean, who gave her the right? If I hadn't seen her go to pieces in front of Ren, I wouldn't have believed it was possible for someone so perfectly put together to fall apart so spectacularly over a boy. It would be like watching Jennifer Aniston have a meltdown at the self-checkout because she didn't know how to scan a banana. It simply did not make sense.

What did make sense were her feelings for Ren. He was perfect crush material: handsome, great hair and a set of shoulders so strong and broad he could probably carry an injured sheep several miles for help, and as far as I could tell he was a decent enough man. Admittedly the bar for 'decent enough man' dropped lower every day but he was polite, funny and had yet to start a single sentence with the words 'well actually', which put him ahead of at least half the male population of the planet. The birdwatching thing was a bit leftfield but I definitely preferred the thought of a man standing half-naked in his back garden, looking at hawks, to the idea of a man sitting half-naked on the settee, swearing at a teenager in Slough, playing *Call of Duty*. It would be a pleasure to help him see how wonderful Bel was. I would be performing a service for the good of humanity, bringing together two of the finest examples of the species. I would probably be awarded some sort of Nobel prize.

At the intersection of three winding roads, I pulled up my Maps app to check I was still heading in vaguely the right direction and, since my phone was already in my hand, skipped through a quick tour of the apps. It wasn't that I wanted to check them but I physically couldn't stop myself. It was a statistical impossibility for anyone under the age of fifty to do one and one thing only on their phone without checking at least two other apps immediately after. Anyone with that kind of mental fortitude should be made president of the universe. It would not be me.

There were no texts, no emails, zero action on the DMs; according to the Weather app, it was pissing it down with rain back home. Standard. None of these houses in Suzanne's neighbourhood looked as though they could withstand so much as a shower; one huff, one puff and I could blow them all down. My thumb skipped across the screen to the Facebook icon, summoning my newsfeed with a single tap and searching for Samantha Evans with another. I knew it was stupid, masochistic even, but since when did that stop anyone from doing anything? The feminine urge to self-sabotage, I was powerless against it. Samantha's profile appeared on my screen with a gentle pop and right away, I felt the entire weight of my breakfast in my stomach. You couldn't blame her for making her profile public – she was getting married soon, she was well within her rights to want to celebrate. But there was an argument to be made against posting a soft-focus photo of her and my ex dressed in cheap, knock-off Sleeping Beauty and Prince Charming costumes alongside the caption 'Twelve more sleeps until my dream comes true'.

'Keep dreaming,' I muttered, flipping through her other photos as though I hadn't already studied them closely enough to make her my *Mastermind* specialist subject. She looked so happy. Grinning from ear to ear at her sister's wedding, making a heart with her hands against the sunset in Mallorca, weeping at Thomas down on one knee at Disneyland Paris, engagement ring in hand. Imagine proposing marriage with Goofy in the background. Dearest Samantha, love of my life, keeper of my heart, will you do me the honour of becoming my wife and does anyone know whether or not this thing hovering behind me is a cow or a dog?

Swiping out of the app, I threw my phone into the bottom of my bag and marched on up the hill until my calves burned, mad at Mark Zuckerberg, mad at Steve Jobs, mad at Thomas and Samantha and Goofy and most of all, mad at myself.

Everyone looks happy on Facebook, I reminded myself. Hadn't I posted joy-filled footage of me and Thomas on every platform from Twitter to TikTok? No one knew what went on behind closed doors. How many other women spent their evenings uploading smiling photos while tears streamed down their faces? How many other women thought putting pictures of the good times out in the world would bring them back around again? Was it manifestation or self-delusion? I could practically feel Therese's eyebrow raising at my train of thought from halfway around the world. Magical thinking, don't do it.

'She's made her choice and I'm better off without him,' I declared to a small, pink-breasted bird when it alighted on a tree branch in front of me. Even the sparrows were cuter in LA. It hopped down to the ground beside me before fluttering up to rest on the root of a tree that had broken through the pavement. I wondered what kind of bird it was.

'Meets a hot birdwatcher once, turns into Bill Oddie,' I muttered as my feathered friend flitted up the tree, disappearing into the leaves and out of sight. 'Where are you going? Do you have a movie premiere to get to?'

Shockingly, it did not reply.

'Rude,' I muttered, resting one hand on the trunk of the tree. It was huge, like something out of a fairy tale, all twisting branches and deeply ridged brown bark with roots breaking out of the pavement all the way up the street. In the land of palm trees and cacti, I wasn't expecting something so ancient looking. It felt as though this tree had been and would be here forever.

Behind the tree was a gate and beyond the gate was a driveway, curving around lush green lawns, passing under towering oaks. The driveway, predictably, led to a house, only the word house felt deeply insufficient to describe this dwelling; this was a mansion, a castle even. Its creamy, yellow-tinted walls, half obscured by trailing ivy, rose up out of the trees, and white wooden shutters covered the windows like a parent hiding their child's eyes. I could see the house but the house couldn't see me. Holding my breath, I followed the fence down to an imposing wrought-iron gate to get a better look. Just like Ren, just like Bel, just like my blueberry ricotta pancakes and everything else I'd encountered so far in LA, it was gorgeous. The mansard roof was covered with dove-grey tiles and on the far side of the house there was a rounded tower topped by an actual turret. If a singing candelabra had waved at me from the one window that wasn't shuttered, I wouldn't have been the slightest bit surprised.

Right as I was about to pull out my phone to take a photo, I saw something move inside. Not an enchanted candlestick but a person. A slash of scarlet lipstick and a curtain of steel-coloured hair appeared at a window. It was a woman. I gave her an awkward wave as our eyes met, adding the kind of half-smile we rolled out when we'd been caught doing something we shouldn't be doing, but rather than reply with a wave of her own or, even better, ignoring me completely, she raised her hand and gave me the finger.

I laughed, barking with surprise, as she disappeared from the window, leaving me red-faced and smiling, hoping Suzanne could help put a name to my new hero. As someone who didn't open the door to anyone who didn't call *and* text to confirm their visit at least an hour before their arrival, I couldn't begin to imagine how annoying it must be to have people hanging off your gate and taking photos of your house every day. Like I was doing at that exact second. But it was such a beautiful house, how could anyone walk past it without falling into dreamy romantic fantasies about its residents? I could practically see Katharine Hepburn and Spencer Tracy walking up the front steps in time for cocktail hour.

With an unspoken apology to the coolest senior citizen on the planet, I tore myself away and marched back out onto the road. The long, winding, uphill road. All at once, my legs turned into lead weights, loaded down with pancakes and jet lag, and the choice between dragging myself up the hill or rolling back down to wallow in Suzanne's pool like a sloppy hippo was almost no choice at all. But even as I turned and walked down the hill, away from the mysterious Hollywood chateau, I knew I'd be back sooner rather than later.

'Suze, I completely understand. Work is work, you don't need to apologize.'

Stretched out on a sunlounger by the pool, I put on my best sympathetic face and heroically refrained from yelling 'I KNEW IT' into my phone as my sister remorsefully explained she would in fact not be coming home in two or three or even four days.

'It's such a mess up here,' she said with a grunt, rubbing the delicate skin under her eyes and doing nothing to improve the dark circles I'd watched get steadily worse for the last fifteen years. 'Things in the LA office are completely under control but these idiots don't know their arse from their elbow. This is Seattle, they're all supposed to be geniuses. I wouldn't trust them to make my bed.'

'That's why they pay you the big bucks,' I replied, cheerfully toasting her with my homemade margarita. 'It can't be helped, you'll get back when you get back.'

'About that.'

'Go on.'

'It could be quite a bit longer. I might not get back until next week.'

The left-hand corner of my mouth twitched uncontrollably.

'That's it, you're coming up here,' she ordered. 'I'll book the flights and order a car, you just pack your bags.'

'No, really, it's not a problem,' I insisted even though I didn't entirely believe myself as I said it. 'You're busy, I'm fine. Please don't stress about me, I'm golden.'

Her eyebrows came together in one long furry caterpillar of doubt.

'You're sure? It's no bother, Pheebs, I can have my assistant sort it all out. We'd get you your own room, you wouldn't be an inconvenience.'

'As warm and inviting as that sounds, I'm very sure.' I flipped my phone around to remind my sister of the charms of her garden. 'A private pool, my own hot tub, every streaming service under the sun *and* a personal trainer to take me out for pancakes? Not too shabby for Phoebe.'

When I turned the screen back around there was a ghost of a smile on Suzanne's tired face. 'So you've met Bel?'

'Someone forgot to cancel their morning HIIT workout,' I confirmed. 'Aren't you the same woman who told me cardio was a tool of the patriarchy? Since when do you have a trainer?'

'Since our grandmother died of a major heart attack?'

The hollow rush of grief surprised me the way it always did whenever someone mentioned Gran unexpectedly. Three years gone and it felt like yesterday.

'She was seventy-seven and we've both been checked out, it wasn't anything hereditary,' I said before filling my voice with forced cheer. 'Anyway, you'll be pleased to know Bel took me out for brunch and it was delightful.'

'Really?'

'Mostly,' I replied. 'She offered to take me to the beach tomorrow but I don't know if I really want to go. I might cancel.'

'Our beaches are hideous,' she replied, wrinkling her nose with distaste. 'If you're that desperate to sit in the sand and stare at the sea, I can book you a flight to Hawaii and meet you there when I'm done.'

I stared at my sister through the screen of the iPad. 'Just how much money do you make? Because it's clearly too much.'

Her tell-tale diamond earrings sparkled under her hotel room lights as she laughed. 'Haven't you ever heard the saying never ask a man his salary or a woman her age?'

'Thankfully, no, because it's a stupid saying. Also, you're my sister and I can ask you whatever I want.' Even if you never give me a straight answer, I added silently.

'Whatever, if you've already told Bel you'll go, you're going,' she warned. 'You can't cancel on her. When I had the flu, she really looked after me, you've never seen so much green juice. I think she put an entire field of celery through my blender. You be nice to her.'

'I'm being very nice,' I sniffed. 'When am I not nice?'

She waited for me to answer my own question but I refused to bite.

'All I'm saying is, she doesn't do sarcasm and she takes everything to heart, so tread carefully. The poor thing's had a terrible year – did she tell you she was up for a part in the new *Star Wars* show? Lost out in the final round when she clocked the director in the chops with her lightsaber.'

'That might be the only thing she didn't tell me. Did you know she played second ovary in a tampon commercial three years ago? It's on YouTube, in case you're interested,' I replied, looking down at the open notebook beside me as my sister snorted with laughter. 'Really, Suze, you don't need to worry about me and you don't need to worry about Bel. I will be nice. So nice, I'm going to help her seduce the love of her life.'

The snort of laughter turned into a deep, wary inhale.

'Is that right?'

'Yes,' I confirmed. 'She's in love with your neighbour. Completely obsessed with him.'

Suzanne looked perplexed. 'Are you talking about Ren? Around the corner?'

I nodded.

'Interesting,' she said as she picked at a clump of mascara in the corner of her eye. 'Last I heard, the love of her life was the woman who makes smoothies at

Erewhon in Silver Lake. Which reminds me, do not go to Erewhon in Silver Lake. It's overpriced and awful and full of terrible people paying too much money for terrible things in hope of seeing a terrible celebrity.'

'What kind of terrible celebrity?'

'Justin Bieber goes there.'

'Maybe she didn't want to tell you about Ren because he's your neighbour,' I suggested, scribbling the words 'go to Erewhon in Silver Lake' into my notebook. 'We bumped into him this morning and I can confirm she has a mega crush on that man.'

'Well, you can see why,' Suze admitted. 'The shine went off it for me when he started banging around in his tool shed at the crack of dawn every weekend.'

'And what time are we calling the crack of dawn?'

'No one should be banging and hammering until after midday,' she muttered darkly. Suzanne never had been a fan of an early morning. Or mornings in general. 'Ugh, I've got to go, my boss is on the other line.' She rolled her head backwards as if looking to the wispy clouds above for help. 'I'll talk to you later. And watch what you're doing with Bel. I don't want to have to find a new trainer or move house because you were trying to "help" her.'

'Understood,' I replied. 'Now piss off and talk to your boss.'

'Love you too.' She blew kisses into the screen before wrinkling her nose at the big red box behind me. 'And you'd better not get Cheez-It dust all over my furniture.'

'I won't,' I promised the blank screen as she ended the call.

* * *

Wiping the Cheeze-It dust off her furniture, I rolled forward, cracking my spine as I touched my toes with my phone then rolled back, soaking up the sun. Gran would have loved it here, she always was a sun worshipper. The first sign of anything over eighteen degrees and she was in the back garden, bottle of factor four Malibu tanning oil on one side and a Mills & Boon romance on the other. The hours I'd spent trying to upgrade her sunscreen to at least factor fifteen. What a waste of breath. Margaret Chapman had died as she lived; extremely well-tanned. It was a funny thing, grief. Nothing about it made sense. Suzanne dealt with hers by refusing to stand still. Two weeks after the funeral she moved from London to New York. Six months after that she went to Sydney, with pitstops in Hong Kong and Dubai before she finally settled in LA a year ago. My sister had never needed anyone to anchor her the way I did, people seemed to weigh her down. Without Gran, even three years later, I was still adrift, bumping from one side of the harbour to the other and always threatening to make a break for the open sea.

I needed a distraction, I thought, pushing away the heavy thoughts and reaching for my notebook and pen, writing 'Things I Know About Ren' across the top of the page in my very special, borderline illegible handwriting.

Number one, his name is Ren.

Not a very inspiring start.

Number two, he lives in LA, next door to Suzanne.

Number three, he likes birds. *Really* likes birds.

What else? He was funny and relatively polite and claimed not to be a pervert. He was an alleged vegan. He was the most beautiful, most devastatingly handsome man I had ever set eyes on in my entire life. Which felt a bit long-winded so instead I jotted down the word 'fit' and underlined it seven times to get the point across. But how to speak to his heart? I let the notebook rest in my lap and closed my eyes. What would I say to Ren if I were trying to make him mine?

Once upon a time, I was famous for my love poems. Admittedly my fame was limited to two fairly small and very specific circles – the Year Ten girls at South Border Comprehensive school and later, the greetings card community, but still. My first job at the card company was to come up with poems for the Valentine's line and I nailed the assignment first time, ate it up without even trying. It didn't even feel like bragging, I knew my poems were epic. Probably because I'd been waiting to fall in love ever since I read my first romance novel at the tender age of ten, when I stole my grandmother's copy of *The Doctor Needs a Wife* and secretly read it under the covers at bedtime. Until a tall, dark, handsome man appeared in my life to whisk me off my feet, I poured all my feelings into my work.

And then I met Thomas. He was tall, dark and handsome, exactly what I'd been dreaming of. He was also clever and quick-witted, he always had Gran in stitches. He worked at an accounting firm in Nottingham and we used to joke that we were complete opposites; I was good with words, he was good with numbers and our children would be geniuses. He used to talk about our children a lot in the early days.

Overnight, it felt as if someone had given me a whole new world of words I needed to describe feelings I'd never experienced before, a special, secret edition of the Oxford English Dictionary reserved for people who were truly in love. Reading about romance was one thing but living it was another. I could have written ten epic poems a day when we first met. The way the world sparkled at the edges when he held my hand and melted away completely when he stopped in the middle of the street to kiss me. Nothing felt like a cliché because it was all real: thunderbolts, violins, fireworks, I felt it all.

When things went wrong, I lost all the words. Not just the new words but the old ones too. How could I write from the heart when mine was broken? Now I delegated the Valentine's cards to someone else on my team and kept myself busy with Mother's Day and Father's Day and Bring Your Pet To Work Day. Much easier to write heart-warming sentiments about a theo-retical dog than a theoretical lover when you knew for a fact that love didn't exist.

Not for me anyway.

But, high on pancakes and coffee, I'd made a promise to Bel, so I opened my eyes and stared hard at my notebook. I was going to have to try.

And it could be good for me, I reasoned as I dug back into the Cheez-It box, a way to balance out my karma and get her back on my side. Because, yes, I had admit-tedly tried to break up one couple but now I was attempting to bring another two people together. In the greater scheme of things, I was practically a saint.

'Go ahead and call me Cupid,' I said, wiping my orange hands on Suzanne's white sunlounger and turning over a fresh page.

CHAPTER FIVE

'Is it me or are we driving awfully close to the edge of the cliff?'

'It's you.' Bel tore around another hairpin bend, the back end of my sister's giant car spinning out behind us. 'Trust me, I've driven a car this size around these roads a million times. Once, anyway. You have to be confident, accidents only happen when you're too anxious.'

'I am almost positive that is not true.'

I clenched at an oncoming lorry and held my breath to make myself and the car thinner. Suzanne's SUV will be faster than my Honda Fit, Bel said. Suzanne's SUV will be safer, Bel said. I couldn't decide who was stupider; her for suggesting it or me for believing.

'Is there any chance we could slow down a bit?'

She answered by pressing her foot against the accelerator. 'The good beaches get busy early,' she replied. 'If we don't make it by nine, we won't find a space in the parking lot and we'll have to walk.'

'I don't mind,' I said. 'Better to get there late and walk, than drive off the edge of a cliff and never walk again.'

'No one in LA walks,' Bel laughed. 'If I'd known you were weird about heights I would have taken the five to the ten to the PCH but it's so much quicker to do the 101 at this time. I guess we could take the one back, it depends what time we leave.'

'You realize you're talking a completely foreign language?' I said as a neon-pink Range Rover hurtled towards us, swerving into its own lane only at the very last minute.

She laughed and turned up the car stereo, drowning out the honking horns of the other cars. 'You'll get used to it. There's no weather to talk about so we're obsessed with traffic instead. You gotta know your freeways if you're going to make it in LA.'

'And that's why there's no catchy song about Los Angeles to sing at karaoke,' I quipped. '"If you can make it to your destination in one piece, you'll make it anywhere" doesn't have the same ring to it.'

'We'll make it,' Bel trilled. 'And just so you know, we do have a song, it's called "I Love LA" and it's so good but there's like, a conspiracy against it? It was written by the guy who wrote the song for *Toy Story*?'

Winding down the window, she stuck her arm outside, surfing the air as we tore through the hills.

'Next stop, Malibu!'

'Next stop, a bottle of Malibu,' I whispered, slumping down in my seat and praying we would arrive at our destination very, very soon.

* * *

'Oh my God,' I breathed as I kicked off my flip-flops and buried my toes in the sand. 'Did we die? Are we in heaven?'

'Welcome to El Matador,' Bel draped one arm around my shoulder and leaned her head against mine. 'My favourite beach in the whole world.'

I'd never been much of a beach person. Beaches meant sunburn and sand in unpleasant places, too many people and not enough snacks. I liked my water clean, contained and within fifty feet of a usable toilet. But this was different. After filling half the tiny car park with Suzanne's monster truck, we struggled down a death trap of a wooden staircase but the moment I set eyes on the beach, I understood it would be worth the inevitable arse workout on the way back up. There was nothing but gold sand, blue ocean and Bel's beaming face, and it was so quiet, all I could hear was the reassuring roll of the water. White-crested waves roaring in and sighing on their way back out. Perfection.

'You like?' Bel spread her arms wide as if to give me the whole beach as a gift.

'I love,' I replied. 'It's amazing.'

'It only gets better.' She flashed a grin and cocked her head over her shoulder. 'Come on, follow me.'

'OK, but unless you're taking me to the Tenth Annual Hollywood Chris Convention, I don't know how you're going to beat this,' I said, chasing after her regardless.

We walked on packed sand towards a huge rock formation that cut the beach in half, an archway worn away by centuries of persistent waves. A true testament to the power of nagging. I lowered my head and stepped into the cool, creamy silence underneath the arch, breathing in the briny scent of the water, listening to the waves as they echoed off the rocks. It was like sitting inside a magical seashell, just the shimmer of the sand and the push-pull of the sea. I'd never felt so at peace. It was official, Ariel was an idiot. Imagine wanting to give all this up for a man?

'This might be a silly question, but why aren't there a million people here?' I asked in hushed, reverential tones.

'It gets busier, we won't be alone for long,' Bel replied, running her fingertips over the wet, glistening rocks. 'But you saw the parking lot, it's tiny. Most folks see that it's full and keep on driving to another beach. Plus there's nothing to do here, a lot of people prefer Zuma or Will Rogers – they're bigger, they have snack bars, volleyball, stuff like that.'

'Ooh, let's never go there,' I said with great enthusiasm. 'If I lived in LA, I would come here every day.'

'You say that, but you wouldn't.'

She stepped out from under the arch, back into the mellow sunshine, and with some reluctance, I followed. More beach, more peace, more quiet, me, Bel and a couple of healthy looking seagulls I hoped wouldn't come any closer.

'Everyone thinks they'll go to the beach all the time when they move to California,' she said as she shook out her towel. 'But I never do unless I have someone visiting. So thank you for reminding me all this beauty is right on my doorstep, give or take a forty-minute drive. Two hours in traffic.'

'I don't know why anyone would choose to sit in their house and stare at a screen when they could be sitting here, looking at this,' I said, laying out my towel next to hers as she laughed out loud.

'Since when did people make choices that make sense?'

She wasn't wrong.

I uncapped my sunscreen, ready to spray every available inch of flesh, and Bel peeled off her oversized T-shirt and bike shorts to reveal two of the smallest pieces of fabric to have ever been successfully sold as a swimsuit. A pair of teabags strung together on dental floss would have offered more coverage. Naturally, she looked incredible.

'We should take photos before the sun gets too bright,' she declared, twisting her lush dark hair into an effortlessly chic topknot. 'This beach was made for thirst traps and it's always a good idea to stock up when you get the chance.'

'Tell me again how you have no luck with people you're attracted to?' I secured my unwashed hair with a snap of a banana clip. What kind of person washed their hair to go to the beach? The hot kind. 'Bel, in case you hadn't noticed, you really are beautiful.'

'This is just a body, everyone has one,' she slapped herself on the stomach, leaving a red handprint on the tanned, toned flesh. 'It doesn't matter how you look if you can't string a sentence together.'

'I, like Ursula before me, would argue that is entirely untrue,' I said. 'I'm sure there are plenty of people who couldn't care less about what comes out of your mouth as long as they could still look at you.'

'And would you want to date one of those people?'

'Possibly,' I replied. 'If they were very rich and not completely hideous.'

She peered at me over the rim of her Ray-Ban sunglasses. 'Trust me, you wouldn't. I've dealt with more than my fair share of "shut up and look pretty" guys. When you're not allowed to talk, all you can do is listen and you do not want to hear what those men are saying.'

'For someone who can't string a sentence together in front of a random boy, you're extremely insightful,' I said. 'Gorgeous and clever? How dare you?'

She sat up on her knees and held her hands out for my sunscreen. 'My whole life, people have told me I'm pretty,' she said as she sprayed her arms and legs. 'And that's nice to hear, right? I'm not stupid, I know it makes life easier if people think you're attractive, but it doesn't feel good to be valued only for the way I look and have everyone assume I'm dumb. I'm not saying I'm a genius but I'm not just this peppy, pretty vacant thing people want to believe I am.'

The weight of my own assumptions settled on my shoulders like a rock.

'I'm sorry. We're all jealous,' I said. 'I for one think you're an incredible person.'

'That's nice of you to say,' she replied as she fussed with the strap of her bikini top. 'Most of the time I try to rise above it but when you've been hearing the same thing for so long . . . I guess sometimes I start to believe it too. It's harder to ignore the voice in your head than the ones outside it.'

Her words were featherlight but they cut through me like a knife. I knew that voice all too well.

'It only takes one very convincing person to make you believe the worst,' I told her. 'And changing your own mind isn't easy.'

'There are always going to be assholes in the world,' Bel said, sighing at the inevitable. 'We have to help each other, you know? It's the only way to beat the system.'

'Speaking of helping . . .' I leaned back on my elbows and wiggled my toes in the sand. 'I've been thinking about you and Ren. What if you wrote him a love letter?'

She pushed her Wayfarers into her hair and made a face.

'Or, what if we remember this is the twenty-first century?'

'No, it's a great idea!' I protested. 'If he's really into books like you say he is, I think he'll be into it. A love letter would definitely get his attention.'

'As well as the attention of the LAPD.' She waved a hand to dismiss the notion. 'Pheebs, it's giving super stalker. I was thinking we take some fire photos on the beach, I post them on main then slide into his DMs so they're the first thing he sees when he checks my page. We can chat a little online, get to know one another and then, once I'm comfortable enough to form a sentence around him, we smash.'

'And they say there's no romance these days.' I shook my head at her plan. 'How is sending someone a DM less stalkery than sending them a letter?'

'DMs don't require your home address. They give the FBI way less to go on.'

'It's not stalking, you work for his neighbour. It's not like you've been following him or anything.' I looked over at her when she didn't answer. 'Bel, it's not like you've been following him or anything, is it?'

'Is it following if I also needed to get gas, go to the grocery store and drive across town to collect some timber?'

'Why would you need timber?'

She paused, her shiny top teeth digging into her full bottom lip. 'For reasons.'

'I'm going to pretend you didn't tell me any of that,' I said, moving on. 'A love letter from the right person is the most wonderful thing in the world. It's a better way to start things than a DM. What are you going to do, screenshot your inbox to show your grandkids?'

I could tell from the look on her face that was exactly her plan.

'I just don't think I'm a love letter person,' Bel said as she rolled onto her stomach. 'They're cheesy.'

'What if Ren isn't a DM person? He might not even check his messages.'

'It has been a while since he posted,' she admitted, chewing on the inside of her cheek. 'And the last three posts were all photos of birds?'

'I cannot overstate how much he likes birds,' I said, cutting the air with my hand. 'If that's a deal-breaker, speak now or forever hold your peace because seriously, he loves them.'

'If that's the weirdest thing he's into, he will be the most normal guy I ever dated,' she replied. 'You're seeing him later, right?'

'Yes.' I nodded, a tiny beat of anticipation flickering in my chest. It wasn't often I got to hang out with very beautiful men. In fact, the last man I spent any kind of time with was Malcolm the electrician. Malcolm was not only Not Hot, he also charged by the hour and two hundred pounds later, the light in my downstairs toilet still didn't bloody well work.

'So you guys hang out, look at birds, and as long as he's not a secret super creep, you put in a good word for your old pal, Bel.' She clasped her hands together in front of her, eyes huge and pleading. 'And if you're totally, one hundo per cent certain he's a love letter kind of a guy, we'll go with your plan.'

'What if he is some kind of secret super creep and I'm stuck spending the evening with him?' I asked.

'Hey, it's your plan,' she replied, flipping her sunglasses back down. 'You want to get doughnuts on the way back? I know a great place not far from here.'

'Yes, please,' I replied, already drafting the letter in my head. Shall I compare thee to a Red-tailed Hawk? How do I love thee? Let me count the birds. A Common Bushtit by any other name would smell as sweet?

Maybe not.

'And to think when I woke up, the only thing I had to look forward to was a pap smear,' Bel said happily. 'And now look at us? Beach, doughnuts, fall in love.'

'Not bad for a Wednesday,' I agreed, smiling at the ocean as the waves rushed in to greet us before running back out to sea. 'Not too bad at all.'

'Have the best time tonight,' Bel yelled as she scrambled out of Suzanne's tank and back into her own normal-sized vehicle. 'Don't forget to tell Ren how great I am and how much I love vegan food and birds and books.'

'Do you love vegan food, birds and books?'

'I don't *not* love them.'

It was more than most relationships had to go on.

'And text me everything!' she yelled over the sound of her engine.

I gave her two thumbs up as she pulled away, blasting unexpected death metal as she went.

'Still waters,' I muttered, fishing around in my bag for my keys.

Suzanne kept her house chilled to a frosty 65 degrees and the freezing cold tiled floor felt like heaven on my bare feet. The morning had been bliss, reading, chatting, occasionally venturing into the water before collapsing back on my towel with a packet of Ruffles. Well before I was ready to leave, Bel's phone tinkled into life, breaking the spell. One of her clients had a dog-walking emergency and so, we were forced to abandon our beach day because a Bichon Frise in Bel Air needed to get his steps in.

Still sunshine drunk, I hazily pulled out my phone to find a new message from my sister. I'd sent her a photo of the chateau I discovered the day before to see if she knew anything about it and apparently, she did.

OMG the witch's house

Not an actual witch, just an arsehole

As far as I know. Cd b a witch?

Her mail gets delivered to me all the time, house numbers v similar and she's SO RUDE

2 x packages for her on table near front door – cd you drop off?

David, I need the engagement numbers for Q1 vs Q2 before the 2pm meeting AS REQUESTED YESTERDAY

Sorry, last one not for u

'God help David,' I mumbled, slipping my feet back into my shoes and grabbing two small boxes from the console table in the hallway.

It took exactly seven minutes to walk from Suzanne's house, 4001 Parva Avenue, to 4101 Parva Avenue, the home of a Ms M. Moore, and even though I was only going to drop off her post, a little bubble of excitement swelled in my stomach. I was full of questions. Would the middle-finger flasher be there again? Was she Ms M. Moore? And how was I supposed to get the bloody packages up to the house in the first place?

The huge wrought-iron gate at the end of the driveway was locked.

'Hello?' I bent down to speak into a rusty intercom. The buttons and speaker were almost completely hidden by prickly vines and it very much looked as though no one had used it in a long time. 'I'm here to deliver a package for Ms M. Moore?'

There was a crackle of static as the speaker activated. 'Bring them to me.'

Short, sweet, straight to the point.

'Hi, yes, hello?' I replied to the disembodied voice. 'Sorry, but the front gate is locked and I can't see another way in?'

Another crackle, another command.

'Bring the packages to me.'

'Bring them to you how?' I asked, equal parts loud, confused and polite, the perfect cocktail of a Brit abroad.

A screech tore through the speaker and I reared backwards, almost falling over.

'You have five minutes.'

And then it went silent.

'Not creepy at all,' I said, staring at the rusty little box, not quite sure what I'd got myself into.

Prowling the perimeter of the property gave nothing away. The gates were bolted into tall, concrete walls topped with less-than-inviting six-inch spikes which meant climbing over was not an option, especially since I couldn't remember when I had my last tetanus jab. But what about climbing over the gate itself? Tucking my two little packages into my pockets, I calculated a route: climb the tree, shuffle along a branch and hop over the gate. It didn't look too difficult; when we were kids, Suzanne and I used to climb trees all the time. Yes, it was twenty years ago, but climbing a tree was like riding a bike, you never forgot how. Although, much like riding a bike, I suspected the injuries might hurt a lot more at thirty-three than they did at thirteen if my plan went tits-up.

I set the toe of my trainers against a helpful knot in the tree trunk and scrambled up to the first branch that looked strong enough to hold my weight. There had already been so much more climbing on this trip than I'd anticipated. If only Ren was around to hoist me up on his shoulders again or even better, call one of his hawks down to grab the packages and deliver them by bird mail. But no, I was on my own for this one.

Thankfully the branch was sturdy and thick and I was able to pull myself along towards the gate with relative ease, grateful for the lack of witnesses on the deserted street. Bel was right, literally no one walked in LA.

'OK, this is higher than I thought,' I muttered, hanging a good seven feet above the ground as the branch began to bend under me. 'Not an ideal situation.'

But it was too late to turn back now. I reached out with one exploratory foot, making sure I was definitely on the other side of the gate, and when I heard a cracking sound coming from the tree, I knew it was time to either jump or fall. Before I could second-guess myself, I let go of the branch and hurled myself at the ground, landing in an inelegant heap next to two small, somewhat battered packages.

'At least I had a nice relaxing morning,' I said, groaning as I stood to dust myself down and make sure all my bones were still intact. They were. I had done it. I had defeated the gate. I had climbed a tree like my ancestors before me, there was nothing I could not do.

Coasting on my new-found power, I marched up the driveway, ignoring the beautiful gardens, the elegant rose bushes and ornamental ponds, focused on nothing but my mission. I would deliver these bloody boxes if it was the last thing I ever did and if I had to climb back up the tree to get out, there was a good chance it would be.

There she was. An older woman sat outside the house, enormous sunglasses covering most of her face, a green silk turban on her head, matching caftan covering her body and a long, lacquered cigarette holder held between her pursed lips. Without a word, she pressed a big red button on a small black box. Behind me, I heard a loud mechanical whirr as the foreboding gates of 4101 Parva Avenue opened slowly.

'Did you hear me on the intercom?' I asked, confused.

The woman gave a single nod.

'And you saw me climbing over the gate?'

Another nod.

'But you decided not to open them?'

'I considered it,' she said in a slow, husky drawl. 'But where was the fun in that?'

I didn't know whether to laugh or cry.

'Some of your packages were delivered to my sister's house,' I said, tiptoeing along the fine line between just about normal and completely hysterical. 'She asked me to drop them off.'

Behind the sunglasses, I saw one eyebrow arch. 'Interesting. She usually throws them over the gate.'

Even though I couldn't confirm or deny the accusation, it did sound like something Suzanne would do.

'Today you're getting special delivery,' I explained. 'Here you go.'

'I don't want them today,' the woman replied, standing abruptly. 'Bring them back tomorrow evening at seven.' She turned to go back inside, holding up the little black box and pressing the big red button again. 'It takes exactly forty-five seconds for the gates to close. If you don't want to climb back over the wall, I'd start running.'

And with that, she went inside, slamming the door behind her.

'And now we know why the postman delivers your packages to us instead of bringing them here,' I grunted before breaking into a sprint and sliding through the closing gates a moment before they clanged shut. An invisible lock clattered into place and I collapsed on the side of the road in a sweating, shaking heap, barely able to breathe and still holding on to two small packages addressed to a Ms M. Moore.

CHAPTER SIX

It took me a while to recover from my visit to the Moore house but the imminent threat of a visiting Ren was enough to spur me into action. I'd cleaned all the bathrooms (why on earth did Suzanne need five toilets for one person?) and ordered in every vegan-friendly foodstuff stocked at the local supermarket. It was a lot of food. If you could dream it, the vegan artisans of Los Angeles could make it. At dead on the dot of 6 p.m., I sat down on the sofa and stared at the front door.

Ren had said six-ish but that was one whole day ago. What time he showed up would tell me a lot about the kind of person he was. I wasn't a monster, five minutes late was OK. Ten minutes was pushing it and I'd been raised to believe anything over fifteen minutes was taking the piss. More than half an hour past the appointed time and I would need a signed affidavit from government officials to confirm you had played a pivotal role in the preservation of humanity or don't bother coming at all.

'Waiting for someone?'

Jumping a clear foot off the settee, I turned to see Ren lurking behind me, framed by the open sliding glass doors of Suzanne's living room.

'Are you trying to give me a heart attack?' I paused to make sure I hadn't actually wet myself before I stood to greet him. 'Also nice to see you, do come in, have you ever heard of a front door?'

'This was one of the walk around and ring the buzzer situations, huh?' he replied as he held out a bottle of wine and a fancy printed paper bag. 'I'm sorry. I brought alcohol and cake, if that helps at all?'

'It does,' I said, grabbing both the wine and the cake. 'It helps a lot.'

With his hands free, Ren smiled and pointed at my outfit. 'I see you got the jeans and T-shirt memo. We match.'

He was right. Both of us had opted for the classics: blue jeans, white T-shirts, navy Converse. But where my ASOS jeans were snug and my Free People T-shirt loose, Ren's straight leg Levis hung low on his hips and the ultra-thin cotton of his crew neck tee clung to his body, coasting over every curve and plane. His skin glowed and his dark hair was damp, giving him the distinct look of a character from a nineties romcom who had been up since dawn, building a log cabin for disadvantaged orphans before rushing into the shower and pulling on the first items of clothing he could find so he could still make our date on time.

Not that this was a date.

This was a strictly platonic meeting of two adults so one of said adults could look at some birds while the other conducted a subtle interrogation then manipulated the first into falling in love with her older sister's personal trainer.

A perfectly normal Wednesday evening.

'I got some food in case you're hungry,' I said, gesturing to the feast I'd laid out on the kitchen counter. 'You mentioned you were vegan so it's vegan.'

Truly, I was a poet.

'Good memory.' Ren poked through the assorted snacks, his hand hovering over a cookie and a carrot stick. I breathed a sigh of relief when he went for the cookie. I refused to allow Bel to pursue a man who actively chose a carrot over double chocolate chip. 'Thank you for being so considerate. My folks still think I'm being difficult.'

'Aren't you though?' I teased with a scrunched-up smile.

'Yes,' he replied, laughing. 'I'm a fair-weather vegan if I'm being honest. My ex was vegan so I kind of took it up by default. I love dairy but it does not love me so I mostly avoid it and wow you did not need to know any of that.'

'The faux veganism, the ex or the lactose intolerance?'

He took a bite of the cookie and held his hand over his mouth while he chewed. 'Got it, overshare confirmed.'

'Let's go outside and look for your hawk,' I suggested, crossing the room to head out the way he came in. 'I thought I saw her earlier but it could have been an owl. Or a pigeon.'

He looked at me, less than impressed. 'How does someone mix up a hawk, an owl and a pigeon? I know you're not an expert but come on.'

I turned to give him my sternest frown. 'Can you tell me the difference between lactic, glycolic and salicylic acid?'

'Maybe I'll just shut my mouth before I get myself into any more trouble,' he replied with a playful glint in his green eyes.

'Every day is a school day,' I said as I led him outside. We could definitely add a good sense of humour to my list of things to know about Ren. He also got bonus points for bringing wine *and* cake, and I had to admit, I was more than a little curious to know more about this ex of his that he'd mentioned so readily.

I probably knew more than enough about his lactose intolerance.

'How are you liking LA so far?' he asked as he leaned forward and rested his forearms against the fence at the bottom of Suzanne's garden.

'So far, so good.' I fixed my hair behind my ears to anchor it down against the early evening breeze. 'My friend, Bel, took me to Malibu this morning. It's so beautiful out there.'

'It really is,' he agreed. 'Although I can't remember the last time I went.'

I clucked with disapproval. 'Bel said the same thing and you should both be ashamed of yourselves. Imagine having something that perfect on your doorstep and never going to see it.'

'You know how it is, we never appreciate what's right in front of us,' Ren said, turning away from the view and smiling down at me instead. 'I've never been to the UK but I'm sure it's just as beautiful where you live?'

'Oh, extremely beautiful,' I lied, safe in the knowledge he would never find himself in my village but also wondering which he'd find more aesthetically pleasing, the burnt-out pub that still hadn't been knocked down or the ancient slag heap round the back of the closed down coal mine. 'But it's very different to LA.'

'Everywhere is different to LA.'

His eyes lit up in a way that made me so jealous of the city, I wished it had a shin so I could kick it. No one had ever looked that way when they were talking about me.

'There's something special here,' he said. 'Sure, the city has its problems, a lot of things here are a mess, but I've never been anywhere else that makes me feel the way LA does.'

'And what way is that?' I asked.

'Like you could do anything,' he answered, awestruck by his own hometown. 'Be anyone, achieve all your dreams. Everything feels possible here.'

Something else to add to the list. Ren was passionate about the things that he loved and looking at him then, watching him watch the city below, I completely understood how Bel had fallen for him. What must it feel like to have someone adore you so completely?

'I thought that was New York,' I said when I remembered it was my turn to speak. 'Rumour has it, if you can make it there, you can make it anywhere.'

He frowned and shook his head. 'I lived in New York for a while. More like if you can make it there, you're either a billionaire or a sociopath.'

'That's not nearly as catchy, is it? What if you're a billionaire and a sociopath?'

'Then you'll fit in great,' he said, his smile sliding back into place. His face didn't look right without it. 'New Yorkers *are* New York, the people make the city. For me, LA isn't about the people, people come and go all the time. It's about the tension. Los Angeles is contradiction, that's what makes it so exciting.'

'Really?' I replied, looking down at all the big houses with their tennis courts and swimming pools. What did these people have to be tense about? 'I spend most of my time trying to avoid tension.'

'You don't think there's such a thing as good tension?'

He turned to look at me, hitting me with the full force of those deep green eyes, and I suddenly found it very hard to swallow.

'Think about it. Here we are in the middle of one of the biggest cities in America and at the same time, we're lost in the woods, looking for a red-tailed hawk. How is that possible? This morning you were on a deserted beach but if we wanted to, we could drive up a mountain and be swimming in a glacial lake before bedtime. You can go to Beverly Hills and pay a thousand dollars for a steak or get five bucks' worth of tacos from a truck outside the drugstore and they will both be the best meal you ever ate in your life. That's the kind of tension I'm talking about.'

'Oh well, when you put it like that,' I said, swept up in his enthusiasm once again. 'Now please tell me more about the tacos.'

'I know I'm biased but I do believe this is the greatest city in the world.' He cast a loving eye out over his town, exhaling a contented sigh. 'Maybe it's because I grew up here or because this is where my grandfather came to make a better life for his family, but I've always felt like there's magic in Los Angeles. There's nowhere else I'd rather be.'

Even though I knew it was rude, I couldn't help but stare at him. His eyes had turned a deep, dark emerald, dancing with memories I wished I could share. Imagine feeling so much passion for a place. Imagine feeling so much passion about anything. Nothing even scratched the surface for me these days; feelings were too dangerous. Everyone let you down eventually. Even the local pizza place had taken my favourite tuna pizza off the menu. I didn't, couldn't and wouldn't trust anyone. But in that moment, standing beside Ren, I almost wished things were different.

'If you love LA so much, what took you to New York?' I asked, shaking off the shadows of my dark mood.

I had to find out as much about him as I possibly could. For research purposes. For Bel. And also because I could listen to the sound of his voice until the end of time and never get bored of it. There was a depth and a richness to his words that made my whole body tingle, a voice deep enough to sink into and lose yourself. But not in a threatening way, like the man who did all the movie trailers. It was deep, warm and welcoming.

'Curiosity mostly. I grew up here but we moved to Maine when I was fifteen, to be closer to my mom's family. I still came back every summer to see my grandparents, but I had to have my teenage rebellion, same as everyone else. New York was the obvious option.'

'You've got to be careful with curiosity,' I cautioned,

more to myself than him. 'It'll get you in all kinds of trouble.'

He nudged me with his elbow and a spark shot up my spine. 'Sometimes it's good trouble. Sometimes it's worth it.'

'And when did you move back to LA?' I asked, twisting my body away from him. It had been far too long since I'd felt the touch of another human being. One brush of a man's elbow and I was practically a puddle. I pressed a finger to the spot on my elbow, still flaming from his touch. Maybe I was allergic to him. Perhaps I should take a Piriton just in case.

'I didn't,' he said. 'Technically, I still live in Maine although I don't have a place there right now. My grandpa died a year ago and I'm here to fix up the house so my brother can get more out of a developer who's going to knock it down and build an ugly modern block in its place because he doesn't care what it means to me and my dad.'

Well, I did ask.

'I assumed this was your house,' I admitted, regretting my assumptions for the second time in one day. 'Can't you and your dad tell him you don't want to sell the house?'

'Hector has convinced my dad selling it is the best thing to do, so it's me versus them,' he replied. He clasped his hands together and I saw the muscles in his forearms tense up. 'Mi abuelo built this place when he moved here from Mexico; all he ever wanted was for it to stay in the family. I talked to a few brokers about renting it out but property taxes in California are crazy and an old place like this, it's a money pit. I'm supposed to fix the place up, tidy the garden and make sure we get the best price, but I've been doing some restoration work while I can. Bringing the house back to life before someone knocks her down.'

'Sorry, I didn't mean to bring up bad stuff. I know families are complicated,' I peered down at the quaint little cottage below. Did it know how much trouble it was causing?

'No, I'm sorry, I shouldn't have dumped that on you.' Ren shook his head, restoring his easy smile as he shifted his weight from one foot to the other. 'Now you see why I like birds so much. There's no drama with birds. Actually, there is a little but it doesn't usually involve shitting all over your grandfather's final wishes so your brother can make a quick buck.'

'You don't know that,' I said, nodding at a couple of birds as they swooped down in front of us. 'What about those parrots we saw? They could be fully embroiled in some *Succession*-style drama about who's going to take over the family seed business and you'd never know.'

'You're right, I have been blind to their rich inner lives,' Ren chuckled and a tiny jolt of happiness ran through me when he gave me a grin. 'That goldfinch over there is clearly a Kendall.'

'And whatever that thing is, it's got Roman written all over it,' I pointed at a twitchy, bright-eyed bird with light grey feathers and dark grey wings as it bounced from foot to foot at the end of the terrace. 'Cheek of the devil, that one.'

'With nothing but love, I can confidently say mockingbirds suck,' he confirmed, and the grey bird gave an impertinent trill and flew away in protest. 'You said you saw our girl earlier? The red-tail?'

'Let's be honest, it could have been Big Bird for all I know,' I admitted. 'Have you had any sightings?'

'Not since Monday but I've been busy with the house.'

He looked off into the trees and I remembered that was why he was here, to look for the hawk's nest, not to hang out with me. And I was supposed to be talking up Bel, not mooning over the way his pupils had dilated, turning his emerald eyes into something deeper and darker and even more inviting.

'I've got a question,' I piped up, my squeaky voice cutting through the atmosphere like a rusty bread knife. 'How do you feel about love letters?'

Ren looked back at me, deep, dark, inviting eyes clouded over with more than a little confusion. 'Sorry, what?'

'It's my friend, Bel, she really likes you and she's written you a love letter.' I was talking too loud and too fast but I couldn't stop myself. 'Which I think is very old school and romantic and not at all weird and much nicer than sending someone a DM.'

'I never check my DMs anyway,' Ren replied and I took an internal victory lap. 'But wow, a love letter.' He cupped the back of his neck, squinting as he processed the information. 'No one ever wrote me a love letter before. That's kind of . . . romantic?'

'So romantic,' I agreed. 'And Bel is amazing, one of the most incredible women I've ever met. You should definitely ask her out.'

'I should?'

'Yes,' I nodded. 'Shall we call her right now?'

'Shouldn't I meet her first?'

'You've already met her. She was at brunch with me yesterday. Dark hair, brown eyes, stunningly beautiful.'

He shook his head. 'I don't really remember who you were with . . .'

'She said "snigh" and then hid behind her hair.'

'Oh.' Ren's eyes widened with realization. 'Ohhhh.'

'She was nervous,' I added quickly. 'Completely swept away by you, love at first sight, totally smitten, so she wrote you a letter but she was worried it might come off as a bit intense, which I said was ridiculous because who wouldn't like to get a love letter so I said I would ask you but, short version, Bel really likes you.' I forced the corners of my mouth into what I hoped was a convincing smile. 'And I think you'd like her too.'

'That is a lot of information,' he said, backing away from me and moving over towards my sister's firepit because of course she had a firepit. 'She really said it was love at first sight?'

'She said a lot of things, I could be mixed up,' I replied, following slowly without making any sudden moves. Was that too much? Had I gone too far? I didn't want to scare him away. 'The main takeaway is that she really likes you and she's written you this love letter and you should take her on a date.'

He clasped his hands together, resting his elbows on his knees, manspreading on the sofa in honour of his ancestors. Even the good ones regressed in times of stress.

'Have you read it?' he asked.

'Have I read what?'

'The love letter?'

'Have I read the love letter?' I looked so flabbergasted at the idea, I was surely in contention for an Oscar. 'No! It's a very personal thing, I would never, nothing to do with me, no sir.'

'Well, can I read it?' he asked.

You can when I've written it, I thought.

'She was going to drop it off but she got caught up at work,' I replied. 'There was an emergency only she could take care of.'

And in certain circles, I was positive that making sure Mr Fluffkins got his walk *was* considered an emergency.

Ren wiped a hand over his face, eyebrows raised, still altogether too surprised at the thought someone might take one look at him and fall head over heels. 'You know, my grandparents always said they fell in love at first sight. They met at a dance, got engaged a month later and married six months after that. I guess there's a part of me that always wondered what that must be like, to see someone and to just know.'

'Part of me wonders what it would be like to climb Everest, doesn't mean I'm going to find out,' I said, momentarily forgetting my mission. 'But I'm sure it does happen. Sometimes.'

'So you don't believe in it?' He folded his arms across his chest, the white sleeves of his T-shirt straining against his brown skin. 'We have ourselves a cynic.'

'It's a pretty thought,' I replied. 'And I love that it has happened to two people as wonderful as you and Bel.'

His grin faded away into something more thoughtful as he held my gaze, his face bathed in golden light. It was offensive how beautiful he was. Just sitting this close to him had even my stony heart skipping enough beats to set off the warning on my Apple watch.

'Phoebe,' he started to say. 'I don't know—'

'Look!' I leapt to my feet, cutting him off as a large shadow swept over the terrace. 'There she is.'

Circling above us was the red-tailed hawk.

'Do you think she was there the whole time?' I asked, cupping a hand over my eyes to get a better look. 'Watching in the woods like a creepy little madam?'

'If she was, she sure knows how to pick her moments,' he replied, eyes still on me. I flushed from head to toe, awash with an uncomfortable warmth I didn't quite know what to do with.

'There, in that tree, do you see?' Ren pointed upwards to a tree behind his house. 'That's the nest, looks like a bundle of grey sticks.'

It was almost impossible to see the wood for the literal trees, but I searched and searched until the nest came into focus like a magic eye picture. As soon as I saw it, I couldn't see anything else. The hawk swooped down into the tree, its branches rustling and protesting her arrival until everything settled and I lost her again.

'You think Bel likes birds?' Ren asked in a voice so low and soft, it felt like a caress.

'I think she loves them,' I replied, ignoring the whisper of doubt that gnawed at my bones. Was this a good idea?

'My grandpa always said our house was lucky for love. Maybe it's my turn.' The left side of his mouth quirked upwards to form a dimple in his cheek, a charmingly resigned half-smile. 'I guess I'm going on a date with your friend.'

'She's going to be so happy,' I said, hugging my arms around myself as he looked back out into the trees. 'You won't regret it.'

But I had a horrible feeling I might.

CHAPTER SEVEN

'When you asked if I could help you with a job, I assumed you meant the dog walking,' I held up a pink bikini top and gulped. 'Are you sure there aren't a couple of Dobermanns out there, dying to stretch their legs?'

Bel bit her quivering bottom lip and hit me, her ridiculous anime eyes glassy and wet. 'I'm so sorry, I would never ask someone I hardly know to do something like this, but I really feel a bond with you and the girl I usually work with has food poisoning and I really need money and no one else was free on such short notice and this is not the kind of gig you can do without full control of your colon.'

'Funny you should say that,' I replied. 'Because I'm not sure I have full control of mine.'

'If you want to back out, I totally understand. Everything happens for a reason, right? So what if I can't pay my rent and have to give up my dreams and lose my shot at true love and move home and live with my parents.'

She really didn't need to throw her arm across her eyes but it did add something to the overall dramatic impact.

'OK, enough, stop.' I held my hands out in front of me to shut her down, eyeballing the rest of my uniform with wary resignation. 'We both know I'm going to do it.'

'You're the most amazing woman I ever met,' Bel cheered, jumping up and down on the spot. Once a cheerleader . . . 'It's gonna be fun, really not work. Now tell me, how's your breaststroke?'

'Do you still get paid if I drown?'

'I think so, but I'd have to check the contract.'

'Then it's good enough,' I pulled off my T-shirt and picked up a pair of purple seashells with as much enthusiasm as I could muster. 'Let's get this over with before I change my mind.'

'It's official,' Bel declared as I lay on the floor of the tiny pool house, thrashing around like a beached whale. 'You're the cutest merperson ever.'

Lots of little girls grew up wishing they could be a Disney princess. Not me. Suzanne was the wannabe Ariel in our house; I couldn't think of anything less appealing than risking my life for love when I had exactly zero successful models of it at home. I always preferred the first fifteen minutes, little town, quiet village, nose stuck in a book. Give me an underwater cave full of stuff over a life on land any day. Which was probably one of the main reasons I was less than thrilled to be forcing my unwilling lower half into a latex mermaid tail on Thursday afternoon. I'd only been in LA since Monday and had already packed more into the last three days than the last three years at home, but when Bel called, distraught, I remembered what Suzanne said about her having a hard year and couldn't bring myself to say no.

Naturally, she slipped effortlessly into her tail without the help of baby oil or baby powder, both of which I had slathered all over my legs at her suggestion, only for them to mingle together and congeal into some kind of clumpy baby slop. There was a reason neither Johnson nor Johnson had ever thought to combine the two.

'I can't believe I said yes to this,' I grunted as the tail finally snapped into place around my soft stomach. 'How long is the party?'

'We do two forty-minute shifts then we're done.' Bel, who looked as though she had been born with a tail, sat a few feet away, weaving strands of silver glitter through her long brunette braid. 'We have a ten-minute break in the middle in case you need to pee or eat or something.'

'Eat? Solid food?' I looked down at the tail, cutting deep into the tender flesh of my midriff. 'I don't think so. And if I have to go to the loo, it'll be sloshing around inside the tail until I take it off.'

'You wouldn't be the first person to pee in a tail,' she chuckled before seeing my eyebrows shoot up my forehead. 'But not in that one. That one has definitely never been peed in.'

I stared at myself in the mirror. How did someone go from writing St Patrick's Day limericks to dressing up as a mermaid to entertain a bunch of kids at a birthday party in the space of a week?

'This is the stupidest thing I have ever done,' I declared.

And given my recent behaviour, that was really saying something.

'Wish I could say the same,' Bel replied. 'Trust me, it's going to be the easiest five hundred bucks you ever made. My first time, I was so nervous, but the children are always so sweet. They want to believe you're a mermaid, all you have to do is let them.'

'If they believe this, they'll believe anything,' I said, rolling over and resting my sweaty head on the cool tiles. The tail was so tight I hardly dared breathe out all the way for fear of splitting it wide open and exposing said children to an untimely lesson about the importance of bikini waxing.

'Are you ready?' Bel flexed her flippers and gave her fins a shimmy. 'We need to be in the pool before the kids arrive.'

'No, not even a little bit,' I replied, sitting up with my legs bound tightly together. 'Wait, how are we supposed to get out to the pool?'

'Oh, it's easy.' She slid down from the sofa and inched elegantly across the floor on her behind. 'See?'

'Next time you ask me for a favour, remind me to say no,' I muttered, flubbing along the pool house floor and following her out the door.

Even if I couldn't be the world's most enthusiastic mermaid, I could be enthusiastic about the house where said mermaiding was to take place. It was magnificent. We'd driven high up into the hills, landing in Bel Air, and it felt as though we were on top of the world.

Admittedly, I wasn't West Philadelphia born and raised but I had a sneaking suspicion West Philly wasn't nearly as fancy as this. The house itself was extremely modern, huge concrete and glass blocks stacked on top of each other with floor-to-ceiling glass walls pointing towards the ocean that would require a small army of cleaners to keep them free of fingerprints. I had no doubt the owners could afford one. The grounds were equally impressive, perfect lawns, tennis courts, obligatory winding driveway and of course, the pool. Or, I should say, pools, plural.

There was one regular rectangular pool, one narrow infinity pool that rolled off the edge of the cliff, and one smaller, curvy pool that hosted an honest-to-God water slide that I was dying to try but preferably not in my mermaid costume.

'Tell me again,' Bel said as two men dressed in white slacks and white polo shirts (deeply impractical staff uniforms were always a signifier of the obscenely rich) wordlessly loaded us into little carts like two aquatic sacks of potatoes. 'Exactly what did Ren say?'

'That he thinks love letters are the most incredible romantic things ever in the history of the world,' I replied, paraphrasing just a little. 'And that he wants to meet you.'

She swooned in her cart and flipped her fins. 'This is the most exciting thing that has ever happened to me. He's everything I ever dreamed of and now I have a chance with him all because of you.'

'You're welcome,' I said. 'Don't forget to invite me to the wedding.'

The little nugget of doubt I'd felt the night before had not only lingered but taken root. But there was no need to worry. I was doing a nice thing for a good woman and a hot man. There was no way it could possibly ever come back to bite me in the arse. Even though the last time I thought I was doing a nice thing for a good woman, it didn't so much bite me in the arse as chomp off a whole cheek.

'Bel,' I hissed as the men in white helped us out of the carts by turning them over and dumping us out onto the ground. 'Is that a unicorn?'

She squinted across the lawn then nodded. 'But I don't think it's a real one.'

'No, probably not,' I agreed, not entirely sure whether she was joking or not. 'I cannot believe this is a party for a seven-year-old.'

'Then you should see some of the sweet sixteens I've done.' Her eyes widened with disbelief at her own memory. 'They're carnage. Bel Air teen parties make *Euphoria* look like *Sesame Street*.'

Along with the mermaids and the unicorns, the luckiest-slash-most-spoiled seven-year-old in the world also had a petting zoo, an outdoor mini spa and a bouncy castle, and next to the bouncy castle, a real castle. A to-scale replica of Sleeping Beauty's castle that was the size of most starter homes in the UK sat on the far side of the lawn all tied-up with a gargantuan blue satin bow. How did you even tie a bow that large? Was that a skill you could learn? Did they teach special classes here in how to cater to the one per cent? I stopped myself from asking the question because I didn't quite know what I would do with myself if Bel said yes.

'When I turned sixteen, my mom took me and my two best friends bowling then we got a McDonald's on the way home,' she muttered, casting a dark look over the Bel Air birthday extravaganza.

'A classic birthday choice,' I said, smiling for the first time since she showed me the tail. 'I did the same except we went to Frankie & Benny's.'

'Are you still friends with them?'

'Am I still friends with who?' I asked.

'Frankie and Benny.'

'In a way,' I replied wistfully. 'We don't see each other as much as we used to, but I know they'll always be there for me in my time of need.'

Getting back to the task at hand, I rolled over to the water and if my tail hadn't been too tight to allow it, I would have gasped. The other three pools were wonderful but ours was exquisite. Shallow around the edges and deep, dark blue in the middle with a soft sweeping current that sent tiny waves across the surface, it looked more like a small lake than a swimming pool. No, a grotto. It was the perfect home for a couple of mermaids, even if one of them was completely bricking herself.

Neatly positioned on the gently sloping edge, Bel unfurled her fins and slid into the pool. My entry wasn't quite so elegant. I rolled down the slope, hitting the water with a splash, only stopping when I grabbed hold of a passing fish-shaped floatie. Playing mermaid really was the perfect way to show off my complete and utter lack of upper body strength, but it was too late to worry about quitting that 2015 Instagram arms challenge after only two weeks now.

'Do you really think we could pull it off? This love letter stuff?' Bel asked as I delicately spat out a mouthful of saltwater. Knowing I was in the water but not being able to feel the water was really straining my tenuous grasp on reality, and a mild but growing sense of panic fluttered in my stomach. 'I'm not a great writer, I don't want to mess it up. Every time I think about Ren, I want to puke.'

'It's going to be perfect because I'm going to help you,' I promised, quite close to puking myself. 'All you have to do is think of the things you love about him then dress it up a bit. We probably won't mention the fact he makes you want to vomit.'

She pouted, absently slapping her fins on top of the water.

'The best writing is authentic,' I said. 'You can tell when someone's speaking from the heart, it comes off the page.'

'Is this a good time to tell you I failed English?' Bel said. 'More than once. Can't you just write it for me?'

'No. I'm the conduit not the author,' I replied. 'It has to be your thoughts realized by my words. Think of it as me realizing the artistic expression of your feelings. We're symbiotic, we're working together.'

She sparked into life with a dazzling Hollywood grin. 'So it's a collab! Like I'm Harry Styles and you're Gucci?'

I smiled back, touching a hand to my heart. 'That's the nicest thing anyone's ever said to me.'

'If that's true,' she said with a look of alarm, 'we need to introduce you to some better people.'

There wasn't any time to think on her advice. A loud rumbling sound in the distance wiped the smile right off my face.

'Can you hear that?' I asked, instinctively wrapping an arm around my seashells. 'What is it?'

'Oh, that?' Bel tossed her hair over her shoulder and swung her legs into mermaid position. 'That's the kids.'

It sounded more like a herd of hangry, hangry hippos on their way to an all-you-can-eat buffet.

'How many are coming?' I asked, craning my neck to peek around the rocks. What seemed like a stupid idea ten minutes ago now felt like the biggest mistake I'd ever made.

'I don't know, like, fifty?'

Fifty children? Half a hundred seven-year-olds and there I was, sitting in a foot of water with my legs bound together and a very precarious grip on my bikini top. I knew I should have double knotted.

'I don't think I want to do this,' I said as the unicorn whinnied with distress across the lawn. We were of one mind. 'I'm not a strong swimmer. I shouldn't have agreed to it and—'

'Babe, it's all good.' Bel's tone remained calm and soothing despite the fact the roar was getting louder and louder and louder. 'Here's what you're gonna do, climb up on that rock and they won't be able to reach you. Just toss your hair around, look cute and I'll handle the ones in the water. Trust me, they get bored of us so quick. After five minutes, they'll be making TikToks with the unicorn and rolling their own sushi.'

When I was seven, the closest I came to rolling my own sushi was nicking one of my mum's crab sticks.

'OK,' I muttered as I shuffled along the floor of the pool, reaching the rock as hordes of children streamed across the lawn. 'But why do I feel like they're going to be making sushi out of us?'

Bel was wrong.

None of the kids cared about the sushi.

None of the kids cared about the petting zoo.

They didn't care about the outdoor spa, the bouncy castle or even the real castle. The moment they saw us, they ran straight for the water and the only thing that glistened more than the glitter on their bodies was the violence in their eyes.

'Oh hell no,' Bel yelled as they splashed their way towards us, all grabby hands and screeching voices. 'You do *not* touch the tail.'

I watched from my perch up on the rock, helpless as they overwhelmed her, one arm rising out from under a swarm of swimsuit-clad kiddies.

'Bel!' I shouted. 'Bel! Can you hear me?'

It was a mistake.

At once, the pack's attention turned to me. With alarming speed, they moved as one, clambering up the rocks towards me in a swarm.

'Stay back!' I warned. 'I've got a terrible mermaid disease and if you touch me, you'll turn into a crab.'

Unfortunately they were seven, not stupid.

'Are they real shells?' asked the first little girl to reach the top of the rock, immediately grabbing my boob.

'How did they do the tail?' bellowed the next as she wrapped her arms around my lower half and yanked hard.

'Ow, you little bastards,' I gasped when another appeared behind me and pulled on my hair.

'It's not a wig!' she screeched right into my ear. 'You owe me fifty bucks!'

'The mermaids at Antoli's party were way better,' the first one sulked when I slapped her hand away from my bikini top for the tenth time in ten seconds. 'You're fat.'

'We mermaids don't judge people on the size of their bodies,' I replied. 'We judge them for having stupid names like Antoli.'

And that was when everything went horribly wrong. The rest of the children realized the rock above the pool was not big enough for ten of them *and* a mermaid, and so they made the only logical, sociopathic choice.

They pushed me off.

Even though it wasn't far to fall, I fell hard, plummeting backwards into the deep, dark depths of the pool. If nothing else, it was quiet under the water. Dozens of pairs of legs fluttered above me with bruises on their shins and scabs on their knees, and even though I was quite sure I was about to drown, it was nice to see some things never changed, whether you grew up in South Yorkshire or Southern California. My hair fanned out around my face as I tried to kick my legs, but they were too tightly bound together inside my tail and without them, I couldn't seem to push myself to the surface. Slowly sinking, I waited for my life to flash before my eyes, but for some reason all I could think about was whether or not I'd left my hair straighteners plugged in and that one episode of *Friends* where Rachel and Monica only have one condom. Why would flatmates keep a shared box of condoms in the bathroom? Wouldn't you each have your own box in your room? Why didn't Ross or Richard have a condom in their wallet? And how could Ross even think about doing it when his dad's best friend was planning to plough his little sister in the next room? Alas, I thought as I drifted down to the bottom of the pool and settled on the very bottom, it was destined to remain a mystery.

* * *

'Move out of the way, give me some room!'

I heard voices before I saw shapes, the grass cool on my back and warm air on my skin.

'Phoebe! Phoebe! Can you hear me?'

When I opened my stinging eyes, I saw Bel's face rushing towards mine, preparing to administer mouth to mouth.

'I'm breathing! I'm alive!' I cried, coughing up a mouthful of water. 'No need for any of that.'

'Oh my gosh, you're OK.' She adjusted her trajectory by a couple of inches and planted a huge kiss on my forehead. 'Wild that even when you're about to die, you Brits are still total prudes.'

'Are you all right?' I asked. There were still stars in front of my eyes but I was out of the water, I was going to be OK. 'I saw you go under.'

'Only for a second,' she said. 'I'm so sorry, it's never been like this before. I don't know what happened.'

It was only when I managed to sit up, I realized we had an audience. Dozens of people, all staring at us, the adults with some dismay, the children with unblinking disappointment.

'Spoiled monsters?' I suggested.

'Good guess,' Bel replied.

A small girl, in a neon-pink bikini and a crown that read 'birthday princess', came closer and I smiled as warmly as I could although it wasn't terribly warm given that I'd almost just drowned.

'She's not a real mermaid,' the girl proclaimed as she kicked me right in the arse. 'This party sucks.'

'Well, that's rude,' I said quietly through a very un-mermaid-like grimace. 'If you're not careful, I'll curse you.'

She stuffed a handful of blue candyfloss into her mouth and sneered. 'Mermaids can't curse people.'

'But like you said I'm not a mermaid,' I whispered. 'And you're right. I'm a witch. If you don't behave, I'll cast a spell to make sure no one ever watches any of your TikToks ever again. You'll never make it as an influencer.'

The birthday girl screamed at the top of her lungs, tossing the rest of her candyfloss on the ground and hurling herself at a pair of distressed denim-clad legs.

'What the hell is going on here?'

The distressed denim was attached to a tall man with suspiciously black hair, extremely taut cheeks and a forehead so deeply lined, it gave him the look of an angry Shar Pei. He loomed over us, apoplectic.

'Which one of you threatened my Acorn?' he demanded. 'Who made Acorn cry?'

Acorn? I thought.

'Acorn?' I said.

'One of you told Acorn you were going to curse her,' he went on, his surgically stretched face turning very, very red. 'And no one curses my daughter in my house except for me.'

'Daughter?' I flashed him a surprised and moderately impressed look. Despite his low riding jeans and flashy trainers, I definitely would have guessed grandad. He grunted with frustration and I took a moment to remind myself I didn't need to speak every thought that crossed my mind.

'Why do you keep repeating everything I say?' the man exclaimed. 'Are you an idiot? Are you mentally challenged?'

'No, but we were almost drowned by your kids,' I replied politely, still on the floor, still in a mermaid tail. 'Then lovely little Acorn gave me a literal kick up the arse as a reward for not dying on your property, so that was nice.'

'Mermaids are to be in the water when the children arrive,' the man said, chopping the edge of his left hand against his right palm. 'Mermaids are not to leave the water until the children leave. This was all in your contract. Did the agency not explain it in small enough words for you to understand?'

'Excuse me, sir,' Bel said, offering a winning smile. 'We were in the water but the children got a little overexcited so I had to pull my friend out of the water and—'

'Did I ask to hear your excuses?' the man snapped. Even winning smiles were losers sometimes. He yanked off his rainbow-lensed sunglasses to reveal venomous green eyes, the colour really brought out by a bright red incision scar from his recent facelift that wasn't quite healed. 'No. I asked you to shut up, sit around and look pretty, and you couldn't even manage that, which makes me think you couldn't manage much of anything.'

'You can't talk to her like that,' I said, sitting up as tall as my binding waistband would allow. 'Didn't you hear? We literally could have drowned.'

'And I literally don't care.'

It was clear to see where Acorn got her charm.

I twisted around and cocked my head back towards the pool house. 'Come on, Bel,' I said. 'We're leaving.'

'Good, leave, get out of my house,' the man screamed even though we had only managed to inch about a metre across the lawn. 'Pair of dumb bitches. Don't think you're getting paid.'

'Oh, we're getting paid.'

Bel swung herself around to face him, pointing to all the people, professional and otherwise, taking photos and videos of our showdown. 'Because if you don't pay us, we'll sue. I think maybe you're the one who didn't read our contract which states that no one is permitted to touch the mermaids for the duration of the event.'

'That's bullshit,' he said with a grunt. 'Everyone knows—'

'Also outdoor pools are to be heated to 88 degrees or the mermaid reserves the right to refuse to perform. A parking space is to be provided for each mermaid and mermaids will not tolerate abuse of any kind,' she recited with glee. 'The pool isn't 88 degrees, we had to park on the street and you're an asshole. There's a whole bunch of witnesses holding evidence in their hands and even if you delete their camera rolls, everything on social media is archived for like, ever.'

The man blanched but said nothing.

Bel tipped her head to one side and batted her eyelashes. 'So, will it be Venmo or cash?'

'I really hope someone did get that on film,' I said, marvelling at my friend as the man stalked back through the crowd and disappeared into his house. 'You're incredible.'

'No one tells my friend to shut up and look pretty,' she replied as we shuffled triumphantly back to the pool house.

CHAPTER EIGHT

After sitting in traffic for the best part of two hours, we rolled into Suzanne's driveway with three things I didn't have when I left: a very sore, very red ring around my midriff, a thousand dollars in cash and a newfound respect for Ariel's desire to trade her fins for feet.

'I can't believe he gave us a bonus to go away,' Bel said, cranking up the handbrake. 'What a dream job.'

Tearing my eyes away from the cash in my hands, I gave her a questioning look. 'Apart from where we nearly died?'

'I don't think you understand how much money I don't make. I would take a brush with death for a four-figure cash bonus any day of the week.'

'I would give it back to see you threaten to sue him again,' I replied, stuffing the ten one-hundred-dollar bills into my handbag. A thousand dollars took up less space than I would have hoped. 'You were incredible.'

She looked hugely proud of herself, and rightly so. 'We should go out and celebrate. We got paid, baby!

There's this great rooftop bar downtown, awesome views, cutest guys. What do you say?'

The red ring around my belly burned inside and out. 'What about Ren?' I asked.

'Not for me,' she grinned, punching me in the arm. 'For you! What's a vacation without a little holiday romance?'

Rubbing my stomach, I shook my head. 'I don't think so. One-night stands aren't really my thing.'

'Then keep him for two nights.'

You couldn't fault the woman's logic.

'Let's say casual sex in general,' I replied. 'Not for me. The thought of jumping into bed with someone I've just met doesn't do it for me. There has to be more to it than that.'

'So you're sapiosexual?' she suggested. 'Or demisexual?'

'I'm not sure I know what demisexual is, so let's not step on anyone's identity,' I replied, squeezing the end of my still-wet ponytail. 'I like sex but I like it best when I know and trust the other person well enough to relax and enjoy myself. Going home with a stranger doesn't sound like a good time. I'd spend the whole time stressing out about what they were thinking, whether or not I was doing it wrong, which diseases I needed to get tested for the morning after.'

'Wow, I didn't think they still made people like you,' Bel said with genuine but kind surprise. 'It doesn't have to be that deep, Phoebe. Sometimes sex is just sex, a fun activity for two or more consenting adults.'

I gulped.

'Two or more?'

'OK, you're not ready for that,' she acknowledged. 'But you do know sex is allowed to be a no-strings thing, right?

Yes, Y2K is back but it's really the fashion we're interested in, not the attitudes. There will be no slut-shaming on my watch.'

'Love it for everyone else,' I said, giving a double thumbs up in agreement. 'Doesn't mean it's for me.'

Bel shrugged, holding up her hands in surrender. 'No, totally, everyone's on their own journey. Sex is great cardio though, trust me, I'm a trainer. Nothing works off calories like using a willing partner as a human dildo.'

'You have such a way with words,' I replied, clutching at my imaginary pearls as she honked with laughter. 'I can't believe you think you need help writing a love letter.'

'You see? You're so funny, you're like the funniest person I ever met. The men here would eat you up.'

'And that's a good thing?'

'Can be,' she said. 'If they're good at it.'

'I think you're confusing men looking for sex with literally anyone else alive,' I said, ignoring her suggestive eyebrow dance. 'I've seen the women around here – they all look like they're sixteen and think flesh-toned cycling shorts and a crop top constitute a complete outfit. They're hot, Bel, properly, objectively hot. I am a pale, pasty, failed mermaid who considers the return of low-rise jeans to be a crime against humanity.'

She leaned her head back against the headrest, lips pursed, eyes narrowed. 'There's a lot of different kinds of hot. Last time I checked, there wasn't a regulatory committee that agrees on one single, official definition.'

'I think you'll find there is,' I scoffed. 'It's called the internet and it convenes daily.'

'Let's go out,' Bel said again, stretching out all her

vowels with belligerence. 'We had a near-death experience, we have to celebrate. With shots.'

'That's not a rule.'

'It's a new rule, I just made it.'

'Maybe another night,' I told her as I opened the car door. 'I still have to go and drop off those packages and this mermaid needs her beauty sleep.'

'But the hot men,' Bel whined. 'You're depriving the studs of LA a chance to get to know you.'

I laughed, shooting for a carefree chuckle but landing closer to a glove puppet being savagely attacked by an angry squirrel. The thought of going out-out with Bel made my skin itch and I wasn't proud of the fact. She was gorgeous in an immediate way. Even though there was a lot more under the surface, the surface was more than attractive enough on its own. No one would ever have to get to know her first or gradually fall for her personality. She'd never have to wow someone with a witty joke and hope they would eventually, one day, see her as something more than a friend. She and I were very different people.

Because you're boring, whispered the unwelcome voice in my head. You're dull. You're so ordinary. No one cares what you think.

'—you're cute and funny, you have a great accent, and what a butt.'

When I snapped back to the real conversation I was having with a real person, Bel was still counting off my attributes on her fingers.

'Any man would be lucky to have you,' she declared. 'Even for one or two nights.'

'Sorry,' I said, running out of polite ways to say no. 'I'm really tired. All that mermaiding took it out of me,

I think I'm going to curl up with a good book and get an early night.'

'So, Suzanne told me not to ask you, but is this about your ex?'

I crystallized at the mention of him, the sweet, warm safety I felt when I was with Bel transforming into something brittle and breakable.

'My ex?'

'Yeah, Suzie kinda mentioned he's getting married soon?' she added. 'And maybe you're not like, totally completely over him? And maybe that's why you came out to visit?'

'That's not how it is at all,' I replied, switching my eyes away as I tapped myself down for the house keys. 'I couldn't be more over him if I tried.'

'She said you haven't dated anyone else since you guys broke up?'

'It hasn't been that long.'

'You don't think two years is long?'

So Suzanne didn't like to talk about herself but she didn't mind sharing hot takes on my personal life with complete strangers? Good to know.

'OK,' I said, opening the door and spilling out onto the pavement. I couldn't get out of the car fast enough. 'I really need a wee and I'm going to be late to my other thing so I'm going to go. Thanks for the lift and saving my life and stuff.'

'Wait, what about the love letter?' Bel called as the ground rushed up to meet my feet. 'I didn't even give you my list of things I love about Ren!'

'Text it to me,' I shouted over my shoulder as I scrambled upstairs to the front door, forced my key into the lock and closed it quickly behind me. The sound of my heartbeat pounded in my ears in contrast to the serene silence of the house.

The thought of Suzanne and Bel sitting around her kitchen table, gossiping about me, turned my blood into acid. I could only imagine the other lies and half-truths that were doing the rounds. After Gran died, more than a few of my friends drifted away. It wasn't their fault and I didn't blame them; they didn't know what to say and I didn't know what I wanted them to say. I'd never lost anyone before and it was dizzying, exhausting, a fresh wave of grief knocking me off my feet every single time I managed to get up. Mum and I weren't close, Suzanne was far away and the only person who kept me rooted in my life was gone forever. Not even I could come up with a card to suit that occasion. The right words didn't exist.

Instead I doubled down on what I had left, desperate to hold on to it. Thomas. I made him my whole world and in return, he closed the curtains, locked the doors and kept everyone else away. I didn't realize how dangerous that was until it was too late. It took hardly any effort on his part to convince me he was the only thing I had left in the world and months later, when I finally found the strength to stop drinking his poison, almost all my friends were gone. The thought of having to beg them all to come back and explain what had happened, my grief, my mistakes, the misery he put me through when I was at my weakest, was too much.

So I didn't.

Dumping my handbag on the kitchen table, I opened

a cupboard door just to slam it shut again, the sound echoing all the way through the beautiful, silent house.

The very thought that I was still in love with him. My sister didn't have a clue.

CHAPTER NINE

'Hello, my old nemesis.'

I patted the trunk of the tree outside Ms M. Moore's house, having arrived promptly at the appointed time. My hair was washed, my shoes were clean and my frayed temper somewhat soothed. It took an entire tub of Ben & Jerry's and a straight hour of watching eyeliner hacks on TikTok in the hot tub, but my rage was almost all gone.

At least the gates were open this time; not all the way open, but just wide enough for me to squeeze through with her packages, a box of chocolates and a bottle of wine. I came prepared, partly because Gran raised me never to show up to anyone's house empty-handed, but also because I was half-expecting her to snatch the packages out my arms with a stick then send me on my way and if she did, I was going home, getting back in the hot tub and drinking the entire bottle of wine while stuffing the chocolates straight down my gullet.

There was no doorbell on the front door, just an old-fashioned brass doorknocker in true murder house-style. So far, so ominous. Jiggling the tote bag on my shoulder, I knocked and I waited. The last time I was here, there wasn't much time to enjoy the gardens, what with climbing a tree and running for the gate and whatnot, but today I had a moment to take it all in. The house was surrounded by beautifully manicured green lawns and rose bushes so overloaded with blooms, if their scent hadn't been so overwhelming, I might have thought they were fake. Right in front of the house, a circular gravel driveway curved around a stone fountain, ready for a vintage Rolls-Royce or some other classic car to roll up with some satin-clad 1940s Hollywood starlet spilling out the back into the arms of a tall, handsome, possibly gay leading man she was contractually obliged to be seen with three times a week.

While I was busy daydreaming about the perils of the studio system, the front door to the house opened and in the dim light I saw the silhouette of its presumed owner loom into sight.

'Hello,' I said when she did not move or speak. 'I'm Phoebe Chapman? I came yesterday? You asked me to bring your parcels back today?'

'Yes, I recall,' she replied. 'I'm old, not an imbecile.'

'Noted.' My lips inched upwards in an awkward smile. 'Would you like me to leave them here or should I bring them in?'

'You may bring them inside,' the woman replied, moving back through the shadows of the entryway. 'Follow me.'

* * *

The outside of the house was impressive but the inside was magnificent. Two symmetrical, sweeping staircases filled the entrance hall and a crystal chandelier bigger than my Renault Clio hung from the ceiling. With the windows all shuttered, only the narrowest beams of light were able to slice through the musty air, occasionally catching a crystal tear drop and sending a burst of rainbows dancing across the wall. It was beautiful.

In front of us were three archways, each presenting a different path into darkness.

'This way,' the woman said, choosing the one off to the right, and for reasons I truly did not understand, I trotted right off after her. A very long, very quiet minute later, my host stopped at the end of the hall and opened a door, the sudden burst of light inside dazzling me.

'Come in if you're coming in. And put the boxes on the table.'

'Sorry, yes, thank you,' I muttered, squeezing my eyes shut until they adjusted. 'Couldn't see for a second there.'

'And you're going to apologize and thank me for blinding you?' I heard a thrilled cackle fill the air. 'As though I didn't already know you were British.'

Blinking, I trod carefully until I could see again. And what a sight it was to see. The deep bottle-green wallpaper that looked like silk, the glossy mahogany wood of the furniture, the softly glowing brass accents and plush velvet. French doors opened on to the garden at the back of the house, the wine-coloured drapes that hung on either side of them loosely restrained by matching swags. It was a shock to see a flatscreen television mounted to the wall on one side of the room; anything other than a gramophone felt like an affront. It was like stepping back in time.

'Sit,' the woman instructed.

Like a well-trained dog, I plopped down on the closest seat, resting my tote bag on the tops of my feet, afraid to let such common fabric touch anything in this house. My host eased herself into the chair opposite, affording me my first proper look at her, and I couldn't stop myself from staring. She was old but how old was impossible to say. Her skin was perfectly even and fair, lined with evidence of a life well lived, but her fine bone structure was still there: high cheekbones, long nose, neat chin. Her hair was silver and carefully set, and her bright blue eyes looked sharp enough to cut through steel.

'What's wrong?' she asked. 'Haven't you seen a faded movie star before?'

'I, um, no, you're not, I mean—' I started before giving up. I didn't know what to say. Whatever else she might be, I was certain I'd never seen anyone quite so beautiful.

'Myrna Moore.' She reached one arm across the table, swathed in black silk, and held out her slender hand for me to shake or kiss, I wasn't sure which. 'I'd say it's a pleasure to meet you but I'm too old to lie.'

'I'll just give you your packages and be off,' I said, speaking into my chest as I dug around in the tote bag. 'No problem.'

'If I wanted you to leave, I wouldn't have asked you in.' Her voice was deep and raspy but there was a warmth to it that made the hairs on the back of my neck stand up on end. I could have listened to her read the instruction manual for my air fryer and not get bored. Which reminded me, I really should get round to reading the instruction manual for my air fryer.

'What did you say your name was?'

'Phoebe,' I replied. It felt like a confession. 'Phoebe Chapman.'

Myrna Moore sat back in her chair, one finger lightly pressed against her chin. 'It used to be that I knew everyone around here but I'm not familiar with any Chapmans. You said you've been getting my mail?'

I nodded and handed over my offering of a box of chocolates. Sod it, I was keeping the wine.

'My sister lives at 4001, Suzanne Chapman? Tall, blonde, British? Swears a lot?'

She reached for a gold pendant, flat and round, that hung around her neck and ran it back and forth along its rope-like chain. Every possible part of her was bejewelled; she had gems in her ears and every other finger was decked in diamonds and emeralds and rubies, stacked all the way up to her knuckles.

'The white villa on the crest of the hill? I didn't know Myrtle and Roy had moved.'

'She moved in quite recently. I don't know who she bought it from, sorry.'

'Myrtle and Roy, the Edelsteins,' Myrna said confidently. As if anyone would ever dare to question her. 'They were there a very long time. There was another family in there between them and the Goldfarbs, I forget their names, they didn't stick around long, and before that it was the Salgado family.'

I couldn't not smile, it was just like talking to Gran. She always knew everyone's comings and goings, often before they did. 'You know a lot about the area. Have you lived here a long time?'

'Is sixty-two years a long time?' she asked and I was sure it was a test.

'It's a decent amount,' I replied.

She responded with an almost imperceptible nod. 'Gabriel Salgado built your sister's place the same time my Wally built this house for me,' Myrna said, gesturing around the beautiful room. How much of it had changed since then? My best bet was nothing but the telly. 'I was twenty-one, just married, desperately in love and without a single clue as to how the world works. What I wouldn't give to go back to those days. You must be around that age?'

God bless the good people at Olay.

'Not quite, I'm thirty-three. Almost thirty-four.'

She gave me another look, scrutinizing the fine lines around my eyes I spent too much money trying to plump out. 'It's impossible to tell these days. The fifteen-year-olds look like they're forty and the forty-year-olds could pass for fifteen. The only thing that doesn't change is that women are never happy.' She reached over to a brass bar cart and one by one, transferring a bottle of red, two wine glasses and a corkscrew onto the table between us. 'On the bad days my arthritis gets the best of me and I have to make do with a screw top. Be grateful today is not one of those days.'

'I can help,' I offered, but not quickly enough. Clearly, Myrna had enjoyed plenty of practice opening bottles in her time. She pulled out the cork with a satisfying pop.

'Let me do it while I still can,' she said. 'Once they

hide me away on the old folks' farm, I doubt I'll be allowed to serve myself so much as a cup of coffee.'

I held out my glass as she poured, steady as a rock, and even though I was sure I would regret asking, I couldn't help myself.

'Old folks' farm?'

'They would prefer I call it an assisted living facility but, as I said, I'm too old for lies.' She clinked her very full glass against mine and sat back. 'Now you tell me, Phoebe Chapman of 4001 Parva Avenue, what possessed you to trespass on to my property yesterday?'

'I was just trying to drop off your packages,' I replied, licking the delicious red wine from my lips, Myrna nursing her glass in both hands without drinking. 'I'm sorry, I couldn't see another way in.'

'And you weren't afraid I might have attack dogs or security guards?'

'To be honest, I didn't really think about it,' I admitted. 'You don't get that many attack dogs or security guards where I live.'

'Luckily for you, I have neither.' She held my gaze, looked at the wine on the table and then back at me. 'I prefer to deal with enemies in my own way. They say poison is a coward's weapon, but I prefer to think of it as a ladylike way to kill, don't you agree?'

My eyes opened wide as I choked on my wine, spilling half of what was still in my glass. Myrna tossed back her head and laughed so hard I was afraid she might break a rib.

'Sorry, that was cruel but too good an opportunity to pass up,' she said, wiping a tear from the corner of her eye. 'Really the joke's on me, I'll never get the red wine out of that rug.' She reached for the box of chocolates and popped off the lid. 'Truffles, wonderful, my favourite.'

Leaning back against her chair, she dropped one in her mouth and chewed.

'So to be extra clear, you haven't poisoned me?' I asked, swabbing my mouth with the back of my hand.

She shook her head. 'Too hard to dispose of a body these days.'

Shaking, I put the rest of my wine down, oddly enough not in the mood for it any more. I couldn't decide who was worse, the terrible children who tried to finish me off that morning or Myrna who was surely old enough to know better.

'Quite impressive, the way you got over the wall,' she said, helping herself to another truffle. 'You remind me a little bit of me when I was your age. Perhaps a decade or so younger; by the time I was thirty-three I dressed like an adult.'

'What's wrong with the way I'm dressed?' I pulled at my black linen jumpsuit, searching for a flaw. It was one of the fancier items I'd shoved in my suitcase an hour before I left for the airport, and one of my all-time favourite outfits. I loved it.

'You look like a toddler in mourning. I don't know whether to offer my condolences or offer to change your diaper.'

I hated the jumpsuit and I would never wear it again.

'You said you're a movie star?' I said, utilizing my spectacular talent for changing the subject. 'That must be exciting.'

'You missed out the word faded. I haven't acted in sixty years,' she drawled. 'But yes, it was until it wasn't.'

From the look on her face, I knew there was more to the story and once again, against my better judgement, I found I couldn't stop myself from asking another question.

'So you retired?' I pressed lightly. 'You didn't want to act any more?'

'Pass me those packages,' Myrna ordered. 'That's why you're here after all.'

I wasn't the only one who was good at changing the subject.

She attacked the first box with her corkscrew, tearing through the brown wrapping paper and slashing through the Sellotape as though it had done something to offend her. Fishing around inside, she pulled out a tissue paper package and tossed the box to the ground. It was a tiny glass salt shaker. She held it up to the light to inspect it further, a satisfied sound tickling the back of her throat before she placed it on the coffee table. The second box went the same way, savagely attacked then discarded. This one contained a silver salt shaker.

'They're lovely,' I said for the want of something to say. Even if she'd given me a thousand guesses as to what was inside, I never would have got it. 'Do you collect them?'

'Against my will.' Myrna picked up the second salt shaker and turned it over in her still nimble fingers. 'People send them to me. Still. After all these years.'

'That's . . . nice?'

'I was in a famous picture, *The Waitress*, 1962,' she explained, putting the salt shaker down and swapping it for another chocolate from the box. 'Have you seen it?'

Biting my lip, I shook my head.

'One of the last great noirs in my opinion. I, the titular waitress, was killed at the end.'

'Spoiler alert,' I said, reaching for the truffles.

She tutted and slapped my hand away from the chocolate box. 'Don't blame me for your shameful cinematic education. *The Waitress* is a classic. In the final scene, as I fall to the ground, shot dead by my vengeful ex-lover, my arm extends and the camera closes in on my hand as it slowly opens to reveal the key to the whole story. A salt shaker. The salt shaker that matches the peppermill found at the scene of the crime at the beginning of the movie. It would all make a lot more sense if you'd seen the film instead of rotting your brain on dinosaurs and wizards and whatever other nonsense your generation calls entertainment.'

'I'm sorry, it sounds brilliant,' I offered meekly. This was not the time to tell her I'd seen the *Twilight* saga more than twenty times; she didn't strike me as someone who had an allegiance to Team Edward or Team Jacob.

'My fans began to send these almost as soon as the picture came out. They've slowed down over the years but never completely stopped.'

'How many do you have?' I asked, genuinely curious.

'I've never counted.'

She picked up the salt shakers and stood slowly, her loose black silk shirt and matching palazzo pants rippling as she walked across the room, gesturing for me to come along. 'You tell me, how many do you think are in here?'

She pulled back a curtain to reveal a floor-to-ceiling glass-fronted cabinet built into the wall, each and every inch of shelf space covered in salt shakers. There had to be a thousand, if not tens of thousands. Salt shakers of all different sizes and shapes, made of glass, porcelain, gold and silver. Some were decorated, some were plain, some with words or names of places painted on them, and some bearing a picture of a woman in a blue dress and white apron, who I took to be a very young Myrna Moore.

'This is wild,' I said as she opened the closest cabinet to find a home for the latest additions to her collection. 'People just send them to you?'

'From all over the world.' She stood back to observe her collection, arms folded across her chest. 'I don't get so many these days. It's too difficult now, to find my address, to package the thing, to take it to the post office. If someone can't do something with two taps on their phone, they don't bother, effort is a dirty word. Very few people have the moxie we had in my day.'

My first instinct was to defend the under eighties, but I knew she was at least partially right. I lived and died by my phone and was on first-name terms with at least half the Deliveroo drivers in the greater Nottingham area.

'Very few people would, for example, climb up a tree and jump over a wall to deliver a package.'

The expression on her face was not easy to interpret but, unless I was mistaken, she looked amused. One corner of her mouth ticked upwards and her eyes sparkled, reflecting the light of a trillion salt shakers. Of course, there was also a very good chance I was misreading the situation entirely and she was about to kneecap me with a crowbar for a laugh.

'How are you enjoying the Edelsteins' house?' she asked.

I exhaled with relief as she led us back to our seats,

all my joints intact. 'It's beautiful,' I replied, thinking about all the families she must have seen move in and out over the years. 'Did you happen to know the Garcias who lived in the house next door?'

'Joe and Rosa?' This time her expression was easy to read. A huge, beaming smile took over her whole face. 'Wonderful people. Joe was a builder, like Gabriel. They moved here together, as I recall. Rosa had the most beautiful singing voice and those big brown eyes. I always said that girl could have been a star.'

'I met their grandson,' I told her. 'He's renovating the house.'

The slightest blush warmed my cheeks at the thought of said grandson but thankfully, Myrna didn't seem to notice.

'Takes after his grandfather then.' Her smile faltered as she flexed the fingers on her right hand. 'I was sorry to hear Joe had passed. He built a lot of beautiful houses in this neighbourhood, although I doubt many of them are still standing. They'll knock this place to the ground the moment I'm out of it.'

'Surely not,' I protested, feeling oddly protective of a house I'd only just set foot in. 'Your house is beautiful.'

'Beautiful, old and too expensive to maintain, much like me.' She gave the arm of her chair a loving stroke. 'You can only be one of those things in Los Angeles. She might look impressive to you, but she needs work. New windows, new roof, new plumbing, new air conditioning. Anyone with that kind of money has too much sense to waste it here, and anyone foolish enough to want to waste it wouldn't have the money in the first place.'

'When are you moving?' I asked.

Myrna closed her eyes and exhaled slowly.

'Two weeks.'

It sounded as though she could barely believe it herself.

'Two more weeks and off I go into what my hateful stepchildren like to call God's waiting room. Which, in my opinion, is a very optimistic name. There's a better chance of me being elected president of these United States than a single resident in that place making it past St Peter and through the pearly gates.'

'I'm here for another week,' I said, drinking in the beauty of her sitting room and feeling unexpectedly sad for this fascinating woman. 'Do you think it might be all right if I came to visit again?'

She reached for her pendant, sliding it up and down, and studying my face. 'Sunday would be fine,' she said. 'In the afternoon. Visiting in the mornings is terribly gauche.'

'Not a morning person, got it.'

She pursed her lips and made a small, affirmative noise in the back of her throat.

'I'll expect you at two. And feel free to dress like a grown woman next time.'

'Can't make any promises,' I told her, a quick mental search through my luggage yielding very poor results. 'But I'll try my best.'

'See that you do,' she said, chasing her words with a disappointed but resigned grunt. 'It's the least my home deserves.'

And I had to agree with her there.

* * *

Lindsey Kelk

Bel's list of things she loved about Ren was not quite what I was expecting.

With two feet on the floor of Suzanne's pool and my upper body curled over the side, I studied her text as though it were written in cryptic code.

Like his green eyes

Hot bod

Smart

Seems nice

I hear WAP playing in my head every time I see him

Even though I was pretty sure there was only one *WAP* on either side of the Atlantic, I still googled it to be on the safe side.

'Just the one meaning then,' I muttered as the too-catchy chorus knocked on the doors of my brain. If I let it in, it would never leave and as much as I loved Cardi and Meg, I had a feeling it wasn't the right soundtrack for the greatest, most romantic love letter of all time.

'Siri, play some Motown please?'

I almost clapped with pure delight as Stevie Wonder echoed through the invisible speakers hidden around the garden – I was getting used to Suzanne's swanky LA lifestyle far too easily – and read through Bel's list again. OK, so she wasn't a whizz with words, that wasn't a secret. Just because she wasn't waxing lyrical about his eyes didn't mean her feelings weren't real. Some people saw one colour, some people all the shades. She hadn't spent as much time with him as I had. She didn't know they were so much more than green. Sometimes emerald, sometimes more like fresh-cut grass, or the misty, mossy shade of trees reflected in the water and ringed with pure black, set off by his perfect, burnished bronze skin and fringed with lashes so thick and long, the thought of them fluttering against my cheek as his face came closer to mine made my heart thud in my chest.

Clearing my throat, I rushed back to the present, water swishing around my legs, the early evening sun warm on my shoulders. I was getting myself in the right mindset, that was all.

Green eyes was a much more concise way of saying exactly what I'd come up with. Bel was efficient, nothing wrong with that.

'Hot bod,' I said aloud. 'Seems nice.'

Hot bod went without saying but Ren didn't seem nice, he *was* nice. It was one of the things I liked best about him. He was kind when he didn't have to be, generous with his time, honest and open. He'd gone out of his way to make me feel welcome and if that wasn't nice, I didn't know what was. And then there was the look on his face when I told him about Bel's love letter. He wasn't afraid to show his feelings. Only that letter was still a blank piece of paper because my brain was holding all my words hostage. It was so long since I'd tried anything like this. All my romantic leanings were locked away safely where they couldn't get me into trouble and now I wanted to release them, they were nowhere to be found.

The sun began to slip out of sight, disappearing behind the so-called mountain as I stood in the pool, staring at a tiny puff of a cloud and watching as it turned from white to peach to pink against the powder-blue sky.

'You can do this,' I muttered, reaching for the notebook and pen sat on top of my towel. I tapped the pen against the paper, hoping to shake some sentiment loose. If I were Bel, what would I say to Ren? If I were beautiful and confident and knew he was impatiently waiting to read my words, what would they be? It wasn't just a letter, it was the beginning of a love story, something he could tell their grandchildren about, the way his grandparents had shared their story with him. A vision of an older Ren popped into my mind, three little boys splashing around in his kidney-shaped pool, and sitting on the grass by this salt-and-pepper version of my green-eyed, nice, hot neighbour was a young girl with my blonde hair. She clapped as he pulled out a stack of letters, tied with a red ribbon, slid the first one out of its envelope and read to her.

My pen moved across the page.

Ren.

The very first time I saw you, everything changed. I knew in that moment I'd been living underwater, holding my breath for far too long and watching the world pass by, out of sight, out of reach. Your green eyes brought me to the surface. When you smiled, I remembered how to breathe. All my words escaped in that exhalation and slowly, one by one, I have searched for them, gathering them in my heart so I could put them in this letter, hoping to come close to describing the way I feel.

I never believed in love at first sight until now.

'That's not bad,' I whispered as I read my own words back. 'Pretty much exactly what Bel said.'

A shiver ran down the length of my spine and I pushed the pad and paper away, clear of the pool, slipping deeper into the water until I was in up to my shoulders. Imaginary Ren and his fantasy grandchildren faded away, the little blonde girl replaced with a beautiful brunette. It looked better, more believable.

With a deep breath in, I dipped all the way under water and opened my eyes to watch the sunset, submerged.

CHAPTER TEN

All I wanted from my Friday was peace and quiet.

Bel was too busy pretending to be a burned-out but still impossibly beautiful mother of two in an advert for car insurance to trick me into another near-death situation and Suzanne was still threatening the lives of half the population of Seattle, which left me blissfully alone with only three things on my to-do list.

Eat, sleep and deliver the letter to Ren.

I was looking forward to one of those things much less than the others.

Putting pen to paper had put ideas in my mind and I couldn't seem to shake them loose. All night long, I'd tossed and turned, the false memory of Ren and the little blonde girl chasing me everywhere I went, and when sleep finally found me, my dreams were even worse. In one, I was a waitress, serving Ren coffee in a black-and-white diner, and in another I was a mermaid, he was a merman, and we did unconscionable things in both of them. No matter how many times I told myself they were only dreams, they didn't mean anything, it was impossible to push the thought of MerRen bending me over a coral reef out of my mind.

'They're just dreams,' I said, blinking down at the book in my hands and trying to remember anything that had happened in the last ten pages. 'You can't control your dreams.'

No matter how many hours I spent watching videos about lucid dreaming on TikTok.

It made sense. You write a romantic letter about a man, you're bound to have some residual romantic thoughts, like using a Lush bath bomb and finding glitter all over the house for weeks on end. And I couldn't stop thinking about the letter itself. Was it too much? Not enough? Had I lost the knack? I'd always been so proud of my work but the thought of anyone reading the words on the piece of paper I'd folded three times, slipped inside an envelope and left waiting on the kitchen counter brought me out in a nervous rash.

Eventually, I gave up on the book and swapped it for the remote control and turned on the TV. I had set myself up for the day on Suzanne's sofa, with snacks, cushions and her cashmere blanket. It was time to replace the pictures in my head with pictures on the screen and I knew exactly what I wanted to watch.

'Come on then, Myrna Moore,' I said, pulling up *The Waitress* and pressing play. 'Let's see what you've got.'

The movie was fantastic. Myrna was magnetic on screen; every time the camera came near her, she was all I could see, and the moment it was over, I started the film over again, googling Myrna's name at the same time. The first photo I found was a portrait in black and white, the planes of her face turned towards the light, blonde hair styled in soft waves around her head, glowing like a halo. She looked like a doll with her eyes softly gazing at something off camera and her heart-shaped mouth curved into an almost smile. Mona Lisa had nothing on her. The second photo was a still from *The Waitress*. Even in her unflattering uniform and sensible shoes, she radiated an untouchable kind of glamour. A few more taps on a few more links uncovered an absolute treasure trove: Myrna at the Oscars, Myrna on Catalina Island, Myrna and Liz at the premiere of *Cleopatra*, Myrna and Marilyn drinking martinis at Musso & Frank's. And then I was introduced to her husband, Wally Steadson. He wasn't anything special to look at and he had to be a good twenty years older than her, but from the look in his eyes, there was never a man more in love than Wally on his wedding day. The first photo was of their courthouse ceremony, Wally in a suit, Myrna in a sexy little dress, then Myrna and Wally on their Palm Springs honeymoon, Myrna and Wally in Las Vegas with Elvis. Myrna and Wally laughing in every single picture. Then it all changed. There was one single image of a black-clad Myrna climbing into a car at the Forest Lawn cemetery after Wally's funeral and after that, nothing. She disappeared. I couldn't find a single photograph of Myrna taken after 1965. She never acted in another film, was never pictured attending another event. It was as though she'd vanished, not just from Hollywood but off the face of the earth altogether.

'Myrna Moore, the mystery,' I whispered as my eyes drifted back to the huge flatscreen TV to see the woman herself raise one eyebrow and smile back at me from sixty years ago.

It was early evening by the time I dragged myself out of the house and round the corner to deliver Ren's letter. To her credit, Bel had only texted me fifteen times to ask if he had it, what he'd said, how he'd looked when I gave it to him and whether or not he was shirtless at the time. I could only put it off for so long.

There were so many different types of houses in Los Feliz: Spanish villas, modernist blocks, craftsmen bungalows and so many more I didn't even know how to describe. As I strolled down the hill and around the corner, I realized I'd never really seen the front of Ren's storybook cottage. It was tucked away amongst the trees with a steeply pitched roof and timber framework, and all that was missing was Goldilocks and or the Three Bears. The front of the house was painted the same deep forest green as the back, but it clashed beautifully with the vintage cherry-red flatbed truck parked on the street outside, and even though it was gorgeous, I couldn't help but think he ought to consider trading it in for a horse and cart.

I opened his squeaky gate and made my way up a front path picked out in irregularly shaped paving stones, hopping from one to the next. I felt like Gretel, only without the obnoxious brother and the propensity for eating other people's houses. Even though it would have been quicker for me to climb down the garden stairs for the hand-off, this felt more proper. It also meant I could shove the envelope through the letterbox and run away. I held my breath as I approached the front door, stealth personified. Post and run, no need for me to see Ren at all. I'd added Bel's number to the bottom of the letter so he could call her once he'd read it and my work here would be done. Very, very, very carefully, I lifted the flap of the letterbox, slid the envelope inside and listened as it landed with a dull thud.

Mission accomplished.

'Phoebe?'

The front door opened with a tell-tale creak.

Mission buggered.

'Oh, hello!' I turned around with a face full of cheerful bluster. 'Fancy seeing you here.'

Framed by the doorway, Ren wore nothing but a pair of low-slung grey sweatpants and a smile. I looked to the skies and cursed whichever deity would do this to a girl.

'Did you post this through my door?' he asked, envelope in hand.

'I did,' I confirmed. 'I wasn't sure if you were home, so I thought better to pop it through the door and make sure you got it rather than hold on to it because it's for you so why would I want it because it's the letter. Your letter. Bel's letter. It's the letter Bel wrote for you that I delivered.'

Somehow I found the strength to stop talking and gritted my teeth, baring them all at the same time like I was showing off for the dentist. It was not a sexy look, it was deranged, but Ren didn't seem to notice.

'So, this is my love letter, huh?' He grinned as though

it was all a joke, holding the envelope at arm's length, as though a boxing glove might spring out and bop him on the nose when he opened it.

'The one and only. Anyway, it's teatime, I'm starving,' I said, slapping myself slightly too hard on the stomach. 'I'll leave you in peace.'

But I didn't have the chance to move so much as a single step before he tore it open, pulling out the single sheet of paper. It all seemed to happen in slow motion, the smile fading from his face, replaced by a sense of surprise that warmed into wonder as he went on. It was too much, the way his pupils dilated, the way his breath caught in his chest. His lips parted, moving soundlessly as his eyes swept over the words, bringing them to life and making them real.

The very first time I saw you, everything changed.

As he read the letter, I heard the words in my own head, in my own voice. It was one thing to scribble it down the night before, high on an intense day of meeting Myrna, dressing up as a mermaid and nearly drowning in a rich man's swimming pool, but it felt deeply wrong to watch him reading the letter, believing those words were all from Bel.

It felt like a lie.

My stomach plummeted, churning and melting at the same time, and the knees that had managed to hold me up for more than thirty years threatened to go full Bambi-on-ice at any moment.

'Bye then,' I called, my voice cracking as I backed away towards the gate. 'See you later.'

'Wait!' He looked up from the letter with a flushed, red face. 'This is . . . wow.'

Frozen on the spot, my chest tight, I cleared my throat before I tried to speak. 'I'm assuming wow is a good thing?'

Ren looked at me with so much joy and I almost crumbled away to dust. I wasn't prepared for it, his reaction or my own.

'I don't really know what to say,' he replied with more honesty than I deserved. 'I never thought something like this would happen for me.'

I started at the sharp sting of my fingernails as they dug deep into my palms. I hadn't even realized I was making a fist. What was I doing? Why was this so hard? Why didn't he have a top on?

'You should call her,' I said, backing even further away. Call her and leave me out of it.

'Yeah, I will.' Shirtless Ren folded the letter with so much care and slid it back into its envelope before placing it on a small glass-topped table by the door. 'Hey, did you say you're hungry?'

'Starving was the word I used.' I pressed a hand against my belly but the grumbling happening inside had nothing to do with missing a meal. 'Better go and eat something before my stomach lining starts devouring itself.'

'Making anything good?'

'I thought I might attempt to master mac and cheese,' I said. 'Learn the true ways of your people.'

Still shirtless, he shook his head. 'No way. It's Friday night, you're on vacation. If you don't have plans, we should do something fun.'

All I had to do was say I had plans.

'Where are we going?' I asked.

'We're in Hollywood, baby.' Ren snapped his fingers and shot at me with double finger guns. 'I'm taking you to see the stars.'

'So, tell me,' I said, hugging a stuffed-to-bursting picnic basket to my body. 'Do you often take people for a picnic in a cemetery?'

'Only if they're really lucky.' Ren steered his truck carefully around the curving roads, driving at a very respectful pace which was nice given that we were literally surrounded by gravestones. 'Welcome to Hollywood Forever, you're gonna love it.'

'Thank you, that doesn't add to the horror movie vibes at all.'

He looked as though he had something else to say, a snappy comeback lit up behind his eyes, but instead, he carried on smiling and parked up at the side of the road.

'Wait there, let me get the door,' he instructed, hopping out of the truck and pocketing his keys.

'I'm not completely useless,' I replied. Chivalry made me uneasy. 'I can open a door myself.'

Only I couldn't, no matter how hard I tried. On the other side of the glass, Ren watched with amusement.

'It won't open,' I called, tapping on the window.

'I know,' he replied, tapping back. 'That's why I said I would get it.'

'And there was me, thinking you were being a gentleman,' I muttered as he flipped the outside handle and opened the door.

He offered me his hand to help me down from the cabin, his skin rough and hot as his fingers curled tightly around mine, and I felt another flutter in the pit of my stomach that I did not care for.

'I am a gentleman,' he said in a low voice. 'Most of the time.'

'Is it a seasonal thing or do the hours differ daily?' I asked, shaking off his hand and my unexpected, unwelcome reaction.

'All changes are at the discretion of the management. Wanna go see some dead people?'

'Oh, go on then,' I returned, handing him the picnic basket and falling into step at his side, Ren's woody, warm skin scent carrying me on into the cemetery.

'This is one of my favourite places in the whole city,' Ren said as we crossed the grass to find our footpath. He nodded at a security guard who barely even flinched as we strolled by, very busy looking at his phone while I concentrated on not thinking about what, or who, was underneath my feet. 'It's so quiet and peaceful. Makes for a great place to come and think.'

'It's quiet,' I replied with a shiver, 'because everybody is dead.'

'Touché.'

The soles of my flip-flops thowcked against my feet and I cringed with every single step. If I'd known where we were going, I'd have insisted on going home to change into a closed toe. Wearing flip-flops to a cemetery had to be the most disrespectful thing in the whole world; I was sure at least a hundred of the people underfoot were spinning in their graves.

'It's not just a cemetery, they do a bunch of cool things here.' Ren pointed straight ahead as we took a left turn.

'Down there by the big white building, they have bands play all the time. They do movie screenings, yoga classes, all kinds of stuff.'

'Bringing a whole new meaning to corpse pose,' I muttered, brightening slightly when he laughed.

Cemeteries were never at the top of my must-visit list but as we walked on, I saw that Ren was right. Hollywood Forever was more peaceful than morbid, settling my frayed nerves with a pleasantly serene atmosphere, and even though I couldn't help but keep an eye out for non-sparkly vampires or boilersuit-wearing psychopaths in hockey masks, I was able to appreciate the beauty of the place. We walked past an actual lake, complete with happy-looking ducks, following each other around two by two, and the architecture of the monuments was stunning, as long as you didn't think too much about the residents enjoying their very long naps inside.

'OK, I take it all back,' I admitted. 'This place is gorgeous. Thank you for bringing me here and sorry for being such an ungrateful mare earlier.'

Ren slowed for a second and gave me a reassuring, maybe even slightly surprised smile. 'It's cool. You don't have to apologize.'

Chewing the inside of my cheek, I wasn't sure what to say next. It would not have been cool for me to complain if Thomas had done something for me, even if I was half-joking. But Ren was not Thomas, far from it. Ren was kind and open and had abs you could grate cheese on, a strangely erotic thought.

'Yet another totally random thing in the middle of the city,' I said, pushing away visions of me, Ren and a family-sized block of Cathedral City. Hunger would do terrible things to a girl. 'This place is huge. How is it so huge?'

'LA doesn't make any sense,' he replied fondly. 'It used to be even bigger, but the owner sold a bunch of land to build Paramount Studios and the super crappy strip mall out front. And no, they did not exhume the bodies.'

'So you're telling me it's one hundred per cent haunted.'

'I would not use the AutoZone out front if my life depended on it.'

A big open space came into view and I saw a handful of other people perched on picnic blankets in twos and threes, smiling, laughing and generally enjoying themselves. A perfectly ordinary Friday night chilling out in the cemetery. Why not?

'This must be the most fun place to be buried ever,' I remarked, not at all checking out his backside when Ren bent over to unfurl a red-and-black plaid picnic blanket. If I did, it was just for a moment. For research purposes.

'Kind of like being laid to rest in the middle of a very cool party with an extremely exclusive guestlist,' he agreed. 'Not the worst place to end up.'

While nothing could ever approach the glory of an M&S picky tea, Ren's spread was very, very close. A crusty baguette, vegan cheese, fresh hummus, sliced avocado, cherry tomatoes, grapes, nuts and a brown paper bag with 'chocolate chip shortbread cookies' scrawled across it in marker pen which I had to physically force myself to ignore for fear of grabbing them out of his hand and sprinting across the cemetery to keep them all to myself. Sitting down without flashing my knickers was a chore, the nap dress I'd been lounging around in all day not really designed to be worn in civilized company. Not that there was anything civilized about the way I intended to inhale all this food.

'You just happened to have all this in the fridge?'

'Yup.'

'Do you have any flaws?' I asked, watching him fill two plastic glasses with chilled white wine from a black Yeti water bottle. 'Go on, give me something. This really isn't fair.'

He chuckled, concentrating as he tried not to spill. Should have let me do it, I had never knowingly spilled a drop of alcohol in my life. 'I've got plenty of 'em. Sometimes I fall asleep still wearing my socks and take them off in the night so there's a pile of dirty socks that live at the bottom of my bed underneath the sheets.'

'How do you live with yourself?' I breathed.

'I hate doing dishes. I'd only use paper plates if it wasn't so bad for the environment.'

'So scandalous.'

'I hate waking up. If I didn't set my alarm clock, I could sleep until noon at least, every single day. I can be stubborn, a little inflexible, and I like my own company a little too much.'

'As in you don't leave the house or you massively fancy yourself?' I asked.

With a self-deprecating smile, he flexed a bicep. 'What's not to love?'

It was a wonder I didn't spontaneously combust there and then.

'I'll let it pass because you brought cookies,' I replied, looking away in an effort to compose myself. 'Even if you do sleep in your socks, this is an excellent spread.'

'Why thank you,' he replied with a shallow bow. 'Maybe it looks good laid out like this but it's all I had in the house. I've been pretty much living on snacks, sandwiches and takeout for the last six months.'

He handed me one of the glasses and I raised it in his direction before taking a sip. 'In fairness, you've got very good takeaways here. When I first moved into my house, the options were so limited, there was a very real danger of me turning into a sweet and sour chicken ball.'

'You don't like to cook?' Ren crossed his long legs, the stiff fabric of his jeans stretching over his thick thighs. I gulped down a bigger swig of wine than intended.

'Actually, I do. I got out of the habit when . . .' I paused, pulling a few blades of grass out of the ground to make a little pile at the side of the blanket. 'When I moved.'

No need to offer information he hadn't asked for.

'I cooked more when I was with Shawna, my ex,' he replied. 'Doesn't seem worth the hassle when it's just me.'

The way he spoke about his past relationship was so casual, so matter of fact. I used to be with someone, now I'm not. No drama, no stress, a thing that happened and was over now. I wondered what it must be like.

Looking around at the other picnickers, I caught the eye of a woman staring at Ren. She was too far away for me to hear what her group was saying but when our eyes met, she gave me a guilty little smile then turned away. Did she think Ren and I were a couple? For the first time, I saw us from the outside, a man and a woman sharing a picnic on a Friday night. It was the natural assumption. The thought made me melt a little at the edges even if it was ridiculous.

'Ever see any good birds here?' I asked, turning my back on the woman and her friends.

'Are you kidding me? So many.' Ren wiped his mouth with the back of his hand, a spark glinting in his eyes as he began listing them off on his fingers. 'You've got all the regulars, then there's the ducks and swans in the lake, a couple of peacocks who stroll around, the occasional goose. One time, I saw an incredible Cooper's hawk hanging out on top of the Johnny Ramone statue.'

'Creepy,' I replied happily. 'But also cool.'

'There are a bunch of other animals too. Last time I was here I saw turtles in the pond and we've got all the LA classics: possums, squirrels, so many raccoons. There used to be a couple of cats who lived here too. This place is kind of a zoo. But not an actual zoo, that's over in Griffith Park.'

'Suzanne used to love the zoo,' I said, flashing back to long days in plastic raincoats, my hands full of animal feed. 'I wonder if she ever goes there.'

Ren looked doubtful. 'The same Suzanne who made Santiago the gardener cry?'

'He wouldn't be the first and I don't think he'll be the last,' I replied. 'Suze really wants everyone to think she's a double-hard bastard but she's got a soft centre. It's hard to find but it's there.'

He reached out for the baguette and tore off a hunk of bread. 'The problem with soft centres is you have to chew them up or break your teeth to get to them.'

I rolled onto my stomach, tucking my skirt securely

underneath my hips, and picked out a handful of nuts. 'You, Ren Garcia, are very wise.'

'I used to think the same thing about my brother,' he replied, tossing tiny chunks of his bread across the lawn towards a trio of the same little pink-breasted birds I'd seen outside Myrna's house. 'Until I found out he's solid rock all the way through.'

'I always wanted a big brother but Suzanne wasn't a bad trade. All the bullies at school were terrified of her,' I told him. 'Is your brother older or younger?'

'Older. By five years. He turned forty last month and his wife was plenty mad that I didn't come back for the party.'

'You didn't fancy a family shindig?'

He stretched out onto his back, hands cradling his head, and crossed one leg over the other, his foot furiously tapping at the air.

'There was too much work to do on the house to fly back east for one party.'

It was an excuse. Maybe not an outright lie but not the whole truth either. I could tell from the way his forehead crumpled, like there was a heavy weight pushing it down from the crown of his head.

'My mom and dad are pretty intense about work,' he added when I didn't respond right away. 'They're both second generation, only children of immigrants. Making money is the only measure of success as far as they're concerned. I get it, their parents came with nothing, had to kill themselves for every penny and they want to make them proud, honour their memory. Every generation wants to see the next one do better than they did.'

'Doing better doesn't always mean making more money,' I said, even though everyone I knew considered super successful Suzanne to be doing a lot better than I was and I was fully aware of the fact.

'Try telling that to my dad.'

He stilled his tapping foot and gave a long, heavy sigh.

'My brother got into real estate when he was still in college and made a mint. He's a natural, you know? So I tried it out but selling houses wasn't for me. I fell in love with the homes themselves instead of the commission. Every time I had to show a developer around a place, knowing they were going to tear it down, I felt sick inside. A house is a living thing, you can feel all the lives that have been lived inside those four walls, every story. I couldn't get past it so I started renovating the houses instead. I'd worked for my grandpa every summer since I was fourteen and for a year after high school, I had a pretty good idea of what I was doing, but it didn't bring in enough money for my brother. No matter what I did, the offers from the developer were always higher than the offers from regular buyers. So Hector is the favourite, bringing in high six figures every year, and I'm the black sheep who doesn't have a college degree and manages to get by.'

'Not to be rude but surely there is money to be made in renovating houses?' I asked. I was no fool, I'd seen an awful lot of *Homes Under the Hammer*. 'Surely it's a pretty well-paid profession as long as you're not shit.'

'I'm proud to say I'm not shit,' Ren replied, almost smiling. 'But I take too long and I spend too much. The good money is in flipping a place, not restoring it. What I make doesn't even come close to Hector's income or what they make. Mom and Dad don't get why I want to work harder to make less money. Loving your job doesn't come into it.'

'Well, I think renovating houses is very cool,' I declared. 'And it's amazing that you're restoring your grandfather's house.'

The almost smile graduated to a full-fledged grin but he didn't say anything, and if I'd learned nothing else from my previous relationship, it was when to leave someone or something alone. No good ever came from pushing. Instead I watched the wispy white clouds above us reflected in Ren's dark green eyes then lay down on one side, taking in my surroundings, the lush grass, the palm trees that lined the pathways, the laughter coming from the group of friends behind me. It really was a lovely place even though it felt strange to say that about a graveyard, albeit a very fancy one.

'Whatever you're thinking about must be incredibly intense,' Ren said, breaking my train of thought. 'Care to share?'

'Burying people length-wise,' I replied. 'Why do we do it? It makes no sense.'

The laughter that escaped his mouth was loud enough to wake the dead.

'I'm serious!' I said, slapping him on the arm. 'Why don't we bury people standing up? It would take up less space, wouldn't it? People just can't be arsed to dig a deeper hole.'

'How would you keep them standing up though?' he asked. 'You know, don't answer that, I'm afraid of what you might say.'

'Where there's a will there's a way,' I said. Somewhere in the last ten minutes I'd forgotten to try to relax and actually relaxed. It had been so long, I'd almost forgotten how good it felt not to be on edge. 'What about you?' I tossed a grape at his face, missing his mouth by a mile. 'What were you thinking about?'

He picked up my fallen grape, squeezed it gently between his thumb and forefinger then placed it on his tongue and I suddenly found myself in the unexpected and unusual position of being jealous of fruit.

'Do you think Bel would want to meet me tomorrow night?'

I tore into the bag of chocolate chip cookies and stuffed one into my mouth, whole. So much for relaxation.

'I don't know,' I replied, hand held over my very full mouth. 'Probably.'

'That's what I was thinking about.' He helped himself to a cookie from the bag, breaking it in half before taking a bite. 'I want to do something special. Any ideas?'

'Hire Adele to sing for her?'

'A little out of my budget.'

'Ariana Grande?'

'Is she cheaper than Adele?'

'Probably not,' I admitted and even though I'd asked, even though I was the mastermind behind this whole thing, I was oddly irritated to be talking about it. 'What if you write a message in the sky with one of those little planes?'

'Out of my budget *and* bad for the environment.'

'Really?'

'So terrible. Crazy carbon footprint.' Ren nodded. 'Come on, Phoebe, you're the one who got me into this. I want to do something incredible. Something she'll never forget.'

I was the one.

This was all on me.

'I don't think she needs big flashy gestures; she'd love something like this,' I said, his face lighting up, and I knew I'd got it right. 'Maybe not here though,' I added quickly. 'I don't think a cemetery is Bel's speed.'

Now that was an outright lie. Bel would probably love a quirky date amongst the dead but I allowed myself to be selfish about this one thing. I wanted to keep our evening all to myself.

'I guess not every woman would be into a graveyard picnic,' he acknowledged before settling back on the blanket. 'You're right, low-key is the way to go. It's about the two of us getting to know each other. It doesn't need to be flashy, it should be . . . intimate.'

Somewhere across the lawn, a peacock screeched loudly on my behalf.

'Thanks, Phoebe,' Ren added. 'You're a pal.'

'Don't mention it,' I replied, pouring myself more wine with one hand and reaching for another cookie with the other. 'Anything for a friend.'

CHAPTER ELEVEN

The scene was set.

Ren's back garden sparkled with the string lights I'd spent all afternoon trailing up and down the yard while dozens upon dozens of white candles of varying heights glowed inside tall, protective hurricane vases because there was nothing sexy about a forest fire. Except for firemen and even they were bound to be mad at you if they found out you'd caused it yourself. To make things feel cosier, I'd covered the poolside furniture with beautiful cashmere throws that would hopefully return to my sister's house unscathed, set a bottle of champagne in a silver ice bucket and cued up my most romantic Spotify playlist, the one I used to listen to when I was writing my Valentine's cards. I hadn't listened to it in years but the moment the first song whispered through his speakers, I knew it was the right choice. The garden felt like a secret, the string lights and candles glowing with the promise of magic. Even the sunset had put on a show, igniting the sky with a thousand flames, red and orange and pink burning up the clouds above us.

Everything was perfect.

And it was all for Bel.

'Whoa, is this really my backyard?' Ren padded out of his house barefoot, his mouth hanging open. His worn blue jeans and grey T-shirt looked so soft, moving with his body as he came over to give me a hug. I held my breath against his signature scent but it was a pointless exercise; when he released me to inspect the food set out on the coffee table, I was drowning in him.

'Phoebe, I don't know how to thank you, this is above and beyond,' he said, picking up a pink macaron and examining it closely. 'You did all this while I was out buying timber?'

'No big deal,' I replied. 'It took no time at all, I hardly lifted a finger.'

It had taken five hours, a big chunk of my mermaid dollars and most of my will to live, not to mention blood, sweat *and* tears when I dropped one of the hurricane vases on my big toe. The effect was enough to sweep anyone off their feet, let alone someone who had already texted me to ask whether or not I thought she should bother wearing underwear.

'You're wasted in copywriting – you should get into the events business.' He put down the macaron and popped the cap on one of the two bottles of beer he was carrying before handing it to me. 'When you said you'd help smarten up the yard, I wasn't expecting this.'

'You said you wanted it to be special,' I told him, the cold condensation on the beer bottle soothing my hot, dry hands. 'I'd like to think someone would do the same for me.'

He didn't say anything, just tipped the bottle of beer to his lips and took a long, deep drink.

The confusing emotional stew I'd felt the night before at the cemetery hadn't eased off at all over the course of the day and I was so full of feelings, I felt like I might burst. I was happy for Bel, my new friend who had literally saved my life, and happy for Ren because he deserved someone who cared as deeply about him as she did. Then there was a good shot of pride. I'd done good work, my love letter had been a success and the garden really did look beautiful and I was pleased with that too, but underneath, there was the quiet thrum of something less altruistic. A loose green thread that threatened to unravel the rest. I was jealous. Jealous of the unguarded excitement in Ren's voice when he talked about Bel. Jealous of the eggplant emojis in her last ten texts. Jealous of the champagne and the strawberries and the fact that none of this was for me. My eyes lingered on Ren, drinking him in as the string lights danced in his dark eyes and it hit me again.

I was jealous.

In the back pocket of my jeans, my phone vibrated and a tidal wave of guilt flooded through me.

'It's Bel,' I said, holding my handset aloft as my heart sank. 'She's here. I'll go and get her.'

'Phoebe, you've done more than enough,' he protested. 'I'll go, you go enjoy your evening.'

'No, no, you stay here, pour the champagne,' I shook my head as I hustled past him, practically running to the side gate. 'I'm going out that way anyway, it's no bother. You don't want me here on your date.'

And what's more, I didn't want me there.

Leaving Ren behind, I powered through his front garden to find a wide-eyed Bel waiting in the street. Her hair was curled with casual perfection, subtle make-up expertly applied, and she was dressed in a tiny handkerchief dress, tied around her neck and skimming her body like a sigh. Bel Johnson was a vision. A vision who looked like she was about to bring up her breakfast, lunch and dinner.

'What do you mean, you don't know if you can do this?' I hissed, holding my phone up in front of her face, so she could read her own text. 'Everything's ready, he's waiting for you.'

'What if he hates me?' she whimpered. 'What if he thinks I'm dumb? This is a bad idea, I'm going to text him and cancel.'

She pulled a dinky little flip phone out of a dinky little handbag, only letting out the tiniest shriek when I slapped it out of her hands. The thought of him getting her text, wondering what was wrong and feeling so disappointed was all too much.

'You can't cancel now,' I said, clutching her phone tightly. 'We've been through this. He won't think you're dumb, because you're not dumb. It's going to be amazing and you're going to have the best time.'

When I wasn't climbing up ladders, hanging lights and vastly misjudging how long it would take to drive five miles to pick up pastries, I'd spent most of my day on the phone, coaching Bel for her date. General conversation starters, topics Ren was already passionate about, what to dig into and what to avoid. The last time we'd spoken, she was raring to go but now she was staring back at me as though I'd just told her Hannibal Lecter was coming up for a glass of wine and a light snack.

I took a deep breath and held both of her hands in mine, giving her a gentle but encouraging squeeze. 'All you have to do is remember the questions we talked about, like a script, remember? Everyone likes to talk about themselves.'

'You don't,' she pointed out.

'Everyone else likes to talk about themselves.'

'Your sister doesn't.'

'Most people like to talk about themselves. We've been over it a million times: birds, books, grandpa, renovating houses, how much he loves LA. Get him started and it'll be easy.'

'Oh, I know!' she exclaimed, squeezed my hands tightly. 'You should stay! You can hang out and drink with us!'

'Bel,' I said as kindly as I could. 'You sent this man an intensely romantic love letter. You told him he is the air you breathe and your reason for living. Don't you think it would be a bit weird if you bring a friend on your first date?'

'Remind me what else was in there?' she whispered. 'Did it say anything about his abs?'

I prised my hands free, wiggling the feeling back into my fingers. 'I don't think it referenced them specifically.'

She began pacing up and down the street, the silky fabric of her dress shimmering across her body as she moved, and my heart lurched. Imagine looking like Bel, being as lovely as she was, as kind as she was, and still believing you weren't good enough. What hope was there for the rest of us?

'Please stay,' she begged. 'I'm gonna mess it up if you leave me on my own. I'll say the wrong thing, I'll do something stupid, I always do.'

As much as I wanted to fight it, there was something about Bel that tugged directly on my heartstrings. This wasn't an act, she really was scared, and whether I started with good intentions or not, it was all because of me. It was my scheming that put us all here.

'I'm only upstairs if you need me,' I said. 'Text me if you get desperate.'

'You'll be home?' she asked with huge eyes. 'I can call you?'

'Yes,' I promised, handing back her tiny phone. 'And just so you know, you look beautiful.'

Her eyes filled with gratitude but she still didn't look quite certain. 'I don't know, Pheebs, what if he hates me?'

Shaking my head, I forced out the words that were stuck in my throat.

'Bel,' I said. 'He's going to love you.'

Flat on my belly, I peeked through a gap in the fence at the edge of Suzanne's terrace. Not so much spying as observing. As the matchmaker, I had a personal responsibility to make sure this went well. I was Cupid in a pair of cut-offs, only Machiavellian because I cared, and so far it was going terribly.

Ren looked ecstatic, Bel less so. I watched as she shifted her weight from foot to foot, one arm stick-straight at her side, the other crossed over her body and gripping the opposing elbow for dear life.

'Can I get you a drink?' Ren asked. He reached for the chilled bottle in the ice bucket and poured even before she gave her enthusiastic approval. 'I hope you like it. I don't really know that much about champagne but it's supposed to be good.'

'If it's fizzy and wet, I'll drink it,' she replied, proving the statement to be true by emptying her glass in three chugs.

'That dress is . . .' He shook his head as though he didn't have quite the right words. 'You look beautiful.'

Slamming her glass down on the table, she gave him a thumbs up.

Ren took a step towards her.

Bel immediately took a step back.

I covered my eyes with my hands and groaned.

'These are for you.'

When I opened my eyes, I saw him handing her the beautiful bunch of peonies I picked up from the florist on Hillhurst. I knew she loved peonies, she'd told me she loved peonies, but there she was, staring at the peonies as though he was trying to hand her a fistful of rattlesnakes.

'Thank you,' she said, finally taking the bouquet and holding it in front of her like a reluctant bride. 'Flowers are great.'

Flowers. Are. Great.

'Another drink?' Ren suggested.

'Oh, gosh, yes,' Bel agreed readily, dumping the bouquet on the table beside her champagne flute. 'Do you have anything stronger?'

'Uh, sure,' he replied, even though he really didn't sound very sure 'What were you thinking?'

She held out her hands as though it was obvious. 'Nothing breaks the ice like tequila, amirite?'

Now it was his turn to back away. 'I think there's a bottle inside. Give me a minute to hunt it down?'

'Take all the time you need!' she yelled. 'No rush!'

As soon as he was out of sight, she sprinted to my end of the garden. Pressing my face through the slats of the fence, I gave her the biggest grin I could muster.

'It's going great!' I lied. 'You're nailing it.'

'It's the worst date I've ever been on,' she countered in a very loud whisper. 'And one time, at Six Flags, a guy puked on the rollercoaster and it hit me in the face. Phoebe, this is worse than the time a guy puked in my face.'

No matter how I felt, there was no joy to be found in Bel's misery.

'It's only stressful because it means so much to you,' I told her. 'He's just a man. A very attractive man with nice forearms and not horrible feet, which I admit is a miracle, but he's still just a man and of all the things he could be doing this evening, he wanted to spend it with you.'

'You're so good at this,' she marvelled. 'Have you ever thought about being a life coach?'

'No,' I replied. 'Because it's not a real job. Now get back down there, ask him questions, pay him compliments, the rest is easy. You are amazing, Bel Johnson, and he is lucky you're giving him this tiny little slice of your time.'

'But I don't want to give him a tiny little slice of my time,' she pointed down at her barely concealed crotch. 'I want to give him my—'

'Found it,' Ren called as he sauntered out of his house. Bel spun around, hands behind her back, while I pressed myself flat against the floor.

'You OK?' he asked as she strolled back down the garden.

'Yup,' Bel replied brightly. 'I thought I saw a, um . . .'

Hawk, I said in my head. Tell him you thought you saw a hawk.

'I thought I saw a monkey.'

I raised my head just enough to see the look of disbelief on Ren's face.

'You thought you saw a monkey?' he asked. 'In my backyard?'

'Yeah.' She turned and pointed away from my general direction. 'It was kind of moving around over by the shed but when I went to check it wasn't a monkey after all.'

'Then what was it?'

'A bear?'

He froze, his mouth slightly open as if he was waiting for the right words to present themselves.

'But it's gone now,' Bel added. 'Whatever it was, monkey, bear, Kristen Stewart. She lives around here, did you know that? Such a tiny human. Did you find the tequila?'

'Yes,' Ren said, moving on as Bel's shoulders sloped with relief or resignation, I wasn't sure. 'The bottle is kinda dusty. I don't know how long my grandpa had it but he didn't waste his time on bad tequila.'

'Doesn't matter. Pour it.'

He did as he was told and I wondered how I could get Bel to lob a shot up to me. Below, the two of them raised their drinks, Ren taking a sip while Bel tossed hers all the way back.

'It's a beautiful evening.' He looked out at the gorgeous sunset while she stuck out her tongue and shuddered before hastily refilling her glass all the way up to the rim. 'That sunset is something else.'

'It really is,' she said. 'It's so . . . orange.'

When he didn't reply, she tapped her nails against the glass, shifting anxiously from foot to foot. 'Do you like hiking?' she asked.

From my perch on the terrace, I sent her a mental high five. Questions! She was asking questions!

'Or what about swimming?' she added before Ren had a chance to answer. 'Or the beach. Travelling? Do you travel ever?'

Correction, she was asking every question ever, all at the same time.

'Yeah, I guess yes to all those things,' Ren replied. 'But you know, I would really love to talk to you about your letter. It kind of took me by surprise.'

'Because sending a letter is cheesy and it made me look like a stalker?'

I gently knocked my forehead against the floor of the balcony.

'Because most people send some lame message when they meet someone,' he replied. 'To be so brave and vulnerable, it honestly blew me away. You blew me away. That's why I was surprised.'

'Oh,' she said. 'Cool.'

Bel reached for the bottle of tequila and poured another shot while Ren stared at her like a Magic Eye picture, trying to work out exactly what he was looking at.

'The things you said about looking at the world from underwater,' he added. 'That's exactly how I feel. I must have read that line a hundred times since yesterday, I don't know how you managed to put my feelings into words.'

'Well, I'm a big swimmer,' Bel said, pointing to his pool. 'And I read this thing about Kate Winslet learning to hold her breath for ten minutes when they were filming *Avatar* so I've been trying to do that too. In case she ever needs a stunt double.'

To be fair, she'd said it would go badly and it was going so, so badly.

'I just remembered, I have to go get something from my car,' she announced very, very loudly as she walk-ran over to his side gate. 'Don't go anywhere, I won't be long, but also don't follow me because everything is totally fine.'

With a weary sigh, I slithered all the way across the terrace, through the house and back around the corner to find Bel waiting in front of her car.

'Phoebe, it's the worst date ever,' she wailed, right as my phone chimed with a new text alert. 'You have to get me out of here.'

I opened my messages and winced.

Hey, not to be rude but are you sure this is the same person who wrote the letter?

'I will admit it's not going brilliantly.' I slid my phone back in my pocket before she could see Ren's text. 'What are you doing?'

'Tequila shots mostly.' She groaned loudly, bottom lip quivering. 'I don't know what's wrong, you said ask him questions, I asked him questions.'

'I didn't mean ask him all the questions at once,' I said as she wailed into her hands. 'Most people wait for an answer before they move on to the next one. It's a date, not a pub quiz.'

'I've had a glass of champagne and two shots of tequila. That's usually enough for me to charm the pants off a plant pot,' Bel said before turning to me with accusatory eyes. 'You said he was easy to talk to.'

I had said that. Because he was easy to talk to, for me.

'The last couple of years have been so shitty, everything has been so difficult.' Her dark curls fell forward, covering her face as she looked down at her feet. 'I'm broke, I hate my apartment, my acting career is in the toilet and ever since my cool roommate moved back to Ohio, I've been so lonely. Then I saw Ren and for the first time it was like, pow.'

'Love at first sight,' I said softly.

'I was going to say it felt like my vagina exploded, but sure.'

There was no response I could come up with for that.

'It's been months, Phoebe, months of trying to work up the courage to speak to him, and now I have my shot and I'm throwing it away. I'm going to lose the love of my life because I can't string a simple sentence together,' she said, her voice softening. 'If only you could help me like you did with the letter, until we're comfortable with one another.'

'What do you want me to do,' I asked. 'Hide in the bushes and feed you lines?'

She lifted her head, looking at me like she'd just figured out how to get the ads out of her Instagram feed and I heard alarm bells ringing in my ears.

'I am not hiding in the bushes and feeding you lines.'

'Not in the bushes,' she replied, pointing at my phone. 'You can stay on the terrace.'

'Because that's so much more dignified?'

Clasping her hands together under her chin, she looked at me with huge, pleading eyes.

'No.'

'Please?'

'No.'

'Please?'

'How would it even work?' I asked. It was embarrassing how quickly I caved. It was impossible to say no to those big brown eyes of hers. 'You can't exactly put me on speaker without him noticing.'

'You can hear us from the terrace, right?' Bel said with renewed enthusiasm as she produced a shiny white AirPod from her tiny bag, tucking it into her ear. 'Then it's simple. You call me, I'll wear my Airpod so I can hear you, and you tell me what to say. It'll be like we're on a movie and I'm the actor and you're the script supervisor feeding me lines. Actors do it all the time.'

'They do?' I was both shocked and appalled.

'The sucky ones,' she nodded. 'All I have to do is fix my hair.'

She combed her long dark curls over to one side and wove them into a loose braid that covered her ear. The AirPod disappeared completely.

'This seems very risky,' I muttered, brushing my hands through my own, straight blonde hair. 'What if he sees the thing in your ear?'

'I'll tell him I forgot it was there. He already thinks

167

I'm a total ditz, it won't be too much of a stretch. OK,
call me.'

Half convinced this was doomed to failure and half
cat-killingly-curious to see if it could work, I swiped
through to her details and hit the call icon.

'Can you hear me?' I asked. 'Testing, testing, I must
be an idiot.'

She tapped at her ear, the tip of her tongue poking
out the corner of her mouth. 'It's totally going to work.
It has to, Pheebs, he completes me.'

That was it. I was defenceless against a nineties romcom.

'Like Jerry Maguire,' I said, smiling.

'No, it's a line from Austin Powers,' Bel replied. 'You
know, Dr Evil and Mini-Me?'

'Go on, go, before he thinks you've run away,' I
ordered, marching back up to Suzanne's house as Bel
skipped away. This was, beyond a shadow of a doubt,
one of the stupidest things I had ever done. More stupid
than the time I tried to make a sanitary towel out of
toilet roll and safety clips in year eight. More stupid
than the time I wiped out the entire office computer
network by trying to open nude photos of Chris Evans
and accidentally downloaded a virus instead.

Possibly even more stupid than turning up to my
ex-boyfriend's fiancée's hen night and attempting to
convince her not to marry him.

But this wasn't the time to dwell on my terrible
decisions, it was time to make them. When I got to the
edge of the terrace, Bel was back in the garden below
and Ren was waiting patiently on his little outdoor
loveseat, an open bottle of red wine in front of him. I
tucked my hair behind my ears and set my phone on

the floor in front of me, speaker on, volume down, like the world's shittest James Bond.

'Did I miss anything?' Bel asked as she positioned herself next to him on the sofa, slipping off her shoes and curling her bare feet underneath her body.

'I saw a great egret flying overhead,' Ren replied.

'Oh yeah? What was so great about it?'

'A great egret is a kind of bird,' I whispered urgently into the phone and Bel's spine stiffened slightly.

'I'm joking.' She laughed and cocked her head to one side, curling her hand around the exposed side of her lovely neck. 'I love birds, don't you?'

'I do,' Ren said, sounding almost suspicious.

'Ask him what he loves about them,' I instructed.

'What do you love about them?'

Ren leaned forward to pour Bel a glass of wine. 'My grandpa didn't have money growing up, I mean, he had nothing, but even when he was broke and living on whatever he could get his hands on, the one thing he always had was birdwatching. It's the perfect hobby. It doesn't cost anything, there are no barriers to keep people out and when you start looking for birds, you see them everywhere.'

'That's because they are everywhere,' she reasoned. 'Mostly hanging out by the car wash on Fig waiting to shit on my clean car.'

Ren laughed and handed her the glass, his breath catching as their fingers touched.

'From their perspective, your car is in the way of their shit,' he said, challenging her with raised eyebrows. 'Birds have been here way longer than we have. They're practically dinosaurs.'

'Really?' she gushed, looking utterly dazzled. 'That's incredible. I can't believe you knew that without looking it up, you must be the smartest man in the whole world.'

'All right, tone it down a bit,' I muttered into the phone. 'I said pay him compliments not kiss his arse.'

'I mean, wow,' she said, raking her hand through her hair and throwing me a discreet thumbs up. 'Maybe you could teach me about it sometime.'

'That could be fun.' Ren tipped his face upwards, the pinks and reds of the dusky sunset giving way to the blues and purples of the night. 'I love the way it connects me to my grandpa, looking up at the same sky, watching for the same birds. One day, I'd like to think I'll teach my kids about it and pass it along. You don't worry about stuff when you're watching the birds. They remind me to look up. Everything around us is so crazy all the time but there they are, cruising above it all.'

'It must be amazing,' I murmured without thinking. 'To soar above the world and see everything at once.'

'It must be amazing,' Bel echoed in a breathy whisper. 'To soar above the world and see everything at once.'

'My thoughts exactly.' Ren looked back at her and she looked at him and I stared at the two of them. Those were my words, they weren't meant for her.

'What's your favourite bird?' Ren asked, his deep, warm voice suddenly soft and promising.

'Uh, my favourite, I don't know,' she stammered, pressing her hand against her hair. 'What *is* my favourite bird?'

'A hummingbird,' I answered quickly, pushing my unwelcome feelings down down down. 'I saw my first one the other day, it was nuts.'

Below me Bel snapped her fingers as though the answer had just come to her and technically, it had. 'A hummingbird. I saw my first one the other day and it was nuts.'

'You saw your first hummingbird the other day?' he repeated. 'But you live here, right? You don't see them all the time?'

'Yeah, I do, I meant, um, what did I mean?'

'Every time you see one it's like the first time,' I babbled, heart in my mouth.

'Every time I see one, it's like the first time,' she said. She moved her arm from the back of her neck onto Ren's shoulder and the rest of my words tripped off her tongue like silk. 'They're like magic. Wings moving too fast for us to see them, in motion and motionless at the same time. So fragile and fleeting and precious.'

She was truly an excellent actress.

'You have such a way with words,' Ren said, openly staring at her now, entranced.

'Weird, Phoebe said the same thing,' she replied, reaching out to move the hair out of his eyes.

'Phoebe?' Ren murmured. 'Oh yeah, Phoebe.'

She leaned in towards him and I held my breath until it burned. I watched as Ren pulled her into his lap, a low moan echoing over the phone and through the air as their lips met. Three loud beeps snapped me out of my trance and I let out all the air in my lungs with a ragged gasp as a small, white piece of plastic fell from Bel's fingers, onto the ground behind the sofa, confirming my contribution to the evening was complete.

It was wrong to watch but I couldn't look away. The reality of what I had done smashed into my body, hammering the truth into every cell and atom.

'She really loves him,' I reminded myself as I crawled away, staying low on my hands and knees until I reached the living room. 'You did a good thing for good people.'

Why then, I wondered as I dragged myself onto the sofa, the vision of Ren leaning in to kiss my friend playing over and over and over in mind. Why was it that every time I did something for the greater good, I ended up alone? Not that it mattered, there was no chance now, and now there was no chance, I could finally admit the truth to myself.

I was falling for him as well.

CHAPTER TWELVE

'My husband was smoother than a greased-up dolphin,' Myrna said happily as she led me on a tour of her mansion. 'Slick, handsome, so charming. I knew he was the one the first time I met him.'

'How old were you?' I asked, practically swooning over the dining room. No need to ask if any of these pieces came from West Elm; more likely West Elm came to Myrna's house for inspiration. 'When you met?'

'Nineteen. He was thirty-eight. No one batted so much as an eyelid.'

'Different times?' I reasoned. 'I suppose it was OK back then.'

'Not really, but all the men were doing it and we didn't have the power to stop them.' She held out her left hand and admired the chunk of sapphire that decorated her ring finger. 'I was one of the lucky ones. I loved my Wally something fierce and he loved me right back. You'd be surprised at how rare that was.'

'Still fairly rare,' I told her. 'So I don't think I would.'

Ever since I woke up on the settee Sunday morning, all I'd been able to think about was Bel and Ren, Ren and Bel. It was usually easier in the light of day. Thoughts that haunted you in the night were never quite so scary with the sun teasing them out of the shadows, but this was the exception to prove the rule. I'd done everything I could think of to distract myself. I filled an ASOS shopping basket with hundreds of pounds of clothes I would never actually buy. I hate-watched a house tour of my least favourite influencer's new ten-million-dollar home. I even attempted to Do Exercise, but none of it worked. I liked him, I liked him so much. As absurd and pointless as it was, facts were facts. I liked Ren but because of me, Ren was with Bel and no number of house tours, kneeling push-ups or Free People bralettes could change that.

'We built this house when we got married, Wally's wedding gift to me.' Myrna closed the door on the dining room and walked me into a bigger, brighter sitting room than the one I'd visited on Thursday, full of exquisite furniture as well as a baby grand piano, which sat expectantly in the corner. 'Do you play?' she asked when she saw me staring.

'I had lessons when I was little but no, not really,' I replied. I was too terrified to touch it, my common little fingers were not worthy.

'Wally had a plan,' she said, running her own finger-tips over the glossy wood. 'He always had a plan. We agreed, I would take a break from the movies and "just have fun", those were his exact words. Then when we were good and ready, we would knuckle down to the real work and start a family. But life doesn't work according to your plans no matter how well they might be laid, as we soon found out.'

'Wally passed away?' I prompted gently.

Myrna sat on the bench in front of the piano, transferring her weight on to an ebony walking stick with an ornate golden ball set into the top to lower herself down.

'He got drunk as a skunk and fell down the goddamn stairs.' She lifted the lid of the piano and tinkled two high keys. 'The doctors declared it a coronary incident to save face, but I was the one who almost had a heart attack when I found him the next morning. He was a drunken fool, always had been. He died the way he lived: good and liquored up.'

Not sure what to say, I played it safe and said nothing.

'Don't feel bad, it was no secret Wally liked the sauce,' she added. 'But he could have been a little more careful around the staircase, he designed the damn thing after all. I should have put in those godawful baby gates. Naturally, the hideous children from his first marriage claimed I'd pushed him for the insurance money, but they'd watched *Double Indemnity* one too many times. That money was as much mine as his, I came from a good family, I made a decent salary at the studio and I was sensible with my savings. And if I'd killed him, I'd have come up with something a damn sight more creative than pushing a drunk fool down the stairs.'

Rolling up the ostrich feather-trimmed sleeve of her midnight-blue silk pyjamas, she began to play properly. Naturally, she was magnificent. I smoothed down a wrinkle in my skirt as she closed her eyes, lost in the music. Following Myrna's orders, I'd dressed up to visit.

None of my clothes were right, so I'd borrowed from Suzanne's wardrobe. My sister only ever wore white tops, black bottoms and variations on that theme, but for reasons best known to her and her late night online shopping, her walk-in wardrobe was packed with unworn clothes in bold, bright colours, all with the tags still hanging from their sleeves. I'd chosen a long cream-coloured dress with a pretty rose print and a neat square neckline, something feminine I thought my host might approve of, but when I arrived, I was informed I looked like a gypsy come to steal the shingles off the roof. I did not care for the description and Myrna did not care to learn the word gypsy was considered a slur.

'It must have been hard, losing the love of your life so young,' I said, clapping as the song trailed off. 'No wonder you became a, um . . . you know.'

'A what?' she stilled her hands over the keys and smiled. 'A recluse? A hermit? Darling, I mourned Wally but I didn't shut myself away from the world on purpose. You'd be surprised how few people want to hire the wife of their dead pal for their movie, no matter how beautiful or talented she might be. I was tainted. Overnight I went from a rising star to Wally's widow, and officially no longer an ingenue. Once I saw how it would be, I announced that I had retired from acting and, soon enough, everyone forgot about me. I did it on my terms, as I always had.'

'People forget about you very quickly if you let them,' I said, perching on the very edge of a pistachio-green brocade upholstered couch. 'I'm sorry.'

She closed the lid of the piano and used the walking stick to pull herself up to standing. 'Don't be. Not everyone wants to be famous forever. Now, would you like to see the pool? According to the vulture of a real estate broker my stepchildren appointed, it's something of a showpiece.'

'Sounds delightful,' I said, finding a smile as she guided me out into the garden.

'You're telling me that's a swimming pool? You can actually swim in there?'

'Can, did and do. Everyone who was anyone in the fifties and sixties skinny-dipped in there. A few nobodies as well, but the less said about them, the better.'

I'd never seen anything like it. A series of three long, narrow pools, each with its own dancing fountain, beckoned us down the sprawling estate and into what looked like a not insignificant manmade lake. The water was a deep, unreal blue and it was surrounded by enough foliage to make the whole thing feel completely private and secluded, despite the fact we were only a five-minute drive from the closest 7-Eleven.

'The estate agent might be a vulture but he's not wrong about this,' I admitted, flapping the fabric of my dress around my legs. It was a hot day and the water looked so inviting, part of me was dying to tear off my frock and hurl myself in.

'Wally hated the modern ones,' Myrna said, starting down the paved footpath towards the lake. 'He wanted something that looked like it had been here all along. These were my idea.' She tapped the edge of one of the narrow pools with the tip of her cane. 'They have the same thing at the Hearst Estate in Beverly Hills. We were visiting one day and I thought, why shouldn't I have that?'

I could not relate. Imagine popping into the home of one of the richest men in the world and thinking, I quite fancy that for myself. It was like going to visit Jeff Bezos and buying yourself a spaceship on the way home.

'Why not me?' Myrna said, pleased as punch. 'Good words to live by.'

Why not me? I could think of a million reasons.

I turned and looked back at her house, her palace as it glowed softly in the afternoon sun, and it hit me all at once. I was very, very far from home.

'And what about you, Phoebe Chapman?' she said. 'All I know about you is you're visiting your sister even though she's out of town, and you have far too much free time on your hands. What's your story?'

'Me?' I quickly shook my head. 'I don't have a story.'

'That's a lie. Everyone has a story.'

'Then let's just say, compared to yours,' I replied, 'it's very dull. No one has ever even suspected me of pushing my husband downstairs.'

Myrna placed her cane in front of her, resting both hands on top of it. 'You're still young by today's standards, there's plenty of time for that. Lana was in her late thirties when her daughter "allegedly" finished off her lover, but from what I heard at the time, he had it coming.'

And there was something else for me to google when I got home.

We walked back to the house; Myrna settled in a large rattan chair outside the French doors and silently invited me to take the one next to it. She knocked her stick against the side of her chair, the rhythmic tapping making my heart rate spike.

'You said something before,' she said, cutting into me with laser-guided precision, 'about people forgetting you. That sounds like a story.'

'You don't miss a trick, do you?' I leaned forward and picked at a loose thread on the cuff of Suzanne's dress, ignoring Myrna, whose blue eyes were twinkling with victory. 'It really isn't very interesting. No one's invested in my life, other than my sister and the good people at Netflix who like to check in on me every five hours or so, bless them.'

'What you mean is you don't want to tell me,' she replied. 'That's too bad, darling, because the price of entry to the Myrna Moore museum is a pound of flesh and I'm afraid I will extract it one way or another. Besides, I'm a marvellous person to confide in – who am I going to tell? My godawful stepchildren? The woman who comes to do my nails? I'm the perfect person to hear your sins; no one cares what I have to say and, even if they did, I'm so old, I'm practically dust.'

'You could tweet about it?' I suggested.

She gave me the filthiest possible look. 'The internet is the reason civilization is crumbling all around us. Name one good thing that ever came of it?'

I opened my mouth to answer but it was more difficult than I expected it to be. It really was pretty bad when you thought about it.

'Oh, I know,' I said eagerly. 'Ryan Reynolds. He's an international treasure. King of the internet, love his Instagram.'

'The sweet Canadian boy who did a picture with Sandy Bullock?' She was appeased. 'He used to have a home around here, over on Nottingham Avenue, I believe.

He came to visit once, big fan of my films, he said. Didn't much care for the wife, sour-faced thing. I heard they got divorced and I was glad.'

She smiled at a memory I would have given anything to share.

'Well, if you spent more time on the internet, you'd know he's remarried and has a load of kids and his new wife is truly perfect,' I informed her, taking out my phone and searching for photographic evidence. Myrna leaned forward and squinted at the screen, eventually nodding her approval.

'Fabulous, now, tell me why everyone has forgotten you.'

In a different life, she would have made a fantastic detective.

'There's really nothing to talk about,' I said one more time, on the off-chance she might give up, but the inquisitive spark behind her eyes was going nowhere. 'Fine. I used to have a boyfriend and we broke up and all of my friends were really his friends so now we don't see each other. That's about it.'

'No, it isn't,' she decided. 'Tell me about the boyfriend.'

Running my tongue over my teeth, I took a big breath in.

'I'd rather not.'

Myrna reached inside her shirt for her necklace, the same round gold disc she always wore for my visits, and turned it over and over in her slender fingers. 'Then I will tell *you* a story about being forgotten.' The sun bounced off the pendant, shooting a tiny spotlight across the garden. 'I never wanted to be famous. Not when I was little Reby Greenberg from Long Island. Not when my father's job moved the family to Los Angeles and not even when the director, William Mitchell, spotted me drinking milkshakes at the Brown Derby with my friends. I thought being an actress would be fun; it wasn't. I thought I'd meet thrilling people; I didn't. There were good times but mostly it was hard work and heartbreak, trying to fend off the worst of men without running yourself out of a job at the same time. Then I met Wally and none of it mattered any more. Not because a man completed me but because our being together gave me the opportunity to step away from something that was making me deeply unhappy, even though most every other girl in the world would have killed to be in my shoes. My tiny, tight, pinching shoes, chosen for me by men who couldn't walk a yard in them, let alone a mile.'

After an entire day spent watching her films, it was easy for me to imagine her back then, her bouncing blonde ponytail and red lips, cruising around Los Angeles in some baby-blue convertible with the top down. But it was easy to picture the other parts too. I knew those parts. Most women did, one way or another. How had we managed to lose the magical moments from the past but kept so many of the shitty bits? Times were changing but not quickly enough.

'What about after you lost Wally?' I asked, curling my toes inside my trainers. 'What happened then?'

Slowly, as though she had never been rushed in her life, Myrna picked up a waiting packet of cigarettes from the side table and shook one loose, putting it between her lips before picking up a box of matches. With the box in her left hand and a match in her right, she struck one against the other. It sparked into life on the first go. She took a long, slow drag on the cigarette and blew it out in a pale blue cloud that rose into the air and evaporated over her estate.

'They paint me as a recluse because it's easier than admitting the truth,' she said before taking another drag. 'After Wally was gone, as I said, I did try to go back to acting, not because I wanted to but because I thought I ought to. So they did me a favour really. When the job offers didn't come pouring in, I was thrilled to walk away, but it was impossible for people to comprehend how I could turn my back on it all so easily. They couldn't understand why I might not want to spend my time with men who would be called monsters today, why I didn't fight tooth and nail, give up everything I had to get back in. They say a million girls would kill for the opportunities I had, but what they don't like to talk about are the girls who died for them. Myrna Moore might be nothing but a footnote but that's fine by me. What was it Irene Dunne said? Acting is not important, living is. A terrible stick in the mud, but she was right about that.'

I reached for the box of matches and ran my nail lightly against the rough edge. 'That's exactly how I feel. Like a footnote, like someone people used to know. When it comes down to it, I really don't have any friends.'

The glowing orange tip of her cigarette danced threateningly in the air. 'I don't have any friends because all of mine are dead,' she said. 'What's your excuse? Make new ones.'

I stared at the matchbox, yellow and red, and traced the three stars on the front with the tip of my finger.

My matchbox at home was yellow too but without the stars. Everything here was the same but different.

'If the people I've known for years didn't care about me enough to stay in my life,' I replied, thinking back to one of my early conversations with Therese, 'why would anyone else bother?'

'Those people were imbeciles and you're better off without them. You seem perfectly reasonable to me.' Myrna flicked her ash into a heavy onyx ashtray. 'And I am a fantastic judge of character. I despise almost everyone I meet.'

After a moment's silence, she whistled, long and low. 'That boyfriend of yours really did a number on you, didn't he?'

I slowly pushed the inside tray of the matchbox almost all the way out in one direction and then all the way back in the other. 'It wasn't the greatest love story of all time,' I confirmed, red-faced and frowning.

'I will only say this,' she leaned across the table and her cigarette smoke drifted into my eyes, teasing tears that were looking for a reason to fall. 'Do not allow yourself to get used to being alone. Solitude is charming at first; Wally always used to say silence was my favourite song. Now it's deafening and I cannot switch it off. I don't believe in regrets, but it would be nice to have more people in my life.' She inhaled and tipped her head slightly to the left. 'Tolerable people,' she added. 'Of which there are so few.'

'Maybe you'll make friends at the assisted living facility?' I suggested.

'Does a dog make friends when you put it in the kennels?' she scoffed. 'Scratch that, dogs are idiots. I love them but they're idiots, they'd make friends with a glazed ham if it winked at them the right way.'

Stubbing the half-smoked cigarette out in the ashtray, she looked back at the house, a wistful turn to her features. 'I'm loath to leave the place, really I am, but it's too big for me now. Those horrible children are right, rattling around on my own is simply no good. This house was built for a long-gone time; perhaps it should make way for something new.'

The thought of it was too sad and I took a moment, imagining all the happiness, and most importantly, all the parties that had taken place here over the years. What I wouldn't have given to spend one hour with Wally and Myrna in their prime.

'You should have one last bash before you go,' I said, only half-joking. 'The house is so Gatsby, it would be a shame not to. One big blowout before you leave.'

Myrna wilted back in her chair, touching a hand to her forehead. 'I'll never understand the fascination with that nonsensical book. Why would Buchanan have Gatsby over for dinner when he knew he was in love with his wife? Why did they all drive into the city together to argue in a hotel room? Sad little story, full of sad little men. Nothing great about any of them. Give me a good romance novel any day,' she said. 'Some of the newer ones are genuinely arousing.'

Myrna rose, her slippered feet and gold-tipped cane moving back inside the house, and I hopped to my feet, mildly alarmed but extremely curious to see her library,

'Even if I did have a party, I wouldn't know whom to invite,' she said. 'I can only think of seven living people I can stomach for more than fifteen minutes at a time and that includes you.'

'You could invite your neighbours?' I suggested, feeling oddly proud of myself. 'You said you used to know everyone around here. Wouldn't it be nice to see who lives here now, before you leave?'

She stared at me for a long moment, the feathers at her cuffs blowing underneath the air conditioning.

'Also Ryan Reynolds,' I added. 'And Ryan Gosling. Invite all the Ryans.'

'I'll think on it.' She opened a different door to the one we'd come in with the tip of her cane, and nodded down a dark hallway. 'Do you want to see the secret bowling alley in the basement or not? I can't promise it isn't haunted; it's the only spot in the house where the boys were left to their own devices, and God only knows what they got up to. Rock spent aeons down there and never did get any better at bowling.'

'Can't think of anything I'd like more,' I said, all sorts of theories popping into my head as I followed her into the darkness.

CHAPTER THIRTEEN

Monday morning announced itself with a ringing phone and the sound of someone banging on the front door both at the same time, and I really didn't feel like dealing with either.

It was late when I left Myrna's. I stayed until her assistant arrived to help wrap up her day which, from what I could tell, consisted of changing into another pair of fabulous pyjamas, taking a dozen different supplements and drinking a gin martini that she requested be made 'as dirty as Nixon'. It was icon behaviour. Less iconic was the thumping in my head that pounded in time with the banging on the door. Just because Myrna drank double martinis before bed didn't mean I should. Or could. Or ever would again.

'OK, I'm here, I'm here,' I muttered, reaching for my phone. It was Suzanne and I knew it was Suzanne before I even saw her name on the screen because I'd assigned Justin Bieber's 'Baby' to her calls, an earworm so annoying it would force me to answer it immediately whether I wanted to or not.

'Hello?'

'You're up early, I didn't think you'd answer.'

'Because you're calling early,' I said through a yawn, hobbling downstairs to get the door. 'Why did you ring if you didn't think I'd answer?'

'There's this miraculous thing called voicemail,' she replied. Suzanne the Smartarse. 'What is that noise? Is there construction outside? Is it the zombie apocalypse?'

'No zombies,' I replied, fiddling with the locks and chains and bolts; I already had a very good idea as to who it might be. 'Unfortunately.'

'You locked me out!' Bel blew air kisses at both of my cheeks as she bounced through the door and breezed past me, down the corridor and into the kitchen. 'I didn't even know you could bolt that door, Suzy never does.'

'That's because "Suzy" is an idiot,' I said loud enough for both of them to hear. 'Can I help you with something?'

'Who is it?' Suzanne asked impatiently. 'Is it Bel? I'm assuming it's Bel.'

'No, it's Jennifer Aniston,' I replied. 'She's taking me out for brunch with Courtney Cox and Lisa Kudrow.'

Bel hopped up on the kitchen counter. 'Wouldn't that be amazing? A li'l *Friends* reunion moment? I would love that.'

'Put me on speaker,' Suzanne ordered. 'I want to talk to both of you.'

Too tired (and hungover) to argue, I did as I was told, combing my hands through my tangled hair and wiping last night's mascara from under my eyes. I looked like one of the racoons I'd found rifling through the rubbish when I got home from Myrna's. Small and scruffy with dark rings around our eyes, we both appeared harmless but could potentially kill if looked at the wrong way.

'Hi, Bel,' Suzanne cooed in a sing-song voice I hadn't heard since the time she had to tell Gran she'd crashed the car. 'I miss you! How are you doing?'

'You miss her?' I said, wondering if I'd woken up in the twilight zone. 'You've only been gone a week. I live on the other side of the world and you've literally never told me you miss me.'

'Have you ever woken me up with freshly baked morning buns?'

'If you're talking about that time we had to share a bed at Cousin Jo's wedding and you woke up with my bum in your face, that's on you for insisting we top and tail it.'

'You do your workout and you get morning buns,' Bel said, booping the phone as though it was my sister's nose. 'Mmm, morning buns. Phoebe, we should go get some.'

'You should get some, I should go back to bed,' I replied, pressing my fingertips into my temples. 'Lovely to see you, don't let the door hit you in the arse on the way out. Suzanne, what time does your flight land, where is your Toilet Duck and do you have any Berocca?'

'You're not going back to bed,' Bel said. 'I came to pick you up to go hiking.'

'And the Toilet Duck is in the mud room, I haven't got any Berocca and I called to tell you I won't be back until Wednesday,' Suzanne added. 'I was going to suggest you treat yourself to a spa day on me but now

I don't have to because you're going hiking with Bel! As soon as you've cleaned the toilet.'

'Hold on.' I pinched the bridge of my nose, praying that the automatic coffee maker I hadn't been able to switch off had come up trumps this morning. 'I don't remember anything about hiking?'

'That's because Ren and I planned it yesterday.' Bel swayed from side to side, shimmying her shoulders in a slinky little dance. 'Or he planned it and texted me and I said you should come too.'

'That sounds so great!' Suze crowed down the phone. 'You two have fun, or three, I should say. I have to get into the office before Elon Musk tries to buy us or clone us or move us all to Mars. Enjoy your hike.'

Suzanne rang off and Bel beamed at me from the top of the kitchen counter, altogether too close to my sister's pristine knife block to be fully clear of danger.

'I can't believe you didn't call me yesterday,' she said, flipping the end of her glossy ponytail. 'Don't you want to hear all about my date?'

'I already heard all about your date,' I reminded her, taking myself over to a safer space near the fridge. 'I was on your date.'

'No, I mean after that part.' She raised her hand to her face and leaned forward to whisper a secret. 'We kissed.'

Happy, sad and insanely jealous, I opened the fridge and fished out a bottle of freshly squeezed orange juice, wondering if it was too early for another martini. 'Scandalous.'

'But that's all we did,' she added, swinging her legs back and forth. 'I went for a little over the clothes action but he's a romantic, he wants to go slow. It was very chaste, girl scout promise.'

'Were you ever a girl scout?' I asked.

'No, but I have a girl scout uniform?'

To be filed under things I didn't really need to know.

'So why do you want me to third wheel it on your date?' I poured then chugged an entire glass of juice. Orange juice was good. Orange juice was calming. 'Also, shouldn't at least one of you be working? How come no one ever works in this town?'

'We're all self-employed.' She held out her hands for the orange juice, wiggling her fingers, and took a swig straight from the bottle. 'I rescheduled some things, nothing that can't wait a day, and Ren works for himself. He like, builds houses, did you know he builds houses?'

'Yes, I know Ren builds houses.'

'With his bare hands.'

'I imagine he sometimes wears gloves.'

She tilted her pretty face upwards with consideration. 'I don't know, he has these calluses but they're not like CrossFit calluses, they're like manly calluses, like he's been chopping down trees or—'

'You said you're going hiking?' I cut her off before she could go into any more detail about Ren's hands. There was a limit to the uplifting power of orange juice.

'Yeah, I'm not sure where,' she replied, tapping the Apple watch on her wrist and hopping down from the counter. 'But we're leaving in thirty minutes.' She straightened her sports bra and adjusted the matching leggings. This time they were a deep forest green and she had a blue and brown plaid shirt tied around her waist to match the pristine-looking hiking boots on her feet. 'Ren overslept, that boy is not an early bird.'

'You're leaving in thirty minutes,' I corrected, noting one more thing Ren and I had in common. 'I'm going back to bed. And what's a mud room?'

'Please, Phoebe?' She hit me with those big brown eyes again and I felt my resolve weaken. 'Saturday night only went so well because of you. If you hadn't told me what to say, I never would have got this far. I think you would really enjoy it or I wouldn't ask, and I know Ren would love to see you.'

And I would really love to see Ren.

'Hiking sounds very intense,' I said as I put the empty bottle of orange juice back in the fridge for Suzanne to deal with. She loved it when I did that. 'Don't you need walking boots and backpacks and sticks and things? I've only got my trainers.'

'We're not going to climb a mountain, it's more like a nice outdoor stroll,' she replied, teaming her most wheedling tone with her most convincing smile. 'The only reason I'm wearing these boots is because they look great with this outfit. I don't do those crazy hikes, only the cute fun ones.'

'I don't know,' I said, looking out at the sparkling swimming pool. 'I had big plans today.'

'To do what?'

'Nothing.'

'No, I'm sorry, I'm putting my foot down,' Bel said, shifting into personal trainer mode. 'You have to come hiking, you need to get outside and get some fresh air. It's an LA rite of passage. And I promise I can control myself, there will be no PDA. There will be minimum PDA. I'll warn you when to look away.'

I was torn. Some fresh air might be nice and hiking was on my LA bucket list. Better to go with people than end up getting lost, running out of water and being eaten by a family of mountain lions which was truly the best-case scenario I could come up with when I thought about venturing into the wilderness alone. But even the mildest suggestion of PDA was enough to make me reconsider. We all had to go sometime, what better way than to feed a family in need? Really, it would be stupid not to go. Petty. Was I really going to let my little holiday crush on Ren get in the way of having a nice time? Because that's all it was really, a crush. He wasn't even my type. I'd always gone for Clark Kent over Superman, an indoor cat kind of a man. How could I possibly be in love with a lactose intolerant, semi-vegan twitcher? The bird watching kind, not the streamer. That definitely would have been enough to put me off.

'Please, Phoebe?' Bel pleaded and pressed her hands to her heart. 'I'll never ask you for anything else ever again even though I think maybe I said that when I asked you to help me with the mermaid thing, but this time I really mean it.'

'Fine,' I replied as she jumped up and down, clapping her hands. 'But are you sure I'll be safe hiking in trainers?'

Pulling me into a hug, she gave a quiet cheer, the muted roar of an invisible crowd. 'I, Bel Johnson, super swear and pinky promise you will be one hundred per cent safe and will not even fear for your life for one single second.'

'You promise?' I asked, looking down at her sturdy hiking boots then over at my waiting Converse in the corner of the room.

'Yes,' she replied, straight-faced, all business. 'I guarantee you will not die on this hike.'

'I'm going to die on this hike.'

'You're not going to die,' Ren said. 'Switzer is one of the safest hikes in the Angeles Forest. You'll be fine. Even in your sneakers.'

I gave Bel the glaring of a lifetime. Somehow, in less than half an hour, we had left Los Angeles, the second largest city in the United States of America, and found ourselves deep in the wilderness and I was not prepared.

'It's an easy hike, I swear. We're going to walk along the floor of the canyon, hop over the river a couple times, climb up the side of the canyon then back down to the surprise at the end.' He handed me a pair of shiny silver walking sticks that matched the ones resting by his feet. 'Then we turn around and come back.'

'How long will that take?' I asked, flicking the catch on one of the sticks exactly the way Ren had and promptly breaking it in two.

'Maybe three hours?' He picked up the two poles of my walking stick, slotted them together and fastened the catch before handing it back. 'It's about four and a half miles in all but we'll want to hang out for a while in the middle.'

Three hours. Almost as long as *Avatar*. I.e. too long.

'Um, how high does it go?' Bel asked.

I looked back and saw her usually sunny face was oddly pale.

193

'It's not so high,' Ren said, kneeling down to double-knot his well-worn boots and looking up at her through a mess of shiny dark hair. I could have sworn there were little cartoon love hearts flapping around his head. 'Maybe feels a little steep coming back but that's only for a few minutes.'

'It looks high.'

'You're a trainer, you're in amazing shape, it'll be a breeze for you.' He gave a dazzling smile and clapped his hands together. 'We all ready?'

I eyed the uneven dirt path that ran alongside the river. 'I would like to remind everyone once again that I have no health insurance so if I fall, please leave me for the wolves.'

'More likely bears,' Ren said amiably, resting his hands on my shoulders and gently pushing me onto the path. 'Maybe mountain lions. Definitely coyotes.'

'This gets better and better,' I said, choosing to believe he was joking but still tightening my hair into a bear-proof topknot. No need to give Yogi and Boo Boo something easy to grab on to.

'Oh no!'

Ren and I turned at the same time to see the third member of our troop sprawled out on the ground, clutching her leg.

'Bel!' Ren was by her side in less than a second and with shaking hands I pulled out my phone, ready to dial for an ambulance. 'What happened?'

She shrieked the moment he touched her ankle. 'I don't know, maybe I rolled it? One second I was fine and the next, I was on the floor.'

'Can you stand?' he asked as he helped her up to her

one good foot. With a heroic sniff, Bel tested her weight on the bad ankle before collapsing into Ren's arms.

'I don't think so,' she said through barely restrained tears. 'Why did this have to happen to me? Today of all days? Why, God, why?'

Now, I knew Bel was a good actress. I'd seen her in action on Saturday night, but this was not that. She was hammier than Porky the Pig. I'd seen drag queens lip-sync for their lives with more subtlety.

'There's no way I'm going to be able to climb up the side of the canyon,' she said, her bottom lip trembling. 'You'll have to go on without me.'

But Ren shook his head. 'We have to get you to the ER. What if that ankle is broken?'

'But it isn't,' she replied altogether too quickly. 'I mean, I really don't think it is because I can still kind of move it a little even though it hurts a lot. I just need to rest.'

'Why don't we unlace your boot and have a look?' I suggested. 'See if it's swollen?'

'You're not supposed to!' Bel yelled, slapping my hand away from her shoelace. 'I took a first aid course that said to leave the boot tied until you can get help; don't you dare touch it!'

She was faking it. She'd dragged me out of bed to climb up a mountain with her boyfriend and now she didn't want to do it.

'If it's that bad, I'd really like to get you to a doctor,' Ren said, frowning. 'Even if it's not broken, you could have a torn ligament.'

Bel hobbled over to a picnic table and threw herself onto the uneven planks of wood like a Victorian spinster taking to her fainting couch. All she needed was some smelling salts and a case of consumption and you wouldn't be able to tell the difference.

'It's not that serious, I can tell, but I don't want to slow you down. Please, go on without me.' She held both his hands in hers, a single, selfless tear running down her cheek. Anyone would have thought she was asking us to leave her behind enemy lines. 'You said you'd been planning this hike for weeks, I don't want to ruin it for you and I don't want to ruin Phoebe's day. We can go hiking any time, she only has a few more days of vacation.'

He looked back at me and I traded my suspicious face for an easy smile before he noticed.

'I really hate the thought of leaving you.' He cupped her face with his hand, his thumb stroking the tear from her cheekbone, and a surge of something sour shot through me. 'You're sure you don't mind waiting for us?'

'Not at all.'

'You're really going to sit here on your own?' I asked. 'For three hours?'

With slightly too much ease, she swung her legs up onto the bench and stretched out, unzipping a neon-pink bumbag.

'I'll meditate,' she replied before holding up her phone. 'Plus I have a bunch of stuff downloaded on Netflix. I figured we wouldn't have a signal out here.'

How convenient.

'If you're sure, I guess we'll see you in a couple of hours,' Ren said as he handed her the car keys. 'And be on the lookout for bears.'

'You will,' she replied sweetly. 'You're joking about the bears, right?'

He hoisted his backpack over his shoulders and bent down to kiss her gently on the lips. Bel pressed her hands against the sides of his face and sighed happily as they parted, eyes still locked on one another.

Your feelings for Ren are just a crush, I reminded myself as I started off down the trail on my own, seething with jealousy. You were upset when Harry Styles started going out with Olivia Wilde as well, but you got over that soon enough. I would get over Ren eventually.

'As long as you don't fall off the side of a mountain first,' I said cheerfully as I ploughed ahead, onwards and upwards.

CHAPTER FOURTEEN

'You planning to do this without me?'

Ren jogged up at the side of me and nudged me with his walking sticks. I marched on, one foot in front of the other.

'Just giving you some alone time,' I replied. 'No one wants their creepy mate watching them kiss their new girlfriend.'

'It's a little early to be throwing the word girlfriend around.' He tucked his thumbs into the straps of his backpack, his cheeks flushed. 'We've only had one date.'

'But you like her?'

'I do,' he replied readily. 'She's so . . .' He looked up to the trees for help completing his sentence. 'She's not what I expected. Unpredictable.'

I hoisted my backpack up onto my shoulders and nodded. 'You mean like how she keeps letting herself in my house without knocking?'

He laughed but didn't correct me.

We turned a corner and found ourselves deep in the

dense woods, dappled sunlight flickering through the trees to light our way. It was beautiful and if I hadn't already stepped in a puddle and soaked one foot all the way through to my socks, I would have been utterly charmed.

'I know it's only been one date, but I can't figure her out,' Ren said. 'Some of the things she says, I can't tell if she's joking or not. Nothing about her makes sense.'

'Since when did other people make sense?' I stepped carefully over a creek to avoid another piss-wet-through shoe. 'What exactly are you trying to figure out?'

'You really want to know?'

No, I thought, I really don't.

'Yes,' I said. 'I really do.'

'It's the letter. The one you delivered.'

Oh good, no way this could go badly.

'What about the letter?' I asked, with a gulp.

The sound of his sigh settled softly in the woods.

'I fell in love with it.'

'Oh,' I replied as I walked face first into a tree. 'OK.'

'I know it sounds dumb but I've always been kind of an old romantic.' Ren shook his head as he spoke, as though even he couldn't believe what he was saying, too distracted to notice me picking bits of branch out of my hair. 'My grandpa said I was an old soul when I was a kid; I liked watching old movies with him, listening to old music. Even my job. You don't get that many people into carpentry these days, you know?'

'It's the oldest profession in the world,' I replied sagely, before realizing what I'd said. 'Wait, no, that's something else.'

'I think I was born in the wrong decade,' he went on, grinning at my fumble. 'I always figured that's why

I had such bad luck with dating. There was more feeling in Bel's letter than my entire two-year relationship with Shawna.'

'It's just a letter,' I said too quickly, my words falling all over each other. 'How much can you know about a person from one letter?'

He chuckled and shook his head. 'Now I know you didn't read it.'

Technically he was right. I didn't read it, I bloody well wrote it.

Ahead of us, the trail forked off in two different directions, reminding me of the shadowy hallways in Myrna's mansion. One path led further into the woods with birds singing and sunshine lighting the way. The other turned upwards, shaded, slippery, narrow and precarious. Without having to ask, I already knew which way we were going.

'It's not that she sent me a letter, it's the fact she wrote it in the first place,' Ren carried on talking as though he wasn't walking us directly into a scene from every single horror movie ever made. 'Anyone can get in touch with anyone today. I could DM Ana de Armas right now and tell her I think she's hot, but to write someone a real letter and pour out your feelings in this beautiful, poetic way? This is how it used to be. You had to put your heart on the line if you wanted to tell someone how you felt, you couldn't hide behind a screen then delete the conversation if it didn't go your way.'

'So what I'm hearing is you think Ana de Armas is hot?'

'*Everyone* thinks Ana de Armas is hot.'

He wasn't wrong.

'But hot doesn't compare to honesty and vulnerability.'

A deep, burning heat set fire to my face and it had nothing to do with the hike.

'Can't hurt that Bel's not too hard to look at,' I said, huffing a little as we started up the incline proper. 'No one's going to kick her out of bed for eating biscuits.'

Ren looked back at me over his shoulder, confused.

'Cookies,' I clarified, fishing my sunglasses out of my backpack. 'Sorry, sometimes I forget it's a different language.'

'Bel is beautiful,' he agreed, as if there was any other option. 'But there are a lot of beautiful people in this town.'

'You're telling me. It's like there's a global hot girl convention only it's every day,' I grumbled. 'They honestly should warn you about it when you book your flights.'

Ren laughed as I panted my way up the steeply rising trail. My calves burned as we shot up above the trees in a few metres and our previously cool, green path through the woods turned into a rocky, sun-bleached mountain hike. So much for a cute little walk; this was hot and hard, and if anyone tried to take a photo of me in this state, I would push them into the canyon.

'Like I said, you're going to think it's dumb,' Ren said. 'But I fell for the letter, I fell for Bel's words. I don't think it would matter what she looked like.'

I stopped in my tracks, partly because I was completely out of breath and all the muscles in my legs had seized up at once, and partly because I couldn't laugh and climb at the same time.

'That is such a load of rubbish,' I said, pressing my hand into my ribs to stave off a stitch. 'You would have fallen in love with her no matter what she looked like? Ren, please.'

I didn't think I'd ever seen him looking annoyed before but there was a first time for everything.

'It's true,' he insisted, chin lifted with defiance. 'You don't have to believe me, but it is.'

'No, it isn't,' I argued. 'And there's no way to test the theory because conveniently, Bel is absolutely bloody gorgeous. You cannot stand there and tell me you would have loved the person who wrote that letter even if they'd turned out to be . . .'

'Turned out to be what?' Ren asked, one of his walking poles wedged into the cliffside.

Me.

If they turned out to be me.

'See? You don't even have an answer,' he added. 'Because you're a cynic and I'm a romantic.'

'No, you're a liar,' I replied. 'What if she was ugly? A proper children-scaring, dogs-howling, mirror-breaking uggo?'

'Attractive is subjective. Everyone has something beautiful in them.'

'What if she worked in a chicken factory and always smelled like innards?'

'That sounds like a very specific example and maybe something you need to work through with a therapist.'

'What if she turned out to be Boris Johnson in a wig?'

He pulled a bottle of water from his backpack and held it out to me. 'This is a pointless conversation,' he said as I snatched the bottle and chugged. 'Bel is beautiful, inside and out.'

I had to admit he was right about that; she was a beautiful person. When she wasn't letting herself into the house, faking an ankle injury to get out of a hike or convincing me to strap my legs together in a latex mermaid tail.

'What I can't figure out is why she can't relax and be herself with me. One minute, she's Comedy Bel, playing everything for laughs, and the next, she's Love Letter Bel, all lyrical and romantic. Maybe she has to hide that part of herself with other people, but she doesn't have to pretend with me. I want the woman who wrote the letter.'

I never thought I would be so thankful for a dangerous, crumbling track that had been worn into the side of a mountain with a fifty-foot sheer drop on the other side, but in that moment, there was nowhere else I'd rather be. The path demanded too much attention, was too steep and narrow for Ren to turn around and see the look on my face.

What had I done?

'How far until we get to the top?' I asked, keeping my eyes on the ground.

'There's maybe ten more minutes of incline then we're back downhill for a while.' He stopped as the path curved to the left, placing one hand on the rock face to steady himself. 'Wanna take a break?'

A handful of pebbles skittered off the edge of the trail as I slid past him to lead the way. I wanted to be up front, I didn't want to follow any more.

'Just curious.' I pointed onwards with one of my sticks. 'Let's keep going.'

'You're in charge,' he said, his boots crunching the ground a safe distance behind me. 'What you say goes.'

'If you say so,' I replied, marching on.

* * *

'Didn't I tell you it would be worth it?' Ren asked.

'You did,' I said, turning slow circles to make sure I saw everything. 'And it almost is.'

'Only almost?'

Hands on my hips, I was determined not to smile. 'It's going to take more than a waterfall to make up for a rattlesnake attack.'

Even though I wasn't exactly an outside girlie, I grew up countryside-adjacent and I'd spent more than my fair share of time in nature. There were woods all around our village that we weren't supposed to play in but did anyway, and at least once a year Gran dragged me and Suzanne off to Sherwood Forest or some National Trust park during the school holidays, even though we mostly spent the entire outing beating each other up. Fresh air makes children feral.

But this was something else.

After hiking up the rocky trail for so long I thought my calves would pop clean off my legs, we eventually came back down the other side, swallowed up by the trees again and moving swiftly along the floor of the canyon until we came to Ren's surprise. An actual, honest to goodness waterfall, the first real waterfall I'd ever seen, and I loved it completely. The water cascaded down the side of the mountain, rushing into a small pool below and shushing everything around us.

Ren dropped his backpack on the ground and shook his head, eyes glinting. 'It was a piece of rope. I only said watch out in case it was a rattlesnake.'

'The possibility of a rattlesnake is bad enough,' I replied pointedly. 'But I will admit, this isn't bad.'

It was the understatement of a lifetime.

Even though the sun was high, it couldn't quite make it through the canopy of tall oaks and sycamores, casting the whole clearing in a peaceful green glow. The air was clean and sweet with the scent of wood and earth and everything fresh. It was magical. There was no other word for it. I felt like an otherworldly creature who belonged in the forest, a dryad or a wood nymph or a hobbit ready for its second breakfast.

'OK, but what do you really think?' Ren asked, breaking the silence but not the spell.

'I think LA needs to stop being so beautiful or I'm never going to leave.' I rested my own backpack on a large flat rock and climbed carefully over to the water's edge. 'Why isn't everyone in a fifty-mile radius here right now? Don't they know about this?'

'They know. Most of them don't care.'

I dipped my hand into the pool, cool and crisp, and the stress of our strenuous ninety-minute hike was instantly washed away. 'I don't understand people here,' I said, watching the reflection of the trees above me ripple away as I fluttered my fingers under the water. 'Stunning beaches on one side of town, forests and mountains and waterfalls on the other, and no one bothers with either?'

'When most people think of LA, they think of Hollywood or Beverly Hills, everywhere that wants to take your money,' Ren explained. 'For me, it's always been about what the city gives away for free. Weirdly, they're the things no one seems to want to take.' He crouched down beside me, his knee barely brushing mine, and I didn't dare move. 'This is one of the first places my grandpa brought me as soon as I was old enough to keep up with him. He went hiking almost every day.'

'Oh, I didn't tell you.' I took my hand out of the water and pulled away, sitting back on my heels. 'I met someone who knew him.'

Ren's face shone in the shade of the clearing. 'You did? Who?'

'Her name's Myrna Moore, she lives in that big old French chateau-looking house at the top of the hill? I dropped off some of her post delivered to Suzanne by mistake and we ended up talking. She mentioned she knew your grandparents. And the people who lived in Suzanne's house. And at least half of Hollywood by the sounds of it.'

'That's wild,' he said with a wistful smile. 'He mentioned her sometimes but I never met her. I didn't know she was still alive, to tell you the truth; I'd love to meet her sometime.'

'You should make it quick,' I said. 'She's moving soon but I bet she'd love to meet you too. Probably. She doesn't seem that keen on people.'

'That would be fantastic.' He punched me lightly on the arm and laughed. 'Look at you, playing matchmaker again.'

'Yes,' I replied weakly. 'Look at me. Or don't, I bet I look like total shit.'

'Nah, you look great.' Ren hopped up to his feet, leaving me crouched in a troll-like ball on the floor. 'It's not often you get this place to yourself, there's usually at least a couple of other people here. We should make the most of it.'

'Shouldn't we get back?' I asked, thinking of Bel all alone on the picnic bench. He was supposed to be here with her, I was only the stand-in.

Ren's response was to peel off his T-shirt and toss it on top of his backpack.

'I'm sure she won't mind waiting ten more minutes. You made it all this way, you've got to swim.'

Swim?

'Is it safe?' I asked as he shucked off his hiking boots.

A nod.

'Are we allowed?' I asked as he unfastened his belt.

A shrug.

'Have you got your trunks?' I asked as he eased his shorts down around his muscular legs to reveal a pair of tight grey boxer briefs.

He pulled off his thick woollen socks and tossed them in my general direction, missing my face by a matter of centimetres and therefore retaining his life.

'Come on, live a little,' Ren said. A challenge. 'When are you going to get another chance to swim in a deserted waterfall?'

He put one foot in the pool and I saw his whole body shiver, the muscles in his back contracting as he took a theatrically loud deep breath then ducked under the water, only to come back up two seconds later, gasping and grinning.

'You're missing out!' he called, splashing his way into the middle of the pool and diving under the water again, re-emerging with a whoop. 'This is incredible!'

'That's funny because from here it just looks cold,' I shouted back. 'I think I'll stay dry, thanks.'

'It's not cold, it's invigorating. Come on, Phoebe.

Either you get in or I'm going to drag you in. Which would you prefer?'

I had to bite my lip to stop myself from asking to be dragged. Jumping into waterfalls wasn't my sort of thing.

'I'm going to count to ten,' he yelled. 'And then you're getting in, one way or another.'

'Why not me?' I murmured to myself as he started to swim back to shore.

Dipping into the post-hike dregs of my determination, I pulled off my socks and shoes and stripped off my leggings, tiptoeing into the water in my vest and knickers. The shock was instantaneous. Dipping my fingers in was cool and refreshing, but to my hot, tired feet, the water was like ice. Worse than ice, it was so cold it burned. Anyone who paid for cryotherapy was a masochist.

'Stop thinking about it and do it,' Ren said when I froze, only in up to my ankles. 'You gotta dive in!'

'Easy for you to say,' I replied, forcing myself to walk deeper and deeper, gasping as the water covered my knees, my waist, then folding my arms over my chest before fully committing my whole body.

'She did it!' He let out a celebratory howl that echoed off the rocks around us. 'Why do women make such a big deal about getting into the water? You'll never know the pain of freezing cold temperatures the way a man does.'

'Are you kidding?' I asked, teeth chattering. 'We have double the shock you do. Men think they're the only ones that suffer because your bits are on the outside when it's much worse for us, we just don't complain as much.'

He came closer, rivulets of water rolling off his bronzed skin, and I couldn't help but notice the beautiful line of his shoulders. 'Bits? You're *so* British.'

Now the initial shock had worn away, I had to admit the water felt amazing. Ren cut through it with expert strokes, the beautiful line of his shoulders not only for show.

'How come you never moved back to LA permanently?' I asked, swiping my wet hair out of my eyes as he floated a few feet away from me. 'You obviously love it here.'

Wiping the water from his face, he grimaced at the question. 'Because I can't afford to? I always thought I'd end up in my grandpa's house but that's not happening now. All I see are memories and all my brother sees is dollar signs.'

'The same thing is happening to Myrna,' I replied. 'Her stepkids are forcing her out. She thinks they'll end up knocking the house down and building something new.'

'And she's probably right.'

His frustrated groan was even louder than the rush of the waterfall. 'Everyone is so obsessed with what comes next, they don't stop to think about the here and now, let alone the past. Myrna, my grandpa, their houses, they're ancient history by LA standards. No one cares.'

'I do,' I said, feeling for smooth, wet pebbles under my toes. 'And you do.'

'Maybe I care too much,' he replied. 'According to my brother I'm a dying breed and I don't think he means it as a compliment.'

Without any kind of plan, I took a step towards him and found myself scrabbling around over loose rocks instead of solid ground. Ren grabbed my arms to hold me steady and I realized I was floating. I'd lost my footing completely. He held on to me and I held on to him, keeping my head above the surface. Just barely.

'More like one of a kind,' I said, the heat of his hands burning my skin through the freezing cold water. I felt the pressure of his thumb rubbing along the bones of my wrist and all my clever, pretty words scattered into the wind. 'I love that you care.'

'Then maybe we're two of a kind,' he replied. 'Me and you.'

Ren belonged in the forest.

His golden-brown skin shone in the water and his emerald eyes were almost jet black, pupils dilating in the muted sunlight. Slowly, he released his grip on my arm but instead of pulling away, he slid his hand up and down the delicate skin of my forearm until his palm pressed against mine, our fingers intertwining on their own. I found my footing, the ground certain underneath me, and the two of us stood in the water, half-submerged, face-to-face. Behind us, the waterfall poured into the pool, a beautiful force of nature, doing what it would always do until the river ran dry.

'This is such a special place to me,' he said, his words so soft they barely carried over the sound of the water. 'I'm glad I got to share it today.'

I opened my mouth to tell him I felt the same way, that I never wanted to leave but if I really had to, I would never forget this place as long as I lived.

But I wasn't the one he was supposed to be sharing it with.

Letting go of his hand, I took a step backwards and tumbled helplessly under the water, arms and legs flailing madly in slow motion. When I came back up, he was laughing, I was spluttering and whatever had been was gone.

'We should get going,' I said loudly, splashing my way back onto dry land and wringing the water out of my hair. 'Bel's up there waiting for us, it's not fair to leave her on her own.'

Ren stayed where he was, staring at me as I attempted to cover my exposed body with my backpack, feeling far more undressed than I had a moment ago.

'You're right,' he said, still waist deep in the water. 'It's not fair.'

I dragged my leggings up over my damp skin, glad we were in agreement. Although exactly what we agreed on, I wasn't quite sure.

The hike back to the car was much faster than the hike out to the waterfall. Wet, wired and extremely confused, I wanted to go home, get in the shower, eat my body-weight in snacks and go back to bed. Possibly not even in that order, the shower was not a priority.

'There you are, I thought the bears had got you!' Bel chirped, jumping down from the picnic bench where we'd left her and rushing down the path to leap up at Ren. 'I was about to jump-start the car and get out of here.'

'Your ankle's feeling better then?'

She glanced over at me, her arms woven around Ren's neck, legs wrapped around his waist. 'A little,' she said, slowly lowering her feet to the ground. 'I took an ibuprofen. Literally a miracle.'

'Almost as if an angel had come down from heaven and healed you himself,' I replied coolly.

'You missed the most amazing hike,' Ren said, draping an easy arm around her shoulders as we continued on to the car park, the creek trickling alongside us, trees fluttering above. 'There was no one down at the water-fall, we even took a dip.'

She wrinkled her pretty nose and pulled away from him. 'You swam in that filthy pond? Ew. I hope you checked for leeches?'

'Leeches?' I repeated. 'There were leeches in there?'

'There are no leeches in that pool,' Ren promised as I spun around and around like a dog trying to chase its own tail. 'You're good.'

'You know you have to burn them off,' I rambled, patting myself down. 'You can't pull them or they leave their rank little teeth in you. Are you sure there aren't any? I feel like I can feel them?'

'No leeches I can see, but you are pretty gross.' Bel gave us both a cursory sniff before hopping backwards. 'You need to shower. Right now.'

Ren laughed at the look of disgust on her face but I knew she wasn't joking. Mostly because I could smell myself.

'I don't know about you two, but I'm starving,' he said. 'We should get something to eat before we head back. There's a really great barbecue place out in La Cañada; they do the best pulled pork I've had on the West Coast.'

My stomach didn't so much growl as roar. 'The vegan thing really is optional for you, isn't it?' I commented.

'Not that I'm judging, I would very much like to eat the pork.'

'No, sorry, I'm not going anywhere with the two of you looking like that.' Bel crossed her arms as Ren pulled a bungee cord out of his backpack, the keys to his truck fastened safely onto the other end. 'You need to shower, I need to charge my phone and I'm being eaten alive by the mosquitoes out here. We did the nature thing, now it's time to go back to civilization.'

Ren's expression shifted very slightly. It was only because I'd studied it so closely over the last week that I noticed the muscles in his jaw tighten, his easy smile tensing up fraction by fraction.

'Phoebe,' he said, his tone perfectly neutral. 'Looks like you have the deciding vote.'

'Oh my God,' Bel groaned. 'Sometimes I hate democracy.'

'Maybe it would be more fun to go out after we've showered,' I replied, even as my stomach screamed like a banshee at the thought of passing up lashings of delicious pig. 'Bel's right, I do smell a bit ripe. Maybe heading home first is a better idea?'

'The *best* idea.' She hopped into the front seat of the truck the moment Ren unlocked the door. 'We're going to have to wind down all the windows so I don't have to smell you guys.'

I followed Ren around to the back of the truck, heaving my rucksack in beside his, watching as he fastened them down with bungee cords.

'All good?' I asked.

'All great.'

But he didn't look as though he meant it.

'Let's head home,' he said. 'Apparently I need a shower.'

'Apparently we both do,' I replied, reciprocating in kind. 'Thank you for today, I never would have come here if it wasn't for you.'

He didn't respond. Instead he pulled on the bungee cord to test its grip, his features weighed down with something heavy, like he was trying to crack a puzzle but didn't like the solution he'd come up with.

'I think today was something I'll remember forever,' I added. 'For the rest of my life.'

'Me too,' he replied. 'Today was special.'

His voice was strained, almost as though it hurt to say it, and I felt something begin to crystallize in the air between us until a loud, sharp car horn sliced through the forest.

'Hey, you guys?' Bel called from the front passenger seat, her hand pressing down on the centre of the steering wheel. 'I need to pee so bad and the bathrooms here are not an option. Can we please leave already?'

'She's not wrong about those toilets, better not keep her waiting,' I said, sidestepping Ren to climb into the back seat, an unsettling feeling buzzing in the tips of my frozen fingers and toes while Bel played with the stereo.

I fastened my seatbelt as he gunned the engine and slowly backed the truck out of the car park, leaving the hiking trail, our waterfall and everything that had and hadn't happened far, far behind.

CHAPTER FIFTEEN

'Thanks again for today,' I said loudly as we pulled up in front of Suzanne's house half an hour later. It had been one of the longest half hours of my life, no one but Bel uttering a single word, all the way home. 'I'm going home for a long, hot shower.' I scurried out from the back seat and retrieved my backpack, holding it in front of me like a shield.

'You're not hungry?' Bel asked, hopping out of the cab and onto the ground. 'I thought maybe we could get pizza.'

Ren closed his door gently, wincing as she slammed hers shut. 'How about Hail Mary?' he suggested.

'No, they don't deliver,' Bel cocked her head to one side, her fresh ponytail swishing in the breeze. 'What about Tomato Pie?'

'I don't mind going to pick it up,' Ren said. 'They're not far away.'

'But delivery is so much easier,' she countered. 'Why go to the hassle?'

'Because I'm happy to make the effort for something good?' he replied, climbing back into the truck. With a stiff wave, he pulled away from the kerb and drove down the street, the sound of the vintage engine echoing through the neighbourhood.

'It's like he wants to make his life more difficult,' Bel said, pouting with frustration. 'Like, why doesn't he get a new truck? That thing must cost a million dollars to run and you know it's going to break down eventually.'

'I think it was his grandad's?' I replied, poking around in my bag for my house keys. 'You can't put a value on sentimental things like that.'

'Yeah, you can, it's about fifty grand, I looked online.' She raised an eyebrow as she let down her hair and shook it loose around her shoulders. 'What?'

'Nothing,' I said as I started up the steps to the house, Bel close behind. 'It might be a good idea to be a bit more supportive of your soulmate's family stuff though – it's important to him.'

'Then it's important to me,' she announced, slipping her arm through mine before immediately pulling away. 'As is you taking a shower ASAP.'

Even when she made it very clear she'd rather roll around in fox shit than touch me with a ten-foot pole, I couldn't be mad at her. There was something about Bel that made you want to protect her. She didn't have a malicious bone in her body and I simply could not imagine her ever doing anything to hurt another human being on purpose. She simply wasn't wired that way. I opened the front door and she skipped inside.

'I'd say make yourself at home but that's clearly not an issue.'

'Way ahead of you,' she replied, helping herself to half the contents of the fridge while I plugged my phone into the charger that lived next to the never-been-used oven. 'Now go clean up before I turn the hose on you.'

And since I wasn't sure if it was an empty threat or not, I ran all the way upstairs, just in case.

I knew Suzanne's en suite bathroom must be something special when it was the only room that wasn't included in the house tour, but I hadn't expected to find a complete spa on the other side of her bedroom. It was bigger than my living room and kitchen combined and full of natural light that streamed from huge floor-to-ceiling windows fitted with one-way glass so you could see out but no one else could see in. I had always been a bath girl. I loved a good soak, any time of day or night. Happy? Take a bath. Sad? Take a bath. Too hot? Cool bath. Too cold? Hot bath. Baths were the answer to most of life's problems, but against all odds, the deep soaking tub that curved like a giant pebble in the centre of the room, so big it almost put the swimming pool to shame, was not the most impressive thing in this room. My sister had built the greatest shower known to man. In fact, it wasn't a shower so much as a harnessed monsoon where you could lather, rinse and repeat. With the push of a button and the turn of a knob, the heavens opened and half the bathroom was consumed with a warm, eucalyptus-scented downpour and it was all I could do not to jump in, fully clothed.

I closed my eyes and waited for the water to drown out all my unwelcome thoughts. The way Ren's muscles moved under his skin when he shrugged off his shirt. How his eyes came alive in the forest. The way I felt when he took my hand in the waterfall pool, and the slightest, tiniest possibility that he might have felt something too?

It was no good. What kind of friend helped someone get together with the man of their dreams then started lusting after him herself? A shit friend, that's what kind. It was time for a reality check. If life was a TV show, I was a guest star, the quirky British neighbour who popped in for one short storyline before disappearing forever. Ren and Bel were the regulars. They could recast my role if they needed more help.

I squeezed an obscene amount of Suzanne's designer shampoo into my palm and lathered up my hair. The answer was not complicated. I simply would not think about Ren. I would not think about his thick, gorgeous hair or his broad chest or his fine, high cheekbones. I would not think about the way his hiking shorts clung to his body or how his strong legs glistened with sweat as we climbed higher up the hiking trail. And I definitely wouldn't entertain the idea of what might have happened if I'd told him the letter was from me instead of Bel, or if I hadn't pulled away at the waterfall but instead pulled him closer and moved his hand between my legs and – I didn't realize how shallow my breath had become or how my heart was racing until I had to reach for the wall to steady myself. With my palms flat against the glass, I closed my eyes, taking deep and controlled breaths until I was steady again.

'I simply will not think about it,' I repeated into the water. 'Because there's nothing to think about.'

There. Problem solved.

* * *

'Ren's amazing pizza won't be ready for at least another thirty minutes,' Bel said without looking up from her phone as I padded across the kitchen with bare, clean feet. 'Told you we should have gotten Tomato Pie.'

'What are you reading?' I asked, opening the fridge to choose between one of the eight different flavours of fizzy water. The people of Los Angeles bloody loved their fizzy water.

'Nothing, just scrolling.' She put down her phone and dropped her head back against the sofa with a smile. 'Did you have fun this morning?'

'I don't know if I'd call it fun,' I replied. 'It was an experience.'

'It was a sneak attack,' she huffed. 'I told you, cute hikes only. If he'd told me he wanted to climb a mountain then jump in a leech-infested lake, I'd have said no Lyme disease for me thank you.'

'Lyme disease?' I pressed a hand against my forehead as I settled on the stool across from her, pulling down the long sleeves of my light hoodie. Was the house colder than usual or did I have the chills?

'But I'm glad I went,' she added. 'It's important to share common interests with your partner.'

I put a pin in my Lyme disease panic and reached for a bag of crisps to stave off my hunger pangs. If a packet of Red Hot Cheetos couldn't sort me out, nothing would. 'But you didn't actually hike. I don't know if driving to the location together counts as sharing an interest.'

'It's also important to have separate interests to help you grow as people.' Bel untied the plaid shirt still around her waist and slipped it over her shoulders. 'Is it me or is it cold in here?'

I rubbed my gooseflesh thighs, relieved.

'And I wanted to say thank you for coming. I'm so bad at platonic relationships; I get into this super toxic cycle where I do something for the other person then they do something for me, then I have to do another thing for them and it like, never ends. It's so unhealthy and co-dependent.'

I took a gulp of my water, waiting to see if she was joking. She was not. 'I could be wrong but I think you just described friendship. The doing nice things for each other bit is a foundational element.'

Bel shook her head. 'No, it's a toxic cycle. I saw it on TikTok.'

'I don't want you to freak out,' I lowered my voice in case our phones heard my blasphemy. 'But not everything you see on TikTok is true.'

She scoffed loudly and snatched away my snacks. 'OK, *Mom*. You got a bunch of messages while you were in the shower by the way. And someone who wasn't the mailman put a note through the door, which is super weird.'

She pointed at a small, cream-coloured envelope on the kitchen counter, next to where my phone was charging, the lock screen wallpapered with Instagram notifications.

'And you didn't think to mention it until now?'

'I was distracted by how pretty you look when you're not covered in hike dirt,' she said sweetly. 'Also I was scrolling and I forgot.'

I shuffled back off my stool, crossing the kitchen to open the letter first. A thick sheet of monogrammed paper slid out of the envelope, a brief note written in elegant blue ink.

Perhaps a party is in order.
I will expect you tomorrow to discuss.
10.30 am
MM

'Who's sending you notes? Mr Bridgerton?' Bel asked.

'That would be Lord Bridgerton to you,' I replied, stashing the letter back in the envelope. 'It's from Myrna, the actress I told you about, who lives up the road?'

'The old lady who said you dressed like a toddler?'

Because of course that was the part she remembered.

'So who was blowing up your phone?' she asked without waiting for confirmation. 'It did not stop buzzing for like, ten whole minutes.'

Without a clue, I swiped it into life, an unfamiliar number on the screen.

Heard you're on holiday

Remember that time we went to Crete?

Hope you're having fun

But not too much fun

I dropped the phone like it was white-hot.

'Phoebe, what is it? Did something happen?' Bel jumped up from the sofa and bolted over to my side. 'You're not breathing – breathe, OK? Just breathe.'

'It's my ex,' I said, shaking my head again and again, as though I could undo my brain and set the messages back to unread. 'My ex messaged me.'

Waiting for my nod of permission, she picked up my phone and scanned the screen, her eyes flicking back and forth.

'I know you said you don't want to talk about it, but for this to make sense, I think you have to. These look pretty chill, Pheebs. I've had more aggressive texts from my dry cleaner.'

'Did your dry cleaner ruin your life?' I asked.

'He ruined my favourite little black dress and that's kind of the same thing,' she replied. 'What are the chances I'll ever find another Chanel cocktail dress for a hundred bucks at Goodwill? Slim to none, Phoebe, slim to none.'

'OK, yes, that is bad,' I admitted. 'But not as bad as Thomas.'

She turned the phone over and placed it face down. 'This is the guy who's getting married this weekend?'

'Yes.'

'And you still have feelings for him?'

It wasn't what she said, it was the way she said it. The same way everyone said it. Not quite pitying but there was a definite implication that whatever was wrong was my fault and I needed to let it go.

'Yes, I have feelings for him,' I replied. 'I hate him.'

She placed one hand on my shoulder, a reassuring weight that did nothing to help. 'Babe, I can see you're angry but you shouldn't hate people. It's like that old religious saying, "anger leads to hate and hate leads to the dark side", you know?'

'I know that's from *Star Wars*,' I replied, allowing my bottled up rage to flow through me until I was sure I could shoot lightning bolts out of my fingers.

222

'You're not listening, Bel. I really, really, really hate him. I hate him more than I hate going to the post office. I hate him more than making tea then finding out the milk has gone off.' I closed my eyes and made little fists, letting it all pour out. 'I hate him more than one of those little hygienic seals they put inside a bottle of shampoo that you only find when you're already in the shower.'

'Whoa,' Bel gasped.

At last. She understood.

'He is not a good person. Those are not chill messages, they are reminders that he exists. He's twisting the knife, it's his second favourite hobby after sticking it in your back in the first place.'

'Let's sit down,' Bel suggested, leading me away from the kitchen and all its sharp objects, across the big airy room to the sofa.

'Can you tell me what happened between the two of you?' she asked as I sank into the comfy cushions. 'I'd like to help if I can.'

'I appreciate it, really I do, but I've had help.' I scrunched the deep pile of the rug between my toes, left foot first then right foot, trying to remember all the tools Therese had taught me. Be present, concentrate on what's happening right now. 'But short of help hiding his body, I'm not sure there's anything else anyone can do.'

'Phoebe.' She knelt down on the floor in front of me, hands on my knees as they bounced up and down. 'You don't have to talk about it if you don't want to, but if you do, it all stays here with me. I won't tell anyone and I won't judge. I won't even react if you don't want me to.'

Closing my eyes, I fished through my feelings, trying to decide what was safe, what to share, where to start.

'He's not funny,' I said, the first trickle to find its way out of the floodgates. 'Even when we first met, I never thought he was funny. He calls Facebook "The Book of Face", he's obsessed with Piers Morgan and he looks like a sentient ham.'

'Thomas or Piers Morgan?'

'Either or.'

'Ham can be persuasive,' Bel reasoned. 'I've been charmed by ham before.'

'Yes, that's it. He's charming.' I held my hands out in front of me as though I was trying to crush the air between them. 'Everyone thinks he's so brilliant but they only see him in small doses. If they'd lived with him, they'd know he's the biggest arsehole to walk the earth since, well, let's stick with Piers Morgan, and that's probably not even fair to Piers.'

Bel sat beside me, patient and kind, not saying anything, not doing anything, quietly waiting for me to continue.

'Honestly, the whole story is very predictable and depressing,' I looked her right in the eye so she knew I meant it. 'He was amazing when we first started going out, then when we moved in together, he got more controlling, more manipulative. Instead of telling me I was beautiful and clever and funny, like he did in the beginning, it was "oh wow, you've made an effort today". Once he told me I was lucky fat arses had come into fashion, and instead of telling him to piss off, I laughed and agreed with him. I didn't eat proper food for a week after that.'

Bel covered my hand with her own but stayed quiet.

'When Gran died and Suzanne left the country, I was on my own and he knew it. He never got angry or violent, he was too clever for that. It was more subtle, bringing me down, complaining about my friends, reminding me how lucky I was to have someone like him.' I stopped as the fury rose up inside me again and pushed out a long, slow breath. 'I'd really rather not go into the specifics but it was dark.'

'You don't have to,' she replied. 'I believe you.'

Three such powerful words.

'I never thought something like that would happen to me,' I said with a rueful smile for silly past Phoebe. 'You see it all the time on TV, don't you? And you think, why don't they leave? Why can't they see what's going on? I thought I was too clever to fall for it but no, I walked right in and I stayed.'

'Until you left,' she reminded me. 'What changed?'

'I wish I could tell you there was a specific moment,' I said, eyes on my feet. The polish on my left little toe was chipped. I needed a pedicure. 'But there wasn't. One day I woke up and I knew I couldn't carry on, a random Wednesday, middle of the week. Nothing special about it at all. I called a helpline, they put me in touch with someone and she managed to fit me in the same day.'

'You went to see a therapist?'

I nodded. 'I'd thought about it before, when Gran died, but it's so hard to get things moving with your doctor. Turns out there are a lot of people who need help and I was at the bottom of a very long list. So I did some research online, found an organization that could help and that's how I met Therese. I never thought I'd be the sort of person who needed a therapist but now I can't imagine my life without her. The moment I walked into her office, I knew I had to leave him. I packed a bag that afternoon and was gone before he finished work.'

Bel squeezed my hand gently. 'I'm sorry. It can't have been easy to leave, you're so brave.'

'It was harder to think about it than it was to actually do it,' I replied, squeezing back. 'Because if I thought about it, I had to admit he didn't really love me, and if he didn't love me then I didn't have anyone.'

'You had Suzanne?'

I looked around my sister's house. Neat, tidy, clean, neutral. A place for everything, everything in its place.

'I did. But I didn't know how to tell her. She was out of the country by then. We would text all the time but we didn't talk often. The idea of calling her and admitting how stupid I'd been . . . it was too much. Besides, I was scared I'd lose her too.'

'I get it,' she replied. 'No need to explain. I'm so proud of you for asking for help when you needed it, I've been there, it's not easy.'

'Well, before you pop the champagne, it wasn't quite such a tidy ending,' I confessed, picking up one of Suzanne's plump cushions and fluffing it in my lap. 'A few months later, I found out he'd started seeing someone else. Therese helped me get through it and I did a really good job of putting it out of my mind. Even when he messaged me from time to time, like today, I deleted them and blocked his number or the account or whatever. I was doing so well. Until . . .'

'I know I said you didn't have to tell me anything you don't want to,' Bel breathed. 'But don't you dare leave me hanging here.'

'Fine, but I'm holding you to the no judgement part,' I warned. 'It was about a year ago, I saw her at the supermarket. I knew it was her, obviously I'd stalked her social media.'

'Obviously.'

'I didn't say anything because what would I say? Then he appeared and I left. Dropped my basket and walked out.'

'Totally understandable.'

'And then I saw them again,' I said with a sigh, the mental image coming back all too easily. 'Same supermarket a couple of months ago, only she looked like a totally different person. She'd grown her hair out long, she was wearing the kind of dress he always wanted me to wear which was totally not supermarket appropriate, by the way, and, God, Bel, she just looked so sad. She looked exactly like I did when I was with him. And I knew he was doing the same thing to her that he did to me.'

I paused for a moment to rub my hand against the soft fabric of the cushion and register the cool air on my skin. I was here, in LA, in Suzanne's house. Not there, not then. I could tell the story and be OK. 'So I decided I had to talk to her.'

'Oh.'

'And in hindsight,' I added slowly, 'I can see there is a chance I shouldn't have tried to have that conversation on her hen night.'

'Oh.'

227

'But it was the only time I knew he definitely wouldn't be there,' I protested. 'One of my old friends posted about it on Facebook and all logic went out the window. Off I went, convinced I was doing the right thing, found the bar, followed her to the toilets, gave her the fright of her life.'

'Ohhh,' Bel said, gnawing on her thumbnail. 'Yikes.'

'All I said was if she needed someone to talk to, I would be there for her, but she freaked out and ran off and now everyone thinks I'm still obsessed with him and they're getting married at the weekend.' I put the cushion down and craned my neck over my shoulder. 'Do you fancy a drink? I really fancy a drink.'

'What did Therese say?' Bel asked cautiously as I tugged at the little straps dangling from the neck of my sweatshirt.

'Nothing. I'd stopped seeing her a month before,' I said with a feather-light laugh. 'I thought everything was done, only it wasn't. I was over Thomas but I wasn't over what he'd done to me. Therese compared it to a river after it runs dry – the water is all gone but it can take years for the landscape to recover, and even when it does, it will never be quite the same as before.'

'I don't know if I can say this emphatically enough,' she replied, pounding a fist into her open palm. 'But *fuck* that guy.'

'Couldn't agree more.' I slumped backwards, all the bones in my body seeming to liquefy at once. If I wasn't exhausted after the hike, I was now. 'All I want is for him to disappear from the planet completely.'

'We could cast a spell,' she suggested brightly. 'I know a pretty great shaman in Laurel Canyon.'

'Let's put a pin in that.'

'Putting a pin in it would be part of the spell.' She stood up, feet hips-width apart, one hand planted on her hip and the other pointing directly at me, part superhero, part girl group member, all Bel. 'Here's what I know. You, Phoebe Chapman, are amazing. You were in a shitty situation, you recognized it, you asked for help and you got out. Not only that but you tried to help another woman when she was in need. It's not your fault she wasn't ready to accept the help, you did your best.'

'Is that something else you learned on TikTok?' I asked, my burning rage simmering down into soothing, warming love for her.

'TikTok is free, therapy is expensive,' she replied. 'You might laugh, but positive affirmations could do you the world of good. Shake out all that negative self-talk you're still carrying around and don't say you're not because you totally are. I can see it in your aura.'

'That's not negative self-talk, it's called being British.' I pulled my feet up underneath me and curled into the cushions as her phone trilled with a text.

'Pizza's ready,' she announced. 'Shall I tell Ren to bring it here?'

God, no, I thought to myself.

'God, no,' I said out loud.

I didn't realize the same words that had gone through my head had come out of my mouth until I saw the look on Bel's face.

'I mean I'm really tired,' I added. 'Can you tell Ren I'm not feeling well or something?'

'Sure thing.' She rose to her feet, slipping her phone

into the waistband of her leggings. 'You want me to come by later, bring you a slice?'

'There's loads of food in the fridge, I'll find something. You don't have to worry about me.'

'I think you'll find I do. We're friends, remember?' Bel sang as she sailed out of the room towards the front door. 'I'll call you tomorrow, don't forget to hydrate!'

Friends. A real, proper, genuine friend.

Wow. It had been a while.

The door closed behind her and my eyelids slipped shut. Between the exercise and the emotional upheaval, I was completely done for.

I pulled a blanket off the back of the settee and draped it over my legs, resting my head on the soft cushion I'd been cradling. A quick nap couldn't hurt. If I closed my eyes for a minute, I'd be refreshed and renewed and ready to do something productive with the rest of my afternoon.

Before I could even finish my thought, I was fast asleep.

CHAPTER SIXTEEN

'The party will be on Friday,' Myrna announced the moment I walked through her door the next morning. 'And your attendance is mandatory.'

'How are we going to plan a party in four days?' I asked, a shimmer of excitement washing over me. I really did love a project. I could get lost in a project. 'Isn't there a lot to do?'

'Oh yes.' She rattled the backs of my legs with her walking stick, driving me into the sitting room like an errant sheep. 'Endless arrangements to be made. Invitations to send, catering to organize, decorations to plan, and none of it is getting any closer to being done with you stood in the middle of the room and staring at me like you've never seen a woman in a vintage Chanel suit before.'

'Probably because I haven't,' I replied. 'It's lovely.'

She pinched at the black and white material of her tweedy two-piece, the classic boxy jacket and demure knee-length skirt tailored to her precise measurements.

I was sure it would spontaneously combust if anyone else even tried it on. Her make-up was flawlessly applied and white bob professionally set. Myrna looked like what she was, Hollywood royalty.

'A Chanel suit is what one wears when one wants to be taken seriously,' she said. 'Or it used to be. Perhaps they sell them to anyone these days. I recall the time I saw Jayne Mansfield in the atelier in Paris and they wouldn't even let her try one on. As Wally used to say, she had too much bosom for her own good and they're hideously unflattering to anyone with curves, but I always did have the hips of a twelve-year-old boy.'

'There's always a silver lining,' I said as she ran a gloved hand over her slender silhouette.

Despite my plans, to do something, anything productive with the rest of my Monday, I somehow managed to sleep all the way through to Tuesday morning. I could almost feel Gran smoothing my hair down and telling me I must have needed it and truly, I did. When I woke up, I deleted the unwelcome texts, blocked the new number and felt a thousand times better. Airing out my anxieties had made them more manageable. I told someone my story and lived to tell the tale, and what's more, she hadn't turned away. Rather, Bel had messaged, offering to come over when she'd finished walking half the dogs in Beverly Hills but that wouldn't be until much later in the day, and Suzanne left a voice note, claiming she was finally returning to LA the following afternoon, which I would believe when I saw her sitting on the sofa. Helping plan a little party, running to the supermarket for chips and dips, a few bottles of wine and some plastic glasses was very appealing, a welcome distraction to take my mind off, well, everything.

But Myrna, it seemed, had other ideas.

'Is this a bad time?' I asked when she slipped her feet into a pair of black patent heels. Sensible heels but heels all the same. 'I thought your note said ten thirty but if you're going somewhere, I can come back later.'

She reached for a rectangular black leather handbag with a long silver chain and hung it carefully from her shoulder without breaking eye contact with the mirror. '*I'm* not going anywhere. We are. Follow me.'

Giving herself a satisfied nod, she marched out into the hall with me close behind, moving faster than was reasonable for an octogenarian in heels using a cane. Either she'd had a very large coffee or an even larger infusion of stem cells, and it was impossible to say which was more likely.

'I can help with the party,' I offered, scooting after her. 'I'm good at organizing things.'

A man in black tails and white gloves who I had never seen before appeared by the front door, holding it open as Myrna approached, and she walked straight outside without breaking stride.

'You've got a butler?' I asked, incredulous. 'Where was he when I arrived?'

'Calling the driver,' she replied as a huge silver Rolls-Royce drove around the side of the house and stopped right in front of us.

'You've got a driver?'

'Darling, don't be so gauche,' she warned as the driver opened the passenger door in his grey uniform and matching peaked cap. 'One does not need help when one has money. If Myrna Moore throws a party, it will be the party of the century. Wally wouldn't want me to go out with a whimper when I deserve a bang.'

Again, I wasn't sure what kind of bang she meant but was certain that if she wanted it, no human on earth would dare say no.

'I've hired the best event planner in town and given him a blank cheque. I expect I'll be bankrupt by morning but what am I saving for? I could be dead before we get the next rainy day in LA. So you see, there is nothing for us to "do" for the party, other than attend.'

I didn't know what to say so I didn't say anything. The last party I went to was a colleague's daughter's first birthday and it ended when the baby's dad (who had one job) bought a knockoff Colin the Caterpillar cake instead of a proper M&S one and the last I'd heard, they were getting divorced.

'Can I ask where we're going?'

She tossed her cane across the back seat and gave me a filthy look while the driver moved swiftly around the back of the car to open the other door for me. I entered head first like Alice down the rabbit hole only to find it wasn't a car at all, it was a hotel room on wheels. Myrna relaxed against the supple cream leather and turned to me with one perfectly arched eyebrow.

'We're going shopping,' she said, not bothering with a seatbelt even as we started off down the driveway. 'If you're going to attend one of my soirees, I'd like to know you will be properly attired.'

'Just so you know,' I replied, hoping to strike the balance between tact and panic, 'I am on a limited budget.'

Myrna pressed a button and a crystal-clear glass screen rose between us and the driver. 'Just so you know, I am not.'

'Yes, but—'

'And I loathe penny pinchers,' she added, glowering at me from across the car.

'How do you feel about shoplifters?'

She peered down at the strappy leather sandals I'd liberated from Suzanne's wardrobe and I felt my toes turn in towards each other like an anxious pigeon. 'I don't hate your shoes today,' she said. 'Congratulations.'

Basking in the warm glow of her compliment, I nodded my thanks, mentally apologizing to my credit card and preparing us both for whatever she had in store.

'Myrna, I look like a Minion.'

The sales assistant raised a hand to hide a snigger, but she wasn't quite fast enough. Displayed on a raised dais in the private dressing room of a Beverly Hills boutique, I lifted my arms and an explosion of blue tulle sprang to life, floating up around the canary-yellow bodice and threatening to swallow me whole.

'I saw that movie,' Myrna sniffed. 'Those horrible little things, running around, up to no good. It reminded me of Congress. But I agree this is not the dress for you.' She turned to the assistant with a smile as sweet as honey. 'Do you have anything a little less formal?' she purred. 'She can't carry something this, shall we say, avant garde? Simple and sophisticated, I think, is what we're going for.'

The woman disappeared through a soft-closing door, leaving us alone with a magnum of champagne, a jug of freshly squeezed orange juice, three different kinds of bottled water and a platter of expensive-looking meat, cheese and fruit that I fully intended to wrap in napkins and stick in my handbag for later when Myrna wasn't looking.

I flopped to the floor and the tulle mushroom cloud masquerading as a dress puffed up around me. 'We must have been to every shop in the city – you didn't like any of the dresses?'

'Nonsense, we've been to three,' she replied. 'And no, I did not. Off the rack has only gotten worse over the years, I should have known better than to expect to find something this easily.'

Straining, I reached for a grape and only a grape and popped it in my mouth. I didn't dare eat anything else until I was out of this extremely restrictive corset. 'I buy most of my clothes online. Shopping gives me anxiety.'

'You don't like shopping; it does not give you anxiety,' she clucked. 'If anything was to trouble your mental well-being, it should be those dungarees you insist on wearing. We ought to set them on fire and bury the remains to ensure no one else has to suffer them.'

'But then I'd have to walk around in my underwear,' I replied. 'Hardly very ladylike.'

'It may be preferable,' Myrna commented. 'And from what I see people wearing these days, entirely de rigueur.'

The plush dressing room smelled like expensive candles and money, and there were racks and racks of gowns Myrna had selected, considered and found wanting, lining the stark white walls, a magpie's nest of gold and silver beading, iridescent sequins and shimmering, liquid fabrics.

'How fancy is your party going to be?' I asked as Myrna reached for her mimosa. Technically, it was a mimosa in that she showed her champagne the jug of orange juice, even if very little made it into the actual glass. 'Shouldn't we be looking for something for you to wear?'

'It's going to be everything a good party should be,' she replied. 'We were famously good entertainers, Wally and I. If he hadn't passed away, I sometimes wonder if that would have been our legacy. Esther Williams jumping into the pool in her gown to perform a routine, Lauren Bacall dancing with Gene Kelly in the ballroom and the Kennedy boys getting up to God only knows what with God knows who in the gardens. And it wouldn't be me, but there are some who will tell you Liz Taylor and Richard Burton consummated their relationship in our greenhouse rather than on the set of *Cleopatra*.'

'And the rest is history,' I exhaled happily. 'What a love story.'

'They married and divorced each other twice and now they're both dead.'

'It's still history,' I pouted. 'So that's what we're going for? Fully clothed swimming and celebrities shagging in between the tomato plants?'

'Don't be vulgar.' Myrna frowned and the delicate, translucent skin of her forehead crinkled like crepe paper. 'But yes.'

'Can't wait,' I said, pushing my luck with a second grape.

'Wally always said it wasn't a proper party unless you'd kissed a stranger or fired a pistol. I fear my kissing days are over, but I do still keep a loaded gun in the house.'

I gulped so hard, I felt my corset protest. 'Now I think about it, I might be busy Friday night.'

'As for what I will wear,' she added, 'I haven't decided yet. All of my custom gowns still fit; they have all been properly preserved. I never did like to plan too far ahead; I imagine I'll decide on the day.'

'Nothing too restrictive,' I suggested as the dressing room door clicked open and the sales assistant returned, drowning in garment bags. 'You want to be able to fire that pistol and get your leg over.'

'The girl's a poet,' Myrna declared with a one-sided smile.

'I'm a copywriter,' I clarified for the nameless assistant. A boutique like this didn't have anything as utilitarian as name badges for the staff. Who needed names when rich people could come in and point at people instead?

'What do you think that is, other than a modern poet?' Myrna replied. 'The idea of a man wandering around with a quill, sleeves billowing in the wind waiting for inspiration to strike is utter nonsense. Know your history, the greats wrote to order just as you do. You mustn't belittle your own work;, it's tacky and beneath you.'

'Your mom is very wise,' the assistant said as she unfurled a full-length red gown so beautiful, if I hadn't already been sitting on the floor, I would have fallen over.

'Oh, no,' I said quickly, looking over at the older woman. 'Myrna isn't my mum.'

'No,' she confirmed. 'I'm her lover.'

The sales assistant froze; the shirred chiffon fabric

she held in her hand fluttered under the air-conditioning vent as Myrna hooted with laughter.

'I think that's the one,' she said, gesturing towards the red dress with her champagne. 'Try it on, darling, I do so love to see you in red.'

'You're a monster,' I told her as the assistant scurried away again.

She raised her glass in a one-woman toast. 'That's a funny way to say thank you but you're welcome nonetheless.'

The dress was stunning. Three slender straps curled around my neck, holding up the cherry-red empire line gown, silk chiffon ruching over the chest and falling in sleek pleats all the way past my feet where the fabric pooled on the floor. It moved when I moved, brushing against my body to suggest the shape underneath it but never clinging.

'It's beautiful, Myrna, but I can't buy this,' I said, running my hands over the fabric. 'Even if I could afford it, which I definitely cannot, I'd only ever wear it once. This dress deserves so much more.'

'The chances of a designer gown sold in LA being worn even once are slim to none,' she replied, rolling her eyes. 'Most of these dresses will be bought or borrowed by stylists, hidden in a closet and never see the light of day. How many people do you see repeating outfits on the red carpet?'

'I don't know, I don't read a lot of celebrity gossip,' I said, hoping she would not ask to see my browser history. 'It's still too much. I'm sure Suzanne has something I can borrow.'

'And I'm sure she doesn't.'

She stood and rattled the door of the dressing room with her cane as I shimmied out of the dress and back into my jeans and T-shirt. 'We'll take the red one, darling,' she said when the apprehensive-looking assistant's head popped inside. 'Take it up by three inches and have it delivered before Friday. Put it on my account.'

I watched the dress, my dress, as it was whisked away by the happiest on-commission sales assistant in the world. 'Myrna, I can't let you buy me that dress.'

'You're not letting me do anything,' she replied. 'I'm buying it because you should have it and because I don't trust you to dress yourself for my party, from your own or your sister's wardrobe.'

'Well, when you put it like that, thank you very much.' I sat on a small velour stool, struggling with the tiny gold buckles of my borrowed sandals. 'Would it be all right if my sister comes as well? You don't need to worry, she goes to posh events all the time, she's a much better dresser than I am.'

'She couldn't be much worse.'

I took it as a yes.

'And why don't you invite Joe and Rosa's grandson?' she suggested. 'It would be nice to meet him. I'm assuming he's a handsome one given the way you blush every time his name comes up. Now hurry up, I've booked a table at the Polo Lounge for tea.'

Cackling to herself, she cruised out of the dressing room to find her Rolls-Royce, leaving me shoeless and speechless.

Myrna Moore never, ever missed a trick.

*   *   *

Even when the days were hot, the LA nights were perfectly cool. At sunset, after a long day of not party planning with Myrna, I finally found myself on the little balcony outside the guest bedroom, flicking through the stack of books I'd brought with me and barely made a dent in. So much for my holiday plan, I thought, tapping my fingernails against the notebook in my lap. Two weeks of reading and eating and flopping around in the pool like that walrus in Denmark who sank all those boats. It really had not worked out that way.

I picked up the first book in my pile, stroking the soft cover, smooth under my fingers. I loved books. I loved words. Gran was a big reader and there were few things I'd ever loved more than a wintery Sunday afternoon spent next to her on the settee, heating on, mugs full of tea, both of us lost in a story. While I would read anything and everything, Margaret Chapman was an avowed romance reader. She had an overwhelming collection in the back bedroom, spanning every subgenre from paranormal romance to doctors and nurses, the fantastical all the way through to the everyday. The one thing they all had in common was a happily ever after.

But it was more than simple escapism. Gran didn't care for horror or thrillers or crime sagas because she'd seen enough unhappiness in her life, losing her husband in her forties, helping Mum through an ugly break-up then practically raising her kids for her; it wasn't an easy life. Why wouldn't she choose to surround herself with love and happiness? All words had power; the ones we read, the ones we spoke and the ones we listened to. I understood that now. We had to be careful which ones we let in.

I pulled my denim jacket around my shoulders as the

evening grew darker and saw a light go on in Ren's house. An upstairs window glowed yellow until the curtains closed and it all went back to black. My heart fluttered in my chest, just knowing he was close by. It was a crush. A harmless crush. I'd been caught off guard by too much sunshine and visible muscle groups. Would I feel this way if we'd met in the car park of Home Bargains on a rainy Wednesday? Obviously not. Poor Ren, I thought; I would get over my crush but he would probably never get to experience the wonder that was Home Bargains. His suffering was much worse than mine.

This was nothing. Even if it felt like something.

I picked up my pen and let it hover tantalizingly over the notebook in my lap.

Who decides when to give it a name? When the whispers in our heart are safe to shout from the rooftops. A fragile, fledging thing, too delicate to share, or brash and brazen and loud, loud, loud.

Let it all out, I told myself. Open all the doors and windows and air your feelings. Write it down and leave it on the page, like Therese always said.

Who decides what to call it? Does it have to last forever? Does it have to be returned in kind, or can it stand alone and still be admired? Different shades of the same colour, light refracted by a diamond. I could be the only one who knows, the only one who saw the sun on your skin and the water reflected in your eyes. I could be the only one who ever knew and it would be enough.

When I put down my pen, the houses in the distance that spent the day as faded charcoal silhouettes, stood out in sharp black relief against the paling sky and the puffball clouds glowed like hot coals. Were the sunsets this beautiful at home? I couldn't remember the last time I'd bothered to look. That was something that would have to change. I re-read my words and pursed my lips together tightly. Hmm. It really didn't feel like nothing.

'It's nothing but a crush,' I said out loud as the solar-powered lights that lined Ren's flowerbeds flickered into life in the garden below and up above all the stars came out of hiding, announcing the end of another day. 'A harmless summer crush.'

I tore the page out of my notebook and folded it into a tight little square before sticking it deep in my jacket pocket where I could touch it but not see it. Where it could be real but not real.

I knew my words had power. Now it was up to me to decide which ones I would listen to.

CHAPTER SEVENTEEN

Suzanne did not stop talking from the moment she walked through the door. By the time she paused for breath, I'd made us both a vanilla caramel iced oat milk latte, eaten an entire chocolate croissant, paid my gas and electric bills on my phone and finally worked a knot out of my necklace that had been there for two and a half years.

'I should leave,' she declared in between sips of her coffee. 'That's what I should do. I should walk into the CEO's office and say, this is not my circus, they are not my monkeys, I do not want to deal with this any more.'

'Nothing worse than other people's monkeys,' I said with as much empathy as I could muster for my very wealthy sister. 'Hopefully they haven't got the pox.'

'They should be put down regardless.' She let her head loll back so far, I thought it might fall off. 'I really should leave.'

'Only one problem,' I pointed out. 'You love your job.'

She pressed her hands against her face and gave a disheartened chuckle.

'I know. What's wrong with me?'

'Nothing.' I placed an obscenely large cinnamon bun on her lap and her face lit up like Christmas. Bel had filled me in on where to get the good stuff; now I too had the power of the Morning Buns. 'It's the way you're made.'

'Love it or not, I've told them not to contact me until Monday. Are you ready for some super-concentrated, extra-special powered-by-guilt sister time?'

'My very favourite kind!' I replied. 'I've got a few plans but nothing we can't work around.'

I was wrong about Suzanne's head. It popped back up like a jack-in-the-box.

'Plans? What plans? What plans?'

'A party on Friday night,' I replied.

'Did Bel invite you?' she asked. 'Can I come?'

'No and yes,' I said, nudging her to take a bite out of the Morning Bun. 'Remember when I delivered those packages to 4101 Parva? It turns out this old – I mean, older lady lives there who used to be an actress and we started talking and I went back to visit and now she's having a big party on Friday night and I think we're sort of friends?'

It wasn't disbelief on my sister's face so much as she was looking at me like I'd had a mental breakdown.

'You made friends with the woman who lives at 4101?'

'Yep, Myrna Moore.'

'And you've been visiting her?'

'That's right.'

'And she's invited you to a party?'

'Technically, the party was my idea,' I admitted. 'She's moving into a retirement home and wants to have one last blowout before she goes.'

'What sort of blowout do you have when you're a hundred years old?' Suzanne scoffed. 'Tea and cakes and haemorrhoid cream?'

'She's eighty-two and from what I've gathered so far it's more likely to be oysters, champagne and poppers, but I can't speak to the haemorrhoid cream. What people put in or on their bum is between them and their god.'

'Fine, I'm officially intrigued,' she replied through a mouthful of warm cinnamon goodness. 'And if you can fit me into your busy schedule this evening, I've got the company season tickets for the Dodgers game tonight.'

Sitting bolt upright, I gave my sister a very serious look. 'Did you just suggest we go to a sporting event?'

'The tickets include free food and drink.'

'Fine, I'm in.' I held my hand up for a high five which she missed spectacularly.

'I've got four tickets,' she added. 'So I invited Bel and told her to bring Ren.'

'Oh good,' I replied. 'Fun.'

What could be more fun than spending several hours outside in a stadium watching a game I didn't understand with my wonderful new friend who I loved and her amazing new boyfriend who I definitely didn't really fancy at all, honest? Nothing. Maybe sticking hot pokers in my eyes but I couldn't think of another single thing.

'Hopefully this one works out for her,' Suze said, standing up to stretch. 'That girl has the worst luck when it comes to dating. She's even worse than you.'

'And how's your love life?' I asked, deflecting the blow. 'I must have missed the queue of men beating a path to the door.'

'Be ready to leave by four,' she replied. Suzanne was pretty good at deflecting herself. 'I want to make sure I get my bobblehead.'

'I don't even know who you are any more,' I yelled after her as she marched inside, throwing up a very sisterly middle-finger salute.

'This place is ridiculous,' I declared when we finally trekked across the acres of car park and arrived at Dodger Stadium. 'It's massive.'

'Almost as big as your mouth,' Suzanne said sweetly as she punched me in the shoulder.

The Chapman girls were not sports people. I didn't have a favourite football team, I couldn't understand rugby and cricket was, to put it politely, for wankers. I was probably being harsh, but the thought of running up and down a field wearing white clothes then drinking tea was completely insane. The only sport Suzanne had ever shown any interest in before now was professional wrestling, and Gran banned us from watching it after a flying elbow off the top of the climbing frame resulted in bruised ribs for me and a broken wrist for Suzanne.

A cheerful man with a weathered face scanned our tickets as I attempted to catch my breath. Perhaps he hadn't had to climb roughly fourteen thousand stairs to get to the gate. 'The game hasn't even started and I'm knackered,' I grumbled. 'How long until we can go home?'

'Game starts at seven.' She was altogether too chipper

for my liking. It wasn't natural. 'We'll probably be home by eleven, half past at the latest.'

'Four hours?' I found myself frozen to the spot, only to be immediately but amiably jostled by twenty different people in oversized white shirts. 'How can a game of rounders last four hours?'

Suzanne grabbed my wrist like a naughty toddler and pulled me out of the flow of traffic. 'Be very careful what you say. People here take their baseball very seriously and I am not getting involved if you get in a fight. I told you when you got into one with that girl in Year Eight, first time, last time.'

'Verity Shenton,' I muttered. 'What a cow.'

'I doubt I'll be able to talk the LAPD around as easily as I did Mr Shackley,' she warned. 'So cheer up and start enjoying yourself.'

'I can't believe you're wearing a baseball cap.' I dropped my head and followed behind like a good little sister. 'You look stupid.'

'You *are* stupid,' she volleyed back. 'Let's find our bloody seats before I change my mind and take you home.'

With a tiny smile, I followed her down the concrete corridor, happy to know some things never changed.

I should have known our seats would be amazing, Suzanne never did anything by halves, but we were so close to the pitch, I could practically see the pores on the faces of the very handsome players and just like that, I was all turned around on baseball.

'You know, a lot of people say there is no defensible excuse for working at your terrible company,' I said to

Suzanne as our beers were delivered right to our seats by a very peppy young man with fantastic teeth. 'But I for one think there might be some benefits to it.'

'No, it's a terrible place and we're all going to hell,' she replied, kicking her legs up on the little ledge in front of us. 'I'm planning to make amends by planting a bug that makes everyone's phone explode the day after I die.'

'Seems a bit dramatic?'

'Fine, I'll leave all my money to charity.'

'I've changed my mind,' I replied. 'Do the phone thing, I want the money.'

'Oh my gosh, Suzie, these seats are amazing!'

There was no time for a snappy Suzanne comeback; Bel bounded down the aisle towards us like a Labrador whose owner had just got back from the war. Behind her, Ren shuffled down the row, a drink in each hand and a constant apology on his lips as he did his best to keep from standing on anyone's feet. Closing my eyes and leaning as far back as I could, I held my breath as he passed by me. Even over the sharp smell of hot dogs and beer and fifty thousand people, his signature scent lingered in the air.

'Your first baseball game!' Bel said, dropping into the seat next to mine. 'Are you excited?'

'Can't say I'm a massively sporty person.' I kept my voice down in fear of upsetting the thousands of rabid fans all around me. 'And the only thing I know about baseball is that first base means kissing and after that I'm confused. I'm assuming they don't actually touch each other up when they get to second and shag when they get a home run?'

'There's always a lot of ass-slapping at these things so don't write the possibility off completely,' she replied. 'Given half a chance, I think they'd do it.'

I peeled off my denim jacket, warmed through by the early evening sun. 'You're officially my baseball mentor. Do you come here a lot?'

She glanced over at Ren, who raised his hand to me in a hello and I waved back. There was no point trying to shout over the roar of the crowd; even one seat away it would have been impossible to make myself heard.

'I love a ball game,' Bel said loudly with a wink in my direction. 'Taking in a game at the ol' park is one of my favourite things in the whole world.' Clasping Ren's hand in hers, her nails painted royal blue and decorated with tiny baseballs, she leaned across the armrest to hiss in my ear. 'I don't get it at all. I've only ever been to one game and I got so drunk, I fell asleep, and when I woke up, everyone was leaving. But I want Ren to think I know my stuff. All the way over here he was talking statistics and throwing out names and I had zero clue what he was talking about.'

'But men love explaining things to their girlfriends, even the good ones,' I whispered back. 'I bet he would have jumped at the chance to baseball-splain.'

'This is why I need you with me all the time,' she said, wincing. 'I can't believe I didn't think of that.'

With Suzanne to my left and Ren to Bel's right, the four of us cheered as the organ played and the Los Angeles Dodgers ran out on to the field.

'I love you and this is amazing and thank you very much for bringing me,' I whispered to Suzanne, a full box of dropped popcorn raining down on us from the section above. 'But do we have to stay for the whole thing?'

'Shut up and try to enjoy yourself,' she replied, sounding more like Gran than ever. 'It's hardly going to be the worst night of your life.'

'Well,' I said, picking popcorn out of my hair. 'We'll see about that.'

'I'm having the greatest night of my life!' I bellowed directly into my sister's ear, three hours and seven innings later. 'Baseball is the most incredible thing on the planet!'

And I wasn't lying. I loved it completely. Baseball wasn't just a game, it was an immersive experience. There were chants, there were songs, there were dances, they even had breaks between the innings where people could play games to win prizes up on the big screen. By the time Suzanne told me to stand up to sing a little song and stretch, I was three giant beers in and deliriously happy. Baseball was my favourite thing ever. I didn't have a clue what was going on but I was obsessed.

'They're doing the wave!' I gushed as thousands of people rose out of their seats, cheering and raising their arms in unison. 'Have you ever seen anything more beautiful?'

'Have you eaten anything besides nachos?' Suzanne asked, giving the most possible big sister energy.

'I may never eat anything other than nachos ever again.' I held out the little plastic baseball cap that had once contained a handful of tortilla chips and some sort of orange 'cheese' for her to see. 'Also, I've had three beers which were very filling.'

'You're going to be so ill tomorrow,' she predicted,

standing up with her handbag tucked under her arm, the spitting image of our gran. 'I'm going to get you something proper to eat, don't even think about ordering another drink.'

'Definitely won't,' I replied with a salute. 'But could you get me a margarita if you see one?'

Even though the evening had turned pleasantly cool, I was very warm. There was a gentle fuzziness at the edges of my vision and all I could do was smile. I felt wonderful, all my cares thousands of miles away.

'It's so cold,' Bel said with a theatrical shiver. 'Ren, are you cold?'

'I'm fine,' he replied, his eyes trained on the field. 'I have a blanket in the truck if you want to go get it?'

Ren was so invested in the game, he hadn't eaten so much as a single nacho. I could not relate. With a subtle eye-roll in my direction, Bel slid down in her seat, lips twisted. Apparently, we had found the boundary of his chivalry and that boundary was the Los Angeles Dodgers. I handed the baseball widow my jacket and with a grateful smile, she slid her arms through the sleeves, digging her hands deep into the pockets.

'So you get three chances to hit it?' I said as I leaned over Suzanne's empty seat and took a discreet sip of her beer. She said I couldn't order another drink, not that I couldn't drink hers. 'And then you're out?'

'Three strikes and you're out,' Ren replied without looking at me. He was still highly focused. 'But if the pitcher throws four balls out of the strike zone and the batter doesn't swing, they walk the batter. And that doesn't take foul balls into consideration.'

'I have no idea what you just said,' I told him as I

clapped my hands in time to the music. Or at least mostly in time to the music. 'And to think people struggle with the offside rule.'

Between us, Bel pulled a tightly folded square of paper out of the pocket of my jacket, flicking it between her fingers. I felt bad for her, it was easy to see she was incredibly bored, but what kind of person could be bored at baseball?

'How come they're wearing belts?' I asked, marvelling at the absurdity. 'Look, that one is wearing a proper leather belt with a buckle. What if he falls over and does himself a mischief?'

'What's this?'

'I don't know, a receipt?' I looked over to see her unfolding the piece of paper she'd found in my pocket and shrugged. 'I thought an old man was trying to give me his phone number yesterday but it was a leaflet for his naked yoga class. If it's that, don't look – there are pictures and they are not good.'

'Who decides when to give it a name?' Bel read out loud. 'When the whispers in our heart are safe to shout from the rooftops.'

Every single muscle in my body clenched at the same time. I felt so tense and dense, I could have stopped a runaway train if you'd thrown me in its path.

'What was that?' Ren's head spun around so fast, the people in the row behind us must have thought he was possessed. 'What did you say?'

'Phoebe?' Bel said, pinching the piece of paper between her thumb and forefinger. 'What is this?'

What is it? I repeated in my head. What is it? What is it?

'Oh, there it is!' I managed to say after far too long, sitting up as my stomach sank. 'Bel, it's the other letter you wrote for Ren. I must have put it in my pocket for safekeeping then forgot it was there. I'm so embarrassed, I thought I'd lost it.'

All at once, Ren didn't seem terribly interested in the baseball any more.

'You wrote me another letter?' he asked.

'I did?' Bel's inflection rose just enough to give both Ren and me pause. 'I mean, yeah, I did.'

'And you left it at mine when you were there on Monday,' I added. 'I found it after you left.'

'After the hike,' she replied, rereading the note, every inch of my skin turning scarlet. 'This was written after the hike.'

'Yes,' I said, biting my bottom lip. 'I'm sorry.'

'No problem,' Bel said lightly, folding the piece of paper in half along a well-worn crease and sticking it back in her pocket. 'Don't sweat it.'

But I was sweating so much, I had very little hope for the natural deodorant I'd swiped from Suzanne's bathroom cabinet.

Ren held out his hand. 'Can I have it?' he asked.

'You want it now?' Bel replied. 'You want to read it here?'

'It's for me, isn't it?' he said, nodding.

'You don't want to read something like that in the middle of a baseball game,' I said, my heavy heart pounding in my ears like a jackhammer. 'This is hardly the right kind of atmosphere for something so . . .'

'Intimate.' Bel finished my sentence for me before standing abruptly, empty peanut shells falling from her lap onto the floor. She stuffed her hands even deeper into the pockets of my jacket, the look on her face inscrutable. Not a good sign for open-book Bel.

'I'm going to check out the store,' she announced, pushing her hair away from her face. 'Anyone need anything?'

'I'm good,' I replied, even though it was far from the truth. She shuffled down the line of seats, arse to face, ran up the stairs and melted away into the crowd. As soon as she was gone, I turned to Ren, my left foot tapping so fast, it was a surprise when I didn't drill my way through the concrete floor. 'So,' I said. 'Tell me more about these foul balls.'

Instead, he threw up his hands, the woman to his left ducking right before he took her eye out.

'I don't get it,' he exclaimed. 'Why wouldn't she want me to read a letter if she wrote it for me?'

Probably because she wanted to read it herself first, I thought, reaching for Suzanne's beer a second time.

'I don't understand, it's like she's two different people,' Ren sighed. 'Why is she pretending with me? Why can't she be real?'

'Could be she's not pretending,' I suggested. 'People are multidimensional, you know.'

But he wasn't listening, already far too busy working through his worst-case scenarios.

'Oh my God,' his face turned ashen. 'What if she didn't want me to read it because that letter wasn't for me? What if that was for someone else?'

'I'm one hundred per cent positive it wasn't written for anyone else,' I said to a fretful Ren with an earnest smile that I hoped was only slightly diminished by the blue-sequinned cowboy hat I'd been wearing for the last two hours. 'She really, really likes you and you only just met, there's still so much to find out about each other. You can't hang your whole heart on one letter.'

'Two letters.'

He shook his head as he slipped out of his seat and into Bel's. 'I don't know what I'm doing.'

His leg pressed against mine and, even though I tried to fight it, I took one breath in and we were back in the woods. All of the fifty thousand people around us, gone.

'Who does?' I replied, pinching my shoulders together.

Ren laughed and leaned in towards me, just enough for his shoulder to rest against mine.

'Sorry, you don't want to hear about all this. Are you having a good time?'

'Fantastic time,' I squeaked. My palms were wet from the condensation on my borrowed beer and clammy from feeling all my feelings, and I wiped them on my jeans when he wasn't looking. 'You?'

'It's a great game,' he said, nodding and shaking his head at the same time, not really answering the question. 'We have a pretty intense rivalry going with the Giants; we swept them in San Francisco, so they're going to want to return the favour tonight.'

'I don't know what any of that means but yes, absolutely,' I yelled over the crowd, one of our players whacking the ball and running for first base. 'Are we still winning?'

'Yeah, but we're going to have to pull our pitcher pretty soon and I don't love our bullpen tonight. Sure could use a three-run homer from Mookie right now.'

'If you say so,' I replied, fizzing happily when he laughed.

Everything went quiet for a moment. One of the players walked out onto the field (not a pitch, according to Ren), positioned himself in a slight squat, pulled back his bat and hit the ball, sending it flying through the air and out into the crowded benches on the far side of the stadium.

'Bloody hell,' I gasped as Ren leapt out of his seat and cheered. 'What happens if it hits someone?'

'You get to keep the ball!' he yelled as though it was a good thing. 'Five zero, baby – let's go, Dodgers!'

All around the stadium, every kind of human celebrated in every kind of way, yelling, waving, clapping, kissing. Even the odd Giants fans dotted in between the vast swathes of Dodger blue seemed OK with it, taking a good-natured jostling from their friends. I couldn't believe they didn't have an away section, but I hadn't heard a single person sing a single note of an offensive song and not once had anyone called the sexual preferences of a player's wife into question. It was all so wholesome. No matter which team you supported, everyone was a baseball fan, the mums, the dads, grandmas and grandads, toddlers, teenagers and even tiny babies who really came into their own when the organist played 'Circle of Life' between the fourth and fifth innings and every proud papa in the place held their progeny aloft and pretended they were Simba.

As the crowd calmed itself, a sweet love song started up through the loudspeaker and the babies on the Jumbotron were replaced by throbbing pink love hearts. A happy-looking couple, who looked thrilled to see their faces blown up twenty feet tall, filled the screen.

'What's happening?' I asked Ren. 'Should I know who they are?'

'It's the Kiss Cam,' he replied. The couple on the Jumbotron kissed then broke apart laughing with everyone cheering them on. 'It's another baseball thing.'

'This game really is so nice,' I sniffed, almost moved to tears as an elderly couple shared a delicate peck on the lips. 'I almost feel bad for always pretending I had period pains to get out of rounders. It's all so lovely.'

The camera cut away from the sweet older couple and landed on a much younger man and woman who immediately launched into the kind of clinch I could only hope their mothers never saw.

'Spoke too soon,' I muttered, looking away. I'd had far too many drinks to see that much of someone else's tongue.

And then everyone around us started yelling.

At first I couldn't understand why the next girl on screen looked so familiar. Blonde hair, blue eyes, over-sized sequinned cowboy hat, nacho stain on her T-shirt. It was only when she raised her hand to her face a split second after I raised my hand to my face I realized what was going on.

There we were, me and Ren, staring up at ourselves in horror on the Jumbotron.

'Oh, no,' I protested pointlessly. 'He's not – we're not—'

But the crowd did not want excuses. The crowd wanted kissing. And the crowd would be appeased or else.

'KISS KISS KISS KISS KISS.'

I turned to Ren in panic but before I could breathe a word, he leaned in towards me, eyes closing as his mouth found mine and every single voice in the stadium exploded in deafening ecstasy.

He kissed me.

It was all over in a second. The camera and the crowd had already moved on, hungry for fresh blood, but I was still trapped in the kiss. The touch of Ren's hand on my face, his hair brushing against my cheek, his soft, full lips gently exploring my own. I was nothing but a mess of sensation and reaction. The scent of him, the feel of him, the taste of him. I gasped when we broke apart, my lips tingling as I stared into his dilated pupils, my breath caught in my chest.

'Phoebe?'

The way he said my name, I could have died.

'Ren?'

I was fixed in time, his forever.

On the field, a man with the bat and a black helmet pulled back his arm and waited, coiled and ready, springing into action the moment the ball was released. The sound of leather on wood reverberated through the stadium, snapping me back to reality, and I was shocked to discover there were still other people around. The ball soared up into the air before landing neatly in a waiting Dodger's catcher's mitt and everyone jumped up to celebrate once again. Everyone except for two people who stayed in their seats, staring at each other, not quite sure what just happened.

One was me.

And the other was Ren.

CHAPTER EIGHTEEN

'It's the first time Bel has cancelled on me ever.' Suzanne picked up an avocado and gave it a speculative squeeze before placing it carefully in the shopping trolley. 'I'm worried about her.'

A dark uneasy feeling churned inside me. This was my fault, I was sure of it.

'Probably not feeling it after last night,' I suggested, mindlessly prodding at a gargantuan beefsteak tomato. 'God knows I've felt better.'

'That's because you drank enough to put the Night's Watch on its arse,' my sister replied as she added a bunch of grapes to our bounty. 'No, something's wrong. Bel never cancels. She even turned up the morning after Burning Man. She was tripping on mushrooms and wearing glitter pasties and a silver thong, but she still turned up.'

Thanks to a very long line for the ladies, Suzanne managed to miss the Kiss Cam debacle and Bel was busy hunting for an Instagram famous fried chicken sandwich only available inside Dodger Stadium which ended up being so spicy, she couldn't even eat it. Our kiss was a secret belonging only to me, Ren and about fifty thousand other people. As soon as Suzanne reappeared, armed with four cinnamon pretzels, Ren moved back to his seat and we did not speak again for the rest of the game.

On the upside, the Dodgers won.

'No, something is definitely up.' Suzanne squinted as she examined a fifteen-dollar bottle of celery juice, putting it back before I had to remind her where she was from. 'She wasn't herself at all, Bel isn't usually on edge like that. And a "sorry can't make it" text? Not likely. When has Bel ever given a short answer when a much longer one would do?' She picked up a jug of orange juice and grinned. 'You know what it is, don't you?'

'She's joined a cult?' I guessed.

'That was last year. She spent a whole week working on a satsuma farm in the valley for fifteen cents a day before she came to her senses.'

'Love satsumas,' I replied, fondling a strawberry-banana-ashwagandha-CBD-THC smoothie and putting it straight back when I saw the price tag. 'God forbid, but maybe she just didn't feel up to it.'

'I'm sure she didn't,' Suzanne commented with a smutty smile on her face. 'Probably too shagged out.'

My stomach lurched and I had to press a hand over my mouth to make sure its contents stayed where they were.

'They were both insanely awkward all night and it was their third date. Ren could hardly look at her, he was probably so nervous.' She dumped a bag of bananas into the trolley in triumph, thrilled with her own powers of deduction. Sherlock Holmes, Jessica Fletcher and the man whose name I couldn't remember from *Diagnosis Murder*, beware. 'They could not get away from us fast enough. Think about it.'

'I'd rather not,' I replied, grabbing a bottle of red wine off the shelf and placing it in the trolley. What kind of supermarket stocked the wine next to the fruit and veg? A genius supermarket, that was what kind. Suzanne automatically picked it up to put it back before scanning the label and returning it to the trolley with a soft grunt of approval.

'The first time with anyone is always weird, even if you're head over heels,' she added. 'You were being weird as well though – anything you want to tell me?'

'You know me, I'm always weird.'

I squinted at a woman in jogging bottoms and a giant Garfield sweater who looked an awful lot like the mum from *Twilight*. It was only when she passed us I realized that was because it *was* the mum from *Twilight*.

'Well, that's true enough,' she said. 'I suppose I should be glad it's going well. If things had gone badly and I had to wait until cover of darkness to roll the bins out for the rest of my life, you'd have been on my shit list forever.'

'Very pleased it's all worked out so nicely for you,' I told her as I rested my belly against the pushbar of the trolley and scooted along, allowing my feet to drag along on the floor. Supermarket trolleys always brought out the toddler in me, no matter what kind of mood I was in. I was simply powerless against them.

'Remind me, how exactly did you help them get together?' she asked, slapping me around the back of the head and taking control of the trolley.

'What are you talking about?' I grabbed a carton of milk out of a massive fridge and waved it in my sister's face. 'Can you even believe the price of milk here? Six dollars for one little carton? That's like paying a fiver for a pint. It's daylight robbery, Suze, you're going to have to move home.'

She reached past me for two bottles of oat milk, narrowing her eyes with suspicion. 'You said you were helping her seduce my neighbour and that he was the love of her life. How did you help exactly?'

'Nothing really. Bit of research, a few conversation pointers.'

'That's it?'

'Yes.'

'Phoebe.'

I gazed into the dairy fridge until the words 'fat-free vanilla almond milk' lost all meaning.

'I may have also helped her write Ren a love letter,' I said eventually. 'Ooh, pea milk? Have you tried this? Is it good?'

'You helped her write a love letter.' Suzanne looked less than impressed. 'What are you, fourteen?'

'It was very romantic, and Ren loved it.'

'Why do I feel like there's a "but" coming?' she asked.

'Because you're a smug know-it-all?'

She smirked as she opened the fridge to select her yoghurts. Imagine hearing that and thinking it was a compliment.

'But,' I added with very necessary emphasis. 'There's a slight, extremely slight, possibility that Ren was expecting Bel to be a bit more like someone who might write a very romantic love letter rather than someone who might send you a voice note while she's on the toilet.'

'She does like to do that.' She stopped for a moment, a giant tub of fat-free, lactose-free, flavour-free joy-free Greek yoghurt in her hand. 'Hang on, did you help her write the letter or did you write the entire thing yourself?'

My face crumpled into a pained expression as I slumped over the handle of the trolley.'I was only trying to help!' I wailed. 'I like Bel so much and she didn't know how to start the conversation so I tried to help but the more I got to know Ren, the more complicated it got because he's so clever and funny and genuine and kind and—'

'Oh my God,' Suzanne shouted, so loud a purple-haired teenager trying to shoplift a bag of peanut butter cups dropped them on the floor and ran straight for the exit. 'You love Ren!'

I panicked, shaking my hands in front of me as though there were no paper towels in the public loos.

'I do not love Ren. Do I think he's handsome and interesting, yes. Do I think about him a lot? More or less all the time. Have I woken up in a cold sweat in the middle of the night because I was dreaming about him doing things to me I will not describe to my sister in the middle of the supermarket? Of course, who hasn't? But that doesn't mean I love him.'

'You literally just described being in love with someone.' She planted her hands on her hips, despairing of me as usual. 'Oh Pheebs, you do love him.'

'It's a crush!' I yelled, opening another fridge and grabbing at multiple cheeses with wild abandon. 'Bel's

feelings are real, she likes him and he likes her and I'm
nursing a silly little crush and now we will never speak
of it again.'

'What makes you think your feelings are any less
valid than Bel's?' she asked. 'Why would you prioritize
someone else's feelings over your own?'

She'd always said she didn't want kids, but it really
was a waste; she had the 'I'm not angry, I'm disappointed' tone down perfectly.

'Because I'm so nice?'

'Because you're a martyr, just like Gran.'

'Don't say shitty things about Gran,' I said, dragging
the front of the trolley behind me as I walked away.
'She wasn't a martyr, she made a lot of sacrifices for
us. I can't even begin to imagine what would have
happened if she hadn't taken us in.'

Suze pulled on the other end of the trolley, forcing
me to stop. 'Has it never occurred to you that Mum
might have handled things on her own?'

'No, because she couldn't,' I replied bluntly. 'I know
you think you could have but no, it hasn't occurred to
me. Why would she stay with Gran if she didn't need to?'

'I don't know,' she admitted. 'Because we've never
talked about it, same as we never talk about the really
important things. Like you turning up to that girl's
hen night.'

I removed the claw clip that was holding up my hair,
retwisted the ponytail and let the clip spring closed
around it, the sharp plastic teeth scraping my skull.

'How do you know about that?'

'Because I used to work with Samantha's cousin,'
Suzanne replied. 'I wasn't going to say anything because

I thought you'd tell me in your own time, but obviously that's not going to happen.'

'It's not as though you go out of your way to tell me about your love life,' I volleyed back. 'I never know anything about your relationships; you haven't mentioned a single man since you broke up with Victor and that was ten years ago. You could be going out with Tom Cruise for all I know.'

Suzanne snorted and folded her arms over her chest.

'Shit, you're not going out with Tom Cruise, are you?' I gasped. 'He'll make you join that weird church and I'm sorry but you wouldn't last a minute there, Suze, you're physically incapable of keeping your mouth shut.'

'Please, I'd be running the place in less than a week,' she scoffed. 'My romantic inclinations are not the issue here. I know you don't want to talk about the break-up, but showing up at someone's hen night and going mental? It's not like you, Phoebe, you're not a confrontational person.'

'Unlike you.'

Once again, she took my insult as a compliment.

'I didn't go to cause trouble,' I said as I stepped to the side so a scared middle-aged man who was far too afraid to interrupt us could get at the bags of shredded mozzarella. 'I was trying to help Samantha.'

'Help her with what?'

It was easier this time. I'd had this conversation once and the world hadn't ended. Admittedly I didn't have it in the dairy aisle of a supermarket in Silver Lake, but beggars couldn't be choosers.

'Samantha's a really nice person,' I said, a hot red rash creeping up my neck as I spoke. 'Thomas isn't.'

There was as much in the words I didn't say as the ones I did. Suzanne's nostrils flared and two red spots appeared in her cheeks.

'Did he do something to you?' she asked with a quiet fury usually reserved for cyclists who rode side by side on a one-lane road. 'Because if he did, I'll have him killed.'

My wonderful sister – not she would kill him, but she would have him killed. She was so good at managing people, she even delegated threats of violence.

'He didn't lay a finger on me,' I told her, flicking the corner of a bag of Doritos. 'And the most important part is I'm out of it now. But she isn't. Maybe Samantha has thicker skin than me, maybe he's nicer to her, who knows? I just wanted her to know there's someone she can talk to, on the off-chance he's still a horrible bully who likes to make women feel like shit and ought to have his tongue cut out and his knob chopped off.'

'Men like that don't change.' Her blue eyes, so like mine, so like Gran's, shone with tears. It was something I hadn't seen in years, not even at the funeral. 'How long did it go on? Was he always like that, did I not see it?'

'No one saw it, he made sure of that, and no, he wasn't always terrible . . . or he was always but he was very good at hiding it at the beginning. I don't know, I'll never know, and thankfully, it's over, at least for me.'

I sucked in my cheeks, determined not to cry. Not in the bloody supermarket. Gran would rise from her grave to drag us both home by our ears.

Suze nodded emphatically, her lips pressed into a tight, pale line. 'We've got to look out for each other,

Pheebs, you're all I've got. I know I'm away a lot and always going on about how busy I am, but I am never, *ever* too busy for you. I wish you'd told me before.'

The second she started crying, I started crying, and a supermarket employee who had been restocking the cream cheese quietly removed himself to the next aisle over.

'I wish I had as well,' I croaked. 'And I wish we weren't having an emotional breakthrough in the middle of the supermarket.'

'It's the nice supermarket, as well,' she choked on her words, swiping at her face with the back of her wrist, attempting to regain her composure. 'I once saw Jon Hamm here buying Pepto-Bismol and loads of toilet paper.'

'Thanks for shattering a dream,' I replied as I pulled her in for a hug right there between the pasture-raised double-yolk organic eggs and the artisanal imported buffalo milk burrata. 'What kind of toilet paper was it?'

'Four-ply,' she wailed into my shoulder, her entire body shaking with tears. 'The really nice stuff.'

'Good for him,' I whispered, stroking her hair. 'He deserves it.'

The last person I would ever expect to find waiting on a doorstep was Myrna Moore and yet, when we pulled into the driveway with our bags and bags of shopping, there she was.

'Phoebe, darling,' she cooed, lifting her enormous sunglasses up over her eyes. 'There you are. I've been ringing the bell for an eternity, I assumed you'd died.'

She looked like an actress playing an actress. Her shades and her cigarette holder accessorized a pristine, ruby velour tracksuit, and her glossy black cane rested against the front door. The silver Rolls-Royce waited dutifully in the street below, its engine purring softly.

'And this must be the sister who prefers to throw my mail over the wall than deliver it in a civilized manner.'

'And you must be the woman who has terrified so many postal workers they daren't attempt to deliver your mail correctly in the first place.' Suzanne set down her shopping bags and held out her hand. 'Suzanne Chapman, pleasure to meet you.'

'Oh, I like her,' Myrna said as she shook my sister's hand. 'Now let me in before I expire in the street and everyone thinks I've turned to drugs.'

'To what do we owe the pleasure, Ms Moore?' Suzanne asked, guiding her into the living room while I fumbled with the fancy instant-boil kettle, wondering which mugs to use, which tea to brew. What would be up to Myrna's exacting standards?

'The party-planning people have taken over my house and I couldn't bear to be around their nonsense one second longer.' She peered around the room with an openly critical eye but made no comment. Practically the highest compliment she could bestow. 'Since your sister was the one who suggested the shindig in the first place, I assumed it would be reasonable for me to take refuge here.'

'We were actually on our way out,' I started to say but Suze cut me off with a sweet smile.

'Phoebe does love to get herself involved in other people's business,' she said. 'You're welcome to stay as long as you like.'

Myrna walked slowly around the open-plan room before deciding on the uncomfortable-looking, high-backed chair I'd assumed was only there for decoration.

'A lot of years have passed since I stood in this house,' she said, her eyes combing the walls, the floors, the ceilings. 'Hasn't changed much from the street but I wouldn't have recognized it from the inside. I imagine that's true of most of the old houses still standing.'

'You should visit Ren,' I suggested, dunking the teabags aggressively in and out of the boiling water. 'I'm sure that hasn't changed too much.'

'Joe Garcia's boy?'

I nodded as I transferred oat milk from the bottle into a tiny jug, placed the tiny jug on a fancy tray and carried everything over to the sitting area.

'Marvellous idea, you'll come with me. Let's go.' Myrna leaned against her cane to pop up to her feet, immediately striding across the room towards the front door. 'Suzanne, dear, I'll see you at the party tomorrow evening. Chop chop, Phoebe, I haven't got all day. Some of us are old, you know, and I refuse to die while wearing a leisure suit.'

Suzanne looked up at me from the settee, trying not to laugh.

'Enjoy the tea,' I muttered, chasing after our guest as she barked my name and leaving my sister to drink three mugs all by herself.

CHAPTER NINETEEN

Since Myrna wasn't getting any younger or more reasonable, we drove, or rather we were driven, around the corner to Ren's house.

'It looks the same from here,' she said, her uniformed driver opening the car door and helping her out. I offered him a grateful smile but was met only with stoic resolve, and followed her onto the uneven pavement, keeping close to her side. So many of the roads were buckled and broken, huge potholes threatening to bugger up unsuspecting vehicles, and I hadn't seen a single stretch of pavement longer than ten feet that wasn't cracked in two or adorned with the protruding root of a tree. Fifty million-dollar houses and fifty-cent pavements, it was unbelievable.

'Rosa planted those apple trees,' Myrna pointed towards a miniature orchard in one corner of the front garden, full of pretty trees bearing small, shiny apples, not quite ready to eat. 'She was a keen gardener. I always saw her out here when I took my daily walks around the neighbourhood, but that was a long time ago.'

'How come?' I unlatched the gate, very much hoping Ren wouldn't be at home. 'You don't like to walk any more?'

'I stopped walking around the neighbourhood when I stopped recognizing the neighbourhood,' she replied. 'The hip replacement doesn't help much either.' She made her way through the garden, her expression cloudy with memories as she paused in front of every plant and tree.

'Rosa died when I was in the hospital. I didn't find out until long after the funeral – can't imagine dropping me a line was at the top of Joe's to-do list. He was never the same without her, but you never are after you lose the love of your life.'

'It's very romantic,' I said. 'But don't you think you might like to meet someone else?'

Myrna looked at me and laughed.

'Oh, you sweet child. I found plenty of someones after Wally died. I was only twenty-three when he died – do you think I lived like a nun? It was the sixties and I was beautiful, it's a wonder I didn't catch something contagious.'

'Good to know,' I replied, rubbing a non-existent itch on my nose. 'Sorry I asked.'

'Men, women and everything in between,' she said, exhaling happily. 'Not a one of them understood me like my husband, it was never really love after him. But the sex was fantastic.'

'Call me crazy but I've got a funny feeling you're going to enjoy yourself in the retirement community,' I commented as she pressed the doorbell for far too long with the head of her cane.

'I've got a feeling you'll take that back before I rattle your legs – oh, this must be Joe's boy!'

The door opened and there he was, in olive-green carpenter pants and a snug grey T-shirt, already darkened with sweat. His face was shiny and he had a hammer in one hand which he quickly shoved into one of the deep pockets.

'Hi?' His eyes flickered between me and Myrna and he rubbed a dirty hand on the back of his trousers. 'Phoebe?'

'Is that a hammer in your pocket or are you just happy to see me?' Myrna said with a seductive wink. 'Don't answer that, darling, nothing you say will be good for my ancient ego. May we come in? If I don't keep moving, my hip will seize up and I'll be forced to curl up and die in the corner of your garden. It'll be no good for house prices, believe me.'

'Ren Garcia, this is Myrna Moore,' I said, mouthing an apology. 'She's the lady I mentioned, who knew your grandparents?'

'And your father.' Without waiting for an official invitation, she walked straight into the house giving it the same considered once-over she gave Suzanne's. 'Michael, wasn't it?'

'Still is,' Ren replied. 'Michael Joseph Garcia.'

'We can go if this isn't a good time,' I offered.

'Not at all,' he said, beckoning me inside with a tilt of his head. 'Good timing is overrated.'

Steeling myself, I stepped over the threshold and Ren closed the door behind me with a gentle click.

* * *

Somehow, the Garcia house managed to be the complete opposite of both Suzanne's bright, white, open-plan villa and Myrna's classic, elegant chateau. It was almost unbearably cosy, all warm dark wood and exposed brick with a huge fireplace at the heart of the room. The windows were small and leaded, peeking out onto the front and back gardens, and the whole place was surrounded with plants and trees and bushes. I half expected to see a deer wander by searching for Snow White and finding me, Myrna and Ren instead. What a disappointing day it would be for that deer.

'It hasn't changed one bit,' Myrna remarked, eyes crinkling with joy, her cheeks barely able to support the breadth of her smile. She pointed across the room with her cane and nodded. 'I used to sit in that rocking chair and read to your father when he was a baby, and over there in the corner, that's where your grandmother would put the Christmas tree.'

'You can still see the marks in the floor from the old metal stand.' Ren took her arm and walked her over to the spot, poking at four small indentations, perfectly placed like points on a compass. 'I still have it in the attic, but we haven't put a tree up in years.'

'That's a shame. Your grandmother loved her Christmas tree, it was always the most beautiful one on the block.' She slid the tip of her cane into the indentations, her smile fading a fraction. She turned to study Ren more closely, squinting into his face. 'You don't look much like your grandfather but I can see Rosa in there. You have her eyes, her hair.'

'Everyone says I'm her double,' he replied, helping her over to the sofa before choosing the chair nearest to her for himself. 'Never was sure if that's a good thing or not.'

'Damned good-looking, that's what you are,' Myrna declared. 'That face is a weapon. Tell me, have you ever thought about acting?'

Ren laughed and I sat in the chair closest to the door, keeping my eyes on Myrna instead of his hands or his lips or the spot where his T-shirt didn't quite meet his trousers, allowing me a glimpse at the skin of his lower back.

'You never met two people more in love than Joe and Rosa.' Myrna eased back against the sofa cushions as though she were travelling back in time. 'You were close with your grandparents?'

'Very,' Ren replied. 'My mom and dad moved us to Maine when I was fifteen, but I spent all my summers here, a bunch of Christmases too. I can't believe we haven't met before; both my grandparents always spoke so highly of you.'

'We most likely have but you would have been too small to recall, and I don't acknowledge children until they're old enough to make a decent martini.' She knocked her cane on the floor and scowled. 'I liked to travel in the summer before I had to rely so much on this thing and I'm ashamed to say I didn't see so much of your grandfather in his later years. I am very sorry for your loss; he was a wonderful man and I don't say that often.'

'She really doesn't,' I confirmed. The highest compliment I'd heard her give anyone was when she told the man at the Polo Lounge her tea wasn't as disappointing as she'd expected.

'Thank you, that means a lot.' He managed a smile, but I could tell it was still hard for him. I understood only too well. 'It's been a rough year without him.'

'Why Maine?' Myrna asked, looking around the room as though searching for an answer to her own question. 'What possessed your parents to move so far away?'

'My mom's family is out there,' he answered. 'They wanted Mom and Dad to take over their business.'

'Which is?'

He wove his fingers together and flexed his hands.

'They own a chain of local fried fish restaurants called Fanny's Famous Fried Fish.'

One corner of Myrna's mouth flickered.

'How charming.'

'Not really,' he replied. 'Now they want me to come back and help out too.'

'And you don't want to be a . . .' Myrna paused, took a breath, then proceeded: 'Restaurateur?'

'Not really. I worked there all through high school and believe me, nothing says homecoming king like a teenage boy who stinks of fried catfish twenty-four-seven.' Ren gestured around the living room, the heavy oak beams, the tiled fireplace, the stucco walls. 'I've always wanted to build things, like my grandpa. Restoring this place is the best job I've ever had. Going through the original plans, seeing how it all fits together, how things used to be done. I feel like I'm getting to know Grandpa in a whole new way.'

Until he caught my gaze, I didn't even realize I was staring at him. I looked away, a fierce heat burning in my cheeks as I studied the grain of the wood in the floorboards. It was painfully awkward, sitting so close to him, behaving so politely and not mentioning the fact he'd laid the greatest kiss of my entire life on me exactly fifteen hours and fourteen minutes ago.

'When my husband passed away, Joe and Rosa took very good care of me,' Myrna said, filling the uncomfortable silence. 'They brought me food, opened the curtains, answered the telephone. All the things I wasn't doing for myself. Some days we didn't even talk; Rosa or Joe or both of them would come by and sit with me. Most people don't know what to say when you're grieving, but all you really want is nothing at all. Just someone. They understood that. They were such a comfort in those days, I've never forgotten. The very definition of good people.'

My eyes prickled, already warmed up and ready to go after Suzanne's supermarket weep. I felt the same way when we lost Gran. Lots of people trying to fill the sad, empty space with well wishes and platitudes but it was all noise.

'That's how I felt when I lost mi abuelo,' he said softly. 'Thank you. Again.'

'Stop thanking me; they're facts, not gifts. Although I do have something for you.' She reached into her Chanel bag and pulled out something small and square, wrapped in tissue paper. 'Rosa painted this to remind me there would be better times. I've kept it by my bed ever since, but I think you should have it now.'

He accepted the parcel and gently, carefully unwrapped it. Inside was a canvas stretched over a frame and on the canvas was a painting of a bird, soaring through the sky.

'She loved to paint,' Myrna said, rising to her feet. 'I can't begin to count the number of afternoons I sat

in that backyard of yours, watching the birds fly overhead with Rosa sketching while your grandfather
banged away in his workshop.' Her eyes wandered
around the room and she smiled at things that were
no longer there. 'It would be a sin to sell this house to
someone who might knock it down, even more so than
mine. We built our house with money, but Joe and Rosa
built this house out of love. It's bedded into the very
walls – can't you feel it?'

The three of us were quiet, Ren and Myrna lost in
memories and me in dreams. She was right, there was
something special here. Even though I'd only just
walked through the door, I felt so at home.

'Enough nostalgia for one day,' Myrna announced,
shifting the energy of the room back to the present day.
'As always, I have things to do.'

'Thank you for coming by, Ms Moore.' Ren propped
his grandmother's painting on the mantelpiece before
taking Myrna's arm in his and walking her back to the
front door. She leaned all her weight against him and
looked back over her shoulder to tip me a wink.

'For as long as the house is still ours, you're welcome
here any time. I'd love to see your home sometime, if
that's possible?'

'It's Myrna, darling,' she insisted. 'And you'll see my
house at the party tomorrow evening, won't you?'

'Party?' Ren repeated. 'What party?'

'Phoebe didn't tell you?'

'Sorry,' I said as she turned back to flash me a
despairing look. 'Might have forgotten to mention it.'

'I'm having a gathering Friday evening at eight, you
are expected,' she said, accidentally on purpose cracking

my shins with her cane as I sidled past out the front door. 'Not that you don't look entirely charming in this ensemble, but dress is evening attire, if you don't mind.'

'I'll be there,' he promised, accepting an enthusiastic kiss on each cheek. 'I think my grandpa's tux will still fit.'

'Don't tell me I need to take you shopping as well?' Myrna replied with a withering look. 'I despair at your generation, I really do.'

'God help her when she gets an eyeful of Gen Z,' I commented as she took herself off to visit the apple trees, leaving me loitering on Ren's doorstep. 'Thank you for . . . I was going to say humouring her, but that's not the right word, is it?'

'I don't think they came up with a word to describe a visit from Myrna Moore yet,' he said. 'What a trip.'

'Can someone please explain how to work this thing?' yelled the woman herself from across the garden where she was striking at the Garcias' rusted old gate with her cane. 'It's easier to break out of Alcatraz. What are you trying to do to a girl?'

'I'd better go,' I said, mirroring Ren's awkward stance. 'But it sounds like I'll see you tomorrow.'

'Sounds like you will. She seems the type to send some goons to get me if I don't show up on time. It's going to be crazy, right?'

'From the stories she's told me, I think it might be,' I replied, managing something like a smile. 'Not the way I imagined I'd be wrapping up my holiday but I'm excited.'

'Wrapping up?' He looked at me in disbelief. 'But you only just got here?'

'It's been nearly two weeks, I leave on Saturday night. I can't decide if it feels like I just got here or I've lived here forever.' I tried not to sound too sad but the more I thought about it, the more it broke my heart. And not only because it meant surviving another airport drive with Suzanne.

'Certainly feels like you belong here,' Ren said softly. 'Our hawk is going to miss you.'

'That fickle little madam?' I laughed. 'I don't think it'll faze her; I haven't even seen her since last week.'

'Maybe you haven't been looking in the right places.'

His eyes darkened with the same heavy, tantalizing look I'd seen at the waterfall, and I stumbled backwards off the bottom step and on to the footpath.

'Hey, before you go.' He dug his hands deep in his pockets, shoulders shrugged up to his ears. 'I wanted to say something, about last night.'

'Oh, no, there's no need,' I said, jumping in quickly. I couldn't think of a single thing I could say that would make the situation better. 'I'm sorry, I should have ignored the camera. I mean, what were they going to do, put me in prison? They can't put you in prison for ignoring a Kiss Cam, can they? Wait, can they?'

I had, after all, heard some very strange things about the justice system in America.

'No, not as far as I know,' he replied. 'But I'm the one who should apologize.'

'Please don't.' I rocked back and forth on my heels, incapable of standing still. 'It's all fine, never happened, just one of those silly things.'

He relaxed his shoulders and his green eyes glowed in the midday sun.

'I don't think they have the right word for this situation either,' he said. 'I didn't mean I wanted to apologize for the kiss—'

'Would you look at the time,' I said loudly, looking down at my watch-less wrist. 'I have to go. Are you seeing Bel tonight? You should bring her to the party. What am I saying, ignore me, none of my business. Must be off, have a great rest of your day!'

'Phoebe, wait,' Ren started but I was already halfway down the path.

'About time,' Myrna said as I aggressively jiggled the rusted catch until it opened. 'Not that I blame you for hanging around; that boy is Joe and Rosa through and through. If I still had two working hips, I'd make a play for him myself.'

'It's not like that, he's dating my friend,' I replied. 'She's amazing. You'll meet her tomorrow night.'

'Let me know which one she is and I'll see if I can't push her downstairs.' Her driver hopped out of the car and opened the passenger door, helping her inside before I could respond. 'I'll see you at the house tomorrow. Six p.m. sharp, a girl is coming to do your hair and make-up.'

'But I don't need—' I started before registering the lift of her eyebrows and the stern turn of her mouth. 'Tomorrow at six.'

The car drove away and even in the shade of the Garcias' trees, it was blisteringly hot, maybe the hottest day since I'd arrived. The air felt like it was on fire, scorching the back of my throat every time I inhaled. You could almost smell it. I turned my face upwards, eyes closed. In two days, I'd be on my way back home to enjoy a nice British summer, so who knew when I'd see the sun again. When I felt my skin sizzle, testing the limits of my SPF, I opened my eyes, sun drunk and ready for home.

Then I saw him.

Ren.

He was still exactly where I'd left him, in the doorway, arms stretched high and his hands resting against the top of his doorframe. He was watching me. He didn't move when my gaze smashed into his, didn't react when I started backwards, every thought in my head written all over my face, naked and exposed. I turned and bolted up the hill but even when I crashed through the front door and locked it behind me, I could still feel his eyes on mine.

'I wondered when you'd be back,' Suzanne called, busily wiping down the kitchen counters as I stood panting with my back pressed against the door. 'I managed to get a table at Mother Wolf for dinner, there's some stuff I want to talk to you about. What do you want to do until then? Spa? Observatory? Get doughnuts from the Farmers Market then go to the Grove and judge all the teenagers' outfits? That one is always more fun with company.'

She looked up, her eyes wide with alarm.

'Phoebe, what's wrong?'

'I don't even know,' I replied. 'I really don't.'

I was shaking, my hands trembling so badly, I didn't even dare take the glass of water Suzanne poured for me. What just happened? Had I dreamt it? The way he had looked at me . . . it was the same way I looked at a tub of Ben & Jerry's Phish Food, like I was going to devour the whole thing and savour every mouthful.

'You saw Ren then?' Suze asked.

'I'm so confused,' I said, nodding and sliding down the door until my bum hit the floor. 'I hate being confused. I've worked really hard to get confusion out of my life. I stopped watching *Doctor Who* because I couldn't work out what was going on any more. All I want is straightforward and simple and happy.'

'Then that settles it,' she said, putting the water down on the counter. 'There's only one place we can go.'

'To a small dark cave a hundred miles away from the nearest living thing?'

She threw down her tea towel and picked up her handbag. 'I'm taking you to the happiest place on earth.'

'A small dark cave a hundred miles away from the nearest living thing?'

'Shut up and get in the car,' she said, clipping me gently around the back of the head. 'You'll see when we get there.'

CHAPTER TWENTY

'I cannot believe we're at Disneyland,' I said as we wandered down Main Street USA, Suze wearing a Minnie Mouse varsity jacket and me, living my best life in a 'first time visitor' badge and a pair of sparkly silver Mickey ears. 'This is so much better than a dark cave. You really are pitching for sister of the year, aren't you?'

'You mean I'm not a shoo-in?' she replied with mock surprise. 'I paid for the Lightning Lane tickets and everything.'

Staring around with the wide-eyed wonder of a sugar-cracked seven-year-old, the strange moment outside Ren's house felt like it had happened a million years ago instead of a few hours earlier. And if I pushed it right back into the darkest corner of my mind and concentrated on literally anything else, I could easily go for three minutes without thinking about him. Five if I had a snack. Even though I could tell she was itching to ask about it, Suzanne wasn't pushing the conversation, and for that, I was grateful.

'This must be the tenth time I've asked since I got here,' I said, taking in the masses of people all around us. 'But how does anyone get anything done in this town?'

'It's a reward for having to put up with all the hot people,' Suzanne explained. 'Yes, I have to see the most beautiful women in the world every time I go out to buy milk, but I can also be eating Mickey beignets in under forty minutes should the mood strike.'

Biting into delicious, overpriced churro, I considered the trade-off. It was fair.

'Never had you pegged as a Disney person,' I said.

'There are only two kinds of people in this world.' She raised her hand to give Donald Duck a nonchalant wave. 'Disney people, and people who don't know they're Disney people. I used to turn my nose up at it as well, but that was before I had one too many *Star Wars*-themed cocktails at eight in the morning and spent the entire day riding The Haunted Mansion drunk.'

'Reflection and growth is such an important part of the human experience,' I said wisely. 'Still, I can't believe we just turned up in the middle of the afternoon. I honestly thought you weren't allowed in a theme park unless you left your house while it was still dark and no one was talking to each other by the time you arrived.'

She shook her head. 'No, turns out you can arrive at any time. Not only that, you can leave whenever you want as well, you don't have to be here for fifteen hours then crawl back to the car tired, emotional and piss-wet through from the log flume.'

'It never was a proper day out unless someone cried in the car on the way back, was it?' I sniffed, misty-eyed with nostalgia. 'Gran threatening to turn the car around and Mum climbing in the back to separate us while we were going eighty down the motorway.'

'Happy days,' she replied. 'And the fact we believe that probably explains more about us as adults than we realize.'

Suzanne stopped in front of the statue of Walt and Mickey, chomping an ear off her Mickey-shaped ice cream while I listened in on a bespectacled man lecturing his girlfriend as to why Disney as a whole was very problematic and they shouldn't really be here at all but since they were, he had to get some blue milk and make his own lightsaber. My mind wandered, each thought drifting into another until I ended up somewhere I didn't want to be. Was everything going to plan with Myrna's party? What would she wear? What would Bel wear? Ren in his grandfather's tux, Ren in the doorway of his house, Ren looking at me across the garden and the kiss, the kiss, the kiss.

'I really miss Gran,' Suzanne said.

I was so shocked, I nearly dropped my churro.

'You do?'

A distressed-looking dad, covered in an assortment of children, cleared the bench beside us and Suzanne promptly plopped down, beating a gaggle of teenagers who stalked off with dark looks on their beautiful faces.

'Of course I do. Just because I don't talk about something all the time doesn't mean I'm not thinking about it.'

I sat down on the bench, not sure what to say next. I'd got so good at keeping my feelings under control, it was difficult to let them loose even when I really wanted to. Instead I watched my sister while she watched the world go by, the same happy glossiness to her that I'd noticed when I first arrived. The little lines in her forehead were smoother than usual, her limbs seemed looser in their sockets, and she'd traded her resting thinking face for an uncomplicated grin.

'You really love it here, don't you?' I said.

She nodded. 'I do. Out of everywhere I've lived, there's something special about LA. Just one thing missing though.'

'A decent freezer shop?'

'Two things then,' she replied, bopping me on the head. 'I meant you.'

It was nice to know someone missed you but miserable to miss them back. I rested my head on her shoulder, soaking in the sisterly bonding.

'You don't think you'll ever come home?'

She put her arm around my shoulder and squeezed. 'I think I am home,' she replied, and I made myself smile for her even though I suddenly felt like having a big cry. 'We should do this every year,' she added. 'We really should.'

'OK, but I might ask Mickey if it's possible to move in,' I said, pointing at the pink castle in front of us with my foot. 'I could live in there. They'd hardly know I'm here, I'm neat, I clean up after myself.'

'No, you aren't, and no, you don't. I mean sister time in general – doesn't have to be Disney but we do have to make it a priority. I don't want to end up like those siblings who only see each other at funerals and weddings.'

I frowned, at her statement and the fact I'd almost finished my churro. 'Everyone we both know is already married. Although there's bound to be a few second weddings coming up soon. Gran never liked the look of our Jo's husband and after that Homer Simpson tie he wore when they got married, I'd have to say I agree with her.'

Ignoring my assessment of our cousin's romantic prospects, Suzanne finished her ice cream and gnawed thoughtfully on the leftover little wooden stick.

'There's something I want to tell you.'

From the set of her jaw and the ominous edge to her voice, I suspected it wasn't her feelings about Jo's husband's regrettable choice in accessories. 'I've been thinking about it ever since we got back from the supermarket.'

I pushed a long, low whistle through my teeth. 'A whole six hours? This must be serious.'

'Be quiet and listen or I'll leave you here to find your own way home.'

'I'm all ears,' I said, instantly regretting that time I deleted the Uber app from my phone in a fit of moral righteousness.

My sister rolled her shoulders and tilted her head from side to side as though she was about to go ten rounds with Rocky Balboa. Even Goofy took a wide berth as he walked by.

'It hurt. To think you felt as though you couldn't tell me something so horrible had happened to you or ask for help at the time – and that's not your fault so don't you dare apologize.'

She held up a warning finger as my mouth opened, the words 'I'm sorry' ready to trip, unbidden, off my tongue.

'It wasn't your fault,' she said again. 'You're not the only one who has kept secrets.'

'If this is about the time you came home drunk and threw up in my Barbie box, I already know it was you and not the dog.'

Something happy nudged at the corners of her mouth and she fiddled with the back of her earring as she spoke, the solitaire diamond spinning around and casting a kaleidoscope of colours on the ground by my feet.

'Probably a bit late but, I'm sorry. My point is we weren't the kind of family to share their feelings or have deep and meaningfuls. I learned the word invulnerable long before I understood what being vulnerable meant. I'm serious, I didn't even know there was an opposite word until I was in my twenties.'

'Still feels like something to be ashamed of,' I admitted. 'And I say that as someone who spends a *lot* of time on Instagram.'

'And I've read every one of Brené Brown's books,' Suzanne said.

'That's such a lie.'

'Fine, I bought two and skimmed one, but that's not the issue here,' she replied. 'The issue is that we ought to be able to be open and honest with each other. About all of it, good stuff, bad stuff, boring stuff. We shouldn't try to tackle everything on our own.'

'I don't think it's always a bad thing,' I said, scrunching my toes inside my shoes. Just talking about being more vulnerable made me feel, well, vulnerable. 'We're the kind of people who are more comfortable knowing we've got our guard up. That's fine.'

'Except we don't know when to take it down,' she suggested gently. 'Pheebs, don't take this the wrong way, but do you not think there's a chance you put your guard up against the wrong people? I'm only saying that because I do it too, and I'm not attacking Gran or Mum, but it's the way we were raised. Not to be a burden. Not to cause a fuss. Sometimes you have to ask for help and that's OK.'

She wasn't wrong. In fact, there was endless evidence that she was completely correct but it still hurt to hear.

'So I want to say this,' Suzanne went on. 'I want to be completely honest with you because you are my sister and I love you no matter what and I know you love me, no matter what.'

'Yes, unconditionally.' I slapped her thigh hard to drive the point home, a smile flickering on my lips when she winced. 'There's nothing you could say or do to change that. Unless you're about to tell me you're packing in your job to sell essential oils online.'

'God no, I'm not a monster,' Suzanne replied. 'I'm gay.'

There we were, perched at the heart of Disneyland on a Thursday afternoon, me and my thirty-seven-year-old sister, who just decided this was the perfect place to come out.

And honestly, why not?

'Oh,' I said, popping the last inch of churro into my mouth. 'OK.'

I chewed in silence, eyes wide, taking my time with every chomp while Suzanne stared at me in disbelief.

'OK?' she repeated. 'I just told you I'm gay and all you have to say is OK?'

Wiping my sugary hands off on my jeans, I juggled all the words running around inside my mind, trying to decide on the best ones to make this right.

'Brilliant time for you to decide you don't have a

snappy comeback,' she muttered. 'Thanks, Phoebe, thanks a lot.'

'I'm thinking!' I replied, reaching out to grab her wrist when she started to stand. 'Sit back down immediately. I'm trying to think of the best thing to say, not whether or not I think it's OK. It's more than OK, it's brilliant! Or it's neither good or bad? I don't know exactly what to say, but I do know I don't want to say the wrong thing. I'm happy you told me and I'm completely on board and I love you. Is that good?'

'Oh,' she said, welling up. 'OK then.'

Suzanne Chapman, in tears, twice in one day. It had to be a record.

'I'm *thrilled*,' I said, doubling down on my enthusiasm as I worked through my reactions. 'A bit surprised, didn't see it coming, and just a heads up, I'm probably going to ask some really insensitive questions.'

'What's new there?' she replied, slapping her hands on her thighs. 'While we're getting everything out into the open, let's go, what do you want to know?'

'It's really all right to ask? You can totally tell me to piss off.'

I wanted to make absolutely sure. This was much more important than the time she told me I could borrow her Juicy Couture tracksuit top but went absolutely spare when I wore it to Alton Towers and brought it back covered in chocolate milkshake.

She turned her whole body towards me and crossed her legs up onto the bench. 'Go for it.'

'How long have you known?'

'Always? When I say gay, what I mean is not straight.' Her shoulders inched down from up around her ears.

'I'm not really sure which label to put on it. Right now, I'm mostly interested in women, but that's not to say I couldn't ever fall for a man. I did love Victor. We didn't break up because I was living a big gay lie; we broke up because he wanted to buy a second-hand Ford Mondeo and a semi-detached bungalow around the corner from his mum while I wanted, well, this.'

She waved her hand around the Magic Kingdom. Poor Victor, I thought. He wanted to settle down and knock out a bunch of kids but my sister was dreaming of tripping the light fantastic with an anthropomorphized mouse. Their love was not meant to be.

'I always knew it wasn't just men for me but I never said anything. You remember how it was when we were kids; we hardly grew up in the most tolerant, enlightened time in history.'

'Not wrong there,' I said, widening my eyes with agreement. Everyone said kids could be cruel but what they really meant were kids can be savage little monsters without a shred of empathy, who haven't realized you absolutely cannot use the most sensitive, difficult things a human is dealing with against them for a laugh. Kids weren't just cruel, they were sociopathic.

'The older I got, the clearer it became, but at the same time, it was more difficult for me to tell anyone,' Suzanne explained. 'Everyone thinks it's so easy to come out now, a cute TikTok or an Instagram post with a green velvet couch, but it doesn't work that way when you're my age. Coming out to the whole world when you're in your thirties is not appealing, Pheebs, you're supposed to be set by then. Everyone's made up their mind about you, everyone knows who you are. And I've read everything there is to read and it's not a one off thing, you don't say 'guess what, I'm queer' and they give you a certificate. You have to do it again and again and again, every single day. I couldn't face it, so I didn't do it. But I'm ready now.'

A marching band swelled behind us and kids screamed and parents yelled and I was feeling so many feelings, altogether too full of sugar and caffeine to process them in any meaningful way. All I wanted to do was bundle her up in a massive hug and cry hysterically because I was so bloody proud of her and loved her so much but she'd only come out, not turned into a completely different human. If I even made a move in that direction, she'd likely slap my legs right out from under me.

'Are you out at all?' I asked instead. 'Does anyone know? Like, here in LA?'

'I'm not not-out,' she replied. 'But I also haven't made a point to discuss it with anyone. I don't really talk about my personal life as you might have noticed.'

I had. I had noticed.

'So you're not seeing anyone?'

She shook her head and switched from fidgeting with her earring to flicking the little wooden stick from her ice cream. 'The being too busy to date thing wasn't a cover-up. I've heard relationships where two women are involved move much faster than straight ones, and I haven't got the time to move someone in after three dates.'

'At least you've got plenty of room.' I pinched her cheek and she swatted me away. 'If I wasn't your sister, I'd go out with you just for the pool and the hot tub.

You're really hot and mostly nice and very rich. They're going to be banging your door down.'

'I should get you to write my Tinder profile,' she said with a bigger, bolder smile than I'd ever seen on her before. 'Oh Christ, I'm going to have to do a Tinder profile.'

'Yes, you are,' I replied gravely. 'The queer gods giveth and they taketh away.'

She clapped her hand on top of mine, slotting our fingers together, and pulled me up to my feet. 'Thank you,' she gasped, exhaling out years of stress I couldn't even start to imagine. 'I can't believe I've been sitting on that for so long.'

'The fact you're queer or that you threw up in my Barbie box?' I asked with a raised eyebrow. 'Don't think I've forgotten.'

'Mind like a steel trap,' she said, laughing long and loud and clear. 'What do you want to do now?'

'My steel trap mind seems to remember you mentioning *Star Wars*-themed cocktails,' I replied. 'I wouldn't mind one of those about now.'

'Come on then.' She yanked on my arm, almost pulling it off, and picked up her pace to a jog. 'Last one at Oga's Cantina buys the Fuzzy Tauntauns!'

'I don't know what that is but I want one,' I yelled after her, holding my Mickey ears securely to my head as we ran, smiling at the sunset, smiling at my sister and so, so proud.

CHAPTER TWENTY-ONE

'I don't know where the two weeks went,' I declared from the comfort of a red velvet chaise longue in Myrna's enormous dressing room. 'How can it be time for me to go home already?'

Across the room at a vanity surrounded by softly glowing white light bulbs, Myrna glowered in my direction, while an anxious-looking make-up artist worked magic on her face.

'You don't leave until tomorrow,' she replied between puffs of powder. 'A lot can happen between now and then.'

'True.' I pressed my fingertips against the cold brass studs that ran along the edges of the chaise. A lot had already happened in the last two weeks.

'Now tell me how we're going to seduce Joe Garcia's boy.'

Ever since I arrived, she'd been like a dog with a bone on the subject of Ren, and if it weren't for the very beautiful red dress that was hanging in the doorway of her walk-in closet, the tray of chocolate-covered strawberries on the side table and the fact I was too British to be so rude, I would have upped and left.

'I don't know how many times I have to tell you,' I replied, shovelling a third strawberry into my mouth. 'He's going out with my friend, Bel, and when you meet her, you'll feel terrible because she's a literal angel and deserves all the happiness in the world.'

'There's every chance I won't even set eyes on her,' Myrna said as she retied the belt on her marabou-trimmed, silk dressing gown. 'The idiot I put in charge tells me he invited two hundred people and almost all of them RSVP'd yes, despite the fact I said no more than one hundred and fifty. Imagine assuming there would be a fifty-person drop-off? For one of my parties? The nerve of that man.'

'Who are the two hundred people?' I asked, genuinely curious. 'I thought you didn't know that many people these days.'

'I don't.' She pushed the make-up artist out of the way to check her work in the mirror. 'Lighten the blush. Ideally, we'll land somewhere between a corpse and a whore.'

The make-up artist whimpered, her hands trembling as she went back into her kit. 'The event people were in charge of the invitations. My only instructions were A list only and no one who has been so much as accused of anything morally objectionable in the last fifty years.'

'I'm amazed they were able to find twenty people let alone two hundred,' I replied as she leaned into the mirror and smoothed a fluffed-up eyebrow. 'Although I suppose a lot depends on your definition of morally objectionable.'

'Given that I find most men breathing to be disquieting these days, I suspect the evening will be something of a clambake.'

'Thank you for teaching me a new word and I can guess what it means so don't worry about a definition.' Her lips curled into a self-satisfied smirk in the make-up chair. 'Although, while we're on the subject, I don't suppose you know anyone I could set my sister up with?'

'Assuming you think I'm too old for her?' she asked. I nodded. She sighed. 'Then no. Besides, don't you think you've done enough matchmaking for one vacation?'

The only suitable response was silence, so I looked away, frowning, as she closed her eyes, smiling.

There were no clocks in Myrna's dressing room, only more perfectly preserved mid-century furniture, impossibly beautiful hand-painted wallpaper and rugs so plush and warm, I couldn't even see my toes when I planted my feet onto the floor. The room was timeless in every sense, but according to my watch, it was almost seven. The party started at eight and I already felt jittery, three-coffees-anxious with a sugar crash pending for good measure.

'What I don't understand,' Myrna said, closing her eyes to allow a light dusting of grey shadow over her lids, 'is why you would help your friend secure the affections of Joe's boy when you want him for yourself?'

'I'm not talking about it.' I tapped the fingers of my left hand against the back of my right, my knees bouncing up and down. 'Who exactly is coming tonight? As a civilian, I think you ought to warn me in case I fangirl someone to death.'

'Look at a single soul the wrong way and you'll be removed,' she replied without a trace of humour. 'And I'm afraid we are talking about it, darling. You forget I was in the same room, I saw the way he looked at you, like he wanted to eat you up with a spoon. Although God only knows why with you in those hideous pants. Do you work part-time as a clown for sick children? That was the only justification I could come up with.'

The tapping intensified. 'Wide-legged jeans are considered very stylish by a lot of people.'

'Since when were lots of people right about anything?' She tutted and brushed the make-up artist's hand away to check the eye make-up. When she didn't insult it, I thought the woman was going to cry with joy. 'Nonetheless, I know what I saw and if he wants to fuck you in that ensemble, he must really want to fuck you.'

'Myrna!'

'Don't Myrna me,' she said. 'I don't want to hear your excuses because I've heard every single one of them and they're thinner than Greta Garbo after six months eating broiled grapefruit for dinner. "I'm leaving tomorrow, we don't really know each other, he's too good-looking", all nonsense. You quite clearly adore him.'

My shoulders were tight with a tension that had been there all day, slowly ratcheting up and up and up until I could hear my collarbones grinding into dust.

'He *is* too good-looking,' I said. 'You saw him. He's gorgeous, too handsome for his own good. Too handsome for me.'

At that, Myrna waved the make-up artist away and snapped her fingers to get my attention.

'That attitude will get you nowhere. The world is full of ugly men who bedded and, even worse, married the most stunning, the most beautiful women.'

I considered her words, sharp as a knife and historically accurate.

'Do you think they sat around thinking, she's far too attractive for me, I really ought to keep my dick in my pants? Because they didn't. The number of movies and television shows where a hideous troll of a man goes home to an earth-shattering example of womanhood astounds me still.'

'Marge is significantly hotter than Homer,' I admitted.

'And that's even before we start talking about the musicians,' she went on. Possibly not a big fan of *The Simpsons*. 'All those foul little boys who don't know how to wash, sitting in their bedrooms writing songs about women who are obsessed with them? Darling, show me these women? No one wanted a bar of them until they stood on stage with a guitar. They wrote it into being. You need to go into life with that kind of attitude. When you tell yourself someone is too handsome, too smart, too whatever it might be, to be interested in you, what you're really saying is that you're not good enough to be with them. And if you're not on your own team, why would anyone else join it?'

She paused for breath, her make-up artist standing to one side, looking as though she didn't know whether to give her a round of applause or burst into tears.

'I know you're right and I'm working on it,' I said. Myrna raised an eyebrow as though that was ever in question. 'But it's hard to change the way you think when you've been thinking that way for a long time.'

'No, it isn't.'

Classic Myrna.

'It really isn't,' she said. 'You make a choice, darling, but it is a practice and you must commit to it every day. A girl can't rely on having someone around to whisper sweet nothings in her ear from sunrise to sunset; it has to come from somewhere else.'

'Instagram?' I guessed.

'Yourself,' Myrna barked, hurling a tube of mascara in my general direction. She was surprisingly strong and impressively accurate for a woman in her eighties. 'Do you think I care what other people say about me?'

'I'm going to go out on a limb and say no.'

'You are the only one who decides what's true about yourself, no one else,' she confirmed. 'Well, you, a judge and a jury, but I'll tell you what I told Jane Fonda. If you're foolish enough to end up on the wrong side of the law, that's on you. Now come here, so we can see what to do with you.'

Reluctantly, I eased myself off the chaise longue and sloped across the room, joining her in front of the mirror.

'We'll ignore your terrible posture because you're doing that on purpose to vex me. When we first met, I told you I was too old to lie, and I haven't gotten any younger since then so please listen up, I hate to repeat myself. I've met your Ren and, as far as I can tell, there is no discernible reason why he shouldn't fall head over heels in love with that woman in the mirror.'

'Are you talking about me or you?' I asked, looking at our side-by-side reflection.

'As much as it pains me to say it, you,' she replied wearily. 'I'm not going to sit here and list myriad wonderful things about you because it would be a waste of what's left of my short and precious life. You already know them. But you think you're protecting yourself by accepting someone else's lies rather than believing your own truth.'

I watched my cheeks turn pink in the mirror.

'Hurts, doesn't it,' Myrna said, sharp and precise. 'The truth so often does.'

'You could have a very successful second career on TikTok,' I told her. 'Tough Love with Myrna Moore.'

'I'd rather scoop out my own eyes with a caviar spoon.' She slapped my wrist with a paper fan. 'And don't think I don't know when you're trying to change the subject. How can you be so certain the boy's heart doesn't beat only for you if you didn't give him a chance to tell you? And please don't try to answer that because it was a rhetorical question. If you want him, speak up and claim him.'

'You're missing something here,' I said. 'However I might feel about him and however he might feel about me—' She opened her mouth to speak but I kept going, risking my life to make my point. 'Ren is spoken for. He's with Bel now and there's no way on earth I would ever do anything to hurt her, so I'm just going to have to learn my lesson and live with it.'

'And you think you can, do you?' Myrna asked. 'Live with it, I mean.'

I thought about getting in Suzanne's car and driving away. I thought about the plane taking off and flying me halfway around the world. I thought about logging on to my computer on Monday morning and trying to write hilarious and heartfelt captions for British Sandwich

301

week all while Ren existed on the other side of the planet, hiking and bird watching and doing any number of things that didn't include ever kissing me again.

'That's what I thought.'

I didn't say anything. I didn't have to.

Myrna looked to the make-up artist, who was still cowering at her elbow. 'This will do.'

'So glad you like it,' the make-up artist whispered as she reached for her cane and rose out of the chair.

Wrapped in her robe and wearing more jewels than Thanos, Myrna was a sight to behold. It all made sense. Wally never stood a chance against her. I gulped as she fixed me with a gimlet eye and just for a moment, I felt as though we were in one of her pictures. The colour seeped out of the room and there she stood in black and white, all the more formidable for it.

'Tell me,' she said. 'Did you ever hear the saying, it's the fate of glass to break?'

'No,' I replied as I took my turn in the make-up chair, half-expecting a man in a trilby and a trench coat to burst through the door with a pistol in his hand. 'What does it mean?'

She pointed at the vanity in front of me. 'I've had that mirror for more than sixty years but one day, perhaps today, perhaps a hundred years from now, it will shatter into a million pieces. What might be unthinkable now is inevitable.'

'What if I roll it up in bubble wrap and never, ever move it?' I countered. 'Should be pretty safe then.'

'What's the use of a mirror if you can't look into it?' she countered. 'You can't fight fate, Phoebe, darling. There's only ever one winner in that bout.'

Right on cue, she spun around and with a dramatic flourish, disappeared into her walk-in closet, leaving me with many more questions and absolutely no answers, staring at myself in the unbroken mirror.

CHAPTER TWENTY-TWO

'Is that really my little sister?'

Suzanne took a step back and applauded as I descended Myrna's staircase an hour later. My red gown fluttered as I moved, the silk sliding against my skin with the softest whisper, and I vowed never to wear my scratchy Primark tracksuit bottoms ever again as long as I lived. Or at least until I had no other clean clothes and couldn't be bothered to put a wash on. The make-up artist had worked wonders on my face. I looked like the sort of woman who never stayed up eating Cheetos and watching Architectural Digest house tours until 3 a.m. but slept eight hours every night and drank gallons of the fifteen-dollar celery juice I made Suzanne put back in the supermarket.

'When I got changed, I realized I had my knickers on inside out,' I told her, accepting a delicate kiss on the cheek. 'So yes.'

'Well, you look incredible. Rachel Leigh Cook in the red dress in *She's All That* incredible and also before that because she was always gorgeous.'

'And you're hotter than post-makeover Anne Hathaway in *The Devil Wears Prada* and *The Princess Diaries*,' I said as I doffed an invisible cap.

She tutted loudly. 'There's no wonder women feel so shit about themselves. Anne Hathaway did not need a makeover in either film.'

'I don't think we need to feel too bad for her, but you can always go and offer your condolences in person if you want.' I pointed at a tall, gorgeous brunette across the room. 'But that really is a killer dress.'

'This old thing?' Suze smoothed the figure-hugging black velvet of her strapless dress over her hips, her shoulders shining in the artfully designed low light of the lobby. 'I bought it for some work charity event a couple of years ago and quite frankly it was wasted on them. Never attempt to dress up for a middle-aged man who wears the same hoodie seven days a week.'

Even though everyone had told me no one turned up to anything on time in Los Angeles, it was only just after eight and guests were already streaming through the doors, beautiful car after beautiful car pulling up to the front of the house and dropping off people I only ever expected to see on movie screens. Thanks to the security guards prowling the street, no one had managed to climb over the wall (today), but I could see the flash-bulbs popping in the distance, trying to see through the tinted windows of the limos. It was a strange feeling, being surrounded by so many familiar strangers. I knew them but they didn't have a clue about me.

A waiter hovered in front of us with a full tray of champagne coupes. Suzanne, ever the big sister, carefully picked two glasses and took a sip from each.

'They're very full,' she said before handing one to me. 'Don't go spilling it on that dress.'

I rolled my eyes but accepted the drink, turning back to the entrance right as one of our favourite divas tottered in, head to toe in silver sequins, white fur stole slung low on her arms. Suzanne grabbed my hand and squeezed tightly without saying a word.

'I know, I see her,' I whispered. 'Do you think she'll sing?'

'I'm not even sure she can breathe in that frock,' she replied as the chanteuse teetered forward on vertiginous heels. 'But I wouldn't bet against it, especially if Myrna asks. I think *I'd* sing if she told me to, and let's not forget I'm the only person who has ever been asked to stop mid-song on karaoke night at Popworld.'

'"Someone Like You" is a very difficult song,' I offered with great diplomacy.

'It's getting crowded in here,' Suzanne said, wafting herself with her evening bag as another Oscar winning actor arrived and tripped up Myrna's stairs. He was shorter than I'd imagined. They all were. We were leaving this party with a lifetime's supply of celebrity anecdotes. Or at least one or two stories to submit to DeuxMoi. 'Shall we have a look around?'

'Let's go out to the gardens,' I suggested. 'You've got to see them before it all starts popping off.'

'OK, but I would also like to see them while it's all popping off,' she said, linking our arms and allowing me to lead the way.

The party planners might not have realized quite how popular Myrna's event was going to be, but they had done a spectacular job decorating. All the dust sheets had been removed and replaced with soft, golden light. Everything sparkled like it was brand new, only not new now, new in 1961, and it was easy to imagine we'd all been taken back in time the moment we crossed the threshold. Soft jazz played through invisible speakers, a raspy voice over a tinkling piano, undercutting the happy buzz of conversation and ever-present fizz of champagne. There were so many flowers, red roses, Myrna's favourites, as well as delicate touches of jasmine and iris to scent the room. It smelled as though the whole house had been very lightly spritzed with Chanel No. 5.

I nodded politely at a short, smiley man I vaguely recognized as the husband of a housewife as we passed by him, onto the patio and into the night. The A listers kept on coming but there were only two people I was really watching for.

'Have you heard from Bel or Ren?'

I hated it when my sister read my mind.

'No,' I replied. 'Have you?'

'Bel texted to apologize for cancelling our session. I said I'd see her tonight but I haven't heard back. She's not one to miss out on a party though, I'm sure she'll be here.'

'You know her better than I do,' I replied, realizing at once that it was true.

Just because I liked her, didn't mean I knew her. Offering to help set her up with Ren had been a huge mistake, and not just because of my feelings. If I could go back in time to that very first morning, I'd do it all differently. Introduce the two of them then step back, stay out of the way. Hindsight truly was a wonderful thing. Now all I needed was a time machine and we'd be set.

'Are you kidding me?' Suzanne yelled when we reached the bottom of the garden. 'That's a swimming pool?'

'Isn't it stunning?' I confirmed. 'The stories Myrna has told me, honestly, if those trees could talk.'

She moved across the grass as though drawn to the deep blue water, her eyes glassy and full. 'I'm just going to dip a toe in,' she whispered. 'It's too beautiful, I have to. Also these shoes are killing me. Whatever possessed me to wear four-inch heels?'

'Suze, we've only been here half an hour, it's too early for skinny dipping,' I warned. 'If you want to keep your job, at least wait until it's properly dark.'

She held up a hand to signal that she'd heard me but I knew the words hadn't fully registered. Not that I blamed her – there was something about that pool that could make even the most committed never-nude change their ways. Avoiding the siren song of the siren sapphire waters, I took myself over to the edge of the lawn where wooden loungers had been set up in groups of twos and threes, creating a tiny sanctuary away from the party, but no one had needed it. Yet.

Behind us, the house glowed with life, looking more incredible than ever and thrilled to be used for its true and proper purpose. It hadn't seen a party like this in more than fifty years and if Myrna was right, which she usually was, it would never see another. It didn't bear thinking about.

The little black evening bag Myrna had insisted I use rather than carrying my lipstick in my pocket 'like a pack donkey', vibrated in my left hand and I immediately threw myself on top of it like an unexploded grenade, looking around to make sure I hadn't been seen. Phones were banned from the party. All the guests arriving through the front door and all the staff coming through the back had been searched, a certain multi-Grammy award winner having her gold iPhone wrenched from her hand with a separation anxiety-stricken sob. But I didn't arrive through the front or back door. I came down the staircase from the dressing room and I was the only person at the party who still had their phone.

More than a little afraid one of Myrna's security guards would shoot me on sight, I walked over to the very edge of the garden, leaning against a tree and pretending to enjoy the view as I opened my bag and pulled out my phone, swishing my hair over one shoulder to hide the handset. It was still vibrating, silent but insistent, with a UK number I did not recognize.

Had he changed his number again just to torment me? It was possible. He must have felt a disturbance in the force, a ripple in the ether that told him I was happy again and needed knocking down a peg or two.

'Bad luck, dickhead,' I said, steeling myself to answer. 'I'm ready for you this time.'

'Hello, is that Phoebe?'

But I wasn't ready for her.

'Hello?' I replied hesitantly. 'Samantha?'

There was a muffled snuffling on the other end of the line, the sound of someone swallowing, a decision being made.

'Yes,' said a thick, hoarse voice. 'Sorry to call so late, but you said any time and I suppose this counts as any time.'

I did the mental maths. Eight in the evening in LA

was four in the morning in the UK. Four in the morning on her wedding day.

'I absolutely meant it,' I shook my head at the very silly question I was about to ask. 'Are you all right?'

A beat.

'I'm supposed to get married today.'

I closed my eyes and Myrna's party, the Hollywood Hills all melted away, leaving me alone, in an eighties bathroom, smothering my sobs with a hand towel so he wouldn't hear them.

'Are you still there?' Samantha asked, a quiet panic I recognized in her voice. 'I'm sorry, I shouldn't have called, this is so out of order, it's not your problem.'

'Samantha, it's OK, you don't have to apologize,' I said quickly. Time was very much of the essence for Samantha and me. She needed my help and I needed not to upset the security guards Myrna claimed to have found via a contact in 'The Mob' who still owed her a favour. 'I told you to call me and I'm glad you did. I'm here, I'm listening, whatever you need to say, you can say it to me. I won't tell a soul, you're safe.'

It was difficult, trying to keep calm and carry on when what I really wanted to do was leap into the air, fly around the world to pick her up then pop back to the UK and string Thomas up by his predictably small penis. I'd set things straight if I had super powers; they were always wasted on men.

'He hasn't done anything wrong, not really,' she whispered. 'But some of the things he says. I thought it would get better after we got engaged but it's getting worse.'

'I believe you,' I said, reeling with the same rush I felt when Bel said the same words to me. 'I understand.'

But the acknowledgement was too much for her. At once, Samantha's voice brightened like the sun trying to shine through a dirty window. 'It's probably cold feet, isn't it? I'm overreacting, being too sensitive, just like he says.'

'If you really believed that you wouldn't be talking to me now,' I said, channelling Suzanne as best I could, kind but firm. 'Have you talked to anyone else about it?'

Another sob hitched in her throat.

'Who would I tell? Everyone loves him.'

'Your parents? Family?'

'I can't, we're not close like that.'

So he had a type. Blonde hair, blue eyes, open to being manipulated and easy to isolate from everyone they loved. What a guy.

'We were watching telly the other night and I dropped the remote down the back of the settee. We had to pull it out to find it and the settee scratched the floor. It was the tiniest little scratch, you wouldn't be able to see it unless you were looking for it, but he started screaming,' she babbled, all of it pouring out at once. 'He starts pacing up and down, telling me how clumsy and stupid I am, how I can't even change the channel without messing something up. No wonder I'm only a teacher, I'm too stupid to get a proper job. No wonder I was single for so long, I ought to be on my knees, thanking him for marrying me or I'd end up alone in the gutter.'

'I'm so sorry,' I said, wishing there were better words that meant more. 'None of that is true, not a word of it. You're none of those things, Samantha, do not take it to heart.'

'But that is what they say about teachers, isn't it? Those who can, do, those who can't, teach. And I *was* single for a long time.'

I knew what she was doing, because I'd done the same thing. She wanted to believe it, she was debating with herself as much as me, trying to make sense of it and finding truth that wasn't there. I'd heard all I needed to hear.

'Samantha, it's four o'clock in the morning on the day you're supposed to get married and you're calling your fiancé's ex-girlfriend to ask if him abusing you is normal. It isn't. It's not normal.' I paused to let her speak but she didn't say anything. She didn't hang up either. 'If you need somewhere to go to think things over, you can go to my house. It's the last place he'd expect you to be. There's a key hidden underneath a little red plant pot in the back garden, I'll text you the address.'

Still no reply, just stuttered breathing.

'You can still get out of this,' I said. 'Telling someone is the hardest part, trust me, I know.'

'I just needed to talk to someone.' She spoke through tears that sounded like they were coming thick and fast, no way to hold them back now. 'You were the only person I could think of.'

'We all need someone to talk to,' I assured her, thinking about my sister, Myrna, Bel. And me. How many people were drifting through life, feeling this alone? 'You can talk to me any time you need, twenty-four-seven, round the clock, and I'm texting you my address right now. Apologies in advance for the state of the house and take a pint of milk for tea because I've been away for two weeks and whatever is in the fridge will be rancid by now.'

'I'd better go,' she said, committing to nothing. 'It's really late. Or early.'

'Both, I suppose,' I replied. 'Depends on your perspective.'

I looked back out on the sparkling city below me. Half past four in the morning there, half past eight in the evening here, but the truth was still the truth.

'Thank you,' she said. 'And sorry.'

'Don't apologize,' I replied. Had I got through? Was it enough? 'Remember, the key is under the smallest red plant pot. Call any time.'

She hung up without saying goodbye. I stared at the blank screen as though it might give me a window into her world if I concentrated hard enough. Picking up the phone must have been hard. Cancelling the wedding at the last minute would be even harder. But getting out while she still could would be worth all that pain and more.

I raised my champagne in a toast to Samantha and wiped away a tear I hadn't felt escape. It was the last tear Thomas would ever get out of me and that was worth celebrating.

CHAPTER TWENTY-THREE

Until someone got their shit together and turned a DeLorean into a real time machine, there was no way for me to go back in time to see what Myrna and Wally's parties were like in the fifties, but if they were only half as decadent and debauched as this one, it was a wonder she was still alive at eighty-two. Even as an innocent bystander, I was certain the night had taken ten years off my life.

Phoebe from two weeks ago would have gone home the moment she got off the phone with Samantha. She would have made her excuses and taken herself to bed with a cup of tea and a lovely big box of assorted misery, indulging until she felt sick. But this Phoebe, in her red dress and her perfect make-up, decided not to. She made a choice to stay, to be with her sister and celebrate the changes she had made instead of worrying about things she couldn't change, and no one was more surprised than me.

By nine, the sun had set and the moment its watchful gaze left the revellers to their own devices, the devil came out to play. Champagne spilled over pyramids of glasses, luscious truffles were hand-fed to full lips and Myrna was proven right – her air-conditioning system really did need updating if the number of people shedding clothes left, right and centre was anything to go by. At the heart of it all was the hostess herself, bejewelled and wearing an emerald-green dress, high necked and long sleeved, with a soft drape to the back and a long silk skirt that fell almost to the floor but not quite so as not to get caught up around her feet. As practical as she was stylish, she informed me it was essential not to let your skirt get caught up in your shoes, not because you might fall over but in case you had to run from the police. When she moved, I saw a slit running all the way up one side to reveal what she insisted on calling her 'hoofer's legs'. She was iconic.

One by one or two by two, her guests lined up to bend the knee to the queen of the hills, some of the most famous people in the world, starry-eyed and speechless. She sat in her favourite, high-backed chair, receiving them with a healthy mix of grace and glee, smiling at some and seeing off others with a single flicker of her eyebrow. Alongside the actors and singers and industry bigwigs were Myrna's neighbours. I saw the old man who lived two houses down from Suzanne clinking glasses with the mum from a classic nineties sitcom, and a woman I recognized from across the street, barely recognizable without two screaming toddlers strapped into a double pushchair, laughed happily with a tall, handsome former vampire and all I could think was, good for her. Those children were awful.

But there was still no sign of Ren and Bel.

'Let's go and get another drink,' Suzanne suggested.

'You can't spend all night waiting for them, they might not come.'

'I can't make my mind up whether it would be better if they did or didn't,' I admitted, right as a ponytailed teen-actress-turned-music-mogul popped another bottle of champagne on the screaming celebrity hordes. 'Ren really wanted to see Myrna's house, I can't believe he'd pass up the opportunity.'

'You know how new couples can be, they're probably at his place—' she stopped herself from completing the sentence and quickly recalibrated. 'Doing something very chaste while fully clothed.'

'If you really believe that, you've been single for too long,' I said glumly.

'I've been single forever,' she reminded me. 'But I'm going to work on it.'

'Work on it how?' I asked. 'Have you set some annual objectives?'

'I know you're taking the piss out of me, but yes,' she answered, her eyebrows set with determination, blue eyes focused. 'I've hired an executive partnership agency and they're going to send over profiles of several suitable candidates on Monday. Hopefully we can set up some meetings for next week.'

'Stop, stop, it's too romantic,' I swooned. 'My heart can't take it.'

'Shut up and drink your champagne,' she ordered, puckering her lips to stop herself from smiling. 'I'm a very busy woman and I haven't got all day to be swiping through apps and meeting losers who'll go through my bathroom cabinets when they say they're going to the toilet.'

'Everyone does that and don't pretend you don't because we all know the truth.' I glanced over at Myrna's chair. 'Our gracious host implied she'd be interested if you're up for it.'

A delighted bark of a laugh escaped from Suzanne and she traced the rim of her glass with her fingertip, contemplating the offer. 'It's going to have to be a no. She's amazing, obviously, but she would eat me alive, and I don't mean in a good way.'

'The correct answer,' I replied, only slightly worried at the glint in my sister's eyes.

As the music got louder and the lights dimmed lower, any lingering inhibitions popped like the bubbles in the champagne and Myrna got the bacchanal of her dreams. Singing, dancing, touching, bodies pressed against bodies, it was beautiful chaos.

But I didn't care about the party. All I wanted was Ren. With each minute that passed, the need to see him grew stronger until it was almost an obsession. He could already be here, him and Bel lost in the crush of couture, and the thought of leaving the next day without laying my eyes on him one more time was unbearable. Even though I knew it would hurt, I just had to.

I slipped away from the crowd, leaving Suzanne talking with a stunning Black woman I recognized but couldn't quite put my finger on. She was wearing a scrap of pink fabric that clung to her body for dear life, providing just enough coverage to avoid getting arrested, but more importantly, she was looking at my sister like she was the key to the universe and Suzanne looked almost as thrilled with her as she had with her department's latest productivity report. I left the two of them to make heart eye emojis at each other and let myself drift away on the tide of the party, pushed and pulled into the different rooms, moving with the ebb and the flow and ending up in the ballroom. It wasn't a huge ballroom, said the woman who hardly had room to swing a toy cat in her living room, but it was spectacular, the ceilings hand-painted to look like the night sky, all the stars and constellations picked out in what could easily be real gold. There were no windows so it felt safe and secluded, the perfect hideaway, even with a hundred people crammed inside and dancing to the live band. I bobbed along the edge of the room, drinking in everything I saw. There was no need for the free-flowing champagne, just walking around the room was enough to get me drunk.

When Ren and Bel walked in, everyone turned to stare.

Gran liked to say everyone was beautiful when they were happy and the people at this party were ecstatic, but the two of them together were spellbinding. Bel was everything, glowing in a one-shouldered peacock-blue gown, slashed at the waist to reveal inches of midriff and slit all the way up to the matching underwear that teased its existence as she moved. Ren made the perfect foil in a slim-fitting black tuxedo that only made his broad shoulders broader and narrow waist more defined, and a blindingly white shirt beneath to set off the bronzed tone of his complexion. They looked incredible, perfectly cast to star in the rest of their lives together. I stayed exactly where I was, barely breathing and doing my very best to disappear.

Ren whispered something in Bel's ear and walked out, leaving her alone in the spotlight where she belonged.

Completely unable to help myself, I raised a hand when her gaze swept towards me, waving her over to my safe little corner.

'There you are,' she said with a happy exhalation, pressing kisses onto my cheeks. 'I've been looking for you everywhere, this place is too much.'

'Myrna wasn't messing about when she said she wanted to put on a proper farewell bash,' I said, wondering where Ren had gone, when he might come back and whether it might be easier to throw myself off the balcony and into the pool rather than deal with all these confusing feelings.

'It's a whole vibe.' She bopped her head in time to the music. 'You look beautiful.'

'Then you look incredible,' I replied. 'That dress is magnificent.'

'A diamond's got to shine,' she replied, laughing as she tossed flicked hair over her shoulder and struck a dramatic pose. 'But thanks. I bought it from this guy in Calabasas who I'm pretty sure was stealing dry cleaning from the Kardashians. Hey, this is going to sound crazy but I thought I saw someone who looked just like Suzanne making out with someone who looked just like the singer, Juliette.'

I snapped my fingers, relieved to put a name to a face. 'That's who it was. Good for Suze.'

'I'm going to need to know so much more about that later,' Bel said, happy and confused. 'But I need to talk to you. Is there some place quiet we can go?'

My heart leapt out of my chest, bouncing up and down like Tigger after ten espressos.

'It's going to be impossible to have a conversation in here.' I backed away until I had to yell over the music. 'Let's talk tomorrow.'

But Bel wasn't the kind of girl to take no for an answer. She opened her evening bag and pulled out a small square of folded paper.

'I didn't ask you to write this,' she said. 'So what gives?'

It was the letter from the baseball game.

'I'm an overachiever?' I replied, my hand reflexively reaching for my throat as the letter opened on its own in the palm of her hand, unfurling like a lotus flower. 'You can ask Suzanne, always going above and beyond with my homework. It's a back-up letter, in case you needed another.'

'Sorry, Pheebs,' she said. 'I don't believe you.'

'No, that's definitely it.' My words tumbled over themselves as the music grew louder in the background. 'I was writing something else and I thought, what if Bel needs another love letter? So I scribbled it down. Really, just bashed it out, barely even thought about it at all. I can't even remember what I wrote.'

'I ended things with Ren.'

Bel folded the letter back into its neat, safe square and pressed it into my hands as I stared back at her, too stunned to speak. 'It should be easy, right?' she said. 'That's what people say. If we were meant to be together it would feel natural, like when I got my first iPhone. I knew how to use it without even reading the instructions. What's the word?'

'Intuitive,' I suggested, still so shocked.

'I knew you'd know,' Bel said happily. 'Me and Ren, we have nothing to say to each other. I still think he's hot and nice and everything, but the only thing we have in common is you. Why drag it out when he has a chance at something really special with someone else?'

The throb of the music got louder and louder, the dance floor bouncing beneath our feet.

'I can't imagine he'll be short of offers once word gets out he's on the market,' I said, burning up at the thought of a stranger standing in his back garden, running their hands through his hair. Somehow it was much worse than the thought of Ren and Bel.

'I'm talking about you, dummy,' she said, laughing out loud. 'I should have seen it right away but I was too busy fantasizing about a version of a guy that doesn't exist. Ren isn't my fairy-tale ending, he's yours.'

A wave of warmth washed over me, followed by the cold rush of icy shock.

'I figured it out after the game,' she explained, plucking a glass of champagne from a passing waiter's tray in exchange for a smile so devastating, he almost fell over. 'I knew you didn't write that letter for me and I was so mad.'

'I'm sorry,' I said automatically. 'Really sorry.'

'Don't be!' She used her barrel-shaped clutch bag to tap me on the top of the head like a poorly behaved dog. 'Jeez, is that your default setting?'

'Yes?' I replied. 'Sorry.'

'There she goes again,' she huffed happily. 'I wasn't mad at you, I was mad at me. It hit me while I was looking for my chicken sandwich; you and Ren are a better match. I don't care about birds or baseball or hiking, and he doesn't care about acting or fitness or any of the real housewives franchises, not even Beverly Hills and they're local!'

'Well, no one's perfect.' I leaned against the wall to steady myself. Was this really happening?

'The two of you are the same person. You have the

same weird sense of humour, you both love books and you really enjoy talking about your grandparents, which personally I think is a little odd but if you're going to live in the past, you might as well live in it together. You do like him, right?'

'I do,' I confessed. The band doubled their tempo and the room began to spin. 'I like Ren.'

The understatement of the century.

'Here's the thing I realized yesterday,' Bel said before draining her glass of champagne and dumping it on a ledge behind her. 'I was watching TV and *Twilight* was on and pow, it all made sense.'

Like Ren said, she really was unpredictable.

'*Twilight* made it make sense? You think Ren's a vampire?'

'No!' she exclaimed, excitement animating her beautiful face. 'Ren's Bella. The beautiful little idiot who doesn't know how gorgeous she is while everyone else falls over themselves trying to hit it.'

'Not as pale though,' I pointed out. 'Or as clumsy. Or insufferable.'

'She's the worst,' Bel agreed before prodding me in the shoulder. 'You're Edward.'

'I'm the vampire?'

'And I'm Jacob.'

You'd never seen anyone look so pleased with an analogy.

'I thought I was in love with Ren,' she explained. 'And on paper we make a ton of sense like Bella and Jacob. We have fun, we both have great hair and I had a real glow up in high school, just like Taylor Lautner, but I'm not the one. It's you. You're the smart one, you're the one with all the words, and even if you went to Volterra to get the Volturi to kill you, Ren would save you because you're soulmates.'

'You went off the rails a bit towards the end, but I think I follow,' I replied. 'Wait, does that mean you're going to imprint on my baby?'

Bel shrugged. 'Never say never, I'm only twenty-seven; if you had a kid right now, I'd be forty-eight when they turned twenty-one. Perfect second marriage age. Think about it, who would make a better daughter-in-law than me?'

'My theoretical child could do a lot worse,' I admitted. The woman was a wonder. 'I don't know what to say.'

'Say "thank you, Bel, you're right. I am super horny for Ren Garcia and I'm going to go find him right now and climb him like a tree."'

It wasn't the worst idea I'd ever heard.

'What are you waiting for?' she asked, placing her hands on my shoulders and physically turning me to face the door. 'Go find him!'

'Wait, does he know?' I asked, excited and scared and a little bit hungry. I'd hardly eaten all day in fear of not fitting into the dress and I was paying for it now. 'Did you tell him about the letters?'

'No.' She shook her head. 'I figured that part should come from you. We both know you're better with words than I am.'

It was a lot to process. Ren was officially single, I was a vampire, Bel planning to marry my non-existent child. I glanced around the room, looking for a waiter armed with hors d'oeuvres. Typical man, never around when you needed him.

'So.' Bel flashed her dazzling Hollywood smile at me. 'What are you waiting for?'

'What if he doesn't feel the same way?' I whispered.

'I should have known that's what you would say,' she replied. 'But Phoebe, what if he does?'

What if he does.

A new voice popped into my head, bright and hopeful and one I very much wanted to listen to. What if he does? Hope was a thing worth holding on to.

'I wouldn't even know where to start,' I said. Every word I'd ever learned swirled around inside me and none of them were the right ones.

'You've already started.' She closed my hand around the piece of paper in my palm and squeezed. 'All that's left to do is to say it out loud.'

CHAPTER TWENTY-FOUR

Turning my back on the party raging on around me, I slipped past the guests and down one of the dark hallways that led to the rose garden. I needed to be where people weren't, to collect myself and gather my thoughts.

The moon was almost full when I found my spot, a little wooden bench right in the heart of the rose bushes, far enough away from the house for the party to feel like a dream. She cast her milky glow over everything, soothing, calm and crystal, and I held the letter in my hand, my mind so full it felt empty, like a sky full of snow.

'Phoebe, is that you?'

Of all the rose gardens in all the world, he had to walk into mine.

'Hi,' I said without standing. I wasn't sure if my legs would hold me. 'You're here.'

'Where else would I be?' Ren replied in a hushed and reverent tone. 'Can you believe this place? I can't believe Myrna's selling. It should be on the historical register, no one should be allowed to touch it.'

'Did you get a chance to talk to her?' I asked, ignoring the out-of-control thudding that was happening inside my ribs.

He stood a few feet away, his profile edged in luminous white and nodded. 'I did, but just for a second. She insisted I find her later for a dance so maybe we'll talk more then. To be specific, she said a horizontal tango but I think she was joking.'

'She almost certainly wasn't,' I replied, the corners of my letter digging into my palm.

'Some party.' Ren glanced around the gardens, looking everywhere but at me. 'Did you see Bel?'

'I did.'

'Did she tell you our news?'

'She did.'

So eloquent, Phoebe, so articulate. You should be a writer.

He reached one hand up to his hair, the fabric of his jacket straining at the shoulders. 'I guess it's just one of those things, you know? Wasn't meant to be.'

'Some things aren't,' I said with a stutter. 'I'm sorry.'

He'd always been so easy to talk to until now.

'It's for the best anyway.' Ren walked over to the bench and sat down next to me, the fabric of my dress filling the space between us. 'Looks like I'm going to be leaving soon.'

It was not what I had expected him to say. I was the one who was leaving, not him.

'What do you mean?' I asked. 'Leaving for where?'

'My brother called this afternoon. Someone made an offer on the house, all cash, two hundred thousand over ask. He wants me out by Monday.'

'But that only gives you two days,' I protested. 'That's not fair, it's too soon.'

'I know.'

'And there's nothing you can do?'

Ren's jaw tensed and he stared off into the distance. That was his answer.

Above me, a cloud drifted in front of the moon, casting a gentle, promising darkness over the garden. I closed my eyes and inhaled deeply, literally stopping to smell the roses. I usually hated rose-scented things, they were always too heavy and cloying, but Myrna's garden smelled heavenly, the warm sweetness of the flowers cut with Ren's fresh, woodsy scent. It was heartbreaking to think I'd never experience it again.

'I can't believe I have to leave tomorrow,' I said, letting my quiet words linger in the air. 'I really didn't expect to love this place so much, it's not how I imagined it would be at all.'

A smile carved faint lines around his mouth. 'LA is whatever you want it to be,' he replied. 'You get out what you put in. Most people don't see what you saw, they stick to the shiny surface, but if you dig a little deeper that's where the good stuff is.'

'I'm thankful I had you to show me,' I said before clearing my throat. 'And Suzanne and Myrna and Bel,' I added in a garbled rush. 'Not everyone is lucky enough to have so many brilliant tour guides.'

When he looked up at me, his emerald eyes were almost black.

'Not everyone is lucky enough to have someone so incredible to show around.'

All the air disappeared at once, swallowed up by the roses and leaving nothing for the rest of us.

'About you and Bel,' I said, feeling around for a way into the conversation I knew had to happen. 'I'm sorry it didn't work out.'

'Don't be.' Ren leaned forward, resting his forearms on his thighs. A slice of moonlight cut through the clouds to outline the planes of his face and the curve of his full, firm lips. 'This is what happens when you go all in on someone before you really know them. I fell in love with a letter instead of a person, that's on me.'

He fell in love he fell in love he fell in love.

I had always been good at keeping things in their place, mentally at least, and after what happened with Thomas, I'd only got better. Box one feeling away from the other, keep them at a safe distance. Then along came Ren and set it all on fire. All my carefully maintained compartments started to shake, lids flying off boxes, thoughts and feelings running around uncontrolled, and I couldn't seem to grab hold of the words I needed. There was a hurricane happening inside me, all while I sat beside him, not moving, barely breathing.

'I really wanted to be the person she was writing about,' he said, his mouth crooked with his perfect half-smile. 'For someone to see me and know me and love me that way.'

'That's what everyone wants,' I managed to say. 'To be loved for who they are.'

'If everyone wants it, why is it so hard to find?'

I didn't have an answer. He was right. Falling in love should be the easiest thing in the world but we made it so difficult. We laughed at it or diminished it, we put it on a pedestal or ran away when it came calling. The one thing we all wanted and the one thing we all had to give in limitless quantities. Why did we make it so hard?

Ren dipped his head and his hair fell forward in front of his face. It had only been two weeks since we met but it already looked so much longer than it did on that first evening in the garden.

'At least I got my first love letter,' he said, nudging my knee with his and sending a thrilling rush all the way through my body. 'Something to show the nurses in the old folks' home if I'm lucky enough to live that long.'

Maybe it didn't have to be so hard after all.

'Would you like another?'

The words were out of my mouth and away before I realized what I'd said and when he looked up, I was holding the piece of paper out to him. A breeze danced across the lawn and it fluttered as I held it so lightly, almost daring him to take it from me before it blew away forever. Slowly, he moved towards me, crossing into the moonbeam that sliced the space between us, and for a single breath he glowed from head to toe.

'What is this?' he asked, opening it and reading before I had a chance to answer. 'Is it the letter you had at the baseball game? The one Bel didn't want me to see?' His eyes scanned back and forth, two, three, four times, before he looked up at me, his hands trembling.

'Why do you have this?'

'Because I wrote it,' I replied, so brave, so scared, so painfully aware I might never have this chance again.

It was only a short letter, just a few lines really, but Ren studied it as though he was going to be tested on each and every syllable, brow furrowed, lips parted. After what felt like a lifetime, he looked up at me.

'You wrote this?' he asked.

'Yes,' I replied.

'And you wrote the other letter too,' he surmised. 'It's the same handwriting, same style, the same . . .'

He didn't finish the sentence. I wasn't sure if he could.

'Bel really liked you but she didn't know how to tell you,' I explained. 'So I offered to write the letters for her because it was easy for me to talk to you and I wanted to help her but—'

'You tried to help by making a fool of me?'

There wasn't a trace of a smile on his face, nothing but hurt and disappointment, and it struck me dumb.

'You were what, her emotional spy?' he added, every word a challenge. 'Bel sent you to find out the best way to play me? Jesus, Phoebe, all the things I told you about myself, about my family. How much I *loved* that letter. And you two used it against me. This is messed up.'

'It wasn't like that,' I said, trying my best to make him understand. 'She told me how she felt and I just dressed it up a bit. There was no dark agenda or anything, we were doing it because we care about you.'

I was desperate to make him understand but I couldn't get the right words out.

Ren rose from the bench, shaking as he stood.

'We?' he repeated. 'So what, I was dating both of you only I didn't know it?'

'No, that's not it,' I groaned. Every thought and feeling I'd ever had swirled around and around inside my mind and I could see the ones I needed but they were just out of reach. 'Can we start this conversation again? Everything was OK a minute ago, you and Bel already agreed to be friends. There's no real harm done.'

'The real harm was done when you and Bel decided to play me for a fool,' he replied, hurling the letter to the ground. 'Safe travels, Phoebe, I hope you come back to visit again someday. Glad to say I won't be here.'

The evening breeze picked up his letter, my letter, and blew it into the rose bushes as he walked away, hiding the piece of paper away inside a cage of thorns. I could have left it there. I could have gone back to the party and pretended everything was fine like I had a million times before. I could have got on the airplane, flown home and tried my best never to think about Ren again. I could have lived my life without him.

I could have.

But I didn't.

Instead, I took a deep breath in, wincing as I stuck my hand into the roses. Reaching past the beautiful blooms and down into the sharp thorns that protected them, allowing something so beautiful to thrive. The barbs slashed at me as I searched for the letter but I didn't stop until I felt it in my fingers and pulled it back into the light. Dozens of scratches, the same colour as my dress, tracked up and down my arm. The price of retrieving the letter. And even though my arm throbbed, the stings and scratches on my skin were still easier to bear than the wounds Ren's words left behind.

CHAPTER TWENTY-FIVE

I didn't tell Myrna, Suzanne or Bel I was leaving. They would understand. The party may have been a once in a lifetime thing but so was Ren.

'Ren!' I yelled, banging on his front door. 'Please open the door. I'll stay here all night if I have to. Even though I don't have a coat or any water or anything to eat and there are coyotes and raccoons and Suzanne mentioned a mountain lion the other day and—'

The lock turned with a distinctive click but the door didn't open. I waited, counting to ten, before turning the handle to let myself in.

'Hello?' I called, squinting into the unlit hallway. I knew he was angry, but couldn't he have turned at least one light on? 'Ren?'

'Say what you want to say then leave.'

His voice came from upstairs, carrying through the darkness.

'Can you come down?' I asked from the foot of the stairs. 'I don't really want to have to shout all of this.'

'No.'

'Right you are,' I mumbled, feeling my way up the old, creaking staircase.

When I reached the top, I saw a sliver of orange light seeping out from underneath one of the doors and with my heart in my mouth, I knocked gently then pushed it open.

Ren stood in the shadows on the far side of the room, one small lamp lighting the space.

We were in his bedroom.

If the way I felt before was painful, this was agony. He was still in his tux, only with the bow tie hanging loose, three buttons unfastened at his neck, exposing just enough of his throat to make me wonder whether Bel was right, maybe I was a vampire. I definitely had an undeniable urge to press my mouth to his flesh and taste it.

'Well?' Ren said. 'What is it?'

His bedroom was small, the walls wood-panelled and the ceilings low. I stayed where I was, on the other side of the enormous wooden bedframe that separated us. His bed, Ren's bed. Right there, just three steps away from me.

'I offered to write love letters for Bel because she was too nervous to start a conversation with you and I know that sounds absurd when you get to know her, but please try to remember the first word she ever said to you was "snigh".' He pulled at the end of his bow tie, letting it snake around his neck, then tossed it over the back of a chair but didn't say anything. It didn't matter. I was determined to get it all out this time. Even if nothing else came of it, I owed him the truth.

'But I wrote them,' I confessed. 'And I meant every word of them.'

Ren slid his arms out of his jacket, dangling it over a high-backed leather armchair in the low lamplight.

'If that's true, why would you say they were from Bel?' he asked. 'Why would you want me to date her if you had feelings for me?'

'Believe me, I had a lot of different reasons, but they all seem stupid now,' I replied, winding my fingers around one another.

'Such as?'

'Bel liked you first, I'm only here on holiday, you're not my type.' I pressed down on an angry red rose-thorn scratch near my wrist and started at the sting. 'Someone like you would never want someone like me.'

Ren laid his jacket over the back of the chair, smoothing it down carefully, lovingly. I remembered him telling Myrna he would wear his grandfather's tuxedo and I felt a tug in my chest, an irresistible force pulling me to him. Fighting the laws of physics, I stayed right where I was.

'Someone like me,' he echoed as he turned his attention to his cuffs. 'A lame, lonely guy who's stuck in the past, can't make a relationship work, constantly disappoints his family and has been hiding in his grandparents' house for the last year to avoid having to figure out what to do with his life? You mean someone like that?'

'You can't mean that,' I said, watching as he unfastened one cufflink and then the other. 'Do you really not know how amazing you are?'

He met my words with an under-the-breath laugh,

slipping the silver cufflinks into a black velvet box and snapping it shut.

'OK, Phoebe.'

'No, not "OK, Phoebe",' I replied, suddenly furious with him. How dare he not see himself the way I did? Clearing my throat and my mind, I opened my mouth and hoped the right words would come. 'You're considerate. You're kind and genuine. You're so passionate about the things you love.'

He placed one hand on top of his bedpost, first running his fingers over the old wood then pulling on it, testing the sturdiness of the structure.

'Stubborn is the word my family would use.'

'That's just what people say when they know they can't change your mind about something you believe in,' I replied, very much wishing I was that bedpost. 'I've never met anyone like you, Ren. The way you value the past just as much as the future. The way you see the beauty in simple things, in birds, in old houses, in tradition and how you want to share it with everyone.'

The words were coming thick and fast now, I couldn't have stopped myself if I tried.

'You are so completely and utterly yourself in a time when most people are so busy trying to be someone, they don't know who they are,' I told him, practically yelling across the room. 'You couldn't be anyone else if you tried and when I'm with you, I feel like anything is possible, whether I'm jumping into a waterfall or hiking up a mountain or chasing you out of a party and standing in your bedroom to tell you how I feel.' I paused to swallow down my emotions, my voice cracking. 'I have felt so worthless for so long but when I'm with you, I feel like I'm enough.'

The room was full of shadows, muted shades of black and grey and blue, but the bedside lamp etched out his face in a warm orange glow and when he lifted his head I couldn't read the look on his face.

'You,' Ren said. 'Are more than enough.'

His voice was torn at the edges and the rough finish made the hair on the back of my neck stand on end. He moved around the bed at an excruciatingly slow pace until the distance between us had melted away, the unmistakable smell of him mixing with the light, flowery perfume I'd borrowed from Myrna, turning the bedroom into a forest, a mountain. A waterfall.

'The first night we met, I couldn't sleep.' He inched closer towards me until his words existed only in my ear, a secret between the two of us. 'You were so funny and smart and quick, but I figured I'd blown it. Lecturing you about birds when all I wanted to do was kiss you.'

It was everything I could do to stay standing, my breath fast and shallow as his hand curled around mine.

'When you invited me over, I thought maybe I had another chance, but all you wanted to do was set me up with your friend, then you gave me the letter and it was like you'd made my choice for me. You didn't want me but someone else did. Someone who wrote the most beautiful words I'd ever read. I wanted to believe I could inspire those feelings in someone because I have been waiting my whole life to feel that way about someone.'

'They were the easiest words I've ever written,' I said, inhaling sharply as he slid his hand up my arm.

'Jesus, Phoebe, what happened to you?' He examined my cuts and scratches with genuine concern that only made me want him all the more. 'Did you wrestle a coyote on the way over?'

'I lost a fight with a rose bush when I was rescuing this.' I gave him the second letter, pressing it into the palm of his hand. I knew he would keep it safe this time. 'Don't worry, it doesn't hurt.'

A truth and a lie. It did hurt but I couldn't feel anything but him.

Ren took the letter across to a dresser pushed up against the wall and opened a glossy wooden box that sat on top, stowing it safely next to its predecessor.

'When I read the first letter, I heard your voice in my head,' he said, closing it carefully. 'I told myself it was only because you were there, standing in front of me, but I should have known. I should have said something. There were moments when I almost did.'

'When I brought Myrna to visit,' I said. 'At the waterfall.'

'And the game,' he added. 'You can lie to yourself about a lot of things, but you can't lie to yourself about a kiss.'

He raised my forearm to his mouth and gently touched his lips to the tender skin, trailing up my arm, onto my shoulder, up my neck.

'I don't want to lie any more,' I told him as I leaned into the kisses, allowing myself to melt against his warm, solid body. Allowing myself to let go. With one hand curled around the back of my neck and the other travelling down to the small of my back, he held me close.

'Tell me what you do want,' Ren commanded. 'I won't do anything unless you ask me to.'

The promise of what might happen next was almost too much. For so long, my body and my self had been two separate entities and I'd forgotten how to connect the dots, but with his arms around me, safe and warm and protected, I knew there was no need to make this part difficult.

'I want you to kiss me,' I replied.

A slow, gratified smile spread across Ren's face and he nodded just once before his mouth pressed against mine. It was hot and hungry, too desperate to tease me with gentle touches, and I responded in kind. A sharp, delighted gasp escaped from my lips as he pushed me back against the bedroom wall, the sudden shock of it cutting through to the bone, the urgency of his body on mine. It was electric.

'Like this?' he asked, his hands cupping my face as my hair worked its way loose, falling in my eyes and around my shoulders.

'Exactly like that.'

My lips found his again, my mouth opening to his tongue, and I came undone. I tore at his shirt, clawing at the buttons as he pulled at the straps of my dress, both of us ignoring the sound of ripping fabric, neither of us sure what had been destroyed. I couldn't speak for him but I didn't care. I would have torn the entire house apart with my bare hands to get to him in that moment. The delicate, kindling chemistry between us caught fire, roaring into existence and consuming me in white-hot flames, scorching with enough heat to burn down the whole world.

His hands travelled down my body and I surrendered to the sensations, new and unfamiliar, that threatened to take me. Heady, strong, dark desire, the absolute and undeniable need to be consumed by this man in whatever way he pleased. It was a want I didn't recognize but I knew it was my own. I'd hidden myself away in a snarl of thorns for too long, scratching anyone who came too close. Only the thorns didn't only hurt those on the outside. They pricked me every time I tried to move, keeping me safe and keeping me still. But Ren moved through them easily as though he'd always known the way.

'I want this off,' he gasped into my neck as he spun me around roughly and began working on the buttons that held the delicate silk to my body. 'Congratulations on choosing the most complicated dress in America.'

Pressing my hands against the wall, I braced myself, surprised by the sound of my own laugh. 'Myrna chose it,' I said, breathless and aching. 'So you'd think it would be the complete opposite.'

'It's a designer chastity belt,' Ren replied as I pawed at the complicated straps, trying to remember how to unhook them. I had never hated a piece of clothing more.

'Shred it,' I ordered. 'Tear it to pieces.'

'It's too beautiful,' he argued. He gave up on the buttons and rained kisses across my back instead. 'I'll work around it, we already destroyed my shirt.'

'I don't care about the dress,' I replied, barely able to recognize my own frayed, guttural voice. 'You told me to tell you what I want. Ren, I want you. Now.'

He pushed against me as I leaned into him, the evidence of our mutual need pressing into my lower back, and his hands moved around to the front of my body, sliding up from my waist and curving around my breasts, squeezing gently until I moaned. Across the room I saw a mirror and reflected in it, a man and a woman, both with wild eyes, her hair a loose tangle of gold and his shirt hanging off his body, open in the front with a clean rip in the back, torn all the way from the hem up to the collar.

I watched him take a small gold square out of his pocket before unfastening the button at his waistband. I heard the unzipping of his fly. I saw his trousers slip down his bronzed, muscular legs and land in a heap on the floor before he pushed up her dress to find the edge of the thin silk underwear beneath, all that separated them now.

It's the fate of glass to break, I thought as he slipped my underwear to the side and pressed against me. When something unthinkable becomes inevitable. We were inevitable now.

'Is this OK?' Ren whispered. The hot skin of his chest burned against my cool, exposed back.

'Yes,' I replied, my eyes fixed on the couple in the mirror. 'Please don't stop.'

'I won't,' he promised.

And he didn't.

I covered his hand with mine, guiding him exactly where I wanted him, the sound of his groans sending me skittering over the edge and falling so far, so fast, there was no way back. Stars glittered behind my eyes, a delicious, tempting darkness calling out to me as I gave into the hard pressure of his body and the yielding softness of my own, two halves of a whole.

My back arched sharply and we both cried out, Ren wrapping one arm around my waist, the other braced against the wall. I watched us in the mirror, determined to remember every moment of this forever, studying the desire in his eyes, the surprise on his face and the rhythm of his body until the deep, desperate pleasure that had been building inside me pushed every conscious thought out of my mind, leaving nothing but a mess of emotion and reaction. I felt everything: fragile, delicate, brash and brazen, loud and unashamed. Closing my eyes, I gave in to sensation, satisfied to be lost in it, lost in my body, lost in Ren, and I had no desire to ever be found again.

CHAPTER TWENTY-SIX

From the bed, I watched the world shift from black to grey to bright and burning blue. Beside me, Ren slept soundly, long lashes flickering against his cheeks, his breathing soft and slow and even. Everything was perfect.

A red and green hummingbird appeared in the window, its iridescent wings a blur as it hovered in front of me, and I smiled. One more thing I couldn't quite believe about LA, that these incredible little things were flying around all over the place. No wonder people were so much happier here – the thought of saying hello to a hummingbird every morning was a lot more enticing than dodging the pigeons every time I had to cross Market Square. Tiny, colourful miracle bird or scabby, one-legged rats of the sky? It wasn't much of a choice.

In less time than it took to blink, the bird was gone, but I didn't mind. The fact they didn't stick around very long was what made them so special. Some things were more precious because they were fleeting. Rolling over, I turned away from the window and watched the rise and fall of Ren's chest, lost in the deepest sleep. Some things weren't meant to last forever.

It had been a long, incredible night and even though I knew it had to come eventually, the dawn still felt like a betrayal, bringing with it the day I had to leave. With the sky full of stars, everything seemed possible, but now at the soft, uncertain break of day, things were different. I had to go home to England, Ren had to return to Maine. I had a job to get back to and his house was about to be sold. Whether I liked it or not, it was time to face up to real life, and real life wasn't Hollywood parties, designer gowns and unbelievable sex with men who made Zac Efron look like he could stand to hit the gym a bit more regularly. Real life was paying your council tax on time, getting the gutters cleaned before winter and realizing you'd run out of toilet paper right after you sat down for a wee. Real life could never be this blissful.

Even though I'd spent the whole night wide awake, trying to think of a way for us to work, I had nothing. Everyone knew long distance was a fantasy. We'd start off with good intentions, he would call me every day, I would get over my nana-like attitude to phone sex, maybe we'd even visit each other, but eventually it would fall apart, shatter into tears and recriminations, souring what we had, long distance always did. But what choice was there? If only there was a way to tie the night up in a bow and keep it like this forever. But no, as soon as Ren woke up, we'd have to deal with the reality of the morning after.

As soon as Ren woke up . . .

I spotted the glossy wooden box on the dresser and slipped out from under the sheets, searching around the room for my dress. It didn't feel right to do this naked. So quietly, I opened the box, took out one of the two pieces of paper torn from my notebook and picked up a worn-down pencil that sat next to the wooden box. We started with a letter, we should end with one too.

Dear Ren,
This time I don't have the words because I meant all of the others.
You're everything.
I'll never forget you.

I couldn't quite bring myself to sign my name.

Without re-reading even once, I folded the note back up and placed it on my pillow. It almost hurt to look at him, standing close enough to count the freckles on his cheeks and memorize the curve of his cupid's bow. I studied the turn of the arm flung over his head, framing his perfect face, his hand resting lightly in his thick, dark hair. Then I closed the curtains to shut out the sun, picked up his alarm clock and pulled the plug out the back, waiting for the glowing red numbers to fade to black and reminding myself this was for the best.

Setting the clock back on the table, I took one last look at Ren Garcia before tiptoeing out of the room, down the stairs and out the front door, leaving him behind. Fast asleep and dreaming.

'Well, well, well. Look what the cat dragged around the corner and up the hill.'

Suzanne eyed me over an enormous coffee cup, cradled

in her oversized armchair, a bottle of Advil and a plate of dry toast on the coffee table next to her. 'So you're not dead after all. Bel, I owe you twenty dollars.'

It was only a couple of minutes after 8 a.m. when I let myself into the house, tired and sore and confused, but Bel and Suzanne were both up already, wide-awake and waiting.

'Sorry, I meant to message you but my phone died,' I said, pulling said phone out of my bag and plugging it into the waiting charger at the wall as if to prove it. 'And, well, I was a bit busy.'

'I told you!' Bel crowed from her spot on the sofa, dressed in nothing but a bra and a pair of sweatpants that were at least three sizes too big. 'Tell us everything, I want every filthy detail. What was he like? How big is it? Where did he put it?'

'No, too bad, I'm not even acknowledging that last three,' I replied, opening the fridge to search for I wasn't sure what. What beverage was the best cure for self-inflicted heartache?

'That bad?' she pouted in sympathy before a wicked look came into her eyes. 'Or that good?'

'I don't really want to talk about it.'

'Isn't that my line?' Suzanne asked, smiling. But when I didn't smile back, she sat up, her spine stiffening with concern. 'Pheebs, are you OK?'

'Fine,' I lied. 'Better than fine. Also very tired.'

Bel squealed with delight. 'Is Ren coming over?' she asked. 'Should I go get Morning Buns? Should we go out? Are we celebrating?'

I cracked open an iced coffee labelled 'Death Wish Super Jolt Mega Java', taking one sip and one sip only before I understood why there was a skull and cross-bones on the can. One more mouthful and I'd be able to see through time and space.

'Can I go for a shower before we start the Spanish inquisition?' I replied, shaking as I took a second sip. How was this stuff legal?

'You really want to shower straight away?' She stuck out her tongue before chugging from a giant bottle of something called Pedialyte. 'When I hook up with someone I really like, I want to keep them on me for as long as I can.'

'Bel, we're British,' Suzanne said, pulling a face.

'Our gran would dip you in bleach if she'd heard what you just said,' I added. 'In fact, maybe you should shower first.'

'I'm clean, I swear,' she said with a happy exhalation. 'Last night was the most fun I have ever had in my life. I don't think I've made out with so many people.'

'You rebound faster than a trampoline,' Suze replied. 'But it was fun, wasn't it? My night wasn't quite as scandalous as yours but I did give someone my phone number. Not that she'll call.'

'But what if she does?' I asked, borrowing Bel's words of encouragement.

'You'll have to go on a date!' our friend gasped, clutching her imaginary pearls. 'And maybe even have fun and be happy! Oh gosh, Suzie, whatever have you done? Is it too late to get out of it? Maybe you should change your number.'

'You can both piss off,' she muttered. She rubbed her forehead, her sickly complexion clammy and damp, her Californian sheen replaced by a good old-fashioned Midlands hangover. 'At least I didn't go skinny-dipping with half the cast of *Riverdale*.'

'That show got cancelled more than a year ago,' Bel pointed out with a sniff. 'So technically I was skinny-dipping with a group of out-of-work actors.'

I traded my can of rocket fuel coffee for an ice-cold can of Coke, popped the top and chugged, sighing with relief as it sparkled all the way down. Bel cast me a disapproving look but said nothing, knowing full well she would have to prise the can from my cold, dead hands.

'Did anyone see Myrna before they left?' I asked, holding the cool can against my face. 'I didn't get a chance to say goodbye.'

'Too busy banging,' Bel whooped.

'You, Phoebe or Myrna?' Suzanne replied, dry as a bone. 'I didn't. She wasn't around when I left, I did look for her.'

'I really would like to see her before I go,' I said. 'Will we have time to stop in on the way to the airport?'

'Don't see why not. Your flight's at three, isn't it? As long as you're there for midday you'll be fine. We can pop in and see her on the way.'

'Can I come too?' Bel asked. 'I owe that woman an in-person thank you.'

'Same,' Suzanne added. 'Myrna really brought Old Hollywood back to life for one night only.'

'Myrna could bring dinosaurs back to life if she put her mind to it,' I said. 'We'd be overrun with T-Rexes by Christmas if she was so inclined.'

Over on the kitchen counter, I saw the screen of my phone flash into life and fill with a flurry of notifications. Messages from Suzanne and Bel, equally split between demanding to know where I was and encouraging me not to rush home, a deeply unnecessary alert from the airline to confirm my flight and at the bottom, a text from Samantha. I opened it to see a photo of my own front room, a cup of tea steaming on the coffee table, with two words underneath it.

Thank you.

'I can't believe you're leaving today,' Bel said, twisting her hair into a topknot as I set my phone back down on the counter, smiling. 'You should stay longer.'

'If I could, I would,' I replied. 'But I can't.'

'It's really not on,' Suzanne complained as she reached for her dry toast and nibbled the edge before putting it right back down. 'I barely got to see you and now you're bloody leaving.'

Miraculously, I stopped myself from asking exactly whose fault that was.

Rolling over onto her belly and resting her chin in her hands, Bel frowned. 'Where is Ren?' she asked. 'Shouldn't he be here, throwing himself around and sobbing? Or at least trying to give you a quick one before you leave?'

'He's busy,' I said. 'We did the goodbye thing already. Neither of us are big on drama.'

Suzanne crossed her arms over her chest and zeroed in on me with Terminator-esque intensity and I pitied all the people who had to report to my sister. 'There's something you're not telling us. You've got the same look on your face as when you borrowed my Juicy Couture tracksuit top.'

'Suzanne Louise Chapman, that was eighteen years ago, it's time to let it go,' I declared. 'If there was anything to tell you, I'd tell you, but there isn't, so I won't. OK?'

'OK,' they chorused even though from the matching looks of suspicion on their faces, it was anything but.

'Right, I still have to pack and sort myself out,' I told them, ignoring Bel's horrified gasp as I helped myself to a second can of Coke. 'So I'm going to pack, I'm going to shower, I'm going to get dressed and when I come back downstairs, I want to see big fat cheesy smiles all round. I'm not ending this trip looking at a load of sulky faces, so that's an order.'

'Woah, Suze,' Bel breathed. 'She sounds just like you.'

'No,' Suzanne replied, smiling as I dragged myself off upstairs. 'She sounds just like our gran.'

It was the best compliment she could possibly have given me.

'I love LA but does it have to be this hot though?' Bel whined from the deep end of the swimming pool, reaching for one of the medicinal frozen margaritas she'd mixed while I was in the shower.

'It isn't any hotter than yesterday,' Suzanne replied from the shallow end. 'It only feels like it is because we all killed so many brain cells last night, our bodies don't know how to cope.'

It really didn't matter which of them was right; the air was sizzling. I felt like a pile of dry grass, ready to burst into flames at any second, and the only acceptable place to be was in the water.

'We should get out soon,' I said, checking on the time and not liking what I found. 'I want to leave enough time to see Myrna.'

I couldn't see into Ren's garden from the pool but I'd checked before I jumped in. The curtains were still closed. Was he even awake yet?

'I know you said you didn't want to talk about it,' Suzanne said, lifting up her sunglasses to get a better look at me. 'But you were out all night and you came home looking like you'd been ridden hard and put away wet. Surely you're not going to leave without seeing him again?'

'Yes,' I replied. 'I am.'

'So everything is OK but you don't want to see him again?'

'That's correct.'

'Fine. I don't believe you but I won't push it,' she said. 'But say the word and he's a dead man.'

'Then I'll push it,' Bel said, swimming towards us, margarita held up out of the water. 'Because I don't get it. You write those super deep letters, you roll home at eight a.m. walking like you've been riding the bucking bronco at Saddle Ranch Chop House all night, and I don't want to be rude but Phoebe, babe, you should see your face. It's giving Buffy after they brought her back from the dead. What really happened?'

'Nothing,' I said, an unwelcome squeak adding itself to the end of my sentence. 'We talked, I explained about the letters, he was not entirely pleased at first but then we talked it all out and then, you know.'

'Banged it out?' Bel suggested.

'For the love of God,' Suzanne groaned.

'We spent the night together,' I offered diplomatically.

'They banged it out,' Bel said, smiling as she sucked her margarita through a straw. 'All night long.'

'And now I have to go home,' I said. 'So I got up, got dressed and left. What's the point in making it complicated?'

'What did he say when you left?' Suze asked.

'Nothing.' I swirled the rose-gold reusable straw in my slushy drink.

'He must have said something,' Bel pressed. 'Catch you later? Peace out? Thanks for the bang?'

'He didn't say anything because he was asleep when I left,' I muttered, sucking up as much icy tequila as I could stomach as they both exploded in an orgy of dismay.

'You did not!' Bel exclaimed.

'I don't believe you,' Suzanne gasped. 'You walked out on him without saying goodbye?'

'I left a note,' I whispered.

'Phoebe Chapman, fuckboi,' Bel said, shaking her head with grave disapproval. 'You lovebombed that boy and now you're going to ghost. Wow.'

'I don't fully understand what she just said but I do know that's really shitty,' Suze added. 'How would you feel if it was the other way around? If you woke up and he was gone?'

'Like he'd done me a favour,' I replied shortly. 'When he wakes up, he'll find my note—'

'You did *not* leave a note?'

'He'll find my note,' I continued loudly. 'And he'll understand why I left.'

'You're going to walk away,' Suzanne surmised. 'After everything you've been through, you're going to walk away from Ren when, well, I don't actually know him very well, but I've heard good things.'

'He's amazing,' Bel said, patting her on the back to commend the effort. 'They're perfect for each other and Pheebs, you don't have to say anything but if you don't, I'm going to assume the sex was the best sex you've ever had in your life.'

Without leaving enough time for me to breathe, she cheered and sent a wave of water in my direction.

'I KNEW IT.'

'It's not about the sex,' I protested, the pillar box-red glow in my cheeks giving it all away. 'It's about everything else. Long distance doesn't work and I can't go through another horrible break-up.'

'So you're finishing it before it even starts,' Suzanne said. 'Speaking as someone who's made a lifelong habit of that, I've got to be honest with you. It's shit.'

'Then what's the answer?' I asked. I was beginning to feel increasingly unhinged. 'I'm supposed to struggle through a transatlantic relationship and risk getting my heart destroyed again just because there's one man on earth who is gorgeous and funny and kind and interesting and he makes me feel strong and happy and gave me four orgasms in one night and oh my God, what have I done?'

'By Jove,' Bel said in a terrible British accent. 'I think she's got it.'

'What are you doing?' Suzanne yelled as I waded over to the side of the pool and dragged myself out.

'What do you think I'm doing?' I replied, stuffing my feet into my slides and tearing down the garden. 'I'm going to see him!'

I had one wet leg over the fence when his backdoor flew open and Ren emerged, a fury on his face the likes of which I'd never seen. How could I have been so stupid?

'Phoebe, what the hell?' he yelled, striding down his yard as I threw my other leg over the fence. 'You left a note? You were just gonna leave?'

'Yes, but I was coming back,' I replied, hanging off the edge of the terrace, a little puddle of pool water forming below. 'Look, this is me, coming back to talk to you.'

'Did you unplug my alarm clock?'

Straddling the fence, I bit my lip and nodded.

'If the real estate guy hadn't been banging my door down, I would have missed you.' He couldn't even look at me. I couldn't even look at me. The only thing I could do was close my eyes. 'You'd be gone and you weren't even going to say goodbye.'

'I honestly thought it was for the best,' I said. 'I really thought it would be better for both of us and I didn't want a dramatic scene. You know, like this.'

'But what about last night?' His eyes were big and round and dark. 'What about everything we said? And did?'

'I knew it,' I heard Bel hiss, peering upwards to see her and my sister waving from just a few feet away. 'So spicy.'

'You were just gonna leave,' Ren repeated, the words slicing me into ribbons.

Blinking, I glanced down and the ground rushed up towards me.

Karma, I thought, but maybe if I fall and break my leg, I'll get a nicer seat on the plane.

'Ren, I am so sorry,' I replied, threats of cramp shooting along my fingers. Why hadn't I gone round the front? Why couldn't I find the stairs? How had his grandad done this at eighty? 'I was stupid and scared and a bit hungover and last night was so perfect, I didn't want to ruin things.'

His rage was starting to burn itself out. As I looked over my shoulder, I saw him staring up at me, full of hurt.

'You didn't think skipping out on me without a word would ruin things?'

'I thought it would keep a special night special. I was trying to protect us.'

'Not us,' he challenged as one hand lost its grip on the ledge. 'You were trying to protect yourself. If you meant the things you said in your letters, you wouldn't be able to walk away from this.'

'I'm not walking,' I yelled. 'I'm falling!'

He caught me, shirtless and strong, holding me in his arms like the hero on the cover of one of my gran's Mills & Boon novels.

'Well, this is a bit on the nose,' I muttered, swallowing hard as I wrapped my arms around his neck. 'But thank you.'

All the anger and upset in his eyes swirled away, replaced by something even more frightening that I was afraid to name.

'How cheesy would it be if I said I will always be here to catch you?' he asked, his voice cracking at the edges.

'Extremely,' I said, his skin breaking into goosebumps as I curled my fingers in the soft hair at the nape of his neck. 'But I'd be very into it.'

We stayed that way for a long moment, me in Ren's

arms, still soaked through from the pool and dripping onto his grey sweatpants, Bel and Suzanne leaning over the edge of the terrace, slurping on what looked like freshly refilled margaritas.

'I'm so sorry, I never should have left,' I said, pushing my wet hair out of my face and turning my attention back where it belonged. 'I wasn't thinking about us, I was thinking about me and how hard it's going to be to go back to the way things were before I met you.'

'Sorry, but there's no going back,' he replied, lowering his face to mine as I closed my eyes and wet my lips and—

'Oh look,' called a familiar voice. 'It's Phoebe Chapman, half-naked in the arms of that boy she definitely isn't interested in.'

Ren's kiss landed somewhere to the side of my nose as I turned my head to see Myrna Moore standing smirking in the middle of his back garden.

'Darling, put some clothes on,' she said, positively glowing in a scarlet caftan. 'The sixties were a long time ago, you know. And Joe's boy, you really mustn't walk around half-naked. I'm an old woman and my heart can't take it.'

A nervous-looking man in a shiny suit appeared behind her. 'You already know your new neighbours?' he asked.

'For my sins,' she confirmed as Ren lowered me to the ground.

'Myrna, what are you doing here?' I asked, picking up the sweatshirt Bel had helpfully hurled over the edge of the terrace. 'I don't understand.'

'Not as bright as you think, are you?' she replied

before turning a blinding smile on Ren. 'I'm the one who bought your house; I'm afraid I'm the cuckoo in your nest, darling!'

'This,' I heard Bel mutter from a safe distance above us, 'is wild.'

Once again, she was not wrong.

Minutes later, Myrna rapped her cane against the top of Suzanne's outdoor dining table, calling the session to order.

'I have a proposition for you.' She pointed to Ren, who was clutching my left hand almost as tightly as I was holding a new frozen margarita in my right. 'My awful stepchildren were right. My house is too big for me. I'm too old to be rattling around the place by myself, but that doesn't mean I have to slope off to the old folks' farm while they wait for me to die.'

'Myrna,' I began with gentle reproach, but she wasn't interested.

'Don't look at me like that, I won't be patronised,' she said. 'I've got a few more good years in me yet, last night confirmed that for anyone who cared to see it, but I'd rather spend them in my own home than in a hovel, surrounded by decrepit husks.'

'That's exactly what I feel like after your party,' Suzanne said as she handed Myrna a margarita of her own. She took a sip and nodded her approval.

'Good, that means you did it right. Back to the matter at hand. Ren, dear, as I said, I've bought your grandfather's house.'

'You're serious?' he replied. 'You're the one who bought our house?'

'Is he hard of hearing?' she asked, looking at me to confirm. 'Isn't that what I just said?'

Ren's grip tightened around my fingers and I winced. 'You're not going to tear it down?'

'No,' Myrna replied. 'I'm going to live in it. You've done a beautiful job of the restoration and I couldn't stand the thought of some money-grabbing developer destroying something so beloved in the name of a quick buck.'

Bel held her hands against her heart and sighed. 'Oh, Myrna, who knew you were such a sweetie.'

'Another word out of that one and I'll have her flayed,' Myrna warned, Bel's mouth immediately puckering like a cat's arse. 'Ren, the way you brought Joe's house back to life inspired me. Perhaps there is a way to restore my home without razing the whole thing to the ground, despite what the succubus stepchildren say.'

'One hundred per cent. It wouldn't be cheap but it could be done,' Ren replied and I could feel him shaking with excitement. 'I can put you in touch with the people I used for some of the parts I couldn't do on my own if that would help?'

'You will put me in touch with no one.' She stared him dead in the eye and tapped the top of her cane against the ground. 'I want you to do it.'

'Ow!' I squealed as he squeezed my hand so hard, I was sure I heard something crack.

'I'm sorry,' he said, wild-eyed. 'Are you OK?'

'I think you've broken a finger,' I said, putting down my margarita to take a better look.

Myrna stared at me through her sunglasses. 'You're right-handed, aren't you, darling?'

I nodded and nursed my throbbing digits.

'That's your left, nothing for us to worry about.' She turned back to Ren as Suzanne handed me a napkin full of ice from her drink. 'No one will take care of my house as well as you. There will be a project manager salary and you can live in the guest cottage while the restorations are taking place. I've talked it all over with my finance people and they think I'm insane, but there's enough money to do it properly. What do you say?'

'It's a huge undertaking, it could take years,' he said as he gently rubbed my not-broken-but-still-quite-sore hand. 'There's the plumbing, the roof, you probably need the whole place rewired, and finding vintage fixtures for all those rooms won't be easy. I don't know, I've never done anything this major before.'

'There has to be a first time for everything,' she said with a wink in my direction. 'As I'm sure you two know.'

'This is crazy, I – I have to go call my dad,' Ren stood slowly as if he weren't sure his legs would hold him up. 'He's going to be so happy – he never really wanted to sell.'

'Am I to take that as a yes?' Myrna asked.

'It's the biggest yes ever!' He threw his arms out wide in celebration and I couldn't help but think she was wrong about him staying fully clothed all the time. 'Ms Moore, this is incredible, I don't know how to thank you.'

She took a sip of her drink then arched her left eyebrow. 'I believe a diamond ring and a blow job is traditional for two hundred thousand dollars over the asking price, but I'll settle for a handshake.'

Bel and Suzanne both spluttered, coughing their frozen drinks through their nose. I'd been around her enough to reply with a matching raised eyebrow and a sigh.

'Dad is going to be psyched.' Ren kissed me on the cheek before pulling his phone out of the pocket of his sweatpants and tapping away at the screen. 'Thank you, thank you so much!'

'If only all men were so easy to please.' Myrna sipped her margarita and looked around the garden with a cool eye. 'There's enough sugar in here to give a girl diabetes, I think I'll stay for another.'

'When I grow up, I want to be just like her,' I heard Bel whisper to my sister.

Moving into the empty seat beside Myrna before she could beat Bel to death with her cane, I tapped my glass against hers. 'I'm glad you came over,' I said. 'I was hoping to see you before I leave.'

'Leave?' she repeated as though I'd just told her I was running away to join the circus. 'What do you mean, leave?'

'I'm flying home today.' Every time I said it, my heart sank a little deeper. 'We have to leave for the airport in an hour or so.'

'No, I'm sorry but you're not *leaving*,' Myrna spoke as though it was the most ridiculous thing she had ever heard in her life. 'You have to stay.'

'Well, I'd like to, but I paid up front for the whole year's membership at the yoga place in town,' I said weakly. 'Can't stay on holiday forever, can I?'

'Can't you catch a later flight?' Bel suggested. 'Change it to next week?'

'Doesn't quite work like that in real life,' I replied, putting on a brave face. Here was the heartache I was trying to avoid, right on time and ten times as awful as anticipated. 'It's a non-refundable ticket. No changes.'

'Don't be absurd,' Myrna said to me before turning to Bel. 'She's not going anywhere so please try not to look quite so pathetic.'

'I can't just extend my holiday,' I argued. 'I'd need a visa and I have a job at home, I have obligations.'

'Such as?'

I opened my mouth to reply but my mind was a blank.

'She's staying,' Myrna declared when I didn't answer fast enough. 'We'll say you work for me and my lawyers will get you a visa. Someone's going to have to keep an eye on Joe's boy and I can't be expected to stay on top of him twenty-four hours a day, but I'm sure you wouldn't find it too much of a hardship.'

Bel held her hand up for a high five and Myrna gladly obliged.

'Actually, she doesn't need you to get her a visa,' Suzanne said, sounding almost surprised at herself. 'Our dad is American. All she has to do is apply for dual citizenship, that's what I did when I got this job. Mum should have done it when we were kids really, but who can blame her for wanting to pretend he didn't exist? It's a fair amount of paperwork but it's fairly straight-forward, I can help you.'

'Is this true?' Myrna asked. 'Am I to understand the most British woman I ever met in my life is actually half-American?'

I was such an idiot. I'd spent so much time trying

not to think about all the ways our dad had let us down, I'd never bothered to think about the ways he might be able to help us.

'So you could stay?' Bel yelled, jumping up and down in her seat and earning herself a literal slap on the wrists from Myrna. 'You don't have to go home?'

My palms were sweating against my cold glass. Could I?

'It's not that easy,' I said, holding them off while I attempted to gather my thoughts, but my thoughts did not want to be gathered. They moved too fast, irrational and uncontrollable, like a flock of sheep that had been knocking back cans of Red Bull. 'What would I do about a job? How would I live? *Where* would I live?'

'You're a copywriter, not the prime minister.' My sister, as blunt as ever. 'You already work from home – who's to say you couldn't work from here? You're bloody good at your job, Phoebe, they're not going to give you up without a fight. And you'll stay with me; I won't even charge you rent as long as you start bloody well cleaning up after yourself.'

'So what you're saying is I would have to pay rent,' I replied, a hint of a glimmer of hope sparkling inside me. 'I don't know. There isn't a lot of time to think this over, is there? And you can't make major life-changing decisions on a whim.'

Beside me, Myrna let out a derisive scoff. 'In all my years, I've never known anyone so committed to making their own life so difficult and I used to play bridge with Bette Davis.'

'And what about Ren?' Suzanne asked. 'Don't you want to stay for him?'

'Suze, I thought better of you,' I scolded. 'I have to be logical about this. I can't upend my entire life for a man.'

'Forgive me, I didn't realize I was speaking to one of the leading intellectuals of the day,' Myrna said with a small bow in my direction. 'I can't think of anything more sensible. It's called love. People have been doing it for centuries, darling, killed for it, fought wars over it. All *you* have to do is not get on a plane.'

She tapped her empty glass once and Suzanne leapt out of her seat to bring over the pitcher of margaritas. 'The glass is already broken, there's no point trying to put it back together now, you'll only cut yourself.'

'You broke a glass?' Bel said, glancing around the table. 'No one move, I'll go get a dustpan.'

'I can't decide if I love her or if she needs a muzzle,' Myrna said as she stared at my friend. 'Tell me she has good intentions and I'll allow her to exist.'

'The best,' I confirmed. 'You all have the best intentions, I know that, but moving halfway round the world seems like a very big thing to do without thinking it through properly. I don't even know how he would feel about me staying.'

'We all know how he feels about you,' Suzanne said. 'It's disgustingly obvious, so you can pack that in.'

But did we know? Did we really? The last person who said he loved me had lied, and there was no way to know for sure whether or not Ren's feelings were real.

'My dad cried,' Ren announced as he opened the sliding glass doors and strode over to the table, shoulders back, chest puffed out, his own eyes more than a little red. 'Michael Hector Efren Garcia cried. Myrna, I can't thank you enough.'

'Keep that in mind when you're ready to kill me and bury my body under the new rose garden,' she replied, settling into her second margarita. 'By the way, I'd like to add another rose garden.'

'Ren, you have to tell Phoebe,' Bel yelled, unable to keep her mouth shut for one second.

'Tell Phoebe what?' he asked, looking as confused as I felt

'Her dad is American and she could get citizenship and live here forever and don't you think she should cancel her flight and stay?'

She didn't even flinch when I saw Suzanne kick her under the table. I couldn't really complain; I'd done enough meddling in other people's love lives. Looking at Ren, I silently pleaded with him to say the right thing even though I didn't know what it was.

'Did I miss something?' he asked, loosely taking my hand in his. 'What is she talking about?'

'So, technically it seems as though I could stay,' I said carefully and calmly, even though inside I was turning cartwheels. I could stay here in the sun with the palm trees and the terrible traffic and all the different flavours of fizzy water. 'But obviously it's a big decision.'

'Yeah, pretty big,' he agreed, dropping my fingers and planting his hands on his hips. 'Wow.'

'Don't sound too enthusiastic,' I replied with a weak smile.

My heart plummeted into my stomach when he didn't return it.

'Oh my gosh, Ren, tell her she should stay!' Bel shouted before Suzanne finally clapped a hand over her mouth.

'Thank you,' Myrna said. 'I'll order the muzzle as soon as I get home.'

But he didn't tell me anything. Instead he took a big step backwards, and as he moved away, I felt a pull in my belly, like two magnets being prised apart, and gasped at the shock of it.

'I think she should do whatever she wants to do,' Ren said. 'It's Phoebe's decision to make, not ours.'

He was right and I knew it. This couldn't be his decision any more than it could be Myrna's or Bel's or Suzanne's, but my track record of decision-making had taken such a hit in the last few years and I'd made just as many bad ones as good. How was I supposed to know which one this was? Pressing the heels of my hands into my eyes, I breathed in the hot, dry air, trying to memorize the feeling as it filled my lungs.

'It's not that I don't want to stay,' I said. 'But I think I should go home and think about it. Make a sensible decision.'

'So you're sensible now?' Myrna asked, running her pendant back and forth along its chain. I looked away just in case she was trying to hypnotize me. 'Tell me, were you making sensible decisions when you climbed over my gate?'

'Phoebe,' Suzanne admonished. 'You didn't tell me that.'

'And were you being sensible when you jumped off that rock to save me from all those kids at the mermaid party?' Bel added. 'Or when you jumped in that leech-infested waterfall with Ren?'

'OK, I don't think I even want to know about those,' Suze said, shaking her head in despair. 'But I think I can add you to my health insurance, just FYI.'

'This just isn't the sort of thing I would do,' I reasoned, doing my best not to look Ren in the eye as I worked it all through in my head. Gran would never do something so rash, and Mum made hasty decisions only to end up married at nineteen and single again with two kids by twenty-three. But I'd thought long and hard before moving in with Thomas and look where that got me, and the day I left, I didn't think about it at all, I just packed a bag and walked out.

'I don't know,' I said, confidence wavering. 'It's just not me.'

'Phoebe, darling,' Myrna said with unprecedented softness. 'Why not you?'

She stared me right in the eye, no jokes this time.

'This isn't fair,' Ren said finally and I held my breath waiting for him to finish the sentence. 'If Phoebe wants to leave, she wants to leave. We shouldn't make it difficult for her.'

I didn't realize how much I wanted him to ask me to stay until he didn't.

It was all too much. I closed my eyes and saw his body over mine, his brown skin turned liquid gold in the moonlight. I felt his breath against my neck, his hands in my hair, I was overwhelmed by the inimitable scent of him and I thought why not me?

'But if you're going to go,' he added. 'Would it be OK if I drive you to the airport?'

I opened my eyes and I held my breath.

Why not me?

'You really want to drive me to the airport?' I asked. He nodded and I felt my whole body fill with stars. I'd been sensible for long enough.

Whatever this was, whatever it would be, there was only one way to find out. I'd never know what might happen if I didn't let it happen. Ren might break my heart or I might break his or maybe we'd live happily ever after, forever and ever. There was no way of knowing.

I looked up into the trees, searching for our red-tailed hawk. She was nowhere to be seen but that didn't mean she wasn't there.

'That's so kind of you, Ren,' Suzanne said loudly. 'No one willingly volunteers to drive to LAX unless . . .'

'He doesn't need to drive me to the airport,' I interrupted before she could say it. 'Because I'm not going to the airport.'

'You're not going to the airport?' Ren said.

'I'm not going to the airport,' I repeated.

'You're serious?' He looked as though he didn't believe me but Myrna raised her glass in my direction and gave me a wink.

'It's really not that difficult, is it?' I replied. 'All I have to do is not get on a plane.'

With the sound of Bel whooping in the background, Myrna and Suzanne exchanged what were quite frankly incredibly smug expressions, as Ren grabbed hold of my waist and swept me up into his arms, holding on so tightly I could hardly breathe. I yelled as my feet left the ground, it definitely looked better in movies than it felt in real life.

'Be careful!' I warned. 'I've had two margaritas and I'm still very tired from last night; you're putting everyone in a ten-foot radius in serious danger.'

'You're staying?' he asked, lowering me to the ground but keeping his arms wrapped around me. 'You're really going to stay?'

'I'm really going to stay,' I said, losing myself in those green eyes. 'For now.'

'I'm going to do everything I can to make sure you stay forever,' Ren promised before pulling back with an uncertain look on his face. 'That was supposed to sound romantic but did it come off kind of like a threat?'

'Bit of both so let's go with romantic,' I replied, grabbing hold of him and laughing, all the doubt and fear fading away, only the sweetest voices singing in my head.

Who decides? the voice asked. *Who decides when to give it a name and what to call it?*

I do, I replied as I leaned into his kiss, I decide.

And I decided to call it love.

ACKNOWLEDGEMENTS

Thank you to Rowan Lawton for being such a brilliant partner in all this nonsense for so long. I am so lucky to have you and everyone at The Soho Agency. Now go and eat your dinner.

To everyone at HarperCollins, thank you thank you thank you. FIFTEEN YEARS. Wild. Thank you Lynne Drew and Lucy Stewart for all the editorial magic. Thank you to Felicity Denham who remains the best publicist in the business. Maddy Marshall, Emily Merrill, Holly MacDonald, Alice Gomer, Harriet Williams, Kimberley Allsopp, Jean Marie Kelly, Jennifer Dee and everyone else who makes these books A Thing, from typesetting to the warehouse, I appreciate you so much and it's only thanks to you that I've been doing this for a decade and a half.

I also want to thank all the booksellers who are doing such an incredible job out there, especially everyone we met on *The Christmas Wish* tour, you made it a dream come true.

Thank you to Suzanne O'Connor for lending me her name and winning the Young Lives Vs Cancer auction.

As ever, this remains the weirdest job and the writing community is just the best. I'll definitely miss names off this list but truly, I feel so lucky to have you all to DM, chat to, hang out at events with, sob with in the corner over a glass (bottle) of wine, and even just reading your books feels like a gift. You're amazing, thank you: Mhairi McFarlane, Daisy Buchanan, Beth O'Leary, Lia Louis, Marian Keyes, Kate Ruby, Lizzy Dent, Sophie Cousens, Andie J. Christopher, Dorothy Koomson, Chip Pons, Anna Carey, Laura Kay, Kwana Jackson, Sarra Manning, Mike Gayle, Joe Haddow, Nina Pottell, Zoe West, Laura Jane Williams, Suzanne Park, Alisha Rai, Juno Dawson, Lauren Ho, Justin Meyers, Sally Thorne, Emily Henry, Jane Fallon, Sophie Irwin, Holly Smale, Becca Freeman, Jordan Moblo, Cressida McLaughlin, Lucy Vine, Claire Frost, Rosie Walsh, Gillian McAllister, Paige Toon, Giovanna Fletcher, Holly Bourne, Isabelle Broom, Andrea Bartz, Julia Bartz, Leah Konen and so many of other authors, Bookstagrammers, BookTokkers and reviewers who make this job so much fun.

And to the people who keep me going every day, Jeff, Bobby, Rebecca Alimena, Sarah Benton, Della Bolat, Julian Burrell, Jackson Davies, Kevin Dickson, Louise Doyle, Philippa Drewer, Olga Friedman, Emma Gunavardhna, Caroline Hirons, Emma Ingram, Hal Lublin, James McKnight, Eleanor Moran, Kate Prentice, Danielle Radford and forever and ever and ever, Terri White, I'm sorry, I know I owe you all an email. Well, all of you except Jeff. I love you as much as I love Taylor Swift.

Read on for an extract of another of Lindsey's hilarious and heartwarming rom coms . . .

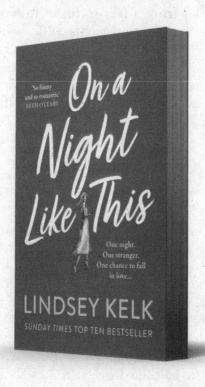

'The kind of book you can't put down, but also want to last forever'

Emily Henry

CHAPTER ONE

'Once upon a time, in a faraway kingdom, there was a woman called Francesca who couldn't be on time to save her life,' Jess announced as I blew through the door of Suzette's Café on Wednesday morning.

'I'm so sorry,' I said, giving her a quick hug before starting to unravel my many winter layers. After an unseasonably mild October, November was not messing around in Sheffield. 'You know I hate being late but Stew said he'd drop me off but his dad called and he had to run and I missed the bus and—'

'Fran.' My best friend pushed a cup of coffee towards me, along with a white paper bag. 'It's fine, relax, I'm joking. Sit down, I ordered for you because I'm so nice.' I dumped my tote bag on the table and smiled as she opened her own bag and inhaled. 'What does she put in these bloody muffins? How are they so good?'

'Best not to ask,' I advised, glancing over to the counter where Suzette was fixing tinsel to the shelves with a threatening-looking staple gun. 'Something we're not supposed to be eating any more, like white sugar or stem cells or crack.'

'All very moreish in their own way,' she replied, breaking off a chunk of muffin before fixing me with a look. 'Are you all right? You two aren't fighting again, are you?'

'I'm fine,' I said, waving away her concerns with the end of my scarf. My hair frizzed up around me in a static halo as I pulled off my bobble hat. 'Just feeling a bit *meh*, that's all.' Jess narrowed her eyes to let me know she didn't quite believe me but wasn't going to force the issue. 'Seriously, I'm so sorry. Are you in a rush?' I asked. 'Or can you stay for a bit?'

She shook her head as she pulled a neon-pink travel mug out of her own tote bag, unscrewed the top and poured her giant coffee inside. 'I've got to run,' she said, the tip of her tongue poking out the corner of her mouth as she poured. 'There are a million meetings today and for some reason, they need me in every bloody one of them. I swear, if I wasn't there, the place would burn to the ground in twenty-four hours.'

Jess was a very cool marketing director who did very cool things at a very cool brewery and, while she complained about her job constantly, I knew she loved it down to her bones.

'No worries,' I repeated. 'Everything's fine.'

'Shall I come round tonight?' she suggested gently. 'Stew's got football practice, hasn't he?'

I nodded, extremely happy with that plan. 'Sounds grand, I'll make dinner. Is there anything you're not eating right now?'

'No, it's too close to Christmas for that,' she replied, screwing the lid back on her cup and dropping it in her bag. 'They've already got the Quality Street open at work, I'll bring you a big purple one.' She scooted around the table to give me a kiss on the cheek. 'What's on your agenda for today?'

'Sitting here and waiting for literally anything to happen?'

'We don't wait for things to happen,' Jess said, white paper muffin bag in one hand, car keys in the other. 'We make them happen!'

'You sound like an Instagram post,' I called after her. 'If you tell me to live, laugh and love, you're not allowed round for tea.'

'More like nap, nom and Netflix,' she shouted back, already halfway out the door. 'See you tonight.'

It had been almost a month since I'd finished my last temping job – a thrilling adventure through the world of data entry for a logistics company in Rotherham – and so far, not a single one of the agencies I was signed up with could find me a new one. Apparently I was 'over-qualified' for almost everything and even though I would have happily wiped Satan's bottom for minimum wage if it meant getting out of the house for eight hours a day, they couldn't find me a thing. All the shops had hired their seasonal staff already and no one else was recruiting this close to Christmas.

Peering through the window of the café, I watched as the shops and businesses turned on their lights, the high street springing to life, the post office, the off-licence, the beauty salon, the bookshop. Everyone else's day was starting while I drank my coffee, ate my muffin and pulled my computer out of my backpack. Everyone had somewhere to go and something to do except for me.

Hands hovering over the ancient laptop as it clicked

and whirred into life, I stared at the two rings I wore every day, the only jewellery I ever wore, really. On my left hand, my engagement ring from Stew, a dainty diamond affair shaped like a flower, that had belonged to his beloved Nana Beryl before it was passed down to me with the most serious of strings attached. And on the third finger of my right hand, my mum's gold wedding band. She'd be so disappointed, I thought, twisting it around and around and around. Susan Cooper hadn't spent so much as a day out of work, a fact she had been fiercely proud of, and the thought of letting her down when she wasn't here any more felt like the worst possible failure.

'Don't wait for things to happen,' I whispered, attempting to stoke a fire that had all but burned out. 'Make them happen.'

With some uncertainty, I slipped my earbuds into my ears and dialled a number I had not dialled in months.

'Vine & Walsh, Rose speaking.'

'Rose, it's Fran, Fran Cooper,' I said, straightening my shoulders and taking a deep, steadying breath. 'How are you?'

'I'm well, thank you, how are you?' The silky southern accent on the other end of the phone sounded surprised to hear from me, which was fair, given that I hadn't been in touch for the best part of a year.

'Really well but still looking for work.' I tapped my fingers against the edge of the table, heart in my mouth. 'I was wondering if you might have anything for me?'

'I'll happily take a look,' Rose replied. 'But I'm fairly certain we don't have anything in your area, unless you've changed your mind about taking work outside South Yorkshire?'

And that was the reason I hadn't been in touch for the best part of a year. Vine & Walsh was an executive recruitment firm, not just your average temp agency, and every time I spoke with Rose, she told me about one incredible job after another and I had to turn each and every one of them down. In my wildest professional fantasies, I was totally jet set. I dreamed of travelling, seeing the world, of waking up to find I was the kind of woman who could pack two weeks-worth of clothes in a carry on and could go from conference room B to the bar to an all-night karaoke party with nothing more than a swipe of red lipstick and a change of earrings, but after we moved back to Sheffield, Stew and I had both agreed we wouldn't travel for work. Admittedly, that deal was made three years ago when we were living in London and there were a lot more jobs to choose from, but a deal is a deal and it was made for a reason, so I kept my ambitions local.

'Sorry, no,' I said as my heart sank slowly back towards my feet. 'Just thought it was worth checking in.'

As Rose let out a quiet, frustrated sigh, a new email from one of the local temp agencies appeared in my inbox. A vet in Brincliffe needed an office manager to do a two-week holiday cover starting Christmas Eve. Utterly depressing and still the best offer I'd had in months.

'There is one thing, and you'd be perfect for it,' Rose said, a note of possibility in her voice. 'It would mean you'd have to travel, but it's very short term and the money is amazing. I need a personal assistant for a very, very – let me say this again – *very* high-profile client.'

LINDSEY KELK

To keep up to date with the latest news, including exclusive extracts, competitions, events and much more, sign up to Lindsey's newsletter at
www.lindseykelk.com

@LindseyKelk